back to single

Evinda Lepins

TATE PUBLISHING
AND ENTERPRISES, LLC

Published by Tate Publishing & Enterprises, LLC
127 E. Trade Center Terrace | Mustang, Oklahoma 73064 USA
1.888.361.9473 | www.tatepublishing.com

Tate Publishing is committed to excellence in the publishing industry. The company reflects the philosophy established by the founders, based on Psalm 68:11,
"The Lord gave the word and great was the company of those who published it."

Book design copyright © 2012 by Tate Publishing, LLC. All rights reserved.
Cover design by Kate Stearman
Interior design by Blake Brasor

Published in the United States of America

ISBN: 978-1-61862-837-4
1. Fiction, Christian, General
2. Fiction, Contemporary Women
12.03.28

foreword

John Ortberg, in his book, Everybody's Normal Till You Get To Know Them, writes, "The irony of the masks is that although we wear them to make other people think well of us, they are drawn to us only when we take them off." This book, though in novel form, is the reflection of someone that took years of her life to peal back the pain, hurt, dysfunction and self- condemnation only to discover freedom, fulfillment and purpose after she was willing to face the very scariest places of her history. It is a compelling narrative of the journey of a woman desperately seeking to make sense of her negative circumstances that continued to repeat themselves. As she began to be able to notice the lives around her, she realized that she was not the only one struggling with this cycle of confusion and self-destruction. From her experiences, she sees that the women in our culture are in deep trouble. She sees the need of women finding their voices and learning how to express themselves when they're hurting, afraid and ashamed. She is hopeful that one person's "story" can make a difference.

"From our pain, comes our calling." This is where the inspiration comes from for the author to write so freely and boldly about her life. She is no longer hiding and running from "what people might think about her," nor is she hiding behind any mask. She speaks freely and boldly in hopes that others will recognize their need to be free from the bondage of their past. She, today, speaks her mind and is not ashamed to be transparent. She gives words for those who know something is wrong in their lives but cannot make sense of their repetitious cycles of self-harm.

This book is emotional, inspirational and transforming. You will not be the same after you've read it.

—Steve Atkinson, M.A.
Atkinson Family Counseling

A Word from the Author and
Acknowledgments

I can't believe it's true; you are finally reading this inspired first novel of the Destination? Joyful! ™ trilogy, and I am excited and humbled at the same time. There is so much to learn and gain in this gift of life, and my honest prayer for you would be that the pages of this novel would speak to your heart about the reality of Old Testament life and the availability and necessity to embrace our God-given New Testament future.

Abba Father, thank You for Your grace that inspires me, holds me, moves me off and away from myself so I may truly continue to take inventory with You, trusting You to reveal and remove that which needs to go, refine that which needs to become pure and strengthen that which is weak in me. Oh, that I would be a mirror of Your reflection and not perched on pride, transparently encouraging others toward You.

Honorary Mom, I just think of you, and I am overwhelmed with tears of thankfulness for His guiding you into and through my life the last twenty-three or so years. I've said this before, and I'll say it again: you are the first person who showed me me unconditional love, despite me, and I know in my heart that He sent you to be the mom that was absent most of my life. I have grown leaps and bounds as a woman because of your patience, your wisdom, your zest for life, and your undying support. You inspire me like no other; you must be an angel!

Nikki Robertson, you are an amazing editor to work with and your signature line rings true: An author writes a book but an editor completes it! I thank God for the gift of you!

My book/event team: Steve, Stephanie, Janine, Dawn, Susie, Sherry, Leigh, Nanny and Kim. There aren't enough pages left for me to write what is in my heart and mind for each of you. He called you to this project and the things that have stemmed from it, and each of you have brought unique gifts to all that we have accomplished with Him and for Him. I am humbled by your love for our Father, and I will never stop thanking Him for the gift of your friendship, your time, and your efforts that have been a wall of support around me. We truly are a team, each member necessary to accomplish what He has called us to do.

Jeff, my son, what an incredibly special gift in my life you are! God has used you to teach me many of the lessons I've learned along the way. I'm overjoyed watching you become the man you were created to be; the father that your son and daughter are learning from and truly adore, and the husband that your beautiful bride, my daughter-in-love, can lean on. I love you with every bit of my mothering heart, more, most!

Bryce and Breanne, my stepson and daughter, both of you have contributed to some lessons that I am still learning! You are a big piece of the puzzle of "family," and my prayer is that some day soon, the pieces will come together to form a beautiful blended family.

Last, but certainly not least, to the man God chose as my husband, the one God has used to remove even more pieces of junk from my trunk, you bring so much to the table, it's hard to put into words, but the most beautiful gift you bring is your agape love for me. I feel it in my bones, in my soul, and oh, what a feeling! I have never experienced this until you. I don't think you realize your importance and your role yet in this journey, but I pray that you will know that I couldn't do this without you. We are on this ride together, and I couldn't be seat-belted to anyone better. You are life, love, and laughter to me.

Dedication

This book you hold in your hands has a special dedication and it just may include you! Many of us are familiar with the term "recovery." In fact, every one of us has had to recover from something, possibly an illness, maybe the loss of a loved one, a financial difficulty, or an unexpected circumstance. The word in and of itself denotes a process and by its very definition demands the same thing. But what about those who dare to recover from the deception of a drug, alcohol, or even a food addiction? Is the definition still the same? I would dare to say it is. See, to recover means to return to the original and/or intended condition.

I find hope in that definition and am comforted by the truth that we all must acknowledge our Creator and the need for our Creator. With that acknowledgement and acceptance comes the courage to meet life on life's terms, one day at a time, hour by hour. With the passing of time out of our addiction, we come to know a love that fills us with unfathomable peace that no other source could offer and we become less and less influenced by the hold it once had.

Perhaps you have thought about recovery as it relates to a life issue that you recognize needs to change, or perhaps you know of someone in some form of recovery. Whatever the case may be, this book is dedicated to anyone in any type of recovery. And as an expression of sincere encouragement and hope, a portion of the proceeds generated from this book will be donated to a recovery group very near and dear to my heart, Teen Challenge. T.C. is an amazing organization dedicated to shining the light in the darkest of recoveries and I will forever be indebted to the seeds they planted and the light they shone in my own son's recovery.

Whatever you're going through, I wish you recovery!

Joyfully,
—Evinda

Table of Contents

The Beginning of the End

"Lacey, I'm not going to make it."

"What do you mean, Peter? Do we need to leave later? Did something come up at the office?" Lacey caught a glimpse of herself in the mirror, and saw that she looked as confused on the outside as she felt on the inside.

"Come on, Lacey, you're not making this any easier."

It felt like an eternity while Lacey waited for him to continue, and finally he spoke again: "I'm not going on the trip, and I'm not coming home. I can't do this anymore. I'll be in touch and let you know when I'll come and get my things."

It was Lacey's turn to pause. "I don't understand. We were going to go away. Why—"

"Lacey, I'm just not happy. I'm not in love with you anymore."

"What do you mean you're not happy?" Lacey asked as she sobbed into the phone.

"I hate it when you cry, but we have to get this over with."

"Get what over with?"

Peter continued with what sounded like a well-rehearsed speech: "Lacey, nothing I do or say is ever going to be good enough for you. You've got Jake, your career as a court reporter, your friends, and your journal. You don't need me anymore."

"But I do—" Lacey tried to stop him unsuccessfully, and the rest of his words hit her like a tornado.

"No, you don't, and I'm realizing I'm okay with that, so I'm just going to file for divorce. It's over. I'll be in touch."

The click and the dial tone reverberated in Lacey's ear, the reality of his words tearing at her heart, engraving pain deep in her soul. She fell to her knees, her sobs projecting her body down to the ground and holding her hostage, landing her in a fetal position.

Peter hung up the phone with a sigh, struggling within himself as he realized that the relief that he thought would surely come after making that phone call was nowhere to be found. He'd been holding his feelings in for so long, and now that they weren't captive inside of him any longer, instead of feeling free, he felt trapped with frustration. He even questioned if he had made a mistake as he thought about the events of the last couple of days. She had been working so hard to get things ready for their ski trip and visit to Mike and Cathy's near Lake Tahoe.

Normally, Peter loved to get away, especially when skiing was involved, but things had been changing for a while, and colliding with the changes were his feelings about Dana. The guilt that lay in the depths of his soul started to make its way to the surface as Peter remembered just this morning how vulnerable Lacey had looked after their intense fight the night before. He had almost told her then. As he was getting ready to leave this morning, he had stolen a quick glance at her and had seen a glimpse of the girl that he had fallen in love with seven years ago. And as he had said good-bye, dreading yet another possible confrontation as he faked his way through his exit, she hadn't yelled, hadn't drilled him with questions to try and get him to talk, nor had she begged him to "communicate" with her. In fact, it was quite the opposite.

As he sat there with his face in his hands, he couldn't figure out what had pushed him away—his own needs or her need to control. All he knew was that whatever it was, it had carved a wedge wider and wider, pulling him into the pool of temptation, and finally, taking him under until he no longer felt pulled but carried further and further away from his marriage.

The sound of someone clearing her throat brought him back to the present. Startled, Peter looked up to see his secretary staring at him.

"Are you all right?" Leanne asked.

"Uh-huh. Why?"

"Because I've told you three times that there's a call for you on line one."

"Who is it?"

"It's someone who says her name is—"

Peter knew exactly who it was and cut her off, dismissing her with a glance as he picked up line one. He was oblivious to the look Leanne gave him as she turned her back and walked away.

"Hello. This is Peter."

"You sound so formal."

Peter's stomach flip-flopped as he heard her voice, and he felt a smile in his heart that spread instantly to his face. "Hey, you," he said, his tone awash with emotion.

"Did you tell her?"

"Yeah, I told her."

"Don't sound so sad." She didn't give him time to respond but got right to the point. "This weekend is all taken care of. The kids' dad is going to pick them up after school, and our place is all reserved. We're going to have a great time. It will be just like old times, only better."

Peter picked up his pen and tapped it on his desk, nervous and excited at the same time. "I'll meet you there after work."

"What time do you think it will be?"

"I'm not sure. I'll get out of here as soon as I can. Probably be between four and five o'clock."

"See you then, babe."

Peter hung up the phone and forced himself to concentrate on his work, using it as an escape from the cloud of guilt that overrode the anticipation of a weekend with his ex-fiancée who had found her way back into his life.

She wasn't sure how long she stayed there, hadn't even realized that she had cried herself to sleep, but the ringing of the telephone brought her back to the present. *What the heck just happened?* Her thoughts blurred together like scrambled eggs. She glanced at the clock and saw that she had been asleep for almost two hours. The phone stopped ringing, and Lacey sat in a daze, not wanting to deal with any of it. She knew she should call Mike and Cathy, but she couldn't find the strength. She had lost control of her world; it had been ripped apart. *Again...why?* She didn't remember it hurting this much, ever. The pain in her heart took her back to the fight they'd had the night before.

Lacey had been working hard in the kitchen putting the finishing touches on the homemade lasagna, bagging the homemade chocolate cookies, and getting the ice chest ready for their trip. She decided to tackle the bills and determine how much spending money they could take. When she had gone online to check their account, she saw a withdrawal made the week before for $120, and another one a few days before that for the same amount. *What the heck?* She had immediately called the bank, convinced that there had to be a mistake. The customer service representative asked her for the account number and the tracing number of each withdrawal. Lacey was on hold for what felt like an eternity, and then the customer service representative was back.

"Mrs. Paulson?"

"Yes."

"Thank you for holding. Both of those withdrawals were made from the ATM machine at the Big Bear Inn, and they were made with your husband's card."

Lacey's heart sank.

"Is there anything else I can assist you with today?"

Lacey sat stunned, unable to speak until the customer service representative repeated: "Is there anything else?"

"No, that's it. Thank you. I just didn't remember those withdrawals."

Lacey hung up the phone, trying desperately not to get sucked into her hyperactive intuition but failing miserably. *His ex-fiancée has been coming around lately acting like she wants to be my friend; he's been openly withdrawn lately; now this.*

And that was the way Peter had found her when he had come home from work. Things had spiraled downhill from there, and when she drilled him about the withdrawals, his excuse had been that he and a few of his coworkers had gone out for drinks at the Big Bear Inn and he had paid for them. Lacey had known immediately that he was lying, not only by his body language and his defensive attitude but the fact that he wasn't a drinker, not really. An occasional social drink here and there, but that was it. Against her better judgment, Lacey had let it drop, but the damage was done.

The morning hadn't brought much sunshine into the situation, either. He seemed to be in a hurry to leave for work. He left over an hour earlier than usual. Lacey had tried to tell herself it was just because he was going to be working a half day, and she had thrown herself into the preparations for the trip, stopping only to call her son, Jake, who was with his dad for the weekend. That had been her only sunshine on a cloudy day, and thinking about him snapped her back to the present.

She looked around the family room where she had collapsed in tears. Nothing was out of place, and everything matched. The many pillows on the couches were made out of the same fabric as the drapes she had sewn. The art that they had collected over the years hung on the walls, staring at her, seeming to shout at her to get up, to go in search of answers. The tears came again, as if in defiance of the shouting, and she lay there, unabashedly weeping while trying to make sense of it all. *You've got to get a grip,* she told herself.

She pulled herself up and walked toward the stairs. As she reached for the first one, she stumbled, blinded by her tears and the feeling of emptiness and sorrow so dense, all she could do was crawl up the stairs, one by one, until she reached the top, and again she willed herself to stand up and walk. Step by step she inched her way toward their bedroom. She stood in the doorway, lost in a sea of pain brought on by the memories of when she had decorated this room. It too, like the living room, was perfect, only this had been their sanctuary. She had really put a lot of TLC into this room, and it showed. The bed was angled right in the center of the wall so it was the first thing you saw when you came in. She smiled, but only for a second, as she caught a glimpse of all the pillows on the bed. Peter used to tease her and call it the bed of pillows. The walls had been painted with a medium shade of dusk, which made the art on the walls look romantically artsy and invited warmth into the room. The adjoining bathroom with its huge bathtub, perfect for bubble baths for two brought the tears again.

She caught a glimpse of herself in the mirror and was dismayed at what stared back at her. She had let herself get lazy when it came to her appearance, and she was so out of shape that her friends, at the risk of hurting her feelings, called her big-boned. Lacey knew it was just a nice way of saying that at 168, five foot two, she was overweight. "Let's face facts—I'm fat," she muttered at her reflection. Her hair, sort of a reddish brown, looked wild and unruly; her face, though she was fortunate to have a good complexion, looked haggard; her big brown eyes looked haunted.

Lacey tore her gaze away from the mirror's painstaking truth, desperately fighting back the threat of more tears. She just couldn't deal with what had just happened; she didn't want to think about Peter and the ruins of the safe, happy life she'd tried so hard to build. She had to find something else to think about. Her gaze settled on her chair, and it beckoned her to sit. She reached for some tissue in the drawer of the nightstand, and her eyes caught the journal that she had been haphazardly keeping for her son. She grabbed it and went to their bed, settling in with all of the pillows, lining them up alongside her to grant her relief from being alone. She opened up the journal to an entry made two years ago and began to read:

> Oh, Jake, life seems to have taken on a different meaning now; it's so much more precious. Your reaction to the news of losing the baby was one of open shock and sadness, which was a confirmation that you really did want a little brother or sister more than I suspected.

The pain of that memory rose to meet Lacey, and she continued to read on, mesmerized by the raw emotions that spoke so loudly on the pages, as if still alive. Through the journal entries she read, there was a theme woven between them, one that wasn't apparent until now. The whole time she and Peter had been married, she had been trying to force a father-son relationship between Jake and Peter, as if Peter could take the place of Jake's real father who was in and out of his life. *Why? Was it because she wanted so much for him to have a better childhood than her own? Or was it that she wanted him to feel loved and accepted unconditionally and not abandoned?*

In search of answers, Lacey read on and came to an entry that described more hard times they all had experienced while remodeling their home, the dream vacation they were planning to take to Hawaii, and the fact that she was pregnant again.

The ringing of the phone brought her back, and she looked at the clock. It was just after noon, the time that they were supposed to be leaving for their trip. She listened as the answering machine picked it up, and Peter's sister's voice came on: "Hey, you guys. I was trying to catch you before you left to tell you to have a great time in Tahoe. I know how much you both need it. Peter, ski that black diamond run for me, okay? Be safe. Love you guys."

It was too much to think about, losing the family she had never had until she had met and married Peter, so she stayed right where she was and continued to read her journal to Jake.

> We were all so excited when we arrived at our hotel in Honolulu. We unpacked and put our clothes away and got ready to go out for our long-awaited lobster dinner. I started spotting. I tried not to panic and told myself I was okay. To make sure, we went to the emergency hospital, and they ordered an ultrasound. I was still convinced that the baby and I were okay, so I asked the technician if you could come in. My sweet son, when you are older, there will be people who ask about your regrets in life. Well, for me, whenever I even think about it, I regret down to my soul having you in there to hear the ultrasound person confirm that the mass on the screen that should have been my baby, your brother or sister, had never formed. Your sobs still reverberate in my heart as I write this. Yes, that is a regret that will stay with me until my own death.

Lacey heard the distant sound of a doorbell, and she went to the hallway window to see who it was. She stood on her toes and looked down. When she saw her sweet neighbor, Katrina, she remembered that she'd forgotten to go over and give her the keys so she could check on their house and get their mail. Lacey let out a sigh. She just couldn't stand the thought of telling her that not only was she not going skiing but that Peter had left her and was never coming back.

Katrina listened to the sound of the second ring of the doorbell. As she stood there, she realized that she hadn't noticed if Peter had come home from work or not. She didn't think so. Lacey had said he was just going to work half a day and then he'd be home so they could leave, but she would be over to give her the keys and say good-bye. *Something's up,* she thought. She reached for the doorbell, and after pushing it one last time, she began to bang on the door. Frustrated, she walked backwards, not turning her back until she had reached the end of the walkway. When she did turn around, she ran across the street to her own house, ran in the door, and straight for the phone.

Lacey walked back to her room and returned to the journal.

> How do I write a year's worth of emotions down on a single page or two of a journal? Things have changed in my field of court reporting. I've been working a lot more than I intended; but then again, I had never owned a court-reporting agency before. The competition in this field is fierce, and I've had to make some cutbacks that have been painful, to say the least, while spending more time at the office and connecting less and less with you and your dad.

There it was again, calling Peter his dad.

> It's almost like I'm running, fast and hard, from the pain of it all. I keep hearing your voice, your words you said to me a couple of weeks after we got back from Hawaii.

Your pain was so blatant, your innocence couldn't mask it: "Mommy, why are you still so sad? You still have me. Isn't that good enough?" Oh, my dearest and only son, you cannot understand, until you have your own child or children, just how much you have completed my life.

Lacey let the journal fall from her hands as she wept at the memories brought to the surface like a wave threatening to drown her. *Did he leave me because I couldn't give him a child? Where and when had it started to take that turn in the wrong direction that had led to such a battlefield with him on one side and me trying to pull him back? How had we come so far, through so much, and drifted so far apart?*

Lacey lay there, ruminating on the journal entries she had read. It had been like riding a tortuous roller coaster, the good times and bad times fluctuating up and down, but the bad times were so much more prevalent, catapulting them in a downward direction. It was all there in black and white, the raw emotional entries of times gone by, and suddenly she remembered that moment in time when she had realized that she had chosen wrong again; she should not have married Peter. That had been the first time she had heard it since she was a little girl—the Voice. Somewhere within her, she heard it, and like the first time all those years ago, it beckoned her to move forward, forward when she felt all alone after being taken from her mom and placed in a foster home; and then forward when she felt all alone in her marriage, and so she had. Shortly after that, she had met the woman who became her honorary mom, a woman who had shown her unconditional love and had given her guidance through her wisdom-packed advice. Lacey knew instinctively that the timing of it all was not coincidental. In her pursuit for understanding, Lacey had gained knowledge and insight from several books on marriage as well as books on child abuse to help her work through her issues of abandonment. She had been determined to get it right, and yet, here she lay, stripped of all her pride, lost in a sea of disappointment and disillusionment, abandoned yet again. "Oh, God, what am I going to do? Where are you now?" Lacey lay there and sobbed her way into a fitful sleep once again.

Disoriented, her pillow still wet from her tears, Lacey woke up to a voice, almost as if it were coming from right next to her, a voice so real she turned and looked to see who was there.

Isaiah 53:4.

She looked around her room, saw the clock on her nightstand, and was startled to see that it was already five o'clock. And then she heard it again: *Isaiah 53:4.* In the background, she heard the shrill sound of the telephone ringing. She couldn't really distinguish how many times it rang, because she was still trying to understand what the Voice was saying. It seemed to get louder and louder, saying the same thing, *Isaiah 53:4.*

What the heck is "Isaiah 53:4?" she asked herself. The phone stopped ringing just as she got up and made her way downstairs. She headed for her bookcase in the office. She didn't remember where she had last seen it, but she knew what she was looking for. She scanned the books on the shelves and opened up the doors to the enclosed part of the bookcase. She scanned from left to right on one shelf and then the bottom shelf. There it was, way in the back. She reached for it and pulled out the dust-covered Bible, her Women's NIV Daily Devotional Bible. It had been such a long time since she had read anything in it, and she didn't even know if there was such a thing as "Isaiah 53:4" in there, but it was worth a try.

After wiping all the dust off, she opened it up to the table of contents, and as she ran her fingers down the books listed, her heart stopped. There it was, Isaiah. Her hands started to shake as she turned the pages, looking for the 53 and then the 4. What she read rendered her speechless: "Surely He carries all of your pain; He dries all of your tears."

S. O. S.—Season of Singleness

(One year later)

Lacey stood in her closet looking at the new clothes she and the girls had shopped for a few weeks ago. She wasn't one for indulging in shopping sprees, but that was exactly what the girls had helped her do. "Out with the old and in with the new," Sophie had said. And Nikki hadn't been much help either in deterring her from the purchases, holding up a skirt here and a shirt there. "Would you look at these Barbie-doll clothes? Girl, you need to eat some carbohydrates. I'll never be able to borrow anything you buy!" And Susie had really surprised them all with the clothes she was bringing into the dressing room, mixing and matching some of the latest styles and labels. Lacey smiled to herself as she remembered that day with all of them—Sophie, Susie, and Nikki. If it weren't for her girlfriends, she didn't know how she would have made it through the last year.

So what do I wear to go clubbing? Lacey was never one to stay undecided, especially when it came to clothes. But then again, she hadn't been out in the single scene for a very long time.

Fifteen minutes and seven outfits later, Lacey had finally set-tled on a pair of black low-rise Chanel pants that flared at the bottom, and an Abercrombie black-beaded halter top, which she pulled up and over her small chest and tied in a way that created the illusion of cleavage. "And now for the shoes," she said aloud. Her gaze fell upon the boxes and boxes of shoes, the array of colors more explosive than any rainbow—white, black, red, blue, yellow, lime green, brown, tan; and not just one of each. Oh, no. There were several styles for each color. "Hmmm," she reached for the black Pradas, a simple but elegant style with one-and-a-half-inch heels. They were surprisingly comfortable and one of her favorites. Apprehensively, she walked to her full-length mirror, muttering under her breath, "It's not like I'm a spring…" The reflection that stared back at her stopped her midsentence and pushed her self-doubts out of reach. The girl that stared back at her was someone she still didn't recognize at five-two, now toned and petite at a size 2 instead of her former size 12, a newly cut hairstyle that was a simple layered cut with bangs that swept down and around her cheekbones with blond- and honey-colored highlights that enhanced her big dark brown eyes.

She put on the finishing touches of her makeup, using a pencil to darken and lift her eyebrows, Bare Minerals blush the color of Bryce Canyon clay to bring out her cheekbones, mascara to thicken her already long and curly eyelashes, and icy pink gloss to help shape her lips; and lastly, she reached for her new favorite perfume, Light Blue by Dolce & Gabanna. The doorbell rang, and she sprayed to the right, to the left, and then all around, put the bottle down, and ran down the stairs, excited to see Nikki. They had met through the court reporting agency that Lacey had joined not quite a year ago, and though the friendship was still new, it was as though they had been friends forever; she was a welcome addition to "the girls." She opened up the door and was rewarded with one of Nikki's famous bear hugs.

"Come on in, girl."

"Peanut"—Nikki's new nickname for Lacey—"just look at you. My gawd, we're gonna be beatin' 'em off with a stick tonight. Looks like I'm gonna get my once-a-year workout in after all."

"You look pretty great yourself, Nikki."

"Yeah, not so bad for a fat-camp graduate, huh?"

"Stop that," Lacey exclaimed. "You're beautiful." Lacey marveled at how Nikki was able to laugh at herself and draw others into her laughter, appearing comfortable with her weight, yet hiding behind it. "Let me just get my purse and jacket, and we can go."

Nikki put her jacket on and reached for her purse.

"So are you ready to come out of hibernation and meet the wolves?"

"Oh, Nikki, I don't want to meet any wolves, maybe dance with them," she said, laughing. "But I think I'm ready to come out of my season of singleness and have a good time with you and the girls. We've got a lot of catching up to do. The last time we were all together was a month ago when we went shopping and had lunch. I wish Susie was coming so she could see this outfit she picked out."

"Well, Peanut, I have a feeling she didn't come because of *him*."

"Yeah, I think you're right. I don't have a good feeling about *him*. Hey, we better get moving. I told Julia we'd meet her there at nine, but we should be okay. Did I tell you she got us a VIP table at this place?"

"Oh my gawd, you didn't tell me I was going out with royalty tonight. How in the heck did she manage that?"

"She's an attorney with connections. What can I say? Besides, I think she spends a lot of time at this place. Let me just grab the directions and lock up, and I'll meet you outside."

Julia parked in her regular parking spot. As she got out of her car, she saw Sophie walking toward her. She waved, locked up her car, and went to meet her. They hugged and complimented each other. "So where's Susie?" Julia asked Sophie.

"She just said she couldn't get away tonight."

Julia refrained from making a sarcastic remark, a rarity for her. "Well, we'll have fun without her. Wait 'til you see how we're going to celebrate Lacey's divorce. I got us a VIP table, right up front, and wait 'til you see the view."

As they made their way toward the club, Sophie marveled at Julia as she took her by the hand, and they walked right past the mob of people waiting in line. "I suppose that VIP table comes with cuts to the front of the line?"

"Absodarnlutely." Julia laughed. "I just need to give these two tickets to the bouncer so he can get them to Lacey and Nikki when they get here."

Sophie stood to the side at the entrance while Julia talked to the bouncer, who looked to be no stranger to Julia. *If he's any indication of what's inside this place…* Sophie thought. Julia made her way back to Sophie and whispered in her ear, "Trust me; it gets better."

A splash of cool air and loud music welcomed them as they made their way in, and Sophie stood beside Julia, impressed when a host, a really hot host, approached them and greeted Julia with not one kiss, but two, one for each cheek, which confirmed Sophie's suspicion that Julia had more than the partner at her firm as a connection. He took them to their table, which had a beautiful view of the back patio and surrounding area that boasted of a long and winding reflecting pool, spiraling waterfalls, and requisite palm trees. Their own table had a big palm-tree umbrella that offered a bit of privacy without shutting anyone or anything out. Sophie looked around and gave Julia a thumbs-up sign as the hot host took their drink orders.

"I'll have my usual, Pierre, and do you have that bottle of champagne chilling?"

"You bet. Just let me know when you want me to bring it out." His gaze turned to Sophie. "And what will the beautiful lady have?"

Sophie smirked at his comment, not easily captured by a guy's charm, and looked up at him. Their eyes locked, and she felt a chill go down her spine that changed her smirk to a smile that warmed her face with a natural blush. "I'll take a pomegranate martini."

"Nice choice. I'll be right back with your first round. By the way, Julia, this first round's on me."

"Thank you, Pierre."

"My pleasure. I'll be right back."

Julia turned her attention to Sophie. "So Lacey told me your son's dad was in a bad motorcycle accident and he's in a coma. Have you told him yet?"

"Yes. I explained it to him a couple of weeks ago, and he wants to go see him. I just don't know if that's a wise thing to do. I mean, it's not like he saw him a lot anyway, but I don't think I want him to remember his dad the way that he is now."

"Well, how did you explain it to him?" Julia asked, curious.

"I told him that his dad had been in a bad motorcycle accident, and because he wasn't wearing his helmet, his brain died but the rest of him is alive and that's why he's asleep all the time. So I think I'm going to wait as long as I can."

"Wow, I don't blame you," Julia affirmed. "It's not going to be easy for you to see him like that, let alone Zach. I mean, I've never had a kid, but I think I would wait as long as I could too." When Sophie's eyes welled up with tears that threatened to fall any second, Julia changed the subject. "So do you think Lacey will like this place?"

"How could she not?" Sophie said, as she turned and looked around her. Her eyes opened wide as she saw that there was a double-decker dance floor. "She's so going to love the dance floors; that's for sure. This was so nice for you to arrange this for her, for all of us."

"Yeah, well, I haven't seen Lacey very much lately, especially since she sold her court reporting agency and began working for that firm in Hollywood.

"Well, I think she's going to love it here."

"Before they get here, let's go check out the eye candy."

"Let's, and can we look for the ladies' room on the way?"

The girls pulled into the parking lot of the Cabana Club, and Lacey's laughter suddenly stopped in her throat. She looked to Nikki. "Wow, would you look at this place. It's beautiful."

Nikki heard a "but" coming in Lacey's tone of voice.

"I can tell something's wrong, Peanut. What's going on?"

"I don't know if I can do this, Nikki."

"Do what?"

"Go in there. Who am I kidding? I just don't think I'm ready for this."

"Now wait a minute, Lacey. You're the one who said we're just getting together with the girls. Don't go getting all twitter-pated on me now. I'm the one who should have her head examined, going to a club with my skinny girlfriends. Now that's worth a laugh and a half. Besides, I'll hold your dance card and make sure that you only dance with a guy I'd take home to mom, and that means, he's got to be Italian."

"Yeah, well, I can't imagine ever taking a guy home again to my adopted mom, let alone your mom, but the Italian doesn't sound half bad," Lacey said with a smile. "Let's go do this, and, Nikki, in case I forget to tell you later, I'm glad there is you."

"I'm glad there's you, Peanut. Now let's get in there."

Julia looked up just in time to see Lacey and Nikki being greeted by Pierre and motioned to Sophie. "Wow, would you look at Lacey all dolled up and tiny standing next to Nikki." As soon as she said it, she realized how it sounded and tried to undo the insult about Nikki. "I didn't realize Lacey had lost so much weight, and Nikki looks great too. I'd kill for skin like hers. She's never going to look her age."

Sophie laughed at Julia's faux pas. "Yeah, Nikki's skin is amazing." She fixed her gaze on Lacey. "Lacey really has taken working out at the gym to a new level. I can't keep up with her, especially since our trainer has talked her into competing for the Ms. Fitness contest."

"How much weight has she lost?" Julia asked enviously.

"I think she's lost thirty-two pounds, four sizes, and a lot of the baggage that came from being dumped for another woman."

Lacey and Nikki descended upon them before Julia could respond. Anyone watching them would have thought that they hadn't seen each other in years as they greeted each other with hugs and laughter. Pierre stood by watching and couldn't help but smile at their reunion. "Julia, would you like me to bring that out now?"

"Yes, it's time to get this party started."

The girls didn't even notice him leave as they all got comfortable around their table and began catching up. Within minutes, Lacey had forgotten why she had been so nervous and was practically dancing in her chair to the beat of the song, taking in her surroundings, including the outside view directly in front of them of the waterfalls and spectacular pool and palm trees. It was breathtaking. The Cabana Club certainly didn't have the typical "meat market" feel of other clubs she had been in years ago. Lacey wasn't sure if it was the upscale-type of club goers or the ambiance, maybe a bit of both, but she liked it so far. She looked to Julia and mouthed "thank you" above the music and the girls' chatter. Julia smiled and leaned in toward Lacey. "I wanted to help you celebrate life after divorce."

"Girls, girls, champagne's here!" announced Pierre as he quickly poured them each a glass. "Allow me the first toast." He looked first at Sophie and, then holding the almost-empty bottle up in Lacey's direction, said: "Welcome to the Cabana Club; it's now a better place for me, to see all your beautiful faces."

"Ahh," the girls said in unison. The girls held up their glasses and clinked them together, and, again, Pierre left unnoticed as the girls toasted to their friendship, to Sophie's change of direction, to Nikki's loss of three pounds, to Julia's connection, and to Lacey's divorce.

Their laughter and toasts to one another could not be heard over the music, but it was definitely obvious to any onlookers that the girls at the front table were having a good time. Ian elbowed his brother and motioned with his eyes in the direction of the girls. Tom looked in their direction, and Ian laughed as he watched his brother's eyes get big and blow out a breath that came back in a whistle that they both heard over the music. "What do you say we send them over a round of drinks?" Ian asked Tom.

"Yeah, I'll split a round with you."

Ian's mouth opened as if to reply, but his voice got caught in midair as he saw her get up off her chair and go dance with a guy that resembled a tall and lanky businessman trying to look comfortable out of a suit. Ian couldn't take his eyes off her. Her tiny and toned body told him that she visited the gym as much as he did. From where he was standing, he could see the laughter that shone in her eyes and sparkled through her dimples. She was full of life and obviously loved to dance, another thing they had in common. He had to see her up close.

Tom, standing next to Ian, followed his brother's gaze and saw immediately why he had wanted to buy the round of drinks.

He slapped Ian on the back. "Hey, bro, I'll go order that round for them."

Lacey returned to her chair and was surprised to see a mixed drink waiting for her. She still had half a glass of champagne left and wasn't planning to drink anything else. "Where did this come from?"

As if rehearsed, the girls all answered with their club code: "Ten o'clock." Lacey looked in the direction and saw two guys holding up their glasses of beer. Lacey followed suit and held up her drink in a gesture of thanks. As soon as she sipped it, she knew what it was. She set it behind her glass of champagne. Her Long Island Ice Tea days were over, and she wasn't about to drink enough to lose control, just enough to take the edge off, which the champagne was doing. She looked back to the girls. "That was nice of them to do that though."

"I don't know that 'nice' has anything to do with it, but this night is definitely getting better," Julia said over the music. "Come on, girls. Let's go dance." They all got up, except for Nikki.

"You guys go ahead. I'll watch our purses and take orders for your dance cards."

Lacey took her by the hand. "No one's going to take our purses, and no one's got a dance card, so let's go, girl."

Out on the dance floor, Lacey couldn't keep her eyes off the guys who bought their drinks. Laughing and dancing, she kept staring in their direction purposefully, moving and grooving to the beat. As the song came to an end, the D.J. announced the line dance to "Achy Breaky Heart" by Billy Ray Cyrus. The crowd broke out in approving applause as they formed a line, side by side. Lacey and Julia stepped up to the front as if to lead because this was their dance and one that they were good at. As the music started, Lacey felt a shoulder bump hers and looked to her left, surprised to see one of the guys that had bought them their drinks right beside her.

"Mind if I join you?" Ian asked over the music.

Not missing a beat of the dance that had already begun, Lacey looked him up and down a couple of times, smiling. "Hey, it's a free dance floor, right, Julia?" Julia answered with a nod, singing "Achy Breaky Heart." When the song ended, they all broke out in cheers and clapping, and the D.J.'s voice broke in: "We're going to slow it down now. It's guys' choice." Lacey quickly turned to leave the dance floor and felt a tap on her shoulder. She turned, and he was so close she could feel his breath on her face.

"Would you like to dance?" Ian asked her.

Lacey's response stopped somewhere in her throat as she looked at him as if for the first time. *This guy's too beautiful. It's only a dance. It's only a dance,* she chided herself. "Sure," she said more confidently than she felt.

He pulled her close, and Lacey tried to relax as she watched the girls leave the dance floor. She felt the beating of his heart, not confusing it with the beat of the music, and tried to pull away just a little bit. He pulled her back into him, gently but firmly, keeping one hand in hers and another around her waist. *Well, at least he's not groping me,* Lacey thought. She rested her head on his shoulder, and for the duration of the song, Lacey allowed herself to not think but just enjoy the feel of his firm body next to hers as he led them around the dance floor, obviously no stranger to the art of dancing.

"Would you look at that," Nikki said to the girls. "They look as if they've been dancing together for years."

"You can say that again," Sophie agreed.

Nikki turned to Sophie. "So what's new with you, gorgeous?"

Sophie's smile brightened at the compliment. "Zack and I are adjusting to my new schedule. Since I've quit court reporting college, I have more time with him."

"Well, that's perfect timing, considering all you guys are going through," Nikki said.

"That's one way of looking at it," Sophie agreed.

"So how's the job going?"

"Actually, real estate is so different now."

Nikki took a sip of her drink. "You mean because of the economy?"

Sophie nodded her head. "There's that, and the fact that everyone's sue-happy so the laws have changed."

"You staying busy, though?"

"Yeah, there's plenty of business. Investors are taking advantage of all the foreclosures and winning at the game of Monopoly because of others' misfortunes. But at least it's a job," Sophie added.

"I'm rooting for you, girl. So, are there any new flames blazing bright in your life?"

"Well, there is a guy I've dated a few times and we seem to have a lot in common, but it's too soon to tell if it's anything serious."

"Good for you," Nikki said enthusiastically. "You deserve to have some fun." And she really meant it. They shared a common bond of being single parents, and Nikki knew that Sophie had really been having a hard time lately, especially with Zach's dad in a coma. Sophie was ten years younger than her, but Nikki had never felt anything but comfortable around her. She envied and admired her unpretentious beauty. At five-six, with long legs and a waist that disappeared when she turned sideways, she was a knockout. She dressed classy and conservatively almost always. Her hair was sexy but simple, cut to fit her heart-shaped face with multi-layers that flowed down in their natural wave and swept in toward the frame of her face, showing off her lips and cheeks, but bringing more attention to her big almond-shaped eyes that were the color of honey. In the months that Nikki had known Sophie, she had come to learn that the inside was just as pretty as the outside, and Sophie had welcomed her into their group with genuine approval.

Sophie leaned over and squeezed Nikki's hand to thank her. Like Nikki, Sophie reflected on their friendship which was entwined with the common thread of single parenting, and she was always grateful for the time they spent together. Nikki had an innate ability to splash her enthusiasm for life on all who came in contact with her in a way that enabled people to see past her excess weight and marvel at her beauty. Her blond and unruly hair framed a round face that was well-defined by her cheekbones and a perfect nose and eyes the color of an inviting pool of refreshing water, big and round as quarters.

As another song started, Lacey returned to the table escorted by Ian, her face flush and her eyes still dancing. "Nikki, Sophie, this is Ian. Where's—"

She was about to ask where Julia was when she appeared. "And this is our friend, Julia," she finished.

"It's nice to meet you, Ian." Reaching for her drink, she held it up to take a sip after thanking him.

Ian looked in the direction of his brother, signaled for him to come over. Tom walked over, and this time, Ian introduced him to the girls. Tom wasted no time after being introduced to Sophie, and asked her to dance.

"Sure." They headed for the dance floor upstairs.

"Hey, Ian, will you dance with me?" Julia asked. He looked to Lacey who quickly turned away not wanting to discourage him, and with a shrug of his shoulders, he nodded, and they followed Tom and Sophie.

"Are you having a good time, Peanut?"

"Yeah, actually, I am. I'm glad we did this. Getting out tonight is going to make tomorrow easier."

"What do you mean? What's happening tomorrow?"

"I've been invited to go skiing with Doug and Martha and their friend from church who just so happens to be a former ski instructor and single. How convenient, huh?"

"Peanut, that should be fun for you, especially since you haven't been able to ski yet this season."

"Yeah, they want to get on the slopes one last time. At least it won't be cold."

"Just promise me you'll take it easy and not go speeding down any black diamond runs, okay?"

"No worries; I don't ski black diamond runs. The last time I went down a black diamond run was when I was with you know who, and I didn't even know it was black diamond until I got off the chairlift and looked down. He thought it was funny, just because he looks like poetry in motion swishing down the hill, but I wound up going down on my butt."

By the time Julia and Sophie returned to the table, Nikki and Lacey were in tears from laughing at Lacey's recount of her black diamond nightmare and Nikki's latest deposition experience. "You've got to hear what happened to her yesterday while she was on the record," Lacey sputtered out in between fits of laughter. Nikki recounted the events of the deposition from the day before, erupting with laughter when she got to the part of her court reporting machine falling over in the middle of an answer full of unmentionable expletives given by the witness. She painted such a visual picture for all of them that brought unrestrained laughter and stories from all of them that kept going into the night.

Lacey woke up to the music from the alarm clock at six thirty, feeling exhausted and refreshed at the same time. The beat of the music brought a smile to her face as she remembered the events of the night before. She had danced and laughed the night away, and it had been good for her ego. Her favorite dance partner, and there had been a few, had been Ian. he had behaved like a perfect gentleman, and he danced in a way that made everyone look at him with awe. And to say he was easy on the eyes was an understatement. *He has to be at least ten years younger than I am,* she thought. "Well, it's not like I'm going to see him again." She got out of bed and headed downstairs toward the smell of her already-brewing Starbucks coffee.

She poured her first cup and filled her thermos so she could retreat to her favorite chair in her office and remembered that she couldn't stay there too long. Doug, Martha, and Jim were coming at eight. This was her favorite part of the day, early morning, when her phone wasn't ringing and the birds were singing. All was peaceful as she sat down to journal. She had started this journal a year ago, after hearing that Voice that had let her know that she wasn't alone and had revived the little seed of faith instilled long ago.

For three months after the phone call that had changed her life forever, Lacey had ridden an emotional roller coaster, enticed by Peter's emotions and confusion, a ride that had them going up and down until it had finally ended and Lacey had been forced to let go of hope in exchange for the divorce papers.

After that, Lacey had put the house up for sale, and it had sold in just two days. So many friends had rallied around her and Jake and helped them pack everything up to put it into storage. Then they moved in with longtime family friends Doug and Martha, their daughter Angela, and their son, Adam, who just happened to be Jake's best friend. The invitation was for as long as it took her to get on her feet. It had been good for Jake, and their home had been a safe nest for Lacey to rest and heal her broken wings and heart.

It had taken six months, and in that time, Lacey started working as an independent court reporter with Del Vicchio and Associates Court Reporting Agency out of North Hollywood, which helped her get their new condo in Rancho Cucamonga.

This second move was easier in an overwhelming kind of way because of all the people who helped: the girls, Doug and Martha and some of their church friends. They had definitely given her a different perspective about church, and she was thinking maybe she'd check it out after all.

By the end of their moving day, everything had been unpacked and put away, furniture placed, the kitchen organized, knick-knacks placed and pictures hung. When everyone had left, it literally looked as though they had been living there for a year.

Lacey looked around her as she poured herself another cup of coffee, reflecting on the whirlwind of her life over the past year. Though the pain wasn't gone by any means, things were working out, and she was on her feet again. Last night had proved that. She was glad she had given in to the girls' relentless efforts of trying to get her out. Just thinking about it brought pen to paper, and Lacey filled the pages of her journal, recapping the night out with the girls and the fun she'd had.

They had been some of the last to leave the Cabana Club. Ian and his brother, Tom, walked them all out to their cars, and Nikki and Lacey were the first to drive away, but not before Lacey noticed Ian and Julia talking at her car. She could have sworn that Julia had handed something to him. Five minutes later, Lacey's cell phone rang, and Julia was on the other end confirming what she had seen. "Hey, I hope you don't mind, but Ian asked for your number and I gave it to him."

"What?" Lacey screamed into her phone.

"Chillax. I just gave him your cell phone number. You should have seen him dancing around while he got the words out of his mouth. He was too cute. I couldn't resist."

"Julia, I can't believe you did that. Maybe he really wanted yours."

"Trust me, I tried to give him mine; he wasn't interested."

"So what did he say?"

Evinda Lepins

"He just asked how long I've known you, if you were single, you know, all the usual stuff. He said he really wanted to get to know you, and then asked for your number."

"And how did you answer all of his questions?"

"I told him that you were single and if he wanted to know anything else, to ask you. Then I gave him your number."

Above Nikki's giggling, Lacey chided Julia, "Yeah, well, don't do me any more favors, Julia. He probably won't call anyway."

"I wouldn't bet on it. Bye for now."

"Ta-ta for now, Julia."

Nikki was still giggling and Lacey turned to her and couldn't help but join her until she realized she would be left wondering if he would call.

"What's so funny?"

"Peanut, the guy was totally smitten with you." As if reading her mind, she continued, "And if he calls, great. If he doesn't, then chalk it up to an ego-boosting time."

"Yeah, I suppose you're right," Lacey said, not wanting to end the night with doubt and insecurity.

It was two-thirty before Lacey was home. By 2:45, she had changed into her oversized T-shirt and removed the traces of makeup before falling into bed. No wonder she was still feeling tired. Saturdays were normally her only day to sleep in, but she was trading sleeping for skiing.

Doug, Martha, and Jim arrived right on time. Lacey heard their horn honk and grabbed the box of items belonging to Peter that had been stored in her garage. He obviously didn't remember leaving them, but Lacey wanted to deliver them personally and exchange the temptation to throw the box away for the chance to see him again.

Doug was holding the trunk of the Excursion open for Lacey when she came outside. He took the box from her and, after putting it in the back, hugged her and asked if she was ready for the day.

"Yes," Lacey said breathlessly. "Let's do this." She turned to make her way into the back seat, and Martha greeted her with a hug.

"Lacey, you remember our friend Jim?" Lacey looked up to see Jim smiling at her as he held the door open for her.

"Yes." And looking at him, she took his outstretched hand and shook it. "It's nice to see you again." They had met a couple of times at Doug and Martha's when she was living with them, and the only thing that stood out in Lacey's memory was that he was a ski instructor. She didn't remember him being so good looking, but then again, she had been in a bubble of pain the few times they had seen each other months ago.

The drive up to Big Bear was like putting on a pair of comfy slippers, but as they pulled into the parking lot of Uni-State funding where Peter worked, the slippers suddenly felt like uncomfortable shoes. Martha looked to Lacey as if sensing her anxiety. "Want me to go with you?"

"No, that's okay. I want to do this."

Jim got out and quickly retrieved the box and handed it to Lacey, giving her a smile to take with her. As Lacey made her way in the front door of the office, she noticed that Peter was the only one at his desk.

Peter looked up. "Can I help you?"

Speechless for a few seconds, Lacey stood there and then broke into a giggle. "Uh, yes, you can." After taking a few steps forward, recognition broke out on Peter's face.

"Is that you?"

"Yeah, it's me. I'm up here with Doug, Martha, and a friend to go skiing so I thought I'd bring you the last of your things." She held the box out; and he stood, almost as if in slow motion, and took the box, not taking his eyes off her. Lacey could feel his gaze try to intrude into her heart so she quickly turned around and headed for the door. She reached for the handle and, with a quick turn of her head and one last look at him, said, "Take care of you, Peter."

"Well?" Martha asked, as soon as the car was moving out of the parking lot.

"He didn't recognize me."

"What do you mean he didn't recognize you?"

"He asked if he could help me. You should have seen the look on his face. It was so worth it. I'm so glad I did it."

A simultaneous sigh filled the car and Doug and Martha exchanged a smile. "You ready to learn how to snowboard, Lacey?" Doug asked.

"After that, I feel like I can do almost anything. I'll give it a try, but I may end up on skis."

"Between Doug and me, we'll have you up and boarding in no time," Jim said confidently.

The weather was perfect with the sun reflecting off the white snow and beating down on them as they made it to the chair-lift for their first bunny run on their snowboards. The clouds were big and puffy against a powder blue sky, and the mountains were a majestic background behind all the tall trees. Lacey was laughing at herself, dragging her snowboard with her goofy foot toward the chair, trying desperately not to fall. A couple of times, Jim had reached out and saved her from falling and then put his arm through hers to help her onto the lift and then off again onto the flat area where they waited for Doug and Martha. Jim bent down and buckled her into her boot and stood up, accidentally bumping into her and knocking her off balance. He grabbed her, and that is how Doug and Martha found them when they glided toward them on their snowboards. The look on Martha's face combined with the shade of red on Jim's face sent Lacey into a contagious laughing spell that put them all at ease as Lacey's snowboarding lesson began with Jim reminding Lacey not to fear falling; it was a part of snowboarding.

Martha laughed in agreement. "That's for sure."

Jim continued, "Now, the most basic thing you need to remember is that you will go in the direction that your board is pointed. If you are not perpendicular to the slope and the nose or the tail of your board is facing more downhill, you will begin sliding in that direction, so to avoid that, you need to lean to the left or the right, depending on which direction you want to go.

"Kind of like you would if you were skateboarding?" Lacey asked, thankful for the times she had spent learning how to skateboard with Jake.

Jim smiled. "Sort of, though snowboarding requires more knee action and skateboarding requires more foot action. Now, let's take your first run. Doug and I will be right behind you to help you. If you get to going too fast and you forget what to do, just fall. It's better than running into something or someone."

Jim and Doug were patient teachers, snowboarding behind her, run after run, reminding her to keep her board perpendicular to the slope so she wouldn't go flying straight down the run, out of control. They were the perfect guides, shouting out signals: "Aim for ten o'clock"; "Watch out straight ahead"; "Lean toward three o'clock." Her butt was sore from learning the art of falling, and her abs hurt from laughing so much at herself. When Jim suggested they stop for lunch, Lacey was starving and jumped at the chance to get off her butt and board.

After lunch, Doug and Martha took off to snowboard on the intermediate runs, and Jim took Lacey back up to the bunny slope. Lacey was feeling more confident now, and though snowboarding was more difficult, the thought of trading in her snowboard for skis was exchanged for the exhilarating feeling of boarding down the slope without falling, the sun smiling down upon her and the wind at her back.

On their way home, they stopped for dinner at Two Guys From Italy Restaurant, and the combination of good food and great company continued to put Lacey at ease as they exchanged snowboarding stories of the day.

"So how's Jake doing?" Jim asked.

Lacey's face lit up at the mere mention of her son. "I miss that little guy. He comes home from his dad's tomorrow. He seems to be adjusting to all the changes life's thrown at him, what with Peter leaving and his dad, Clint, being diagnosed HIV positive."

Doug and Martha looked up, and Jim nearly choked on a bite of his egg plant primavera, trying to hide his shock. "I didn't know. I'm—"

"It's okay," Lacey interrupted. "Actually, we found that out right before Peter left, so he was hit with kind of a double-whammy. But then, moving in with Doug and Martha was good for him, especially since he got to be with his best friend."

"It's been good for Adam, too," Martha offered. "You should see the two of them. They're like the Super Mario Brothers." This brought forth laughter as they talked about a trip they had taken to Solvang last Halloween, and how they had dressed up just like the Super Mario Brothers to go trick-or-treating.

Doug joined in, commenting on Jake's musical talent. "You should hear this boy on the piano, and he's never even had a lesson. We've spent many evenings with me on the guitar and him on the piano."

"Yeah, it's pretty amazing," Martha chimed in. "I'm glad someone's using the piano. Neither Adam nor Angela took to the lessons we paid for so it's been sitting there for years un-played."

Lacey smiled, thinking of some of the fun memories she and Jake had been blessed to make, even after so much pain.

Jim's voice surfaced above the memories. "I'd love to take him and Adam boarding sometime."

Lacey turned her attention to him, touched by the offer. "I'm sure they'd love it, and I bet they could almost keep up with you."

"Doug's told me that they love to board the half-pipe and that they're pretty good at it. They probably could teach me a thing or two."

"They still need someone to pull the reins in on them, though," Doug said. "They can be a little too daring up there. They scare the heck out of me sometimes."

"I can't even watch them," Martha said. Everyone laughed. The rest of the dinner conversation was lively and animated as Martha and Lacey shared stories about Adam and Jake's shenanigans.

On the way home, Lacey slipped into a comfortable silence as Doug, Martha, and Jim talked about plans for a boys' day on the mountain. Lacey listened as the conversation switched to politics, Doug's favorite subject, and the Christian Coalition, a group that Doug was very active in. After a few minutes, her mind wandered to Jake's homecoming tomorrow, and the things that she needed to get done before he came home. When they pulled up into her driveway, Jim offered to walk her to her door.

"That's okay, really," she declined with a big smile. "But thank you." She opened the door and got out and walked quickly to her front door.

Doug's lights shone right on the lock of her door. She put her key in, unlocked the door, turning to wave after she pushed it open. She watched the headlights pull out of the driveway before she closed the door. She let out a sigh of tired contentment and headed up the stairs to get ready for bed.

Minutes later, she pulled the covers down and arranged her pillows all the way down the opposite side of where she slept. Her last thought before drifting off to sleep was the realization that she hadn't even thought about the possibility of Ian calling her.

Who Says Older Is Better?

"Hurry up, Jake. We're going to be late." Lacey waited a few seconds and still heard nothing. She raised her voice a couple of decibels: "Jake, I'll be in the car. Hurry up." She reached for the door. "Please," she added.

This was the worst part of her day, when she had to fight with Jake to get him up and out for school. He definitely wasn't a morning person, and last night certainly hadn't helped things. His plane had been delayed for two hours, and it was eleven o'clock before they had finally made it home.

She started the car and looked down to see Jake's CD holder still on the floor in the front seat. She reached for it and put in Green Day, one of his favorite CDs, and skipped to his favorite song, "Burnout." Finally, halfway through the song, he came grudgingly out of the house. She turned up the volume, and he cracked a smile as he got into the car and hunkered down to try and grab a few more minutes of sleep before school.

They pulled up at 7:23, only seven minutes to spare. Lacey reached over and squeezed Jake's arm. "Rise and shine. We're here."

Jake pulled his head up out of his hood. He looked adorably tired.

"Have an awesome day. Remember, Martha is picking you and Adam up so you guys can hang out for a while. She'll bring you home when I'm done training at the gym tonight, so get your homework done, and when I get home, we can spend some time together."

Jake nodded his head. "Okay. Bye, Mom. Love you."

"More."

"Most," Jake replied, his voice sounding less monotone and more alive. It was a game they played, and it always made them both smile, no matter who ended with "most."

"You win. See you later." Lacey did an illegal U-turn just down the street from the school and sped away toward home. She pulled into her garage, and her cell phone rang. She didn't recognize the number, but answered it anyway. "Hello."

"Lacey?"

It was a guy's voice, but she didn't recognize it. She answered apprehensively. "This is Lacey."

"Lacey, it's me, Ian."

She almost choked on the sip of coffee she had just taken while trying to get out of the car so she decided to stay in the car.

"Are you okay?" he asked.

"Yeah, I'm okay. Sorry about that. I was taking a sip of coffee. I didn't recognize your voice."

"That's okay. Is this a bad time?"

"No, no. I just got home from dropping my son off at school and was going to start getting ready for work."

This time it was Ian's turn to be surprised.

"Are you there?" Lacey asked.

"Uh-huh. I didn't know you had a son."

"Not just a son, but a teenaged son." *That ought to scare him off,* Lacey thought.

"That's cool. So what's he into?"

"Music, skateboarding, girls," Lacey said emphatically.

Ian chuckled.

Lacey could feel his smile pull at her through the phone. "I guess those are the typical things for a fourteen-and-a-half-year-old boy." *I mean, that hasn't been all that long ago for you, right?* Lacey was dying to ask.

Ian responded with another chuckle. "Yeah, only instead of music first, it was sports for me then girls and then music."

Uh-huh, I bet the correct order was girls then sports and music. "Well, music is definitely an outlet for him," Lacey added.

"What does he play?"

"Well, he plays piano, and he's starting to teach himself guitar."

"Wow, that's really impressive. So is he any good on the skateboard?" Ian asked, obviously not scared off in the least.

"As a matter of fact, he is. He's actually trying to get a sponsor right now." A pause hung in the air that felt just a little too uncomfortable for Lacey. "So what are you doing?"

"I'm on my break at work," Ian said, looking at his watch. "Actually, my break is over, so can I call you later?"

"Sure," Lacey replied, trying to quiet the noise of her screaming thoughts.

"Can I call you at home?"

Lacey hesitated, but only for a few seconds. *What the heck,* she thought. "Sure." Lacey could hear his breath coming at a faster pace through the phone. "Do you need the number, or did Julia give you that too?"

Ian laughed. "No—I mean, yes, I need the number, and no, Julia would only give me your cell phone number."

"Now you sound out of breath."

"I'm going back in off my break," he said.

"Oh, I'm sorry," she said, recognizing his need to hurry. She gave him her home number.

"Got it," he said. "I'll talk to you tonight."

"Yeah, talk to you tonight, Ian." Lacey shut her phone, grabbed her coffee, and headed for the house. She came in through the back door and glanced at the clock and decided she had just enough time for her thirty-minute run on the treadmill before getting ready for work. Maybe that would help her burn off some of the anxiety and jitters she was feeling that were not a result of the coffee she had finished off, but because he had called after all.

Beth dialed Lacey's home number first, not sure if she was working or not. Her answering machine came on. "Hi. You've reached Lacey and Jake's voice mail. You know what to do. Wait for the beep, and we'll get back to you." Beth didn't wait for the beep. Instead, she hung up and dialed Lacey's cell phone and listened as it rang and rang. She was about to give up when Lacey answered "hello" almost out of breath.

"Are you okay, honey?" Beth asked nervously.

"I'm great, Mom. I was just on my way into my deposition. You know how crazy it is juggling all this stuff. I'm so sorry I haven't called. I was running all day yesterday, and then Jake's flight was delayed a couple of hours, so we got in really late."

"Well, I won't keep you. I was just getting a little worried since I haven't heard from you in a couple of days. I thought for sure you'd call us after your night out with the girls."

"I know. I have so much to tell you. I'll call you when I'm off the record and on my way home. It shouldn't be too long, okay?"

"Okay, honey. How long do you think your job will be today?"

"I think it's just a little workers' comp deposition, so I shouldn't be more than a couple of hours," she repeated. "I'll call you as soon as I'm done and fill you in on the last couple of days."

"I can't wait to hear. I'll be here at home. Your dad and I don't have any plans today."

Hearing her say good-bye, Bob made his way, hurriedly, to his chair and was sitting there reading *Readers' Digest* when Beth returned. "Did you reach her?" Bob asked.

"Yes. She's fine, just very busy. I guess Jake's plane was delayed a couple of hours last night and they got home really late.

Bob smiled as if to say, "I told you so."

"She said she'd call me as soon as she got off work. She thinks she'll only be on the record for a couple of hours."

Bob let out a sigh of relief. "Well, at least we know she's okay."

"Yeah, she said she had lots to tell me. She sounded good, just a bit tired. I'm just so glad she's out socializing again and recovering from that horrible blow from Peter. I thought for sure the girls weren't going to ever get her to go out again."

"Well, they did, and now you can stop worrying your pretty little head off. What do you say we take Yeager out for a walk?"

"That sounds like a great idea. I think we all could use some exercise."

Lacey checked in at the front desk of the prestigious law firm of Manning and Marder. "Hi, I'm the court reporter on the Harrison Case."

The receptionist looked up at Lacey and smiled. "I'll let them know you're here. Have a seat, and Mr. Thatcher's secretary will be right with you."

Lacey grabbed the named attorney's business card and sat down. No sooner had Lacey gotten comfortable when a tall, professionally dressed brunette came over and greeted Lacey. "I'll take you back to the conference room now."

"Great. Thank you." As soon as Lacey walked into the conference room, she realized that she had misjudged the type of deposition she would be reporting today. There were already four attorneys there, and none of them were her client. Having worked with this firm several times before, she wondered if she was in the wrong conference room. "Good morning, Counsel. While I'm getting set up, can I get a card from each of you and let me know who you represent? And if any one of you has a caption, that would be great. I need just a few minutes to set up." She hoped she sounded calmer than she felt and was relieved when her client walked in just after she had finished setting up her machine and laptop. Good morning, Counsel." Lacey smiled at her client, and he smiled back.

"Good morning, Lacey."

Lacey was startled by his use of her first name but tried not to show it. She sat down and turned on her laptop, noticing that she had been given a caption, and there was a card from each of them. She began inputting the caption into her computer and realized why there were so many attorneys in the room. This wasn't a workers' comp deposition, but a personal injury case involving contractors, construction companies, and from the looks of the caption that included Stanley Ladder Company, another defendant, the case could very well have a product liability component as well.

She looked up in the direction of her client. "Mr. Tulak, are we waiting for any other attorneys?"

"Yes, as a matter of fact…"

The door opened and two more people came in the room. "Make that a 'no.' I think we're all here, except for the deponent." Mr. Tulak introduced himself to the other attorneys as they found seats around the conference table.

Lacey repeated her request for business cards to the newcomers and asked Mr. Tulak, "Counsel, who are we deposing today?"

He spoke so quietly, Lacey had to lean in toward him to make sure she heard him right. "Call me Danny." And without skipping a beat, he said, "We're deposing the person most knowledgeable. Here's the notice so you can get the spelling of his name."

"Thanks, *Danny.*"

He smiled and then turned to talk to his colleagues. Lacey began inputting all the attorneys' names and firm information, as well as whom they represented. She put her cards in the order they were seated, and came up with speaker signs for each of them. Her hands shook as she realized there were going to be eight people involved in the proceeding. *Let's pray they don't try to talk at once.* She looked at each card again so she could come up with some form of speaker identification for each of them. That way when they spoke, they would be correctly identified in the transcript.

She began to input the first thing that came to her mind about each of them into her computer. The closest attorney on her right was Mr. Thatcher, representing the deponent. The first thing that caught Lacey's eye was the fact that he was bald. *Bald. Bald it is,* Lacey decided. One by one, she entered their new names into her computer, laughing at a couple of the code names she'd given them. *They'd freak if they saw how I identified them on this machine every time they spoke,* she thought.

"What's so funny?" Danny asked her.

Lacey almost choked on her own surprise at having been caught smiling for what appeared to be no reason. "I'm just laughing at the mistakes I'm making on my computer. It's a court reporting thing, I guess."

She didn't need to wait for a response from him because the door opened and their missing person walked in.

Mr. Thatcher stood and shook the gentleman's hand. "Good morning, Mr. Jolenwavinski. Why don't we go in my office for a few minutes and I'll look over the documents you brought."

Lacey finished inputting her code names for each attorney into her computer. She had just finished creating the caption pages and putting all of the appearance information in when Mr.

Thatcher and the deponent walked back into the room. Lacey let them get settled and then looked over at her client who indicated she could start. Lacey swore in the witness, and the proceedings began.

When they took their first break, Lacey grabbed her phone from her purse and headed outside. "Hey, Mom, I'm on a quick break and thought I'd call you so you wouldn't worry. I thought it was just going to be a little depo, but apparently I was wrong. I'm on the record with the PMK and we're probably going to go for a couple more hours."

"Well, how's it going? Are you getting everything down okay?"

"Considering there are seven attorneys and a witness with an accent thicker than peanut butter, yeah, I guess so."

"Oh, Lacey, I'm so sorry," Beth said emphatically.

"Is there such a thing as Russian English, Mom?"

Beth chuckled. "Are they at least behaving and waiting their turn?

"A couple of times they've talked right over each other, and I've had to stop them and have them repeat stuff, but they've been pretty professional. I think they're being extra tolerant because they can't understand the witness either."

"You'll get through it. You always do."

"Thanks, Mom. Remind me of that when I'm pulling out my hair and wiping tears of frustration off of my face as I try to edit this thing." They both chuckled. "I'll give you a call on my way home."

"Please do. I still haven't heard about your night out."

"I will," Lacey assured her. "I'll talk to you soon."

Lacey pulled into the 24-Hour Fitness in Rancho Cucamonga and parked in her usual spot. On the way in, she saw a new friend and stopped to talk. "Hey, Seth, how's it going?"

"Not so bad. How's the training going?"

"It's going great."

Seth didn't even hear her. He knew before he even asked because she was definitely looking more and more toned compared to the first time he had laid eyes on her. That had been just two months ago. He smiled at the memory of it. She was saying good-bye to her trainer and hadn't been watching where she was going and bumped into him while he was doing his thing on the bicep machine. He would never forget her warm smile and flustered apology. They had been friends ever since. He liked the fact that she didn't treat him any different from the other guys he saw her talk with despite being half their size. No, she made him feel as if he were six feet tall. She had that way about her; she could make anyone feel so special, and she didn't even realize it.

Lacey could tell his thoughts were obviously somewhere else so she stared at him for a minute and smiled. He was incredibly handsome with sandy brown hair, big green eyes, and a smile that reached out and embraced her. He had a great sense of humor, especially when it came to joking about his short stature, which really didn't bother her. He was fun to be with because of his love for life and it always impressed her that he seemed to have a lot of friends. "Seth?"

"Huh?"

"I said my training is going great."

"I'm sorry. My head was somewhere else."

"So did you decide if you were going to compete in the Las Vegas competition or not?"

"I'm leeeaning toward doing it," he said with a smile.

Giggling at his little joke, Lacey caught his eyes. "Well, I think you should, and besides, it's my first competition, and I need you there. Your being there will make it all the more memorable."

He saw her trainer walking up behind her. "Hey, here comes the slave driver. You better get going."

Lacey turned and saw Harrison walking toward her.

"You ready, Lacey?"

The hard tone of voice and the hardness of his stare, which definitely matched his hard body, told Lacey that he hadn't had a good day and he was in one of his moods. She turned to Seth. "I think this one's going to hurt, but I'd better get it over with."

Seth laughed and looked at Harrison. "Have fun, but don't hurt her too badly." Harrison smiled and tapped him on the back. "Take care, Seth."

Lacey leaned into Seth. "Thanks a lot. I'll talk to you later—if he doesn't kill me, that is." She followed Harrison, and they stopped at the free weight section. He handed her two free weights, fifteen pounds each.

"We're going to work shoulders and abs today. Have you done your cardio yet?"

"I did thirty minutes this morning."

"Good for you," Harrison said a little gruffly.

The way he was acting reminded Lacey of their first session. He had come off so arrogant and ticked off at the world that Lacey had nearly cancelled her remaining sessions. Looking back on it now, she was glad she hadn't. She had pushed through a couple of trainings with him, and after that, he seemed to warm up to her. Lacey had learned a lot about him in the few months they'd been training together. Not only was he gorgeous on the outside—best described as short and stocky with brown hair, huge brown, eyes and a great smile with perfect teeth—he was also funny at times and very honest, sometimes painfully so, which made the decision to compete in the Ms. Fitness contest a bit easier. He certainly wouldn't have recommended her entering it if he didn't believe in her, and Lacey knew him well enough now to know he would never let her get up on stage and make a fool of herself.

"Lacey, are you paying attention?"

"Sorry. I was just reminiscing about the first few training sessions. You seem as grumpy now as you did then. Is everything okay?"

Harrison shook his head and smiled.

"What's so funny?"

"I remember thinking that you had a chip on your shoulder too. But look how far you've come," he said. "This competition is already proving to be good for you. Remember, it's not the prize but the journey you embark upon to attain the prize. Now let's get these shoulders burning."

By six o'clock, Lacey was home, showered, and in the kitchen putting the finishing touches on their salad when she heard Jake come in. "Hey, buddy, how was your day?" The sound of the toilet flushing told her he hadn't heard a word she said. She waited until he came into the kitchen and tried again. "So how was your day?"

"It was just another day, Mom."

Uh-oh, she thought. His tone put her on the defensive. "What's that supposed to mean? Was there anything good about the day, bad about the day? Anything I should know about?"

Jake shot her a look, telling her he hated it when she fired questions at him like that. In fact, lately he hated a lot of things. She could only imagine what he was feeling. After all, he probably would like it if he could just go back to his favorite time, when he, his mom, and his dad were all a family.

Lacey tried to give him a look that said, "Everything's going to be okay," hoping he'd feel guilty for being such a grump.

"Yeah, something did happen that I should probably tell you."

Lacey stopped mixing the salad and looked up.

"Adam got in trouble for defending me today because some jerk was in my face and accusing me of stealing his girlfriend."

Lacey walked up to Jake and elbowed him gently in his ribs. "Does my boy have a new girlfriend, huh, huh?"

Jake didn't respond.

Lacey leaned up against the counter. "So did you steal somebody's girlfriend?"

"No, Mom. The guy was ticked off because I showed him up on the skateboard at lunchtime."

"So how did you handle it?"

"Well, I was going to take a swing at the guy, but Adam stopped me, and the yard duty lady thought we were all fighting so we all got in trouble and had to go sit in the principal's office for the rest of lunch."

Lacey knew she had to choose her words carefully. "Well, that inhales vigorously."

"Mom, you're a dork," Jake said with a smile.

Lacey drank in his smile. "Yeah, well, would you help your dorky mom get the table set for dinner, and unplug the phone so we don't have any interruptions while we eat and hang out."

After dinner, Lacey did the dishes while Jake played the piano. She loved to hear him play and his talent amazed her. He played the piano like Kenny G played the saxophone. Lacey looked up for a minute, the music pulling at her heart, demanding her attention. It was beautiful, but it sounded so sad. Lacey stopped what she was doing and walked to the hallway that joined the formal area and the kitchen. She stood and watched him. It was as though everything that had ever caused him pain was making its way down to several keys simultaneously, one hand creating an awe-inspiring melody, while the other hand was creating the distant but ever-present harmony.

She turned and went back into the kitchen to look over his homework. By the time she coerced him to bed, it was almost nine-thirty. She sat down in her big, comfy chair, exhausted. *What a day*, she thought. It had been a good job and—

Suddenly Lacey remembered she had forgotten to call Mom. "Nuts," she said to the silence. Reaching for her phone, she turned it on and there was no dial tone. "What the…" And then she remembered that she had Jake unplug it at dinner. She was shocked that it was still unplugged. Jake loved to talk on the phone. *Well, it's too late to call her now. I'll do it first thing tomorrow morning*, she thought. She put the phone down and went downstairs to plug it back in. She wasn't even halfway up the stairs when she heard it ring. She ran the rest of the way, hoping that it didn't wake Jake up. He needed all the sleep he could get with the last couple of days he'd had. She made it by the fourth ring and grabbed it, a bit out of breath. "Hello."

"Hey, Lacey, it's me, Ian. Is it too late to call?"

Lacey swore that her heart skipped a beat. In the busyness of her day, she had forgotten to worry if Ian would call or not. "No. I was just running up the stairs so the phone wouldn't wake up Jake."

Ian chuckled. "I have some crazy timing, huh? Last time I caught you drinking your coffee and you choked, and this time you're out of breath from running."

Lacey could hear the smile in his voice, so she knew he was teasing her and not being sarcastic. She made herself comfortable in her chair for the second time that night. "So how was your day?"

"Good. We had some major power outages at a refinery, so I spent most of the day up on a ladder and in the air. But, hey, somebody's got to do it, and that's why they pay us the big bucks."

"I thought I overheard you tell Julia that you're an electrician. Who do you work for?"

"Edison. So how about you, did you have a good day?"

"Yeah, actually it was a good day."

"You're a court reporter, right?"

"Yes, I'm a court reporter. How did you know that? On second thought, don't tell me. Julia told you, right?"

"You guessed it."

"Anyway, it was a good day, a good job. There is something good about every job, really, because I usually learn something new every day I'm on the record."

"I've always wondered how that little machine worked," Ian said. "I had jury duty a couple of months ago, and I remember the judge asked the stenographer to read back something for us, and it was amazing. Is it a bunch of codes and things?"

Lacey appreciated his open curiosity about her job. "No, it's not codes. The machine doesn't even have all of the letters of the alphabet so…"

"So how do you do that, get what everyone is saying?"

Lacey was surprised at his interest and his relevant questions. "Well, everything is written phonetically, and we do a lot of phrasing and abbreviations. It's not easy and some days are better than others, but the more you do it, the better you get."

"So what do you do when there's more than one person talking at the same time?"

"I can get it for a few minutes, but then I have to stop them and ask them to please not speak over each other. The trick is to do it nicely because I usually wait until I can't do it anymore, and I'm pretty frustrated. That happened a lot today, and I was constantly playing a catch-up game, so I was pretty tired."

"Is that a hint? Do you want me to let you go?"

Lacey felt her face turn three shades of red. "Oh, no, I wasn't meaning that at all. Besides, that was only a third of the day. Then there was training and—"

"Training for what?"

Lacey hesitated a second before she answered him, her thoughts returning to that dance the other night, the feel of his hard body up against hers and his symmetrical physique. "Well, I'm competing in a Ms. Fitness show," she said, more confident than she felt.

"Get out. Are you really?"

"Yes, I really am."

"Wow, that's great. When is it?"

"Three months, two weeks, and five days, so there's still plenty of time to back out."

Ian laughed. "But who's counting, right?"

"There's a lot of training for it, and I still can't believe I'm gong through with it."

"You're not going to start looking like a *she* man, are you?"

"That's what everybody says." Lacey laughed. "No, it's not like that. It's not bodybuilding. They judge you on muscle tone, endurance, social interaction; and you have to perform a fitness routine."

Ian let out a sigh of relief. "That's good; I'd hate to date a girl with bigger muscles than mine. Speaking of dating, what are you doing Saturday?"

"Are you asking me out on a date?" Lacey asked, trying not to sound so surprised.

"I'm trying to," Ian said, a smile evident in his voice.

I haven't done this in years. All kinds of thoughts were swirling in her head.

"So are you busy?" Ian asked.

He's so much younger than me. He's going to freak when he sees me in the daylight. "I don't think I've got any plans, but it depends on what my son is up to for the weekend. He probably wouldn't mind hanging out with his best friend for a while."

"Okay. Well, how about if I check back with you in a couple of days, then?"

"Sure. I should know something by Wednesday night," she said, trying not to sound too eager or too excited.

"Then I'll talk to you in a couple of days. Take care, Lacey."

"Good night, Ian." The dial tone said he was gone, but his voice was still reverberating in her mind as she got ready for bed. *Why didn't I just tell him I'd go out with him?* She smiled as she lay her head down before drifting off to sleep.

Ego Booster

Lacey and Jake pulled up in Martha's driveway and barely missed what looked like a sideways triangle made of wood lying in front of the garage. "I guess that's not a good idea," Lacey said, putting the car in reverse.

Jake, who had been pretty quiet up to this point, picked his head up and saw immediately what she was talking about. "Yeah, don't run into that."

"So what is 'that'?"

"It's our skateboard ramp; at least it will be when it's done."

"Well, that sounds pretty cool, but right now can you help me bring some of this stuff in?"

Between the two of them, they managed to carry Lacey's two portable scrapbook organizers, her overnight bag, and Jake's skateboard and overnight bag up the walkway to the front door. Fortunately, they didn't have to put everything down to ring the doorbell because Adam, trying to scare them, opened the door at the same time they had landed on the porch. Both Jake and Adam broke out into a fit of boyish giggles. Lacey loved to watch them. They were such goofs, always making everyone laugh, as well as each other. Martha was right behind Adam. Reaching for Jake first, she embraced him with a big hug and a kiss on the cheek. Jake returned the gestures, and with a smile on his face, dropped his stuff in the entryway inside, and he and Adam ran outside to work on their ramp.

"Here, let me help you with that," Martha offered after giving Lacey a big hug.

"Thanks. I didn't realize I had collected so much stuff, and this is only half of it. I must have a disease called scrapbookitis."

Martha laughed. "Yeah, well, you haven't seen my craft room lately. My scrapbook section is taking over. Aren't you the one that got me hooked on this?"

Lacey laughed, admitting that she had.

Martha smiled. "I'm so glad we're making the time to do this today."

"Yeah, this is like home away from home, and I'm glad I'm here too. I've just really not had anything I've wanted to scrapbook until lately. I mean, I brought the pictures from the last couple of months of things Jake and I have done, the trip we took, a few of Jake and Adam skateboarding."

"Well, that sounds like a good start," Martha said enthusiastically, leading them upstairs to put Lacey's overnight bag in her room.

"And I even have some pictures from last week's night out with the girls, so that's a good start for my new single life, I guess."

"I can't wait to see those."

"Yeah, I met Julia for lunch the other day, and she gave them to me. I hardly remembered any picture-taking."

"From the sounds of things, you were too distracted to remember having your picture taken. So did Julia get a picture of *him*?"

Lacey laughed at the inflection in her voice. "As a matter of fact, yes."

"Well, it's time to begin putting the photos of your new life into a new scrapbook, and maybe when your heart's more whole, you can go back and finish the other book."

They headed downstairs, and Martha quickly changed the subject. "So I want to hear about this guy and how he asked you out. And, by the way, I think it was a great idea to have him pick you up over here, and not just so we can meet him, but for safety's sake, for you and Jake."

Lacey agreed as they made their way into the dining room. Martha already had all of her things spread out on one side of the huge dining table. Lacey didn't know what to say about Ian or the first night she met him. She started unpacking some of her scrapbooking essentials, colored paper, brightly decorated frames, different-colored calligraphy pens, scissors with different-shaped edges, and her glue stick. She still wasn't sure herself why she had agreed to go out with him, but then again, deep down inside, she knew the root was in the redemption of her bruised and beaten ego that Peter had left her with.

"Let's get something to drink before we get started," Martha suggested. They went into the kitchen, and Martha pulled out the pitcher of iced tea. "You're still training for the show, right?" she asked Lacey.

"Yes, I'm still in it, at least training for it."

"I just wanted to make sure before I put real sugar in."

Lacey watched Martha reach for the packets of Splenda and put them on the counter.

Martha poured them both a glass of tea and handed Lacey hers. "You know, I'm not really sure why you're doing this competition, but if it helps get you back on the right track and feeling good about yourself, I'm all for it."

"Thanks, Martha. That really means a lot."

"Oh, and I made us some fat-free treats to munch on later, and our lunch is already in the oven."

Lacey was touched by her friend's thoughtfulness, and she knew that Martha was happiest when in the kitchen, which made it easier to accept her kindness, but she still scolded her half-heartedly. "You shouldn't have, but since you did, what are we having?"

"I baked a spinach quiche for us and I got them some French rolls and cold cuts so they can make their own sandwiches."

Lacey's mouth watered at the thought of Martha's awesome spinach quiche. "You make Martha Stewart look like an amateur, my friend."

They made their way back into the dining room and sat down. Martha looked at Lacey with a twinkle in her eye that bounced off her deep dimples. "Wait until you see some of the pictures I have of our boys."

They worked and talked, sharing photos and ideas for their scrapbook pages and reliving the memories brought back by the photographs. Martha showed Lacey some pictures of the boys' shenanigans when they had a sleepover shortly after they had moved out on their own. There was Jake sound asleep with shaving cream all over his chin, cheeks, and nose; and the next picture showed him after he had scratched his face, and the shaving cream was everywhere.

Martha paused until Lacey's laughter subsided. "Here's the next night when Jake got Adam back." The picture showed Jake holding Adam's finger in a glass of warm water, and Adam had wet himself after only a few minutes.

Martha's narration brought the pictures to life and both Lacey and Martha laughed their way through the first few pages that Martha put together for her family album.

Lacey began with the trip to Magic Mountain with Jake; his dad, Clint; his dad's girlfriend, Jenna; and Adam. Lacey showed Martha the picture of Jake and his dad.

"So what's his girlfriend like?" Martha asked.

"She's got to be the sweetest girl I've met in a long time. It's really hard to be angry at her for what's happened to Clint."

"What do you mean?" Martha asked. "I mean, I know that Clint got the HIV virus from Jenna, but I didn't realize that you harbored feelings of ill will toward her."

"Well, I just wonder why she didn't tell Clint before she slept with him that she suspected that she had the virus because her ex-husband was a hemophiliac."

"Oh," was all Martha could say.

"So now, it's like this domino effect because it affects Jake and his well-being as well as his dad's, so it's just kind of sucky. But like I said, after spending the day with her, I can't stay mad at her and we should get along for the benefit of Jake. Besides, my anger won't make it go away. Living with you for that year, and going to church with you sometimes did teach me something.

"Thanks for saying that, Lacey. I can't imagine what it must be like for them, especially for her."

Lacey was quiet, not used to Martha's display of compassion, especially toward someone who, in her opinion at least, was considered to be the enemy because of all the pain she had caused.

Martha continued, "Can you imagine the guilt she feels, knowing how many lives this has affected, and she's the one that actually has AIDS now? This has to be even more difficult for her. What about her daughter? How old is she?"

"She's a couple years younger than Jake."

"Wow, I just couldn't imagine carrying that cross every day," Martha said sadly. "We take so much for granted."

"You're right; we do take a lot of things for granted." Her own words brought back a memory and Lacey giggled at the picture of the heaping basket of unmated socks and the look of dismay on Martha's face every time she even attempted to mate a few pair.

Martha looked up. "What's so funny?"

"I was just thinking about you and the unmated socks."

They broke out in laughter at the memory. "Yeah, we certainly had enough socks to cover the feet of a whole tribe. You'll be happy to know, I don't do that anymore. I'm trying to change my shopping ways." She handed Lacey some photos of their ski trip just a few weeks ago. "Hey, look at these."

"Those all came out great," Lacey offered.

"Yeah, that's a great one of all of us. Oh, Jim told me to tell you 'hi' and he misses seeing you at church."

"I know, I've got to get back into it."

"He said the offer still stands for him to get together with Jake and Adam."

"What a nice guy."

"Uh-huh," Martha murmured, not looking up from the page she was working on, "He really is. There are a few of those left, you know."

Lacey smiled and finished her Magic Mountain photos, her thoughts still on her son's dad and his dilemma. When she had decorated the pages and made little captions on each of them, she held them up for Martha.

"They all look great. I love that picture of Adam and Jake on the Viper," she said laughing. "They couldn't have got their hair to spike like that if they'd worked on it for an hour and used an entire bottle of gel."

Lacey laughed in agreement and reached for her "moving day" photos. She looked through them all, trying to figure out which ones to put in the scrapbook. She handed them to Martha. "Remember this?"

"How could I forget that day?"

"How did you get so many people to come and help?" Lacey asked, still amazed whenever she thought about it.

"We didn't do anything, Lacey. They just genuinely care about you and Jake and they wanted to help you get settled into your home as quickly and easily as possible. They really live out their faith."

Lacey was quiet, thinking about that last statement, wondering what it must be like to believe in something or someone so emphatically that that faith guided your every step of life; on the other hand, the times she'd been to her church had made it easier to understand. "Well, you were like a moving machine and a home decorator all wrapped up in one," Lacey reminded her as they returned to their pages.

Lacey finished her "moving day" photos and moved on to the skateboard outings with Jake and Adam while Martha worked on her latest family vacation photo pages, each comfortable with the other's company, content to share in the silence.

Outside, Adam and Jake were hunkered down, each holding a side of their ramp while Doug hammered away, attaching the plywood on each side to the triangular piece in the center. Doug loved it when Adam asked for his help with a project, and it seemed as he got older, the projects got bigger. He smiled as he looked at the boys. Jake was like a son to him, and as far as he was concerned, any time Jake wanted his help with something, Doug wouldn't miss the opportunity to be a loving and positive male role model for him. The kid had had too many tough breaks in his short life, and Doug worried about him as though he were his own son. As he thought about Jake, his hammering became more deliberate. Suddenly he was brought out of his thoughts by a scream.

"What the..."

The boys laughed. Adam had pretended he got hit by the hammer, and Doug had fallen for it. They gave each other a high-five.

Doug put the hammer down, shaking his head and joining them with his own one-of-a-kind chuckle. "Come on, boys. We've only got a few more nails to drive in and then what do you say we go in and ask Mom what's for lunch."

The slamming of the front door startled them both, that is, until they heard the boys' voices echoing through the hall. "What's for lunch?" Adam and Jake asked in unison, charging upon them at the table.

Lacey was shocked to realize that they had been working for almost two hours. The clock said twelve-thirty, and the growl in her stomach confirmed it.

Martha stood up and headed toward the kitchen. "You guys get to build your own submarine sandwiches, so I'll get all of the fixings out while you go wash up."

By the time they washed up, Lacey and Martha had everything set out on the table in the family room so everyone could make their own lunch. They sat down, and for the next thirty minutes, Lacey and Martha were entertained by the Three Musketeers, because when Doug was with them, the little boy came out in him and he was as goofy as they were. The only time they got serious was when Martha and Doug asked Lacey if she'd given any more thought to enrolling Jake in Ontario Christian High School. Both boys joined in the conversation, voicing their agreement to give it a try and by the end of lunch, it was unanimous. The boys would start, and hopefully finish, high school at Ontario Christian.

It didn't take the girls long to settle back in to their scrap-booking, each lost in the memories recollected from the photos, and their own creativity that turned their pictures into stories. Martha broke the silence. "So tell me more about Ian."

"Well, as a matter of fact, I was just getting ready to start putting these pictures on a page." Lacey handed her one picture at a time, explaining each memory as she showed them to her.

"Wow, Sophie looks great, and so does Nikki. How are they doing?" Martha asked.

"They're doing great. Sophie is coping with single parenting and making her way through the job transition right now and Nikki is Nikki, still as funny and naïve as ever."

"What about Susie? How come she wasn't there with you guys?"

"She was kind of nonchalant about the reason she couldn't go, but I have a feeling it has something to do with Jimmy. I think things are getting worse instead of better."

"That's too bad. I hope she gets out before it's too late."

"Yeah, you're not the only one." Lacey handed the last two pictures to Martha and laughed openly at the look on her face. Lacey didn't think her eyes could get any bigger, but they did, and usually Lacey could tell by the expression in her eyes what she was thinking, but not this time. "So what do you think?"

Martha cleared her throat and just blurted out the first thing that came to her mind when she saw the pictures. "He looks young," she exclaimed, "young and gorgeous." The last comment said with an approving nod of her head. "And scrumptious," she added.

"Did you just say *scrumptious*?" Lacey asked laughing, though she understood her friend pretty well. She loved to cook and entertain, and therefore, she related so many things to food.

"So with looks like that, I've got to ask, does he have any common sense? Is he arrogant, stuck on himself? What's he like?"

Lacey was still back at the first question. "As a matter of fact, he does come across as rather intelligent. He's an electrician, so he's got to have some smarts. He's very proud of what he does for a living; at least he comes across that way on the phone. Every time we've talked this last week, he's had some electrical emergency and he seems to thrive on it, or in it.

"Uh-huh," Martha said, listening attentively while working on her pictures.

Lacey continued, "And I wouldn't call him arrogant, though he is definitely confident and takes pride in how he looks," she added, remembering a couple of comments from some of their telephone conversations over the last several days.

"Do you guys talk about more than him?" Martha asked accusingly.

Lacey didn't miss the tone in her friend's questions. "Of course we do. In fact, the first couple of conversations we had, he seemed genuinely interested in me, Jake, and court reporting. He even asked some pretty intelligent questions about my job."

"Well, if I seem a bit pessimistic, it's because I'm just watching out for you and Jake. And the fact that he's probably younger than you, at least by the looks of his picture, is a good ego booster for you. There's nothing wrong with dating a younger guy. Just don't go getting serious about him."

"Do you think it's too soon for me to be dating?" Lacey knew that Martha would give her an honest answer.

"I don't think it's too soon at all. You deserve to have some fun. I just would feel better, for your sake, if you were going out with a guy like Jim."

"Jim's nice and all, but..."

"I know... he's not your type. I just don't want to see you give some guy too much power and space in that still-wounded heart of yours."

"Oh, don't you worry. I have a new philosophy for my single life," Lacey said matter-of-factly.

"What kind of a new philosophy?" Martha asked.

"Wine me; dine me; you're never gonna find me," Lacey said, pointing to her heart.

Martha nodded her agreement at Lacey's newfound philosophy. "Just enjoy your season of singleness, Lacey. Besides, there's no such thing as a perfect person, but there is a person perfect for you."

Lacey had to think about that for a minute. "Says who?" It was her turn to be pessimistic.

Martha caught her gaze and just looked up toward the ceiling, which sent Lacey back into her head to ponder all that they'd talked about. The silence was a welcome companion as they worked on the photos, each lost in her own memories.

Jake opened up the door and ran in. "Mom!" he yelled.

Startled, Martha and Lacey looked up just in time to see him run into the dining room. "What's wrong, Jake?"

"Nothing's wrong. You didn't tell me that guy had a Corvette."

"What are you talking about, Jake?"

"That guy you're going out with tonight."

"'That guy' has a name, Jake."

Jake continued as though Lacey hadn't spoken. "He's really cool. He let me and Adam sit in his car and listen to one of my CDs. You should hear that sound system. I can't believe you didn't hear it. We had the volume up all the way to ten, and you could feel the vibrations. It was way cool."

Adam was right beside him. "He's pretty ripped too."

Martha spoke before Lacey could. "What's that supposed to mean?"

Adam and Jake looked at each other and started to laugh, and Jake answered Martha: "It means he's buff, works out," and looking to Lacey, he finished with, "and young."

Was there an emphasis on "young," or am I just imagining it? "Jake, where is he? Did you leave him standing outside?" Lacey sounded as flustered as she felt, but it diminished as she and Martha exchanged smiles and a look that spoke of things that only moms understand.

"He's out there talking with Doug."

Suddenly a bit nervous, Lacey stood up. "Well, I better finish getting ready, then," she said to no one in particular. "Jake, would you let him know I'll be out in a few minutes?"

"Okay. I'm going to take me and Adam's favorite CD out to him and ask if we can listen to it in his—" The rest of the sentence was swallowed up with the slam of the door, and Lacey ran upstairs to finish getting ready.

Martha tiptoed over to the front window to see if she could sneak a peak at Lacey's date, but all she could make out was— Her eyes got big as she took in his car. *Well, if he looks anything like his car...* And then she saw Jake, right there in the front seat with him leaning forward. Martha had been a bit worried about Jake even knowing that his mom was going out on a date, but seeing him now, her concern melted away. Lacey had told her that she had not made a big deal of it when she told Jake; in fact she kind of downplayed it to him. Martha wondered if she had downplayed it to her as well, because she sure hadn't given her a whole lot of information about this guy. All she knew was that he was a good dancer, a good looker, and an electrician. And quite a bit younger.

She made her way upstairs to check on her friend. "Lacey, what color did you say you're wearing? I'm going to look for some jewelry for you."

Just then, Lacey stepped out of her bathroom tentatively. "Does this look okay, Martha?"

Martha turned her gaze from her jewelry box and stood straight up. She couldn't believe that Lacey didn't know she looked great. "I wouldn't say you look just 'okay,'" Martha said a bit seriously. Before Lacey's face fell to the ground, Martha continued, "I'd say you look pretty fantabulous." She was wearing tight, but not too tight, low-rise jeans, a lacey long-sleeved top and boots. When Martha had given her the once-over, she looked Lacey straight in the face and smiled as she handed her a necklace and matching earrings. "Now, here, put these on, and let's finish your hair. You can't keep him waiting too much longer."

They walked to his car, and Lacey turned to wave good-bye to Jake. They were all out there watching them and waving back. Lacey couldn't believe how well it had gone with her friends and her son meeting Ian. She looked up and spoke a silent thank you, grateful that Jake had really taken to Ian and didn't seem to be as upset as he was when she had first told him that she was going out on a date.

Ian reached in front of her and opened her door. "Watch your head," he said with a smile that was still on his face as he slid into the driver's side.

As he pulled away from the curb, the G forces from the acceleration pushed her back in her seat, and she let out a little squeal.

Ian looked over at her and smiled. "You okay?"

"Sure. I just wasn't prepared for that take-off."

Ian refrained from squeezing her leg and, instead, reached over and made a motion to check her seat belt. He was dying and had been dying to squeeze something on her ever since he'd first laid eyes on her. That urge had only intensified when she had come outside to let him know she was ready. She was just as petite and toned as he remembered from the night he met her. The only difference was she seemed a bit more relaxed, and hopefully it was because she was more comfortable with him. Tonight, her look was conservatively sultry. He had no idea how he was going to keep his hands off her, but he could tell that Lacey was not the typical kind of girl you meet in a bar, and he'd definitely need to show some restraint if he wanted to get to know her. "Are you hungry?" he asked to break the silence.

Lacey noticed that he looked right at her when he spoke, and she noticed for the first time that he had eyes the color of Kauai waters. "Well," Lacey stammered, trying to figure out how to tell him she wasn't really hungry, "I had a big lunch so I'm not that hungry right now."

Ian smiled. "Perfect, but I bet you by the time we get there, you will be."

"Where is 'there'?" Lacey asked tentatively.

"I thought we'd head for the beach. You okay with that?"

So he really does listen, Lacey thought, as she remembered that she had told him that the beach was one of her favorite places. "That sounds great," Lacey said, excited to be going to the beach, and at the same time, a little panic-stricken wondering how they would fill the time. *What would they talk about?* she wondered.

As if reading her mind, Ian turned up the stereo, which was playing "Sweet Child of Mine" by Guns and Roses.

Well, you certainly can't tell his age by the music he listens to, Lacey thought. *This is more my era,* she thought to herself. The song came to an end and another Guns and Roses song started, which answered her question. "I was wondering if that was a CD," she said, looking at Ian.

Ian smiled in response and pointed to his CD case. "Here, help yourself," he said over the music.

Lacey busied herself looking through his CDs. He really did have a wide range of music that he listened to, everything from jazz to rock 'n' roll, punk, rap, and top forties. Lacey smiled as she realized that the CD holder she was looking through reminded her of her son's, which pushed the big question to the forefront of her mind but she let it stay there for the moment. She took out the Guns and Roses CD and put in a Journey CD. She cleared her throat, mustering confidence, and then before she could stop herself, "So how old are you, Ian?"

The question obviously caught him off guard. "How old do you think I am?" he asked with a grin on his face.

"Well, do you always answer a question with a question?" Lacey bantered at him good-naturedly.

Ian smiled back. "Not usually," he answered. "Does it bother you that I'm younger than you?"

His boldness caught her off guard and placed her on solid ground in a funny kind of way. Giving him a taste of his own medicine, she shot back with, "Does it bother you that I'm a little older than you?" There, she had admitted in a subtle kind of way that she knew she was older than him. The only thing she didn't admit, nor really know, was just how much older she was. She tapped her foot to the beat of the music as she watched the road fly by.

Ian watched her, drinking her in, her scent, her cute smile that made her eyes dance, and her wittiness was an added bonus. He wasn't looking for anything serious by any means, but something told him she'd be worth going to the next level. His instincts also told him she wasn't going to be putting out anytime soon, and he smiled with surprise as he realized he was okay with that too… for a while.

Being with her was easy, easy on the eyes, and she was easy to talk to. He liked the fact that she was pretty independent but affectionate at the same time. And gullible, wow, was she gullible. He chuckled out loud.

Lacey picked her head up from the head rest. "What's so funny?"

"Nothing's funny. I'm just thinking about you." This time he didn't resist his urge and reached for her knee and squeezed it gently. He looked over at her and winked, and she smiled at him.

By the time Ian paid for parking and pulled into the parking lot, they both were relaxed and having a good time.

Lacey noticed that he took two spots to park, and she couldn't resist baiting him. "What's the matter? You don't want a door-ding?"

Ian chuckled in response and opened his door to get out.

Lacey undid her seat belt as he came to open her door. The ocean breeze reached out and embraced her as she stepped out. Ian shut the door behind her and reached for her jacket and held it out for her. Lacey gave him a point in her mental scorecard. She put her right arm in and turned to put her left arm in and came face to face with him. Her breath caught in her throat as he bent down and gave her the cutest little peck right on the tip of her nose, as if they had done this very thing several times before. She giggled and Ian laughed.

"I just had to do that. You have a cute nose, you know," he said, his eyes bright and his smile dazzling.

Lacey recovered quickly, though she could feel the color on her cheeks from the bittersweet embarrassment, grateful, and yet disappointed that he hadn't drawn her into a long mouth-watering kiss. "No one's ever told me that before," she said a bit breathlessly.

"It's the little things we need to pay attention to, and something tells me there's a lot I need to pay attention to when I'm with you." He stood a few inches taller than her and put his arm around her, gently pulling her to his side and motioning her forward. "I thought we'd go for a walk before dinner."

They walked down the pier, and Lacey was quiet, thinking about what he had just said as well as the planning and thoughtfulness that he had put into their date. They walked that way for a while, comfortable with their silence, the background filled with the sound of the crashing waves. It was intoxicating, Lacey thought, and it would be very easy to get carried away with the sensation of it all, but she resolved to just enjoy the rest of the date with her heart shut.

Lacey watched him drive away and let herself into Doug and Martha's house quietly. The lamp in the living room was still on, and she was expecting one or both of them to be downstairs waiting for her because it really wasn't that late. When she didn't see anyone, she wasn't disappointed that they hadn't waited up for her. She really didn't want to share her night or her thoughts with anyone just yet. She let out a sigh of relief and tiptoed upstairs to the guest room.

About halfway up, she stopped dead in her tracks at the sound of voices. She waited and listened. Apparently the boys were still up, so she went to their door and tapped on it and stuck her head in. They were playing possum. She reached up and pushed the "off" button on the television and walked out of the room, closing the door behind her.

Juggling Act

Lacey reached to knock on the door and jumped when the door opened unexpectedly. Ian stood there, all smiles, looking his usual sexy self. She brought her hand back down and let the breath she'd been holding out in a rush. "You scared me." She wondered if he'd been watching her walk up his driveway, suddenly uncomfortable with the once-over she'd given the front of his house and his yard. She could just imagine what she must have looked like.

Ian reached for her and drew her into his arms, and Lacey forgot about his yard, and everything else, as she threw second-guessing herself to the wind. *This feels so good,* she thought, her arms going around his shoulders and neck easily. She melted into his embrace, which was definitely becoming a familiar and safe place to be over the last couple of weeks.

"Would you like to come in?" Ian asked, as he nuzzled her neck.

"Do you greet all your visitors like that?" Lacey asked jokingly. His response was drowned out by another voice.

"Hey, Lacey, it's good to see you," Tom said. "How are you?"

Lacey masked her surprise at Ian's brother's presence. "I'm great, Tom. How are you?"

"I'm great, actually. Here, let me take your sweater and get you something to drink. What would you like, red or white wine, sparkling water, diet or regular Pepsi, or would you like a beer?" He held his hand out to take her sweater.

Lacey handed it to him and followed them both into the kitchen, wondering if he would be joining them the whole evening or if he was on his way out. "Thanks, Tom. Diet Pepsi's fine." She looked to Ian for some sort of explanation that didn't go unnoticed by Tom, and before Ian could say a word, Tom offered up an explanation.

"I was supposed to have my own date here tonight, but she flaked out on me, so..." He faded off and then added sort of a P.S. "But Ian thought you'd be more comfortable if it was a double date."

Lacey looked up at Ian when she felt his arm go around her waist. Despite being completely embarrassed and frustrated that she was wearing her thoughts on her sleeve, Lacey offered up a nonchalant, "No worries, Tom. I just didn't expect to see you." The red in her cheeks subsided somewhat. She took the glass of Diet Pepsi Tom handed her suddenly aware of an incredibly yummy aroma. "What's cooking?"

Ian finally joined in the conversation. "It does smell good, brother." He squeezed Lacey closer to him. "He's the cook around here, thank God; otherwise, we wouldn't eat near as good."

Tom winked at Lacey. "Flattery will get you fed, my little brother."

"Oh, so that's why he's here," Lacey jokingly chided, remembering Ian telling her that he wasn't much of a cook. She took in her surroundings. The kitchen was cozy and inviting, not what you'd expect of two bachelors. The dining room off to the right was small, but big enough for their modern table that seated six comfortably. There was simple art on the walls, and Lacey marveled at all the plants, very healthy plants that seemed to whisper, "Go ahead; touch me and see if I'm real."

Tom's voice literally stopped her from leaving Ian's embrace and reaching out to touch the plant on the bar. "I do the cooking, and Ian does the decorating. It makes for good teammates, not just roommates."

"Well, who has the green thumb?" Lacey asked, enviously impressed.

Tom looked at his brother and bent down to peak into the oven and check on dinner.

A long awkward silence followed. Lacey turned to face Ian and then finally he spoke up. "Neither one of us can take the credit for the plants. Our mom comes in once a week, and she waters them for us. I've actually caught her talking to them a couple times," he said, laughing.

Well, that answers that question, Lacey surmised. She changed the subject. "So what are we having for dinner, Tom?"

"Marinated garlic chicken, twice baked potatoes, and salad," he said enthusiastically.

"Sounds terrific," she said, looking to Ian.

"Oh, it will be," Ian said, grabbing her by the hand. "Let me take you on a little tour of our place."

Lacey kept her hand in his as he guided her on the tour of the three-bedroom house. She was very impressed with the cleanliness of it and the decorating too. "So who helped you decorate the place, Ian? I don't think I've ever seen such a nice bachelor pad."

Ian chuckled and the matter-of-fact tone laced with confidence didn't quite match the color of red that his face turned when he admitted that his mom had helped him.

"I think that's great, Ian. I know if my son asked me to help decorate his place, I'd do it in a New York minute, and probably pay for it too."

Ian was quick to assure her that he had paid for everything himself. "She went with me on several shopping sprees and offered her opinions. It was fun putting it all together and I know I couldn't have done as nice a job without her," he said. "I didn't want it to look like a typical guys' place."

"So how long has your brother been living with you?"

"Let's see… I've been here almost four years now, and he moved in about two and a half years after I did, so about a year and a half. He was injured while serving in the army and then discharged, lost his fiancée and his house, all in a matter of months, so I wanted to help him get back on his feet."

"Well, he seems to have landed on his feet quite well. He's always so happy when I see him, and now that you've told me that about him, I really am glad he's here tonight. What an interesting pair you are."

Lacey squealed as Ian picked her up and held her close like a baby. "What are you…?"

"And this is my room," he said. He kicked his open suitcase out of his way and lay her down ever so gently. His face was so close to hers she could feel his breath as he kissed first one ear and then the other. She inhaled his scent as she received his kiss.

Lacey was somewhat startled by the little moan that escaped from her throat as he kissed her softly at first and then more insistently. She didn't protest. Instead, she felt her arms reach out and her hands start to rub the hardness of his back, the muscles on his arms. She let herself give in to his kiss, his sexiness rendering her powerless, unable to resist the fervor that was rising.

The sound of shattered glass brought her to her senses. "What was that?" Lacey asked as she wiggled out from under Ian.

Ian, standing now, took her hands and pulled her up easily and swiftly. "Come here, you little 'hard body.' I'm sure it's my brother. He's always breaking something when he's cooking. He probably dropped a wine glass or something," he said nonchalantly. "Let's go see," he said reluctantly. As he turned to lead them out of his bedroom, he nearly stumbled over the suitcase he had kicked earlier.

Lacey looked in it and saw it was partially packed. "So where are you off to?" she asked, not wanting to sound nosy, but definitely curious.

"I'm going on a cruise."

"Wow," Lacey said.

"My buddies and I planned it eight months ago," he explained. He reached to pull her to him, but she had stepped back a step so he hurried on. "My buddy's mom is in the travel business and she got a great deal on it, so we decided to go for it," he added in sort of a monotone.

"You don't sound very excited about going. What's—"

Ian didn't give her a chance to finish but instead reached for her again, and this time she let him pull her close to him. "I'm kind of sorry I booked it now."

Lacey let her hands rest on his chest and looked up at him. "How long you going for?"

Ian stopped burrowing his head in her neck. He was slow to respond. "A week," he groaned as he pulled them apart and took her face in his hands and kissed her on the forehead.

Lacey's pulse began to race, so she stepped back, just a little bit. "Don't be silly. You'll have a great time," Lacey assured him. She knew then that she could never spend a night with this guy; the temptation would be too difficult to resist. She knew her own limits. Making out was one thing, but spending a week on a cruise ship with this guy would probably send her overboard, literally. "Come on. Let's go see how your brother's doing in the kitchen."

Ian took her by the hand, and they walked into the kitchen. Tom was bent down, sweeping the remains of a wine glass into the dustpan. "See, I told you," he said to Lacey, a twinkle of laughter in his eyes.

Tom stood up and walked to the trash to throw his blunder away. "Told her what?" he asked his brother.

"That we have stock in wine glasses." He laughed. The two guys continued to banter back and forth as they got dinner on the table and all sat down. A moment of silence followed, and Tom and Ian exchanged glances, nodded to each other, and they bowed their heads. Tom began to pray. Lacey was stunned into further silence, not even hearing his words until he said, "Amen," which she echoed with her head still bowed. Ian squeezed her knee under the table, and she looked up to see him smiling at her.

"This looks really good, bro," Ian said enthusiastically as he reached for Lacey's plate to serve her first, then his brother and finally himself. The quiet that was present during the prayer was gone, and the guys returned to their brotherly bantering, Lacey joining in every now and then with laughter and a comment or two. She looked up a couple of times to see Ian looking right at her, saying so much with his eyes.

After dinner, Lacey helped with the cleanup and then Ian asked if she wanted to go back in his room to watch T.V. She was about to accept when she heard The Voice, *If you resist temptation, it will flee from you.* She dropped the towel she'd been holding, startled and comforted at the same time. "I'd better go ahead and go so you can get your packing done."

Ian had enjoyed watching Lacey interact with his brother. It had attracted him to her all over again. She had really been a good sport about him being there, especially since he hadn't gotten the chance to tell her beforehand, but then again, he really did think she'd be more comfortable. And she had handled the news of his upcoming cruise so much better than he had imagined, without drama. That alone was huge to him, adding to the list of reasons to spend more time with her before leaving the following Sunday. He'd set it up with her tonight before she left, and just maybe, they could get back to where they were when the glass had shattered.

"Hello," Lacey said, somewhat distracted. She stopped working on her transcript and pulled her eyes away from the computer.

"Hi. May I speak to Ms. Thorton, please?" said the voice on the other end.

All ears, Lacey perked up on her end. "This is she."

"This is Ms. Thompson, the assistant vice principal from Ontario Christian School, and—"

"Oh, hi," Lacey interrupted. "How are you?"

Ms. Thompson continued as if she hadn't heard the question. "I'm calling to let you know that Jake has passed his entrance exams as well as the interview, but we've just received his student file from his current school, and there is something in there that is of grave concern to us."

Lacey held her breath and waited for her to continue.

"I'm sure you can explain it for me. I'm looking at his file now, and apparently he was involved in an altercation during the lunch recess a few weeks ago, and then just recently, he was smoking in the quad and thereafter suspended for three days. We would like to welcome him to our school, but—"

"Wait, I'm so sorry to interrupt you, but before you go on, can I give you a little 'history' to explain this? I mean, I'm not trying to, in any way, justify his behavior; I just want to explain a couple of things about him."

"Well, we know there are always pieces missing to the puzzle, and we can't get the whole picture by looking at just the records. If it makes you feel any better, from what I remember about Jake, he was very pleasant. He seemed to be such a kind kid with a gentle spirit in him and that is why I'm calling you. We don't like to turn potential students away until we have as many of the facts as we can get so we can come to a reasonable conclusion instead of jumping to one."

The compassion that came through the voice on the other end just about sent Lacey over the edge. The last few weeks with Jake had been emotionally draining and exhausting, and if it weren't for the girls and a few dates with Ian, insanity would have been the next off ramp in this journey of singleness and single parenting. For the next several minutes, Lacey discused Jake's painful past with Ms. Thompson, reiterating that she was not excusing his behavior, but just wanting to explain the root of it. She also explained what proactive steps she had taken to try to get Jake to think about his choices before making them, which included dragging him to New Life Vineyard's youth group to give him a different set of friends to hang out with. She ended her spiel with, "And I just know that being enrolled at your school would be a positive influence on him." Lacey took a breath and waited. She was so tired and scared that she didn't know what to do, and everything she had just explained to the vice principal sounded like a hot air balloon filled with a sob story even to her own ears.

"Well," Ms. Thompson began gently, "what we could do is let him start with us, but we'll have to put him on the equivalent of an academic probation."

Lacey let out a sigh, not realizing she'd been holding her breath. "What does that entail?"

Ms. Thompson reiterated the school's policy of no fighting, and their zero tolerance for drugs and alcohol on school property. "We also have a school psychologist that I can check with to see if he'd be willing to meet with him before he actually starts school with us. Would that be something that would be beneficial for him? What do you think?" the vice principal asked.

"Well, I think it would be great, if I could just get him to talk, that is. I mean, it wouldn't do any good unless he was willing to talk, right?"

"That's usually true," Ms. Thompson agreed. "You could ask him if he'd be willing to give that a try and get back to me."

"I'll do that, Ms. Thompson."

"By all means, call me Betty," she said warmly.

Lacey smiled in spite of it all. "Thank you so much for your time and for letting me share with you about all of this. I don't really have anyone I can talk to about Jake except my girlfriends. His father is almost always absent in his life, not just physically but emotionally and monetarily as well. Most of the time I'm so overwhelmed with trying to make ends meet that it's come down to quality of time versus quantity of time, and even that is being interrupted now because of some of the choices he's made." Lacey stopped to catch her breath. "See, here I go again. Sorry about that."

"There's no need to apologize. That's what we're here for. Please, feel free to call me any time, Lacey. I want to help."

"Thank you."

"So this is Friday. Is Monday a good time to get back to me and let me know if he wants to see the psychologist?"

Lacey's thoughts raced for a minute to the weekend ahead. Jake was going to be staying the night with Adam on Saturday so he could go to youth group with him on Sunday, and she was going out with Ian before he left for his cruise. That left Sunday afternoon or tonight and she was in no mood to talk about anything serious with him so soon.

"Are you there, Lacey?" interrupted Ms. Thompson.

"Yes, I'm sorry. I'm just trying to figure out when and how I can approach the subject with him this weekend, but I'll figure it out. I'll get back to you on Monday."

"Okay. I'll talk to you Monday, then. And, Lacey, there's just one more thing I'd like you to remember."

"Yes?"

"He's a Father to the fatherless; He carries all of your pain and, if you let Him, He'll dry all your tears." With that she said good-bye.

Lacey sat perplexed by the woman's last words. The reminder was just too much. She put her head down on her desk and had herself a good cry. She cried for Jake, for what could have been with Jake's father who had exchanged a family for a life of drugs, and Jake was the one who really suffered. He would be fatherless, just like she had been! She cried over his choices, feeling like she had to watch his every move, leaving her little time for herself.

Finally she cried for what could have been with Peter. It was at times like this that she missed him so much and yet deep down in her soul, she knew he never loved her as much as she loved him. What made it even more bittersweet was the realization that she had broken her own rule and allowed herself to need him. It hadn't worked; neither had trying to be a family. She had just wanted it so bad, for her own sake as well as Jake's. She was alone, sick and tired of being alone.

She wasn't sure how long she'd been there with her head down on her arms, but as she raised her head, the gentle words playing in her mind pulled her upright: *I am a Father to the fatherless.* Lacey looked around her office, her eyes wide open with perplexity, her heart thumping against her chest, beating like a drum. *He dries all of your tears; He carries all of your pain.* She heard the words again. "Am I going crazy, or is that *you* again?" She waited and heard nothing, and in spite of hearing nothing, she felt better. "All right, pity party's over." She finished editing her transcript, turned her computer off, and headed for the gym.

"Where you parked, Lacey?" Seth asked.

"I actually parked right in front of you today."

They started heading in the direction of their cars, and Lacey began telling him about a problem she was having with her garbage disposal.

Before Seth could stop himself, he asked her what she was doing later.

Lacey's shoulders sort of slumped. "You okay?" Seth asked.

"Yes and no," she replied somewhat dejectedly.

"What's the 'no' part of that answer?

"It's Jake that I'm worried about."

Seth leaned up against the bumper of his Ford Expedition, and Lacey stood facing him, leaning on the bumper of her car. "So what's going on with the kid?" Seth asked.

"He has a name, Seth," Lacey teased him.

"Yeah, yeah, I know; it's just a habit," he said, chuckling.

"Jake's been doing some pretty stupid stuff lately, kind of acting up. I wonder if it's because I've been going out."

Seth stopped leaning and stretched all of his four foot eleven inches. "What do you mean, you've been going out? You mean with the girls or out on dates?" he asked, his tone obviously curious.

"Well, both, I guess, but more with the girls. I mean, I've had a few dates with this guy who's really young, like twelve years younger, but it's nothing serious. He's really nice, fun to be with, but like the girls said, he's a good ego boost for me right now."

Seth listened, though obviously lost in his thoughts. "So you think Jake's resenting the time you spend with this guy?"

"I'm not sure. Most of the time when I have gone out with him, Jake's hanging out with his best friend, and the first time he was with his dad, but I don't think that's the only thing eating at him," she contemplated aloud but inwardly she questioned the possibility of Jake struggling with her dating.

Seth could tell she wasn't crazy about the guy, but he'd never seen this side of her either. She didn't strike him as a girl who used guys for her own selfish motives. That wasn't the Lacey he was coming to know, at least he didn't think it was, nor did he want it to be.

He continued to listen as Lacey filled him in on Jake's latest shenanigans. He really liked the kid from the first time he had met him, and it had been easy hanging out together the couple of times he had been over to their house. As Lacey conveyed her struggles, he realized he was grateful that he had never had kids. Now more than ever he knew he just wasn't cut out to be a dad, but, he thought, he could be a friend. "Hey, what do you say I come over in a couple of hours and I'll check out the garbage disposal and then we can all go to Home Depot and get whatever we need to fix it."

"You'd really do that?"

"Sure, and after we have some fun at Home Depot, we can go to dinner somewhere, Jake's choice. Sound good?"

"I think that sounds really good, actually," Lacey said, smiling inside and out. "If anyone could make Home Depot a fun experience, it's you."

"Well then, it's a plan, and I'll be over at—"

Lacey interrupted him. "Well, it's four now, so how does six sound?"

"Perfect. I'll see you around six." With that, Seth got in his truck and waved to Lacey as he drove away, realizing he hadn't just made her smile, but he was smiling too! He was actually looking forward to the evening with them.

Lacey made her way into the house with her gym bag and a Starbucks latte for her and a mocha Frappuccino for Jake. She let the door slam behind her—not that she could hear it for the music that was blasting from Jake's room upstairs. She set her bag down and started to make her way upstairs while trying to decipher which CD he was playing. She could tell it was one of the screaming, angry and unintelligible punk groups he liked. She let out a sigh as she made it to his door, and pounded on it, and waited. She pounded again, only this time with her foot. Bingo! Before he could give her an attitude, she thrust the Frappuccino at him. He reached for it and smiled. "Could you turn that down?" she shouted. "Please."

Jake turned away from her and walked toward his stereo. Lacey followed him in, clearing a path with her feet by shoving clothes to the left and other stuff to the right until she made it to his chair in the corner and sat down, not even daring to comment about the mess she had had to clear in order to get there. He plopped onto his bed, obviously where he'd been before she interrupted him. "Thanks for the Frap, Mom."

"You're welcome. So how was—"

"My day at school was the same as it always is," Jake interrupted.

Almost falling for the trap set by his tone of voice, Lacey stopped herself before she responded and thought a minute. She wished she could get inside his head so she could see the things he wasn't saying. Something told her they'd be far more important than trying to understand what he *was* saying. If she nagged him about his negative attitude, she'd never get anywhere with him so she decided to play emotional detective for a bit and do some exploring. She let out a big sigh. *Here goes,* she thought, as she tried to put a smile in her voice. "Actually, today was different, Jake." That got his attention.

"What do you mean?" he asked.

"Well, I did get a call from the school—"

"I didn't do anything wrong," Jake interrupted her, the fear darkening his golden honey-brown eyes to a strong coffee color.

"No, no," Lacey assured him. "Not that school, your new school, you goof." She saw Jake's shoulders drop back down to his normal sloppy posture as he let out a sigh of relief. She looked into his eyes and smiled and watched the darkness literally fade them back to their normal color, softening his expression considerably. She reached out and squeezed his shoulder, realizing in that moment how deep depression had touched his soul, reaching out and invading his actions, changing his personality completely. Lacey longed for her carefree son again, the one that made everyone laugh just being around him. That part of her son seemed to be hiding and rarely came out these days. She took him in her arms and he didn't resist, and for a moment, she said nothing, hoping and praying that her love would speak to his heart and bring that carefree boy back out.

"So, your new school called," she started again as she pulled gently away from him.

As Jake let the words sink in, his face began to light up, beginning with his eyes and spreading to his countenance, causing that famous grin to come out. "So does that mean I passed their stupid tests?" Jake asked, trying not to sound too happy.

"Jake, the tests are not stupid. They're more to figure out where to place you in certain subjects. You don't want to start off the school year in a class way over your head, or for that matter, one that bores you to tears. Anyway, yes, you passed all their tests. Good job," she said as she reached to high-five him.

He responded enthusiastically.

"So what do you say we celebrate?" she asked, deciding that the talk about probation and the possibility of talking to the school psychologist could come later. She made a mental note to call the vice principal on Monday and let her know that for now, they'd have to put talking to the school psychologist on hold. She figured she'd need to make a couple more deposits into his emotional bank before making those withdrawals.

"Don't you have a date tonight?" Jake asked, somewhat dejectedly.

"No, I don't have a date tonight," she mimicked in his tone. "And why did you say it like that? Are you upset about me dating?"

"Well, no."

"Well, *that* sounded believable," she said, catching his eyes and smiling.

"It just makes it more real that my—you and my dad aren't going to get back together."

Lacey was rendered speechless by his words as they pierced her heart. It seemed to be an eternity ago that they'd all been a family. *Why is he bringing it up now?* she wondered. And then she remembered something. "Remember when you were five years old and I explained to you why your dad and I split up?"

Jake leaned forward and put his right hand out and put his first two fingers down on the bed, very close together, as he pretended they were two people walking and repeated what he had never forgotten. "At first mom and dad walked like this, close together, but then as time went on, they changed and grew apart and began walking like this," he finished with his two fingers completely separated. His eyes welled up.

Again, Lacey was unable to speak, this time because of the lump in her throat. "I'm so sorry, Jake, that you had to go through that; that you're still going through that. The truth of it is we're even farther apart now. Your dad has chosen a lifestyle that doesn't include us as a family, but that doesn't change his love for you," she said, fighting the urge to tell him the truth about his dad's choosing drugs over them. "What we have to deal with is things that we can change, honey, and all we can change is ourselves and how we handle life's lemons when they're handed to us. Do we want to suck on them and be sour, or do we want to rise above that and make some lemonade?" She watched as Jake put his fist up to his eyes to wipe away any evidence of tears. She let the awkward moment pass.

Jake put his head down, and Lacey feared that he was tuning her out. *Maybe now isn't a good time to bring it up.* "What do you say we work as a team to make the best of things and try to have some fun, starting in just a couple of hours."

Jake looked up at his mom, flustered.

Lacey recognized the look of embarrassment on his face and figured he probably hadn't heard all of what she'd said.

"What's happening in a couple of hours?" he mumbled.

"Well, Seth's coming over to check out that stinking garbage disposal of ours and figure out what we need to fix it. Then we're going to go to Home Depot to get whatever parts we need. By that time, you'll probably be ready to eat the paint off the walls, so we figured we'd go out to eat, but where we go is your choice." She smiled at him. "Sound good?"

He smiled, and Lacey felt the tension dissipate. She knew that he really liked Seth, or "Little Seth," as he liked to call him.

"Cool," he said, hiding his enthusiasm. "It's not like I have anything else to do."

Lacey knew he was just trying to be nonchalant, so she didn't react. Instead, she stood up and reached for him, pulling him to his feet; she gave in to the urge she'd been fighting earlier and encircled him with her arms and held him close to her heart. As she held him, she knew what she would do about Ian.

By the time they had backed out of the driveway and pulled into the parking lot of Home Depot, Lacey's stomach was hurting from laughing so hard, and she hadn't been the only one laughing. The joking back and forth between Seth and Jake had been music to her ears. And then the humor had really started when Seth started telling Jake about one of her training sessions where he watched her trainer put six plates on each side of the leg lift bar and couldn't tear himself away wondering if she was really going to push those plates all the way up. "She had had to push that bar up so hard with her quads to get the 395 pounds to the top. I just knew she gave herself hemorrhoids." Seth broke out laughing, obviously pleased with his storytelling.

Lacey watched the twinkle in Jake's eyes that accompanied his genuine laughter as he hung on to Seth's every word. It had been such a long time since she had seen him enjoying life with that carefree happiness, immune to the cares of the world, seeing things from a childlike perspective, the way a boy his age still should.

Seth's voice brought her out of her reverie. "Should I park in 'handicapped,' Ms. Fitness, or can you make it from here?"

Lacey groaned as she started to get out of the truck, which started them all laughing again, but she assured him that walking would probably help her soreness. "The farther the better," she retorted. They continued the bantering as they walked around the store. They managed to get everything they needed, despite causing ruckus in the store when Seth and Jake had rammed their cart into a wallpaper display, accidentally, of course.

They were still talking and laughing about it over dinner at Dave & Buster's, which had been both Seth's and Jake's first choice. After dinner, Seth talked Jake into playing pool, and Lacey sat and watched them, cheering for each of them, surprised at Jake's natural ability. Seth still had three balls to pocket but won by default when Jake hit the eight ball in a pocket he hadn't called. "Why don't you guys make it best out of three?" Lacey said, content to sit there and watch them.

They wound up playing four games, each winning two and would have gone for the tie breaker, but Seth had glanced over at Lacey several times, unbeknownst to her, and she had been yawning. He didn't know how she kept the pace she did and still did the mom thing. She was pretty amazing, and he'd had a great time tonight. He walked over to Jake and motioned for him to bend down a bit. "Jake, what do you say we come back for the tie breaker. Your mom looks pretty beat."

Jake looked over at his mom just as she was finishing off a great big yawn and smiled down at Seth. "Only if you promise it will be soon," he said.

"It will be, buddy. Besides, I've got to come over soon so you can help me fix the garbage disposal."

"That's cool," Jake said, not hiding his disappointment about leaving.

"Let's get your mom home," Seth said as he shook Jake's hand.

By the time Lacey got into bed, it was almost eleven o'clock. She was exhausted but happy. She saw her phone blinking indicating that she had voice mail. There was one message, and it was from Ian. He was trying to confirm their date tomorrow night. She groaned at the reminder of what she needed to do. It was going to be hard breaking their date, but that would be the easy part of it. Not only had she decided to break the date, but after talking with Jake, she was convinced that it was time to back out before she got in too deep. It was fun while it lasted, yet she knew it couldn't go anywhere. He had been a great ego booster for her as she made her way out into the world of singles again. He'd probably find someone on that cruise anyway. At least he could without feeling bad about it now because Lacey knew in her heart that he wouldn't have enjoyed cheating on her. He really did seem to have an air of integrity about him. Letting him go on that cruise completely unattached was the right thing to do. It wasn't like she was losing her best friend. No, she still had the girls, and at least now she'd get to see them tomorrow night, if they still wanted to. She would have lots to tell them, too, but the sad thing was she already had the ending to this story, and it wasn't happily ever after, at least not with Ian.

Body Builder

"So what happened?" Nikki asked Lacey, her eyes transparent with disbelief as she looked first to the girls and then to Lacey.

"Let her start at the beginning, Nikki," Susie chided, and Sophie voiced her agreement. Lacey let out a sigh of contentment as she took a sip of her wine. They had all gathered in her living room sprawled out on the couch and the floor like a group of schoolgirls at a slumber party. The stereo was playing in the background but was barely heard above all their chatter. Lacey smiled, caught up in the inquisitiveness of her friends. It was hard to remain sad around them; that was for sure. It was so good to finally be with them again. It had been a long month for all of them without their usual get-togethers, but sometimes that's just the way that it was, impossible to get all their schedules to coincide, especially since they each had a son, that is, except for Susie.

Since they had not gotten together for a while, they had decided to forego their usual happy hour and/or dinner get-together at a restaurant in exchange for just hanging out at Lacey's, with a bottle of wine, or two, and some snacks. They'd get a movie if they ran out of stuff to talk about, but as the night progressed, and the girls got caught up with what was going on in each other's lives, that became more unlikely.

Susie was the first to fill them in on what had been happening with her. She was hanging on by a thread in the love/hate relationship with Jimmy, admitting, though, that she was getting tired of it. "Maybe I'm just restless because I'm not too thrilled with my job either, but at least with my job there is a chance for growth."

"That's definitely a plus," Sophie agreed.

"Yeah, so I'll hang on to the job for a while"—she took a long sip of her wine—"but after fighting with Jimmy for the past three days about coming here tonight, I don't think I'll be hanging on to this no-win relationship."

Nikki was the first to shout her excitement. "Atta girl, Susie."

Sophie and Lacey added their agreement.

Sophie was still seeing Jerry, who she said was a nice escape from the painful situation with her son and his comatose dad. She replayed some of the horrible disagreements she and Zach had been having because she still had not taken him to see his father. "I just can't get over how it is affecting his school work and his whole attitude," she exclaimed, "and it's completely draining me."

"I couldn't imagine…" Lacey admitted.

Sophie changed the subject to her job. "I really like working part time for this developer." She paused and smiled. "He's real sexy," she added.

As soon as she said that, the girls wanted to know more.

Nikki picked up on her tone and the glint in her eyes. "So he's sexy and nice, too? I don't believe it."

Sophie laughed. "Yep, he took me to lunch when I got my first sale." The girls tried to get more information, but Sophie said there wasn't more to tell. "Anyway, I like my job and the hours are perfect because they work around Zach's schedule."

When it was Nikki's turn to tell them what was going on in her life, she had them in fits of laughter talking about another hair-raising experience with her son and his insects and critters.

They all exchanged insect stories, even Susie, who didn't have a son, but she had three nephews and knew how boys could be boys. The best story came from Nikki when she talked about finding a long-lost frog when she opened up the bottom broiler and lo and behold, there he was, flat as a pancake and fried like a chicken.

"So," Nikki continued, "there's still no one special in my life, but then again, I honestly think I like it that way. Besides, I don't think one could sneak past David Michael."

Sophie, who was lying on the couch, sat up and prompted Lacey. "So, tell us, where did your little ego booster take you on that first date?"

Lacey recapped the first date, careful to give them details. "I think what really impressed me is he proved to be a listener, paying attention to the small things when we'd talk, like taking me to the beach because he knew it was my favorite place to be."

They each sat listening, hanging on intensely to every detail as Lacey described the walk on the beach and dinner at the restaurant on the pier.

Susie listened enviously, knowing she'd never experience moments like the ones Lacey was describing if she stayed with Jimmy. Nikki's and Sophie's laughter brought her back into the conversation and she looked at Lacey, the only one not laughing. Susie saw that Lacey's face was the color of cranberries. "What did she ask you? I didn't hear her," she admitted.

"Well, I was just getting ready to talk about our second date, and Nikki asked if he'd kissed me on the first one."

"Well, did he?" Susie repeated, which sent them off on another laughing tangent.

"As a matter of fact, he did," Lacey nearly yelled.

"Well?" the girls chimed in unison, waiting for the details.

"His timing was pretty intuitive on the first kiss, but then the second and third…" As Lacey recalled those moments, she felt a tug of sadness again, but just for a few seconds. She finished her sentence. "Well, he—his kisses just got better and better. I'll leave it at that."

Nikki, unaware of her own naiveté, spoke up. "What do you mean 'his timing'?"

"Well, we were walking on the pier, after stopping for happy hour at the Lighthouse, and we sort of bumped into each other and we came face to face laughing, and it just happened. Anyways, moving on—"

Sophie stood up. "Before you do that, does anyone want a refill?" she asked as she held up her wine glass. They each held up their glass. "Let me just go get the bottle," she said with a smile.

"You might as well open up the second one," Lacey added, enjoying reliving the short-lived season with Ian. Sophie refilled their glasses, and Lacey continued to share the details of the dates she'd been on with Ian and how they ended. When she imitated his pouting look whenever he couldn't get any farther than first base with her, the girls shared another fit of laughter.

"I'm proud of you, girl. I don't know how you hang on to your resolve like that," Sophie interjected.

"Oh, trust me; it wasn't easy, but that didn't stop him from trying. He never gave up, but at least he was a good sport about it. First base was deep enough. If I had let it go farther, no telling when I would've come up for air," she admitted. She went on to tell the girls about the final date at his house, including the scene in his bedroom in the midst of him giving her a tour of their place.

"So what was that like, making out in his bedroom with his brother in the kitchen?" Nikki asked, truly baffled, even more so when the girls burst out laughing not so much at her question, but more at her innocent naiveté.

"Yeah, that might have been a little too weird for me," Sophie piped in.

"Well, to be honest, it was like free-falling. It probably was a good thing that his brother was there," Lacey added emphatically.

Susie's voice broke through the chatter. "So, if it was all so good, why'd you end it with him?"

Lacey wasn't sure if it was her tone or the actual question that put a blanket of silence on the room. She looked up to see all eyes on her, and she struggled as she grasped for that inner conviction that had punched her in the stomach, and hard, almost a month ago after that talk with Jake. She looked up to see their eyes still on her. "It's kind of hard to explain," she stammered.

It wasn't that she didn't want to share it with them, that conviction that had collided with a memory of the past. She just wasn't sure how to share it with them. She was still trying to understand it herself. She had never been promiscuous, and she wasn't about to start now, especially at her age. And yet, the attention sure had been nice, but it wasn't worth risking Jake's well-being. But there was something even more to it than that; she just couldn't quite put her finger on it. It was almost like being blind after seeing, knowing the color of something but not being able to see it to describe and confirm it.

Susie could see that Lacey was struggling and gave her an out. "Well, hey, at least you dumped him before he dumped you," she said, giggling. "That had to have felt good, huh?" She didn't wait for Lacey to answer. "Maybe some day I'll get that kind of courage, and then I think I'm going to swear off men for quite a while." The look of terror on Lacey's face collided with Susie's sudden burst of confidence. "What's wrong, Lacey?" she asked.

"Just what you said about swearing off men triggered something."

Sophie propped herself up again. Nikki leaned forward, and Susie perked up as well. Nikki was the first to speak. "What triggered what, Peanut?"

"Well, it has to do with my first divorce and what happened shortly before I met Peter." Hesitating for a second, she continued, "You guys are never going to believe this, and you have to promise you won't ever share this with anyone, no matter how mad you get at me."

The looks on each of their faces gave away their naked curiosity and eagerness to hear what she had to say. "We promise," they all said simultaneously.

"Well, after I kicked Jake's dad out, I went to school for court reporting." She stopped for a second, unsure if she should continue.

Nikki encouraged her on.

"Well, it was at school that I met this girl, Vanessa, and we became really good friends, too good. She was incredibly helpful and seemingly always available. She was also great with Jake, and she felt like a miraculous cure from a grave disease called a broken and disillusioned heart."

Sophie, the more perceptive of the girls, interrupted Lacey. "Is this going where I think it is going?" She was the more liberal of the four but could not hide her disbelief.

"Let me finish," Lacey answered as gently as she could. She looked to each of them, her gaze resting on Susie. "So anyway, I had *sworn off* men and was very happy just hanging out with her. And, yes, I got sucked into that alternative lifestyle for a little while and almost fell in completely. It was an emotional trip that turned into a trap. I kept telling myself, how could something that feels so right be so wrong?" Lacey wasn't sure if the tears that were quietly trickling down her face were from the pain and shame of reliving it all or the fear of her best friends' reactions.

Nikki stood up and handed her a couple of tissues while offering her unconditional, unspoken encouragement. "Well, we don't know what the ending is, but we do know you're definitely into guys now, so the ending can't be that bad."

Sophie smiled her agreement and held up her glass toward Lacey in a silent toast, encouraging Lacey to continue.

Lacey laughed through her tears, thanked Nikki for the tissues, and gave them all a feeble smile. "So we were at her mom and dad's one night, and after dinner we went into her room and were talking. She was telling me that she needed more from me, and that she was going to have to get out of my life if I couldn't give her what she needed. She was saying this because I had just started going out with this successful real estate agent here in Rancho Cucamonga.

"Suddenly, it was like this light went on in my head. I looked at her and I said, 'I can't, Vanessa. I can't give you what you want.' And then I tried to get up and leave, but she pushed me into her closet."

All of the girls gasped, and Susie asked incredulously, "So what did you do?"

"I couldn't believe it, but she was trying to hold me hostage in her bedroom even though her parents were in their bedroom right down the hall. I finally talked myself out of her room, and had to wrestle her for my car keys as we were walking out. She actually got to my car before me," she said, shaking her head and almost laughing.

"What's so funny?" Susie asked.

"Well, I'm laughing because I still, for the life of me, can't figure out how she beat me to my car because she was at least two of me. I mean, she was a big girl, something like two hundred and ninety pounds."

Nikki interrupted. "See, fat women can run." The girls broke out laughing, dissipating some of the tension but not the anticipation in the room.

Lacey continued, "So she gets to my car before me, gets in, and it took me fifteen minutes to get her out.

"So how did you get her out?" Nikki asked.

"I threatened to go tell her mom and dad that their daughter was a psycho. So she gets out; I get in. I get ready to punch the gas, thinking she was standing to the right of me, and I begin moving and hear a loud thud. I look up, and there she is—on the hood of my car!"

Sophie couldn't believe what she was hearing. "This sounds like that movie *Fatal Attraction*, only it's more like 'fatal attraction of the same sex.'" The girls nodded their heads in disbelieving agreement.

"It gets better," Lacey offered.

"So this is a true story?" Sophie asked in disbelief.

"Cross my heart," she said, motioning to her heart and crossing it.

Nikki brought them back to where Lacey had left off. "So what did you do when you saw her on the hood of your car?"

"I slammed on my brakes. I was so freaked out. I couldn't believe it. I mean, this is something you read about, right? I couldn't believe that it was happening to me."

Sophie spoke up again. "I don't even think I've read anything this creepy. This is unbelievable."

"She kind of slid off to the side when I stopped, which was just a couple of feet from where I had started. I sat there for a few seconds, trying to stop shaking. Well, it was a couple of seconds too long because when I took off again, I didn't know it but she was hanging on to the side of my car. When I saw her in my peripheral vision, I slammed the brakes on again. I know as sure as I'm sitting here with all of you now that the slow-motion picture I got of her falling had to be from God Himself. I saw her head go back ever so slowly, her legs go straight up in the air even slower, and she fell back on her head, although not quite as slow. And then I heard a thud. I screamed and jumped out of the car, yelling her name again and again. When she didn't respond, I announced I was going to get her mom and dad and—*bam!*—she was up and standing. I got back in my car and took off like a bat out of you know where, and I stopped at a gas station to call that guy that I had gone out with but there was no answer."

"What was the guy's name?" Nikki asked.

"His name was Don, and he was—"

Sophie interrupted her. "Why did you have to stop at a gas station? Didn't you have your cell phone?"

"I must have left it at home, because I remember having to stop to make the phone call." Lacey paused for a minute. "But he didn't answer, so I got back in my car and drove home, checking my rearview mirror every other minute. When I got home, I checked all the windows and locked all my doors and got my dog Bo—you remember the big collie I used to have—and went into my room, shut the door, and decided to call my sister. So I'm on the phone with my sister, and you're never going to believe what happens next!"

The girls were still sitting upright, their faces glued on Lacey. She continued, "Vanessa bursts into my bedroom!"

"No, she didn't," Susie nearly screamed.

"Yes, she did," Lacey continued. "I forgot that she still had a key. Anyway, she kept me trapped there for an hour and a half, literally sitting on me to make me listen as she tried to backtrack on the things she'd said while at her parents' house.

"Well, I don't remember how, but I got away, me and Bo, and I took off with my house phone still in my hand and got in my car and went around the corner and down the street to the grocery store. I stopped there because I saw a cop car in the parking lot. So I went up to him and I told him what was going on, and he escorted me back home. As we turned the corner, we see her carrying stuff out of my house, which he made her put back. It was stuff she had bought me. But, anyway, he made her leave since she couldn't prove that she lived there, even though she did most of the time."

Lacey let out a huge sigh as she looked at all of her friends who were obviously engrossed in the story.

Susie's gentle voice broke the silence. "So did she stay away?"

Lacey took a deep breath and shook her head. "Unfortunately, no, she didn't. It was almost a year before she finally stopped haunting me," Lacey continued the story, abbreviating it as much as she could. "After that horrific night, I remember feeling desperately scared and alone. I was desperate to talk to someone to try and make sense of my life and all that had happened and someone told me about this pastor at the Calvary Chapel right down the street from where we were living who offered free counseling."

Nikki sat forward. "I know where that is. I've gone there a few times. What a small world."

Lacey continued, "So I called and made an appointment, and I think it was just a couple of days later that I met with the pastor. I explained to him about my divorce from Jake's dad, the relationship with Vanessa, and he listened. He was pretty nice but more abrupt than nice, especially when I asked him if God was punishing me through Vanessa for my divorcing Jake's dad. He tried to tell me that God wasn't punishing me but that I was reaping what I had sowed. He asked if he could pray with me, and I said, sure. So he prayed with me; I left and never went back." Lacey bit back an overwhelming need to defend her actions. "Sometimes I can't help but wonder why things happen the way that they do, especially when I try so hard to do it all right."

"Sorry, Lacey," Sophie said; "I don't mean to change the subject, but I've got to ask, if she didn't go away, what else did she do?"

Lacey continued, "Well, I started getting threats in my mail, you know, those crazy notes you see where the words are all different styles cut out from different magazine articles? "They said things like, 'I'm watching you,' and 'Don't turn your back or you'll be sorry.' Another one said, 'You've broken something of mine; I'm going to break something of yours.' One of them had some sort of a riddle that I never could figure out. Well, that went on for some time, and I was still in court reporting school, and I was an independent contractor with Princess House Crystal, you know, that home party stuff."

"My mom has a bunch of that stuff," Susie spoke up. Sophie shot her a smile laced with a silent shush.

"Well, one night I was doing my group bingo party at Pizza Chalet in Riverside. I had eight hostesses scheduled and my secretary was there helping me set up, and a big—and I mean *big*—mean-looking Mexican guy came up to me and literally punched me in the face and knocked me to the ground. A few weeks later, I started dating Peter, and that same guy was chasing us in the mountains, trying to run us off the road."

"Didn't you ever call the police?" Nikki almost shouted.

"Oh, I tried many times. The police questioned Vanessa a few times, but she had an alibi every time and they believed her. She was incredibly intelligent and manipulative at the same time. And you talk about likeable; she was so likable. Besides, when this was going on, there weren't any stalking laws like there are now.

"One night I came out from another Princess House show, and my car and my brand-new court reporting machine were stolen. Eventually my machine was returned, but not the car. Then the next week, my sweet collie Bo wound up missing and was never returned. A few days later, Peter came out of his house in the morning to go to work and two of his tires were slashed. About a week passed with nothing happening, and then on the weekend, I was up at Peter's, and I came out in the morning to go to the store, and there was black India ink all over the hood of my car. I mean, it was crazy. And then, shortly before Peter and I got married, it's like she disappeared. Everything stopped."

Everyone was silent for a few moments, and then finally, Susie was the first to speak. "You're lucky to be here alive. She sounds extremely scary."

Sophie and Nikki nodded their heads in silence, the looks on their faces showing their agreement.

"Coming tonight was so worth the fight with Jimmy," she added.

The silence was deafening, and Nikki couldn't take it anymore. "So finish telling us about this breakup with Ego Booster, Lacey."

Evinda Lepins

"Yeah, that was a rabbit trail, huh? Talk about extreme opposites! The breakup with Ian was definitely nothing like that." Lacey went on to explain about the talk that she and Jake had had, and she described the weekend that had felt like a threesome, her, Jake and the shadow of conviction, which had inspired her to make the phone call that had ended it with Ian.

"So how did Ian take it when you broke it off with him?" Sophie asked.

Lacey thought about it for a minute and decided to be totally honest with her friends. "I don't think it bothered him. I think he knew it could never go anywhere. I mean eventually he'll want his own family and I'm certainly not going to do that again, but we both agreed that it was fun while it lasted. It was probably one of the most mature and not-so-emotional endings I've ever experienced with a guy."

Sophie empathized with Lacey. "It's so hard to be out there dating when you have kids involved. It's like your life is not really your own anymore."

"I wouldn't even know how to date," Nikki said. "I have never been on a date with anyone since David Michael's dad. It's just been David Michael and me, and I'm okay with that. Besides, I can always live vicariously through you girls."

"Well, I'm with you, Nikki. I think I'm going to have to get my thrills through them too. Jimmy wouldn't know what a date was if it bit him in the butt. And he definitely doesn't have a romantic bone in his body. His idea of a romantic evening is pizza and beer on a Friday night with a candle lit on the coffee table, one of those candles that are more of an air freshener than any type of romantic ambiance. And I don't dare say anything or there'd be hell to pay."

Lacey asked the question that they were all thinking. "Has he ever hit you, Susie?"

The silence was the only thing heard as Susie paused for a little too long and responded a little too nonchalantly: "Oh, he gets pissed and throws things, you know. It's no big deal."

Lacey could tell they needed to change the subject. Susie had never offered that much information before about her relationship with Jimmy, and she certainly didn't want her to regret it and never open up to them again. "Well, I just don't want to make another mistake when it comes to my love life, especially because now there's Jake's heart involved here, too, not to mention his emotional well-being." She reached for the second bottle of wine that was almost gone, and one by one, topped off their glasses in an effort to lighten the mood. "Here's to meeting life on life's terms," she toasted, and they all raised their glasses.

Silence lingered for just a minute after the toast, and Lacey thought about what she hadn't said because it was buried so deep: *Acceptance and approval, those are the things that bring love and happiness, right? And, yet, that was beginning to clash with what that Voice had been saying.*

"I have another toast," Lacey held up her glass and the girls raised theirs. "To my forever friends: men will come and men will go; they'll even stomp all over your heart, but the beauty of forever friends is that they are ones that never depart."

"Cheers," the girls said in unison, and Lacey basked in the luxury of their acceptance.

"I have another toast," Nikki said. The girls all waited. "Here's to being more like a flower, not deceived by love or bothered by age."

"I'll toast to that," Sophie said.

Lacey let the words sink in and raised her glass with the others. "That was beautiful, Nikki."

Lacey stopped her grocery cart and grabbed her cell phone from her purse. She answered it on the third ring, pausing to look at the number on the caller ID. *This is an odd time for her to be calling.* "Hey, Flo, everything okay?"

Her office manager was quick to assure her. "Yes. I just wanted to give you a heads-up so you can start making arrangements for that big case I was telling you about with the attorney from AIG that is requesting you, remember?"

"Yeah, I think so." Lacey said, not really sure if she did remember. She was in the soup aisle now and grabbed Jake several packages of Top Ramen, his favorite soup.

"Well, it's not starting until next month, nevertheless, his secretary called today to work out some of the details and to confirm that we'd gotten the written request by counsel himself asking that you be the reporter on most if not all of these depos. It—"

Lacey interrupted her. "What do you mean the request by counsel himself?"

"Well, he wrote a P.S. at the bottom of the deposition notice and initialed it."

Who could it be?

Flo continued, "With all the depositions they're setting, it sounds like it's a pretty big case."

"Well, I'm trying to think of who this attorney is," she said while reaching for a can of her favorite soup.

"Well, apparently he's worked with you before. Anyway, the depositions are spread out, but they've said it should go for two or three weeks, Monday through Thursday, all day, every day, and he's hoping to work only half day on Fridays."

Lacey let out a whistle of excitement as she dropped Jake's favorite ice cream in the basket and reached for her Skinny Cow ice cream. "What kind of case is it?"

"I'm pretty sure it's construction defect, although she did say there would be a videotaped deposition of someone not expected to live long enough to testify in trial, so I'm not really sure. Anyway, the money will be good."

"That's exactly what I was thinking. So where are they going to be held?" she asked as she steered her cart to the produce department and grabbed what she thought she remembered she had put on her now missing grocery list.

Flo hesitated before telling her. "Well, that's why I'm calling you now and letting you know, to give you time to prepare for the heavy caseload and make arrangements for your son."

Lacey was touched by her office manager's thoughtfulness.

Flo continued, "Now, most of the depositions are scheduled at his office in L. A." She hurried on when Lacey didn't say anything. "But a few of them actually might be out your way." When Lacey didn't say anything, Flo continued, "Hey, at least you can take the train in every day."

Lacey was already trying to work the logistics out in her mind. "Yeah, that's true. I guess I'd better start working on it. Thanks for the heads-up, Flo."

"You're welcome. Hey, I have your job assignment for tomorrow."

"You do, already?" Lacey asked.

"Yeah. As a matter of fact, tomorrow you have another client request, only it's one of yours from your old agency, Larry Simpson. He actually has a deposition in Santa Barbara—"

She pushed her cart out of the middle of the aisle and stood to one side. "Do I have to go all the way to Santa Barbara?" Lacey interrupted, obviously a bit too loudly according to the look she got from a lady trying to pass her in the aisle.

"Easy, girl," Flo gently scolded. "Let me finish. This one's actually kind of cool. You're going to meet at his office at eight forty-five, and from there you're going to his hangar, and he's going to fly you over to Santa Barbara. He said the actual depo itself shouldn't take more than a couple of hours."

Lacey looked down to see her knuckles turning white from gripping her cart. "Well, seeing that I'm a bit afraid of heights, this definitely ought to be fun," Lacey quipped.

"Do you want me to get someone else to cover it?" Flo asked.

"No, no, it's okay. I'm all about new experiences and overcoming fears these days," Lacey mumbled. "I'll be fine." But it wasn't just the flying part that she was concerned with. The memory from long ago surfaced and Lacey pushed it back and tucked it away for later.

"Well, call me tomorrow after you land."

Lacey flipped her phone closed and put it in her purse. A piece of paper floated out. It was her missing grocery list. She looked at it quickly to make sure that she'd gotten everything and headed to the checkout. By the time she paid for her groceries, they were already bagged and in her cart. She walked to her car and didn't fight it when the memory surfaced again. It was hard to believe it was two years ago when they were both struggling in their marriages and they had almost crossed the line, a line that would have changed their friendship and their lives forever.

"Come on, Lacey. Push it up there. Now hold it for one, two, three…" Lacey let out a groan when she heard him say the number ten. Harrison smiled. "Good job, Lace. That was awesome."

Lacey brought the arms of the leg lift in so she could rest the bar and her legs as she caught her breath.

"So guess how much weight that was?"

"I have no idea, and I don't know if I want to know," Lacey said, still trying to catch her breath.

Harrison's eyes twinkled. "Yeah, you're right. Let's keep it a secret for a while."

His reverse psychology worked. "Okay, tell me how much it was," Lacey begged.

His face broke out into a grin of satisfaction. "That was 410 pounds, 20 more than last time."

Lacey shrieked both with excitement and dismay. "Are you nuts? I don't want to look like a she man," she exclaimed. Suddenly she broke out laughing.

"What's so funny?"

"Nothing, I was just thinking about when Seth told Jake about me doing this leg-press. I wonder what he would have said if he'd just seen that!"

Harrison started laughing, too. "Don't worry; you won't start looking like a 'she man.' We just need to work on the separation and shredding of the quadriceps and hamstring muscles." He shook his head, still smiling. "Believe me; I won't let you get bulky." He handed Lacey her towel and Powerade drink.

Lacey leaned her head back and gulped down quite a bit of the drink and nearly choked when a voice from behind her complimented her on her leg-lifting weight. She turned her head and smiled when she saw Seth's friend, Sam. "Sammy, how the heck are you?" she asked as she hugged him. "You look incredible. Are you getting ready for another show?"

"You look pretty amazing yourself, kiddo." He looked at Harrison and extended his hand. "You're doing great with her, bro."

Harrison smiled a thank you as he shook his hand.

Sam turned his attention to Lacey again. "Yeah, I'm competing in a couple of weeks. So when's your show?"

Lacey was about to give him the countdown when Harrison interrupted. "She has a few months yet."

Sam looked at Lacey, purposefully allowing his gaze to start at her legs and wander around and up in a very nonsexual, appraising way, a way that didn't make Lacey feel as though he was undressing her with his eyes because he was like a big brother. He shook his head in approval. "You're going to be just fine. Seth was even bragging on you the other day, and you know how he hates to brag on anybody."

"He's just being nice," Lacey said somewhat embarrassed but surprised.

Sam squeezed her shoulder and shook his head. "No, I don't think that's it at all, Lacey." He winked at her. "Get back to work. I'll catch up with you another time."

Harrison looked at Lacey and smiled. "I think he's right."

"What's that supposed to mean?"

"I can just tell, from everything you've told me, that your relationship with Seth is changing. Take it from me, Lacey. No guy is going to hang out with a girl and her son, come over to the house as many times as he has to fix this or that, take her son out a couple of times, and call you all the time if he wasn't aiming for something more than a friendship." He looked at Lacey, puzzled by what he saw. "What's wrong? You look like you just lost your best friend."

She bent down to retrieve her fallen towel. When she got back up, she looked at him with an obvious look and said, "I just may have."

"Why do you say that?" he asked, confusion written all over his face.

"He asked me to a birthday party next Saturday night. We've never gone out like *that* before."

"What do you mean 'you've never gone out like *that* before'?" Harrison asked.

"Well, we've always done things in the day time, and it's usually involving Jake and the house, except for his work thing that he asked me to last month. I mean, that was at night, but it was last minute because he didn't want to go alone. But this party Saturday night, first of all, is a casual thing at night at someone's house. And second of all, I'm going to be meeting some pretty close friends of his. I don't know. Something in my gut is telling me it's different, somehow."

"You're over-thinking it, Lacey. Just go and have a good time." When she didn't say anything, he prodded further. "You told him yes, didn't you?"

Lacey leaned into the weight rack and let out a sigh. "Yeah, I did. The funny thing is I didn't even hesitate. I just told him yes almost as soon as he asked me. I mean, we have a great time together, and I'm kind of—I just hope it doesn't change things between us."

"Well, if you want my opinion—"

Lacey interrupted him with one of her looks, but he continued.

"—and even if you don't, from what I know of him, he's a great guy with a big circle of friends. The worst thing that can happen is your own circle of friends gets bigger."

Lacey still couldn't quite shake that feeling down in the pit of her stomach, a feeling that she just couldn't explain. Seth was beginning to take up a lot of space in her head.

Bittersweet Music

"Mom, come out—"Jake said, but stopped when he saw she was on the phone.

Lacey looked up at Jake. "It's my mom," she mouthed and held up her finger to indicate she'd only be a minute.

Jake rolled his eyes, turned, and walked away.

Lacey stopped him. "Mom, hold on a minute." She put her hand over the earpiece and called out to Jake, "Honey, what's wrong?"

He walked back toward her. "Nothing's wrong. We're ready for you to hear our first song and help us pick out a band name."

"Well, there's no need to sound so annoyed. Just give me a couple of minutes to talk with Mom, okay? I promise I won't be long, Jake." She was practically pleading with him now to let her have a few minutes of desperately needed conversation with her mom to help her make sense of her self-inflicted chaos.

Jake stood in the door of her bedroom, hands in his pockets staring at her as if she were an irritating school teacher. She let a little irritation come through in her voice. "Jake, I'll be there in a few minutes; I promise."

Jake shrugged his shoulders and walked away, mumbling, "Whatever."

Lacey shook her head and returned to her conversation with her mom. "Mom, I'm back. Sorry about that. Where was I?"

"You were just catching me up about this job coming up next month that's going to keep you busy and away from home a lot," Beth reminded her.

"Oh, that's right. So now I have to find someone that can give me a hand with Jake after school. I wish you lived closer."

Beth chuckled. "Honey, I don't think he wants to hang out with his adopted grandma. You'll figure out something. You always do. So how was your flying depo with Larry Simpson? Is it easier to work with him now? I mean, it has been almost two years, right?" she added.

"Well, it's still a bit awkward, but I think he realizes that when we were both separated, we were both vulnerable. Thank God we didn't get physical." The relief was evident in her tone as she remembered that short time of separation with Peter, which turned out to be a precursor of the real deal just over a year later.

"So does he know you're divorced now, and what about him?" her mom asked. "You know, it's been a while since you've worked with him."

"Yeah, he knows, and he's actually been divorced longer than I have. He says they weren't able to work it out because she's more interested in her career than him."

"Well, do you think he's still interested?"

"I'm not sure and to be honest with you, I don't want to know, Mom, and I think that's why it was a bit uncomfortable. I don't want it to interfere with our business relationship. Back when we realized that we were starting to cross emotional boundaries, I asked him if he wanted me to send other reporters in the future, and he assured me that we'd be okay to work together. He wouldn't let it interfere, he said." Lacey went on to tell her mom about the flight and the deposition. "And so I guess you could say that it all went without any turbulence, so to speak."

Beth smiled at Lacey's pun. "Oh, you are the witty one. So come on, what is it you're not telling me? I can tell there's something else on your mind. Is it Jake?"

Lacey was startled by her intuition and wisdom. "No, it's not Jake, at least not right at the moment. He seems to be doing okay right now with new friends from the new school and this new band that he started a couple of weeks ago. I think he's found a way to vent some of those pent-up feelings and confusions."

"Then what else could it be? Your job is going great. Jake's in smooth waters right now. What could be so bad?"

Lacey remembered the boys out there waiting for her. "I just wanted your opinion on something. It's about Seth." She went on to explain her fear of jeopardizing their relationship. "It feels like we're starting to shift, and yet we never talk about the change. And tomorrow night we're going to a birthday party of a close friend of his."

"I think that's actually a nice way for a relationship to start, honey. You've built something really nice."

"Exactly, and I don't want to bring the building crashing down around me. I just feel something changing and maybe it's not changing with him but it is for me."

"Just have a good time and think before you leap."

Lacey didn't want to tell her she felt as though she was already midair with Seth and that she didn't know how to stop herself. "I'm sure it will just be another good time with a friend," she said to change the subject. "So how is Dad? Did you guys hear back from the doctor?"

There was a pause. "Mom, are you there?"

"Yes," Beth whispered.

Lacey picked up on it quickly. "Mom, what did he say?"

"It's back, Lacey. The cancer's back."

Lacey felt as though the wind had been knocked out of her, but it was her turn to be strong for this woman who had been like a mother to her ever since they met just a few years ago. In fact, both her and dad had been happy to fill the shoes of the parents she hadn't had growing up. "So when do we start treatment to beat this thing again?" Lacey said, mustering up an attitude of determination and positive thinking.

"We don't, Lacey. It came back with a vengeance. They've given him six months."

Lacey was at a loss for words. Finally, after what felt like an immeasurable amount of time, she spoke. "We'll get through this, Mom." Lacey could hear her mom crying as she choked back her own tears before she hung up.

Lacey sat for a moment in silence. She was sad and stunned, but for the moment, Jake needed her to be Mom. She stood up and made her way out to the garage where the guys were rehearsing.

When she walked out there, they were all laughing at Jake who was jumping up and down, totally rocking out behind his keyboard and a microphone. Their laughter eased her internal sadness. She was glad to see that they weren't waiting for her and that Jake's mood seemed to have switched again, at least to a better place.

When Nikko saw her, he did a special drum roll and that sent them all rocking with their instruments for a few measures, and then as if on cue, they all stopped.

Lacey smiled at Nikko, a goofy and yet quiet kid whose parents were in the midst of a separation.

"Nice drum roll." She smiled at each of them. There was Dave, a fun-loving pastor's kid full of life; he played lead guitar. And Jeremy, the oldest of the group and old beyond his years played base. He too came from a broken home. Adam, who was like a second son to Lacey was not only Jake's best friend, but the sound man, too. "So what are the ideas for the band name?"

They shouted out names, and Lacey stopped them. "So what is it you guys want to tell everyone you stand for?"

Jake was the first to speak up. "We don't want to be like other kids our age, and we don't want to compromise our convictions," he said, wavering in his uncertain convictions.

"Okay." Lacey was stunned at her son's statement. They were all quiet for a few minutes. Lacey was the first to speak. "So how does 'No Compromise' sound?" She could see by the looks on their faces that they were each letting that sink in.

Dave spoke up. "How about 'No Co.' for 'No Compromise'?"

"I love it," Lacey exclaimed! A few beats of musical pandemonium followed some high-fives and laughter.

"Mom, go sit down now and listen to our first song."

Lacey did as Jake directed and got comfortable on a floor pillow. She nodded to Jake to signal she was ready. They started their song, and it sounded so pretty, almost melancholy, just on the verge of sad, and then according to their style, which was a cross between punk and emo, the song got loud and fast. Lacey held back the urge to put her fingers in her ears and sat through the entire two and a half minutes, straining to understand the words that Jake was screaming into the microphone. When it had stopped, the look on Lacey's face must have said a thousand words.

Dave spoke up first. "It was that bad, huh?"

Lacey stumbled for the least painful truth first. "No, it's not that it's bad. I just can't tell what you are all yelling or trying to sing, and aren't the words just as important as the music?"

They looked at each other, and Jake's buried optimism gushed forth. "She's got a point, guys."

"I will say that you definitely have great stage presence…" She glanced at each of them to see if that had registered. A couple of them were smiling, so she continued, "Just work on enunciating your words and bringing the scream down a bit. I mean, I get it; it's the style and considered really cool if you can scream long and loud and all that, but think of the message you're trying to convey." She started to go back inside and glanced at her watch.

"Hey, it's almost dinner time. I'm going to order you a couple of pizzas, so keep practicing and I'll let you know when dinner is ready."

Seth saw her park her car in the driveway from the window upstairs and gave a slight whistle when she got out. She looked good, really good. He lingered a few more seconds as he noticed what she was wearing. She made "casual" look extraordinary. She was wearing dark Levi jeans and a black pullover jersey-type top with a belt that rested at her hips and came down in the front. She looked amazing, and he was looking forward to being with her tonight and introducing her to his friends. Tonight was a turning point for them, a night when he didn't have to share her with Jake, the people at the gym, or with the problems at her condo. The time he spent with her tonight would determine which direction he was headed with her. The connection had been growing for him at a steady pace, and there had been times when he had had to pull back a bit because he felt himself feeling a little too much too fast, but he had never let her know. Maybe tonight that would change. The ringing of the doorbell brought him back to the present and he made his way downstairs.

Lacey looked up when the door flew open and Seth stood there, bigger than life, the smile on his face even bigger. Her heart fluttered at the sight of him, and her smile matched his. "You trying to give me a heart attack?" Lacey said. "I thought you wanted me to meet your friends," she added, the smile on her face evident in her voice.

"Scared ya, huh?" Seth said, motioning her in. "We'll go out through the garage so I can lock up." They made their way down the hall and to the garage, and Seth held the door open for her.

"Hey, that wasn't there before, was it?" Lacey asked, pointing to a collage of pictures on the wall.

Seth's eyes roamed to the direction of her finger. "Oh, that. No, I just hung it today."

Lacey took a minute to look at the photos, marveling at the incredible definition and separation of his legs, abs, arms and back. His body was beautiful, not over-developed like most body builders. Lacey tore her gaze from the person in the collage to the person standing before her now, and again her pulse raced. She shook her head, trying to clear it as she turned and headed for the front door.

Seth followed, trying to get ahead of her so he could open the door. "What are you shaking your head for?"

Lacey had to think of something quick to cover up what she was really thinking. She couldn't tell him *that*. When he got in the truck, she complimented him on the collage. "Out of all the ones you've shown me, I think that one's the best. You look incredible," she added quickly.

Seth backed the truck out and let the garage door come down. "Thank you." He turned to look at her and gave her one of his heart-stopping smiles. "So let me tell you a little bit about the friends you're going to meet tonight."

Lacey leaned back in her seat as he drove and filled her in on facts and funnies of the people she'd be meeting. His face was animated and happy when he talked, especially when he spoke of his best friend and his wife, who the birthday party was for, and their two kids. He told Lacey that he had been there for each of their births and how that had meant a lot to them.

"From the look on your face and the tone in your voice, I'd say that it meant a lot to you too."

Seth laughed. "Well, maybe, but don't tell anyone,"

"Spoken like a true tough guy," she said, leaning over to poke him in the side. "Oh, ticklish, are we?" Lacey asked, already knowing the answer. What she hadn't seen was that Seth had pulled up to his friends' house and he was parking the truck.

Again he laughed and instead of answering her question, he reached over and poked her left side, and she let out a squeal. "Look who's ticklish now," he challenged. "We're here," he added, putting the truck in park and letting himself out. He hurried over to her side and opened her door and reached for her arm to help her out. She was still smiling.

"I love to see you smile," he said.

Lacey's heart raced as he reached for her hand to help her out of the truck. The feel of his hand in hers sent her heart to the races again, making her feel warm all over. She landed on her feet right beside him and was thankful she didn't have to look directly at him in that electrically charged moment.

Seth, obviously feeling the current too, broke the silence. "So this is my friends' place. It's pretty awesome, huh?"

Lacey ignored the sudden awkwardness and looked up at the house in front of her. The sprawling one-story home took up almost a half of a block, which was in contrast to the neighboring areas where the homes were built so close together that one could literally use the rooftops as a means of getting around the neighborhood. She also couldn't help but notice the double two-car garages side by side, and a large, beautifully manicured lawn with gigantic palm trees adorned with white lights spiraling all the way up to the tips of the trunks of each tree; while at the base of the trees were custom brick planters filled with pink, white, yellow, and bright orange orchids and camellias still visible in the dusk light.

"It's incredible. I didn't know this part of Alta Loma existed. What does he do for a living?"

"He's a general contractor, a genius, and a nice guy at that. He's a real hard worker and knows how to enjoy the fruits of his labor," he said. "You'll see," he added, turning up the walkway lined with Malibu lighting. He stopped to wait for her.

"Sorry," Lacey said, as she ran to catch up with him.

"Wait until you see inside." They stood side by side as Seth rang the doorbell. Even though they weren't touching, Lacey could feel the current between them again as she stared at his arms, arms she began to imagine going around her, holding her. She giggled and Seth looked at her.

"What's so funny?" He asked.

Lacey felt her face flush. "Nothing, just excited, I guess," she added for assurance. The thought of feeling the strength of those defined muscles that she had only looked at for months sent a warm rush from her heart all the way down to her toes. When the front door opened, Lacey snapped her head up and out of the cloud she'd been on to see Seth and his friend embrace like long-lost brothers.

"Lacey, this is John, and John, this is Lacey."

Lacey was impressed with John's firm handshake, grateful he wasn't one of those guys who shook a woman's hand like it was a fragile piece of glass that would break if squeezed too tightly. "It's nice to meet you. I've heard so much about you."

"Uh-oh." John laughed. "No telling what this guy's told you." He didn't give Lacey a chance to respond. "Come on in and meet the rest of the gang and my birthday girl."

The music and laughter greeted them as they walked through the long and beautiful entryway. Lacey noticed the mirrors and artwork to her right and the portrait-like photos on her left. The wall was lined with picture after picture and for a moment, Lacey felt her heart fill with bittersweet envy. First there was John and his wife, then the two of them with their first child; then there were portraits of both of their children, and finally, family portraits in the wilderness, on the beach, in the mountains. In every one of the photographs she saw laughter, love, and family, something she'd not had in her own childhood but had tried to grasp with Jake's father… She had even managed to hold it for a couple of years, but then it was quickly snatched away, or so it seemed. She nearly bumped into Seth when she finally looked up.

Seth, who had been talking to John, noticed Lacey was lagging behind. "Come on, kiddo." Seth smiled as he held out his hand for her to take.

Lacey didn't know what caught her by surprise more, the hand Seth extended or the sea of people scattered throughout every room they walked through. She let herself be led in between all the people, trying to relax as Seth introduced her to his friends on the way to finding Karen, John's wife. By the time they made it to the kitchen, Lacey had lost count of how many people Seth had introduced her to, but she was definitely relaxing and enjoying herself, especially when she realized that Seth still had her hand in his.

"Seth, it's so good to see you," Karen exclaimed, looking up from the vegetables she was cutting. "This must be Lacey," she said, leaning over to give Seth a hug.

Seth let go of Lacey's hand to return the hug and then took her hand again. "You guessed right," he said.

Lacey had to raise her head up to look into Karen's face. She stood five feet and eleven inches tall, and her measurements looked like they had to be 36, 24, 36—a.k.a. a perfect body. She had flawless skin, long reddish-brown hair, big green eyes, and a warm genuine smile. She extended her hand to Lacey. "It's so good to finally meet you. Seth's been telling us about you for a while now. It's so nice to put a face with the name."

Lacey choked down her delight of knowing that Seth had been talking to his best friends about her, wishing that she knew Karen well enough to find out exactly what he had been saying. "It's nice to finally meet you too. Seth has told me so much about you and John, and your kids are absolutely adorable." She was still very much aware of Seth beside her as she lifted her hand from his to shake Karen's.

"Can I help you do anything? Besides, it's your birthday."

"No, that's okay, really. I'm just about finished cutting the last of these veggies, and then I can go mingle. Can I get you something to drink, though? We've got sodas, iced tea and water in here, but if you want alcohol, the bar is just down the hall and—"

"I can take her there," Seth said.

"Oh, no, that's okay. I'll just have a Diet Pepsi for now."

Seth helped himself to their refrigerator and took out a Diet Pepsi for Lacey. He winked at her and nudged her elbow. "Let me show you around."

"Yes, please, show her around, Seth, and introduce her to everyone," Karen said, drying her hands on a towel and grabbing a bottle of water. "I'll catch up with you guys in a while. I've got to go find my hubby and say hi to our friends."

Lacey watched her disappear in the crowd, which was definitely larger by now, but when Seth took her hand again to guide her through all of the people who were gathering in groups, it was as though it was just the two of them in the room. She caught his gaze, and he squeezed her hand just as he brought her up to another crowd of people and began to make introductions.

Within a few minutes, Lacey saw a group of girls she knew from the gym.

"I'm going to go say hi to my girlfriends from the body sculpt class. I'll be back in a few minutes."

Seth and John were in the game room with several of the guys waiting for their turn at a game of pool. "She's pretty hot, buddy. Did you say you met her at the gym?"

Seth reached for a pool cue. He smiled as he recounted to his friend that first time he had met Lacey, when she had approached him. "I knew she was the type of person who didn't base friendship on appearances; that my height, or lack of it wasn't an issue for her. So I'm pretty comfortable around her and with our friendship," he said, nodding his head up and down, as if the acceptance of it was still new to him.

"Seth, I can't remember the last time I've seen you this happy and relaxed around a girl." John knew that Seth hadn't been in a relationship in several years, ever since his ex-fiance called off their wedding. John knew that Seth felt his lack of height had taken his possibility of a life with marriage away from him. The whole experience had left him emotionally stranded with walls a mile high protecting his broken heart. "Well, I think she's great, man, and I think it's great that you seem to be good friends, but come on, you have lots of friends. What you need is a *girl* friend."

"I hear you, John. It's just that my mind and my heart are having a tug-of-war," he said shaking his head.

"Dude, you have got to let those walls down. That thing with—what was her name, Heather?"

Seth nodded his head, the pain of the distant memory obvious in his expression.

"Anyway, that happened how many years ago now?" Not waiting for an answer, he continued to push his friend. "She's obviously into you and not shallow like Heather turned out to be. I'd say it's time to jump in, take a chance."

Seth shook his head. "I don't know, man. Maybe I'm comfortable where I'm at, you know?"

"Comfortable? How you going to find love just staying comfortable? Maybe you're just not attracted to her, then," he retorted.

"Oh, no, I'm attracted to her. I know I'm attracted to her."

John smiled but continued to challenge him. "Well, how do you know? Have you explored that at all?"

"No, I haven't. No," Seth emphasized, shaking his head.

"Well, why not? What's stopping you from responding to that attraction, you know, taking it further, first base, second—"

Seth didn't let him finish. "Because I don't know if I'd be able to give her more than that."

"Give her more than what?" John asked, baiting his friend.

Seth looked at John with a dumbfounded look on his face. "More than sex."

"See, you do care for her, but you certainly can't find out how much if you remain just *friends*."

Seth didn't respond right away. Instead, he walked over to the pool table and racked the balls. "The problem with that is she doesn't strike me as a girl that would be content with just a sexual relationship; she'd want more. And to be honest, I think those days are over for me, too. I don't just want to use her for a booty call," he emphasized. "I mean, I know the sex would be great, but…"

John chalked his cue and shook his head. "What do you mean those days are over? You never were like that, at least as long as I've known you."

"Yeah, that's true. I think I'm just projecting. I'd probably want more than that as well, but I…" Seth bent down and aimed for his first shot.

John watched him break. The balls rolled apart, the colors splashing all over the pool table and a couple went into different pockets. "Would you look at that!" John exclaimed. "So what's it going to be, stripes or solids?"

Seth shook his head, appearing to concentrate on the game they were now playing and not the conversation they were having. "I'll take solids."

"Solids it is." John leaned down to take his shot and then another and finally missed after his third turn. "Remember that bachelor party we went to years ago for Hector?

Seth nodded his head.

"Well, do you remember that stripper that was all up in your face and on your lap?"

Seth began to laugh. "Yeah, what was up with that? Did you guys set her up or what? You guys wouldn't admit it then, but come on, you can tell me the truth now."

"Well," John said reluctantly, "maybe." He stopped laughing and continued, "But seriously, you didn't even go for that, so I see what you're saying."

Seth responded with a shot that landed another solid in the left rear pocket. "Besides, she wasn't my type," he added.

"So what is your type?" he asked. "I mean, Lacey looks like she could be your type. You both like to work out, and it shows. She's got a hot little body, by the way."

"No kidding," Seth agreed.

"And from what you've told me, she's not needy. She has a job, which is another plus, right?"

"Yeah, she works."

"What does she do?" John asked and then cursed as he missed his shot.

"She's a court reporter," Seth said, taking his shot and then another, which he missed.

John let out a whistle. "Well then, there you have it: she's not looking for you to support her and her kid, not with a job like that."

Seth nodded his head in agreement and watched as John missed another shot. He pointed with his cue where he wanted his last solid ball to go and leaned down and aimed, shot, and missed. He shook his head in frustration, obviously having a hard time concentrating on his game. "All right, so maybe we have a couple of things in common," he muttered more to himself than John.

John shot the last of his balls in and pointed to the pocket he was hoping the eight ball would go in, shot it, and won the game. John stood up and waited for Seth to congratulate him, but he didn't.

"Maybe she is more my type than I realized."

John shook his head. "Man, if I didn't know better, I'd swear that you're at the edge right now in this thing, teetering toward the jump, and the only one stopping you is you. When and if you decide to jump, let me know. I'll be there for you.

"Yeah, well, we'll see. We'll see."

From across the room, Seth watched Lacey interacting with Karen, John, and a group of their friends. He appreciated, from where he was, how comfortable she looked, laughing and participating in the conversation. She was holding them all captive, probably with another one of her animated stories. Despite all the people around and all the noise of the partiers, Seth couldn't get out of his own head and escape his thoughts as he watched her. The conversation with John had awakened something in him, had brought to the surface feelings that he had been pushing down almost since he had first met Lacey. Now those feelings were colliding with his thoughts of exploring every inch of that hot little body, which was sending him closer to the edge than he had come since losing Heather. He was wrestling with his heart and his head while trying to push back his growing attraction to her. Should he keep pushing down the hope of another chance at love, or should he jump in, at least physically, and change the direction of this thing with Lacey forever? The funny thing about it was he recognized in her that same wall of protection that he had built around his own heart, a wall that took years of self-control to build to avoid being hurt again. Wasn't there a way to jump in without being overtaken? Darned if he knew, but the possibility was getting to be too much to pass up. Who was he kidding? He could no more protect his heart and mind from what he was feeling than fly to the moon. Maybe John was right, but he'd take it one step at a time, taking his time to explore without getting lost, that way the wall would not come shattering down, but would come down slowly. Realizing how he had consented to his own feelings, Seth shook his head and smiled.

"What's so funny, Seth?" John asked.

"Oh, nothing," he said, a bit startled. "I was just thinking. Hey, I didn't even see you come up. Where's Karen?"

"She's trying to round up the girls. What do you say we start gathering everyone for your favorite game? That was one of Karen's main requests for this party, that we'd play your game."

Seth laughed. "Let's do it," he said and followed John as they began to make the rounds in each of the rooms to gather everyone outside to the backyard.

Lacey turned in the direction of the loud voice to see John standing on a chair announcing, "It's time for Seth's favorite game. The crowd broke out in laughter, and Lacey could hear Seth's above everyone else's. She scanned the area, looking in the direction of his laughter, and at the same time, she could feel someone staring at her. She turned and her eyes found his, and they pulled her toward him. The entire walk to Seth, she couldn't tear her gaze from him. He was sitting in a chair surrounded by people. When she reached him, he motioned for her to sit on his lap. She looked around and saw there wasn't another empty chair anyway and pushed past her own hesitation as she sat down on his lap.

There was a definite breeze in the air, and she brushed her own arms to create some warmth. Just as she felt Seth's arms come around her, John motioned for him to join him.

"In honor of Karen's birthday, Seth has agreed to start us off." Everyone cheered him on and began clapping to the beat of the Caribbean music made popular with The Limbo. Lacey jumped up to let Seth go, but he pulled her to him. "Follow me."

She got up again, and this time when Seth got up, she went right behind him, stopping just a step behind him as the music started. She watched, and down and under he went, under the bar that was set on its highest notch for the beginning round of the game. She repeated what he did, and he was waiting for her when she stood up on the other side of the pole. He reached for her hand and they went to the back of the line, laughing at themselves as well as the others. Lacey was free in the moments of just being caught up in the fun of it all, being part of something.

Round two went much like round one, without losing any contestants. Lacey couldn't remember the last time she'd had this much fun. She was giddy with laughter and free from worry. By the time they had completed round three, they had lost five of the forty-five that were playing. Round four proved to be totally devastating, taking out another fifteen people and leaving them with only twenty-five. Seth, of course, was making it look easy, yet it was getting tougher for Lacey but not any less fun. As the pole got lower and the line got shorter, the rounds began moving quicker and quicker, and Lacey lost count of what round it was when she hit the bar and was disqualified. That round took out all but three people. Lacey stood to the side, laughing and watching as the bar got lower and lower and lower and finally, the last one left was Seth. The crowd broke out in hysterics as Seth did a little victory break dance.

"Now I want you to know that this contest was in no way rigged, but we kind of, sort of expected him to win, so, here's your prize, Seth." The crowd was laughing and clapping as John held up a life-sized, five-foot-three-inch blowup doll of J-Lo, one of Seth's favorite fantasy women, and a six-pack of Coronas, his favorite beer. John handed them over to Seth and stood back up on the chair. "So now we'll make our way into the dining room so we can sing 'Happy Birthday' to our birthday girl and break out the cake."

Seth walked into the kitchen carrying a bunch of paper plates and cups and dumped them in the trash. Karen and Lacey were putting the leftover food away and cleaning up the counters and washing dishes. When the last dish had been dried and put away,

Lacey let out a yawn, and put her hand over her mouth, her eyes big as saucers with embarrassment.

"Come on, sleepyhead," Seth said. "I'm going to get her home," he told John and Karen.

"Yeah, go on. You guys have done enough, really," Karen assured Lacey. She looked at her husband, and they both moved at the same time toward the front door.

John gave Seth a pat on the back. "Thanks for all your help, you guys. Come on. We'll walk you out."

Seth held Lacey's door open and helped her step up into the truck. "I forgot my jacket; I'll be right back." Lacey smiled and leaned back into the seat.

By the time he got in on his side, Lacey's head was dangling toward him. He smiled as he stared at her, suddenly finding himself in a tender moment with her but all by himself. She looked so peaceful. He reached across her seat, which definitely took some doing, tapped the electronic adjuster and watched as her seat reclined back. Then he gently moved her head toward the center so she wouldn't wake up with a stiff neck. After getting her into what looked to be a comfortable position, Seth headed for home, his thoughts stuck on how to ask her in once they got there, wondering if she did come in, where it would lead them. The fact that he mentally toyed with all the possibilities the entire twenty miles home revealed that she had gotten under his skin; before he would or could go any further, he had to know if he was under hers.

Lacey awoke to the sound of a garage door closing. She sat up and came to her senses just as it had completely closed. She looked embarrassed and lost, like she was looking for something to say.

"Wow, I can't believe I fell asleep." She laughed. "I must be pretty comfortable around you."

"Hold that thought." He came around to open her door and waited while she gathered her purse and jacket. He helped her down and made sure not to move too far away. When she landed, she landed so close to him that he had to put his arms around her to steady her. "How's that for comfortable?" Her arms went around him in response, and he squeezed her to him for a second, long enough to feel the pounding of her heart, and then took her by the hand. "Let's go inside and fix you a cup of coffee or something. There's no way you can drive home sleepy." He smiled when she didn't resist and led her into the house.

Lacey opened up the door to the bathroom and flipped the light switch. She groaned when she looked in the mirror. She was a mess, both inside and out. Her hair was looking sleepy, and her makeup looked pretty tired too. She put her purse up on the counter and pulled out her comb. She ran it through her hair, quickly teasing the top back part to give it some height. Satisfied with that, she reached around for a couple of squares of toilet paper to wipe the smudges of mascara from under her eyes and blended what was left of her eye shadow. Then she took out her powder and brush to freshen up her face. She put her stuff back in her purse and went to wash her hands. *Why do I care what I look like? Am I trying to impress him? Why didn't I just get in my car and drive off?* The questions lingered in her mind as she washed and dried her hands. She wasn't too sure about the answers to the first two questions, but she knew as sure as she was standing there that the reason she didn't get in her car and go home was because she didn't want to. She wanted to be with him, especially since it seemed as though he wanted her to be. She refolded the towel, remembering how she had felt when Seth had taken her hand at the party a couple of times and then when he had sat her down on his lap. He had made those deliberate moves, and the door of curiosity was now open way too far for her to muster the strength to close it or walk away from it. She took one last look in the mirror, grabbed her purse, and headed out of the bathroom.

Seth must have heard the bathroom door open. "I'm in here," he called.

Lacey headed in the direction of the living room. "What are you watching?" She quickly glanced at his big fifty-two-inch-screen TV and saw the Lakers, perplexity written all over her face.

"I recorded it with TiVo," he answered her unasked question.

"Oh, I was going to say, how are you watching a Lakers game at twelve thirty in the morning?"

"So did you want me to fix you a cup of coffee?" he asked, pushing the pause button.

"No, that's okay. I think I'll just get a bottle of water."

"In that case, go ahead and help yourself," he said, throwing a pillow toward her and smiling when he nearly hit her.

"Thanks a lot," she retorted good-naturedly and tossed the pillow back at him. She watched it land at his feet and turned and made her way to the kitchen. She grabbed a bottle of water out of the refrigerator and took a quick look around. He was definitely a neat-freak kind of guy as she observed the organized, clean counters, the 49ers sports memorabilia on the walls and various shelves, the cleanliness of his floors and the latest and greatest of appliances. Seth's voice startled her.

"Did you find the water okay?" he asked.

"Uh-huh. Did you want me to bring you one?"

"Yeah, since you're already up, sure."

Lacey grabbed another bottle of water and took it to Seth. She sat down on the other end of the couch, suddenly a bit nervous in her own skin again. She concentrated on trying to make herself comfortable. *It's just Seth,* she reminded herself.

Seth took his eyes from the game and looked over at her. "Come over here. You look like you're cold. He patted a spot right next to him, and Lacey scooted over toward him. He reached for his 49ers quilt on the arm of the couch, and before he tossed it out to cover her, he motioned with his other arm for her to scoot closer. The way she was leaning, her head came just at his shoulder. "That's better," he said, and spread out the blanket so it covered her. Satisfied, he rested one arm around her and his other on the arm of the couch.

Seth was comfortable to sit like that for a while, but Lacey's wiggling was speaking volumes. He tried to ignore it, but with her so close, he was obviously struggling to stay focused on the basketball game, stealing looks at her every other minute. After twenty minutes, he stopped the game and turned himself quickly toward her. "Hey, what's going on with you? How come you keep wiggling?" he said in a playful tone. He reached over with his free arm and poked her side. Lacey squealed.

"I owed you that one," he said, laughing, though not at her but more at the surprised look on her face.

She surprised him by poking him back and then the tickling match was on. Minutes later they were on the floor, Seth was sitting on top of Lacey, though not with all his weight, as he held her arms on the ground. "Do you give up?" he asked, out of breath from laughing.

Lacey was out of breath too, and not just from the tickling and wrestling. "Yeah, I give up."

Seth stood up, reached for her hands, pulled her to her feet, and led her back to the couch. The tension that was there earlier was back. Seth leaned his back into the arm of the couch and put his feet up and motioned for Lacey to do the same, and just as if he'd done it many times before, he began rubbing her sock-covered feet, first one and then the other, watching her relax.

They sat like that for a long time, talking into the morning. Seth shared some of his favorite childhood memories of him, his two brothers, and his mom and dad who were all in Wisconsin. He talked about how hard it was every time he went back for a visit and saw how old his parents were getting. "What about you? I haven't ever heard you talk about your family." His eyes bore into hers, encouraging her to share because he was genuinely interested.

Lacey couldn't offer any happy and fun memories of family. "I don't want to be a bummer, but I really don't have too many happy memories from my childhood."

Seth looked shocked and curious at the same time. "What do you mean?"

"Well, to make a long story short, we were taken away from my mom and stepdad when I was twelve and placed in foster care, so I kind of grew up in the system." Lacey could see the questions written in his eyes, but she knew he wouldn't ask them. "So I didn't really get to grow up with my sisters and brothers," she added

"How many sisters and brothers do you have?" he asked lightheartedly, lessening the apparent tension.

"I have two sisters and two brothers, and I'm right in the middle."

"I'm the middle one, too." Seth grinned as he squeezed her foot. "So where did Jake go for the night?" he asked, and she was grateful he changed the subject.

"He's with his dad; I pick him up tomorrow—" Lacey stopped herself when she realized what time it was and then continued, "I mean today, or this evening, I should say, at the train station."

Seth looked up at the clock that said it was 2:07 in the morning. "Wow, I didn't know it was that late. I can't let you drive home now," he said with a smile that spread to his eyes. He moved his legs off the couch and leaned toward her suddenly, catching her off guard. With one hand, he lifted her head to meet his gaze and gently tucked her hair behind her ear with his other hand before bringing her face closer to his.

When Seth led Lacey up the stairs to his bedroom, all of Lacey's spoken and unspoken fears collided with the reality of her rampant passion waiting to be unleashed. He pulled out one of his T-shirts and handed it to her, and as if on cue, she took it and helped herself to his bathroom. She changed quickly, disregarding the warning lights going off in her mind, not wanting to stop and think about what she was doing. The temptation to let go of self-control and get lost in this tide of passion that had been rising all night long was incredibly strong, and as she opened up the door and turned off the light, she knew it was too late to turn back for she had already started giving in to it.

Lacey's drive home from Seth's was an emotional tug of war. On one end was the contentment that comes from a night of spent passion, and on the other was the guilt, shame and embarrassment for giving in to it. She let the tears of remorse come as she replayed their conversation from not even an hour ago, the replay confirming how desperate she had sounded when she had asked about future plans, like a phone call later or could they get together tonight or tomorrow. She had sounded needy, even to her own ears, and he had seen it. The tears came harder as she remembered his nonchalant reply: "We'll see how it goes." His tone had been almost as cold as ice. Where was the fiery passion from the night before? It was like he had flipped a switch. By the time she turned the corner of her street, guilt and humiliation were definitely in the lead in the emotional tug of war, and when Lacey let it sink in that she had just experienced her first one-night stand, the passion definitely became the loser of the game, her guilt and humiliation the winner.

She pulled into her garage and watched as the door came down. She let her head rest on the steering wheel as she pondered her first and last one-night stand. "I am not about to become an official member of the One-Night-Standers' Club," she muttered. She let herself into her condo and was greeted by silence. Putting her keys down on the counter, she made her way upstairs to take a shower, hoping to somehow scrub the night of passion away.

She undressed while the water warmed up. She made her way into the shower and the spray of water splashed down on her head and down her body, causing the rewind button of her mind to be pushed again. She slid down the wall, almost into a praying position, the sound of her sobs meeting the running water, her thoughts screaming louder, telling her she shouldn't have pressed him with questions exploding with need. She wished she could just rewind. But then again, if she could rewind and redo, how much would she undo?

By the time the water started to get cold, she was exhausted from crying and emotionally drained. She turned the water off, grabbed her towel and patted herself dry before dressing in her comfy sweats and T-shirt. All she wanted was to lie down for a nap. She tried, but sleep was a stranger. She tried to hunker down further in her blanket of confusion, but she knew she had to snap out of it. She had to pick Jake up in a few hours, and she couldn't be moping around. She decided that she needed to exert some of her pent-up frustration and sadness.

With a sense of direction, Lacey got up and put a pair of socks on. Without thinking, she grabbed the vacuum and began a rigorous cleaning frenzy, vacuuming the stairs, her room, the hall, the spare bedroom, and when she got to Jake's room, she opened up the door so she could keep going but was forced to turn the vacuum off. It literally looked like a tornado had blown through his room. Stuff was everywhere.

She kicked aside things to get inside the door so she could begin the task of finding the carpet underneath it all. She waded through papers, dirty clothes, clean clothes, empty soda cans, paper plates, books. By the time she had picked up everything off the floor, determined what clothes were dirty and what clothes were clean, put them away, she had filled his trashcan up twice, and her T-shirt was wet with sweat. She tackled his bed next. She removed his pillow so she could pull up his sheet and blankets, and found a pencil on top of a piece of paper. She picked it up and saw the words *I remember the past*. She sat down and stared out the window, wondering if she should read it or just put it back and leave the bed unmade. Her curiosity overcame her, and she read:

> I remember the past. What were worries then? What was pain? I thought I knew, but oh, how ignorant I was. So many times I tried to get it right but failed just before I'd succeed.

"What in the heck is he talking about?" Lacey wondered out loud. "Failed at what?" She continued reading.

> Why? Why are things—no, why is life so much harder for me? Sometimes I don't think it's fair, but neither is this world, so I can't complain. Too many I've let down and too many I've lost trust from.

Who has he let down? she mused.

> It will be a feets to gain it back.

If not for the pain of it all, Lacey would have smiled at his spelling for *feat*. She shook her head and read on.

> I ask myself, how could I have let myself be so corrupted, so worldly, and so evil? And the sad thing is I never thought twice about it.

Lacey could feel the pace of her heart speed up and the guilt rise from her own worldliness and evil deeds. "What have you done, Jake?" She whispered to the silence.

> So to all who believed in me, I'm sorry I let you down and that I like getting high with my dad. To all who loved me, I'm sorry I hurt you. But all of you who care, keep believing and keep the love in your heart because I will cross that red tape with bold black letters that read 'Finish Line,' and I will hear the distinct voice that clearly says, "Well done, my son."

Lacey forgot her own pain as she lost herself in her son's apparent agony, not even cognizant of how quickly she had transferred her own emotions. Anger came knocking, and the thought of Clint getting high with their son sent her blood boiling. Here she kept insisting that he play an active role in Jake's life so they could have a good father-son relationship, and all the while she had been leading her son right into the boxing ring without even realizing it. Betrayal dripped from the ceiling, splashing down on her heart, causing the spot that had once been soft for Clint to harden.

She was in a quandary. She couldn't call Clint just yet to give him a piece of her mind, because the way she had found out, technically, had invaded Jake's privacy. But how was she going to act like she didn't know when she saw Jake? Her world was spinning so out of control, she needed to talk to someone. She picked up the phone. "Mom, please be home," she said to the receiver as she heard the first ring. It rang two more times before she answered.

"Mom, thank God you're home."

"Are you okay, honey?"

"Yes—no." Lacey let the tears fall as she explained to her mom about cleaning Jake's room and the note she had found under his pillow. "So I need some of your words of wisdom, Mom." There was a moment of silence. "Mom, are you there?"

"Yeah, I'm here. I'm just trying to switch gears, actually, because when I saw that it was you calling, I was ready to hear about your date with Seth, so I have to restart my brain, you know?" she said with a chuckle.

At the mention of his name, Lacey wrestled to keep the tears away. "Yeah, well, I'll fill you in on that drama later. I have no idea what I'm going to do about this and I know I can't solve it now, especially because I'm supposed to go pick him up in a couple of hours."

"Are you still going to that church with Martha and Doug?"

"Well, not consistently, but sometimes, yeah. What does that have to do with this?"

"And is Jake still going to the youth group with Adam?" she asked, not stopping to answer Lacey's question.

"Uh-huh, he is," Lacey responded, a bit confused by her mom's questions which seemed to be taking them off track.

"Well, I think it would be a good idea to call the youth pastor and see if you can't get some help from him. See what he says to do about this."

Lacey took about thirty seconds to let that sink in.

"Are you there, Lacey?"

"I'm here, just thinking. That's actually a good idea. Your wisdom is always bailing me out of my confusion. I don't mean to cut this short, Mom, but I've got to go. I'll try to give you a call tomorrow."

"That's okay, honey. You be good to you, okay? And be careful driving. Remember not to drive faster than your angel can fly," she added.

"Thanks again, Mom. I love you."

"Love you lots."

Lacey called Martha next and filled her in on what she had found out about Jake and his dad.

"There has to be something you could do legally, isn't there?" Martha asked, obviously angry.

"I'm sure there is, but I don't know enough about family law to even know where to start, and getting an attorney is not possible financially. Besides, we're talking about a fourteen-year-old kid's emotions. I just don't think there's any easy solution for this, Martha."

"You're probably right, and your mom had a good idea. I just can't believe Clint would do this," she spouted out with exasperation. "Here, let me give you Bruce's number, and just know that I'll keep my eyes and ears wide open when our boys are together."

"Thanks, Martha." They talked for a few more minutes, and when they hung up, Lacey hurried and dialed the number Martha had given her. When the voice mail recording came on, Lacey almost hung up but then decided at the last minute to leave a message. "Hi, my name is Lacey, I'm Jake's mom. I was wondering if you could call me as soon as possible. It's urgent, and it's about Jake, and I really need your help." She left her home phone number and her cell number and reluctantly hung up the phone. She sat and stared at the phone for a long time, willing it to ring, but it didn't.

After a half hour, she got up, threw a sweatshirt over her T-shirt and decided to walk to Starbucks across the street. She grabbed her wallet and cell phone, and headed out the front door, not even bothering to lock it. The air was still crisp for being almost two o'clock, and the sun was shining, but it did little to lift her spirits. She crossed the street. Suddenly, an old habit beckoned to her and she felt as if she were being pulled into the liquor store next to the Starbucks. She approached the counter, paying little attention to the man asking if he could help her. "Yeah, I'll take a pack of Kools Regular, please." Even though smoking had been such a familiar vice from the past, buying them for the first time in a few years was definitely like an out-of-body experience.

She walked next door to Starbucks, ordered her grande Red Eye and then went outside to sit and smoke and wallow in her guilt, now made even worse with the rekindling of an old habit. She wished she could make it all disappear, just like the smoke rings she blew into the air. She looked around to make sure she didn't see anyone she knew, embarrassed by her own weakness, and yet, some of the tension seemed to blow out with the smoke she exhaled, at least it felt like it.

She sat there sipping her coffee, lost in her thoughts. As she reached for another cigarette, her cell phone rang, startling her. She put the cigarette back down. "Hello," she said breathlessly.

"Hi. Lacey?" the voice on the other end asked.

"Yes, this is she."

"Hi, this is Pastor Bruce. I'm returning your call. Sorry it took me a while to get back to you, but I was at church."

As soon as he said he was at church, Lacey remembered it was Sunday. "I'm so sorry. That was pretty stupid of me. It's just that there's so much going on, I've lost track of the days."

"I know how that is," he admitted. "I missed Jake today. Is he okay?"

"He's with his dad." When the words left her mouth, Lacey felt the lump in her throat forming and her eyes welled up. "So I thought he was okay, but he's not." Lacey went on to explain to the pastor what she had discovered while cleaning his room, and then she gave him a bit of their personal history. "So basically, I'm not sure what to do."

"That's a tough one. I've always sensed that he's hurting, and sometimes he even opens up at youth group about his dad and his having AIDS and the fact that he doesn't see him all that often. I didn't know he was going to be seeing him this weekend. He didn't mention it last week."

"Yeah, it was kind of a last-minute thing, and because he gets to see him so little as it is, I didn't have the heart to make a stink about giving us more notice," Lacey admitted.

"Well, if it makes you feel any better, I've never suspected Jake of being high while at youth group." When Lacey didn't respond, he asked her, "So when's he coming home?"

"I have to go pick him up in a couple of hours at the train station."

"I'll tell you what," Bruce offered, "why don't I call him tonight, just talk with him and let him know I missed him, and see if we can't make a plan to go hang out at the skate park."

At the mention of the skate park, Lacey's hope was revived, and she smiled. "He'd love that. I know he would."

"Well, that's what I'll do then."

"That would be great, and thank you so much, Pastor Bruce."

"Just call me Bruce. And, Lacey, can I pray with you?"

Lacey looked over at her pack of cigarettes, sure that he could see them through the phone, so she put them in her pocket. "Uh, sure," she stammered. She bowed her head right where she sat, willing herself to listen to Bruce's words and not her own condemnation that seemed to be screaming at her from every direction. She repeated his "amen," and they talked for a couple more minutes before they hung up.

She sat there lost in something Bruce had said while praying, something about if we confess our sins, that He forgives and forgets them, throws them as far as the east is from the west. Lacey reached for another cigarette. "Yeah, I'd like to forget this last eighteen hours," she muttered as she lit her cigarette. "I'd do it so differently; that's for sure.

She pulled into the parking lot of the train station and saw him. She'd recognize that posture anywhere. She let out a sigh and pushed the words she had read to the back of her mind as she pulled up to the curb and hit her button to roll down the window. "Hey there, handsome, anyone tell you that bad posture will make you old before your time?"

Jake grabbed his bag and opened the door. "Hey, Mom." He smiled, as if he didn't hear her question. He put his suitcase on the backseat and got in.

Lacey waited for him to buckle up, and reached over and gave him a hug. She put the car in gear and pulled out of the train station. "So how was your visit with your dad?"

"Good. Hey, Mom, can Shellie come over for dinner tonight?"

Lacey was glad for the distraction. "That sounds like a great idea, especially since I haven't met her yet." Lacey smiled as she handed him her phone, grateful that she didn't have to do or say anything to keep Jake home for Pastor Bruce's phone call.

WWW@life.help

"Come on, Lacey. Pull your head out," Harrison said a little too loudly. He brought his face down closer to hers. "Do you want to be a walking wounded woman? Since when have I had to catch the weight bar so it doesn't go falling down on your chest?"

Lacey sat up on the bench, startled by his apparent frustration with her. "Maybe you should have let it fall on me," she muttered.

"Oh, stop with the victim thinking, Lacey. Where's it coming from?" He bent down with both arms on the bar of the bench press, bringing himself within inches of her. "There's no way you're gonna be able to compete in this contest if you keep going like this," he added.

Lacey's eyes welled up, and she could feel that tightening sensation that happened in her throat whenever she was going to cry. "I've got to use the restroom. I'll be right back."

"Make it quick. Your time's a-wasting," he said with a hint of sarcasm.

Lacey practically ran to the bathroom and literally ran into the back of someone because she had her head down instead of watching where she was going.

"Well, hello to you, too," a voice spoke.

Lacey looked up to see a blond-haired, green-eyed guy smiling down at her. "Sorry," she muttered and kept on going.

"Hey, you could at least tell me your name so the next time I see you running toward me, I can stop you." He was chuckling when he saw her turn her head. "My name's Daryn, in case you're interested," he added.

She turned back around and kept going. "That's all I need, another body-building, stuck-on-himself, love 'em and leave 'em kind of guy," she muttered as she opened the door to the bathroom. She walked in and nearly collided with a woman coming out. "Sorry," she said and held the door open for her. She made her way to the only empty stall, sat down, and put her head in her hands, choking back the sobs so no one would hear her. *What the heck is wrong with me?* She unrolled several sheets of toilet paper and held it to her face. Within seconds, the tissue was soggy from her tears. When she was all cried out, she sat there for a couple more minutes, mustering up the emotional and physical strength to complete her training appointment with Harrison. She got up and flushed the toilet out of habit. She watched the water go down and wished that the problems in life could be flushed like that, along with the pain. She went to the sink and splashed her face with cold water trying to wash away the red in her eyes. She patted her face dry with a paper towel and let herself out, determined to finish her training session.

Harrison wasn't where she had left him. She looked over to the free-weight section; he wasn't there. She looked down to the biceps and triceps machines, and he wasn't there either. "Where in the heck..." She stopped midsentence. He and Seth were walking out of his office. Seth was walking toward the exit and obviously leaving the gym, and Harrison was walking toward her. *That's just great. Now I'm going to look like an idiot for putting out,* her thoughts screamed right before he reached her.

"Come on. Let's get out of here and go get you some carbohydrates," Harrison commanded more than requested

"I'm not hungry."

"That's too bad; you're gonna eat anyway. I think this training diet is affecting your brain, but we'll soon find out." He steered her to the exit of the gym.

"What's that supposed to mean?" she asked, allowing herself to be led out of the gym.

Harrison stopped abruptly and turned to face her. "Why do you have to mind screw everything, Lacey? Let's just go get something to eat, and see if you feel better."

Lacey wanted desperately to know about what he and Seth had talked about, if he knew why Seth wasn't talking to her anymore. She was sure Harrison had picked up on the not-so-good vibes between her and Seth any time he was close to them in the gym. Emotion overran rationale, and she just blurted it out. "So what were you and Seth talking about?"

Harrison continued as if he hadn't heard her question. "Like I said, I think some carbs will do you good. What do you say we go to your favorite spot?" He smiled and added, "We can talk about it there."

Her stomach growled at the thought of a homemade tortilla stuffed with rice and beans, chicken and cheese from the Kool Kactus, but the desire to know if Seth had said anything about them made her hunger pains seem insignificant. "That does sound kinda good, but I haven't been very hungry these days."

Harrison shrugged his shoulders. "Suit yourself." He turned to walk away, and Lacey stopped him.

"Okay. Let's go. I haven't eaten today anyway, so I probably should try and eat a little something."

"Oh, that's real smart, Lacey, not eating all day," he said, his head shaking in obvious frustration. "Come on. You fly; I'll buy."

"Sounds good." Lacey smiled.

The five-mile drive to Kool Kactus was quick and quiet, except for the sound of the radio, which Harrison had turned up so loud Lacey could feel the beat reverberating through her side speakers.

When she pulled into the parking lot, she turned down the radio before turning off the motor. "They're gonna think some gang members just pulled up." She laughed.

Harrison bent real low in his seat and turned his head toward her. "Hey, esé, what's up?"

His impersonation was really good, and Lacey couldn't help but laugh. They got out of the car and went inside. She told him what she wanted and went and got them a table outside. There was a breeze in the air that mingled with the sun, perfect weather for eating outside. Lacey sat back and let out a sigh as she sat and waited for Harrison and their food.

Harrison came out with their food and drinks and sat down. Lacey handed him his and took her own burrito and unwrapped it halfway. She took her first bite and shook her head.

"What are you shaking your head for?" Harrison asked between bites.

"Because it's so good, and I didn't realize how hungry I was or how much I miss eating here every Saturday. This counting carbs stuff is really hard."

"Yeah, well, just wait; about four to six weeks out, you'll be cut back to seventy-five or a hundred carbohydrates a day, depending how your body fat is looking."

"Well, I'll deal with that then; for now, I just want to enjoy this." They ate in silence for a few minutes, and then Lacey remembered why she really came. "So are you going to tell me what you and Seth talked about?" She knew as soon as she said it that her attempt at nonchalance had failed.

"Well," Harrison started tentatively, "he saw you practically running into the bathroom, and wanted to know if you were okay."

Lacey's heart skipped a beat. "He did?"

"Yeah, and then I decided to ask him straight out what in the heck was going on, since *you* won't tell me," Harrison added, looking right into her eyes.

"Well?" Lacey nearly screamed, ignoring his accusation. "What did he say?" Lacey saw the open hesitation on Harrison's face and was about to start begging, and he interrupted her.

"Actually, I'm not sure I understood what he said, or what he asked, I should say, because now I'm wondering if he was asking me a question so he could get an answer."

Lacey was completely baffled. "What the heck are you talking about?" The sound of a chair being pulled out from the table straight across from them reminded her that they weren't alone. Her cheeks turned the color of the salsa that they were both pouring on their burritos. She leaned in and lowered her voice. "I'm not getting you. What are you trying to say?"

"He asked me, 'Have you ever been with someone you care about, and they called you by the name of their ex?' I was really thinking about what he said, you know, trying to think if Deanna had ever done that to me, and he must have taken it like I wasn't going to answer because he just looked at me and said, 'It's a major buzz kill.'" Harrison paused. "So maybe you're the one to answer that for me, Lacey. What do you think he means by…" He stopped midsentence when he saw Lacey's panicked expression. Her elbows were stuck on the table, her hands still up holding her burrito, and her mouth was stuck open. Harrison watched as her expression changed ever so slowly, and her terror turned to tears. She put the burrito down and reached for a napkin. Harrison had the sense to be quiet for a few seconds longer before he asked her if she was okay.

All Lacey could do was nod her head up and down slowly, as if in a daze, so Harrison continued, "So I take it by the expression on your face that you know what he's talking about. Did you call him 'Peter' or what?"

Lacey was stricken speechless, her mind captured somewhere between that passionate night with Seth and the mention of Peter's name. She looked up at Harrison, barely able to speak, and choked out, "I guess so."

Harrison groaned out loud.

Lacey dropped her head into the palm of her hands until she felt his hand reach for one of hers. "Hey, it's okay. It's not the end of the world," he said, somewhat clumsily. "It's not like you did it in the throes of passion, right?"

Lacey threw her head up and looked right at Harrison. She didn't have to say a word.

This time it was Harrison's turn to look like he'd been punched in the gut.

Lacey broke the silence. "I had no idea. I don't remember doing that, ever, not once the whole night. I must look like a real idiot, huh?" she asked, needing more affirmation or validation than confirmation. "Either that, or a cheap date, huh?"

Harrison picked his head up to catch her eyes. "Lacey, that's ridiculous. Everyone knows you're not like *that*. Besides, you obviously like the guy. It's not like you set out to have a one-night thing with him, and to be honest, I don't think it was that way for him either; otherwise, he wouldn't be acting so offended."

Lacey sat silently, trying to acknowledge the truth of why Seth had blown her off without so much as a phone call since that night. She let out a very heavy sigh. "I can't believe I called him Peter," she murmured. "He isn't anything like him and he certainly wasn't anything like him that night," she added matter-of-factly.

She faded off, lost in the confusion and the guilt. They sat there in silence for a few minutes while Harrison finished up his burrito. Lacey looked at hers and realized her appetite was gone so she wrapped the half-eaten burrito up.

Harrison broke the silence. "So what were you going to say a minute ago?

"I just don't get how he could…" Again she let her sentence go unfinished.

"How he could…?" Harrison tried to get her to continue. She didn't respond. "Okay. Maybe I can help by giving you a guy's perspective."

Lacey started up again as if she hadn't heard Harrison's offer. "Well, after a night like that, how he could just turn it off like a faucet and walk away, leaving me wanting more, more answers, more connection."

"Hey, look at me," Harrison said gently. When she lifted her head, he continued, "That's exactly my point. I don't think he was in it for the sex. His heart was in it, and in his opinion, yours was elsewhere."

Lacey started to open her mouth to defend herself, and Harrison stopped her. "Don't say anything. Just think on that for a while," he said. "I have another trainee in about twenty minutes." He stood and scooted his chair back, and Lacey joined him, willing her heart to follow.

The sound of the piano greeted her when she walked in the house. Lacey's spirits lifted, and she smiled from the inside out, just as she did every time she heard Jake play. She put her keys on the counter quietly, willing him to not hear her so he would continue playing. She turned the corner to see him, and watched his hands move over the keys, methodically at times and at other times picking up the pace just a bit. She realized that this music was new. She had never heard him play this before, but then again, he was always creating music, but he never really wrote it down. He played what he was feeling. She leaned her head into the wall, closed her eyes, trying to gauge his mood from his music. The melody was definitely sad, but there were slight shadows of light-heartedness, near-happy undertones as the chorus seemed to pick up tempo. The sound of his voice startled her, and she strained to hear what he was singing, unfortunately creating a shadow that he saw. The music stopped abruptly and Jake turned to her, knocking a piece of paper off the piano.

"Mom, you scared the be-jeebers out of me."

"So that's a new one, huh?"

Jake hung his head. "Yeah, it is, sort of," he muttered as he bent down to pick up the fallen piece of paper and turned it over on the piano.

"Well, I was going to say, when I heard you start to sing, I was surprised because I don't think I've ever heard you put words to your music, Jake. And even though I couldn't quite hear what you were singing, it sounded really good," Lacey confessed openly. Quietly, she wondered what the words really were. "It seems you have a talent for putting your feelings down on paper," she added and then quickly wished she could take that last sentence back. She was in no way ready to deal with the note she'd found almost two weeks ago now.

"What's that supposed to mean?" Jake asked, with a definite defensive melody now in his tone.

Lacey decided the better thing to do was to ignore his question and take the edge off. "Hey, what's the 'tude for? I'm just paying you a compliment. I think it's awesome that you can put words to music that you write, that's all. And I'm also thinking it's great that you finally put something down on paper. You know, you may be a star one day," she said with a hint of a smile.

Jake rewarded her with a boyish smile as he hung his head somewhat sheepishly. "Thanks, Mom." He pulled the cover down over the keys and stood up and walked toward her holding his arms out to hug her.

"What are you stopping for?" Lacey asked as she returned his embrace.

"Why do you smell like cigarettes?"

Lacey pulled herself out of his embrace and though she danced with the thought of a fib, she looked him straight in the eyes. "Because I've started up again," she admitted. And then to take the focus off her, she added, "Don't you ever start this nasty habit, Jake. It haunts your mind like a constant shadow." He didn't say anything, and Lacey tried to read the emotions on his face, in his eyes. It was almost like he wanted to confess something and then decided against it. She wished she could explain what had driven her to them again, but it would come out as an excuse, and there was no justifying this nasty habit, not even in her own mind.

The silence was so thick it was suffocating. Lacey was desperate to know what was going on in his head but at a loss to even know how to find out.

"I just don't want to lose you, too," Jake finally spoke.

Lacey didn't know what to do with the naked vulnerability he was showing her. She reached for him and held him close. "I'm not going anywhere, honey." Choking in all the emotion, she changed the subject: "So what do you say we get a movie after dinner?" She squeezed him before pulling away.

"No thanks, Mom. I've got some homework," he said, heading for the kitchen.

Lacey didn't know whether to continue with what they had been talking about or let it go and enjoy the fact that he was willing to do his homework without putting up a fight. Maybe she'd learn how to handle these situations better with the counselor that Pastor Bruce had referred her to. She offered up a silent thanks to Pastor Bruce for the time he'd been spending with Jake. "Well, dinner will be ready in about twenty minutes. How about some more music while I'm getting it ready."

He didn't answer.

"Pleeeeeease."

Jake grabbed a Pepsi from the refrigerator and popped it open. "I can do that," he said agreeably and headed back to the piano.

Lacey saw the sign and made a last-minute left turn into the narrow driveway of the Patterson Family Counseling building and nearly collided with an oncoming car. She waved to say she was sorry and drove to the back to find a parking spot. She pulled the keys out of the ignition and saw that she was two minutes late. *Great, what a first impression,* she thought as she made her way to the front of the office building. On the door was inscribed the words, "Psychology based on Theology, Counseling with Biblical Principles." She walked into a small waiting area that looked much like a cozy and comfortable living room, inviting with its two bookcases to the left bursting with books and various knick-knacks, obviously sentimental. In the corner there was a recliner and beside it a little table with more knickknacks and over on the other side, a leather two-seater couch. The door leading into the main offices was closed so Lacey sat down and continued to check the surroundings out.

Within a few minutes, she heard voices, and then the door opened and a couple walked out. A man remained standing at the door and turned his eyes toward her. "Are you Lacey?" he asked.

Lacey stood and extended her hand. "That's me."

"I'm Daniel. Come on in."

Lacey followed him down the hall and into his office, which was a lot more comfortable than she'd expected, with a big solid oak desk on one wall and a beautiful Gibson guitar on a stand in one corner. *Jake would love that,* she thought. She looked to the wall immediately to her right and saw another leather couch so she went and sat down, as if she'd been there several times before.

Daniel handed her a clipboard that had a couple of forms on it and an attached pen. "This is just a little pre-treatment survey to help me get to know you a little bit before we get started." He bent down so he could flip the first page over and pointed to a section on the reverse of the form. "And this second form is some insurance information. I'll be right down the hall if you have any questions." He turned and walked out of the room, and Lacey was left to fill out the questionnaire.

She leaned back into the couch and filled in all of her contact information. Parent(s) substance abuse assessment. Lacey checked the "alcohol" box for her estranged mother and wrote beside it "alcoholic." She also added "chronic smoker." She moved on to her own substance abuse assessment. For "alcohol" she checked "socially." For "cigarettes" she grudgingly answered "daily." For "caffeine"—*that's a no-brainer, but I don't see the right answer; where's the word intravenously?*—"daily" got the checkmark. "Other drugs," she put "never."

Please rate how much you were affected by the following in the past week, Lacey read to herself. "Concerns about your body or physical health," she read aloud. She paused as she looked at the choices. *N/A it is.* Okay. "Thoughts or behaviors you do over and over again." She let herself think about that one for a minute. *That's a no-brainer: stupid choices in men.* "N/A" got checked again. "Unusually high energy." She contemplated the choices and again put "N/A." If anything, she was grateful that she seldom ran out of energy until it was time for bed, and then it was like her battery just gave out. The next question hit a nerve: "Feeling sad, blue, or depressed." *Hmm* she thought and checked "extremely." She finished up the section, which included questions about anger, hostility, and/or irritability, which got a "mildly" checkmark, and the "fears of things or places," "belief that others want to hurt you," "drinking too much," or "using drugs" all got "not applicable."

Lacey let out a big sigh as she saw the final section, which asked for a rating in various areas with the choices being: "N/A, cannot function, serious problems, moderate problems, mild problems," and finally, "no problems." "Oh this ought to be fun," she muttered, "so many choices." For "On your job," she put "no problems." The next one punched her in the gut, but she reminded herself that she was here about Jake and parenting him so she checked off "N/A" for marital or significant other relationship," and then scribbled the word "single" right beside it. "Family relationships" was a category with a few questions, and Lacey could feel her shoulders tightening and her neck hurting. She scooted up to the edge of the couch and leaned forward as she quickly looked ahead to the questions. She quickly filled in "two" and "two" for brothers and sisters and had to stop and really think a minute about their ages; she'd forgotten because of not growing up with them. She answered a few more questions in the sibling section and then went to the immediate family section. For "How many children, ages, and gender" she answered "one, male, fourteen." *Certainly couldn't handle more than one.* "Do any of your children suffer from…" She checked the "depression" box as well as the box for "drugs," as she let out a heavy sigh and wrote in the word marijuana beside the box for "drugs."

She read the next question, which made her insides twist: "Were there any traumatic events growing up?" *Uh, yeah, let me see; where do I begin? My mom married a fat loser when I was six years old, who helped her beat the crap out of all of us at least three times a week, and when she was sleeping or not looking, he molested us for, oh, about six years or so. Is that considered traumatic?* Lacey almost giggled as she imagined what the counselor's expression would be if she were to really write that down. She opted for the "serious problems" box and drew an arrow and wrote at the bottom of the page, "due to physical, emotional and sexual abuse." She went to the next box and checked off "no problems" for the query of relationships outside of family. *Except for men,* she thought bitterly.

She forced herself to complete the rest of the form, which asked for any present medical conditions and medications, to which she replied "None." The next question made her eyebrows raise: "religious preference: atheist, Catholic, Protestant, agnostic, none of the above." Lacey stared at the question and read the choices again, pondering the choices. She knew she wasn't Catholic. Lacey felt herself sit back again on the couch as she let her mind wander to a flashback that the question had brought to the surface.

Daniel walked down the hall toward his office, pausing slightly at the door that he had left cracked open. He thought he had heard talking, but he didn't hear anything now. He knocked a couple of times and then slightly pushed the door open. "Are you almost—" he hadn't noticed her sitting there in almost a trance-like position until she jerked as if startled. "Did I scare you?" he asked gently.

Lacey shook her head and sat forward. "No. Well, not really. I was just answering that last question about religious prefer-ence, and it reminded me of something. I guess I was sort of daydreaming."

"Care to share?" he asked.

Lacey appreciated his smile and genuine interest. She sat back and began talking about the flashback. "Actually, it was kind of weird. I have so few memories from my childhood, especially fond ones, but I was reminded of my Aunt Penney. My broth-ers and sisters and I used to stay with her a lot of weekends as kids, until I turned twelve. Then all hell broke loose, and it was years before I saw her or them again. Anyway, every Sunday, we would walk to church, or I should say marched to church," Lacey said, smiling at the memory. "She was like a drill sergeant on those walks, but I always thought she was, like, one of God's spies. Thinking back, now I think she could have been one of His angels."

Daniel watched the emotions on her face. "You looked almost surprised right now. Did you have another flashback?" he asked.

"No, it wasn't that. I just…"

Daniel picked up on her hesitation and decided to pry just a little bit more. "You just what?" he repeated gently.

Lacey didn't know if she should tell him about the Voice she'd heard several times over the last year and a half for fear that he'd think she was really crazy. At the same time, she didn't want to sound abrupt by changing the subject and risk losing what she had just realized. She started again. "I just realized that for as long as I can remember, I've always believed there was a God."

"Well, that's how you can answer that last question then. As a matter of fact, that's a very true and accurate answer. Most people believe in *a* god, Lacey, and hopefully as we go along, your perception of who He is will become clearer, but we'll definitely explore that as we go."

Lacey was a bit puzzled by the counselor's words, but obediently bent down to scribble her answer for the last question. She didn't check any box but instead, wrote the words: "I've always believed in God." She handed the clipboard back to Daniel. "Here you go."

Daniel took the clipboard and turned to the insurance page. "Do you have your insurance card?" he asked, looking at the blank page.

Lacey dug in her wallet for her insurance card. She handed it to him without saying anything.

Daniel handed the clipboard back to her. "Do me a favor and sign at the bottom while I—"

Lacey stared at the blank page, which was asking for insurance information. "I forgot to fill this out. I'm sorry," Lacey offered apologetically.

"That's okay. I'll copy your card, and I'll fill it out for you so we can get started."

Daniel sat down in his chair directly across from her, just a couple of feet away. There was a moment of silence that seemed to stretch out into several moments as he looked over the form. Lacey noticed the puzzled look on his face, and she felt her gut sort of twist.

"I usually like to start backwards and work our way up the form but I noticed you didn't answer the last question which is: 'What brings you here today?'"

His tone was neither critical nor condescending, just matter of fact, but Lacey could still feel her cheeks burn with a flood of embarrassment. "I didn't even think to turn the form over," she admitted. "I guess my most immediate concern right now is my son." The words "my son" seemed to echo back to Lacey and moved her to tears as she recounted the last year and a half's events to the counselor.

He listened intently. At times, Lacey noticed that he made some notes, and every now and then he would interject, asking a question about her childhood, offering a validating comment, inquiring more about her relationships with men in the past, encouraging Lacey to continue, until it was time to stop, and even that was done gently when he asked her if he could close their time with prayer. They discussed her next appointment, and he walked her to the door and said good-bye.

Lacey walked to her car and got in. She sat there for a few minutes thinking about the last forty-five minutes in the counselor's office. She realized that though she had gone in there needing help concerning Jake, the things he had asked had stirred up some deeply hidden things having nothing to do with him, really, but more about her. Memories that she thought were long gone had turned out to only be hidden, she realized, and they had resurfaced with some of the counselor's questions. *Despite the fact that he has given me a lot to think about, I feel better,* she acknowledged.

"Who was that, Mom?" Jake asked.

"It was Nikki letting me know where we're going to meet this Saturday."

"Does that mean I get to go to Adam's then?"

Lacey leaned into the kitchen cabinet and placed one elbow down on the counter, hoping the gesture would ease the tension she felt. "Well, actually, we're meeting at Sophie's so I was wondering if you'd want to go with me and hang out with David Michael and Zach. What do you think?" Lacey answered his question with her own, remembering what the counselor had said about helping him with choices while giving him the freedom to make them.

"Can Adam come?" Jake responded with still another question.

"Well…" Lacey said, dragging it out while she thought about it.

Jake came around to where she was and put his arms around her, kissing her on the forehead several times in between his words, "please," kiss-kiss, "please," kiss-kiss, until they were both giggling. The words he'd written weren't quite out of her mind and threatened to steal the moment. It took all of her self-control to keep quiet as she pulled away gently

"I don't see a problem with it, but since it's not our house, maybe you should call Sophie and see if she'd mind. Better yet, before you do that, you should call Zach and see if he'd be okay with it." She felt Jake back up and when she looked up, he was reaching for the phone.

"What's his number again, Mom?"

Lacey recited the number for him. "Let me know what they say. I'm going to get some laundry started." She turned and headed up the stairs and heard Jake talking with Zach. A sudden thought stopped her in the doorway of her bedroom. *I wish I could tell Sophie about Jake smoking pot but I know I can't because of Zach.* And as it sank deeper into her consciousness, another one followed: *And there's no way I can ask her to help out while I'm in L. A.* The domino effect was overwhelming.

She turned and walked into Jake's room and grabbed his basket full of dirty clothes and went to her room and pulled her own hamper out. She sorted through her basket first, throwing the colors to one side and the whites to the other. When she had finished, she began to do the same with Jake's. She reached for the last pair of pants, shook them out and pulled out a book of matches from his back pocket. She stood holding them and staring at them, shaking her head in dismay and frustration. She let the pair of pants fall to the floor while keeping hold of the matches. "Now what do I do?" she spoke in the silence, the question running simultaneously with another question: why he had them in the first place. She absentmindedly kicked the fallen pants into the appropriate pile. The thoughts of how she would confront him about this as well as him getting high with his dad were stomping in her mind so loud that she had to sit down on the bench at the foot of her bed.

She leaned back into the foot of the bed and held her head back, looking up. It was then that she heard it again, the Voice, and she sat up and looked around. *Do not be anxious about the worries of tomorrow for I will take care of your tomorrow.* Lacey looked around the room. "That's easy for you to say," she nearly yelled as she stood up and put her hands on her hips, like she was ready for a fight.

"Mom?" Jake yelled.

Lacey nearly jumped at the sound of his voice and quickly made her way out to the hall and the stairs.

"Who are you talking to?" he asked.

Too exasperated to be embarrassed about being caught talking to herself, Lacey blurted out the first thing that came to her mind. "I don't know." The temptation to just let it all out almost swept her away. Jake's voice reeled her back in.

"Well, are you okay?" he asked.

The question evoked a new dilemma, that of lie or truth, reality or perception. The need to know the truth won out, and Lacey held up her hand and revealed the book of matches. "No, I'm really not okay," she countered.

Jake stood there and didn't flinch.

"Why do you have matches in your pants pocket?" she nearly screamed.

"Because me and some kids were trying to burn a message on the tables in the courtyard at school," he yelled back defiantly. "What did you think I had them for?" his question more an accusation than anything.

Lacey's shoulders slumped with relief, not sure if she believed him because she wanted to or because his reason had caught her by surprise and threatened to unravel her intuition about his smoking pot again. But she couldn't tell him that. "I wasn't sure," she stammered. "I guess since I've started smoking again, I was assuming the worst from you. I'm sorry, buddy. That was my bad."

Jake's posture softened at her admission and he began to turn away.

"So what did Zach say about you bringing Adam?" Lacey said, trying to offer a truce between them.

Jake came back to the foot of the stairs and looked up at her. "He said it was cool. So what time should I tell Adam we'll pick him up?"

"Sophie said to be there around three, so we'll pick Adam up around two thirty, and that way I can say hi to Martha."

Lacey let the bar down, suddenly conscious of somebody staring at her. She looked up and saw a familiar face but couldn't remember where she had seen him before. She was still trying to recall it when she realized that he was making his way over to her. *Oh, great. I should've worn my 'Don't talk to me if you're male' sign.* Lacey swore silently.

"Hey, Lacey, how's your workout going?"

Lacey was taken aback. "Do I know you?" she asked him, her tone a bit sarcastic.

His smile reeked of arrogance. "Well, let's just say that we've 'run' into each other." He laughed. "No pun intended."

"Oh, you," is all she could get out as she tried not to look at him.

He held his hand out. "Well, anyway, I'm Daryn."

His confidence bothered Lacey for some reason, but she decided to play nice. She extended her hand. "It's nice to meet you, Daryn." *I guess.*

"Do you mind if I work out with you? I could spot you. You shouldn't be doing this much weight without a spotter anyway."

Lacey didn't have the strength to argue, but she didn't want to lead him on either, so all she said was, "Whatever."

That was enough for Daryn, who not only spotted her on the chest press, but followed her over to her next chest exercise, assuring her that she needed his help. About fifteen minutes into the workout, Lacey learned that he had a son close to Jake's age, that he was a used-car salesman, that he rode a Harley, and that working out at the gym was a way of life for him.

"Are you always this confident?" Lacey finally asked somewhat exasperated with his whole demeanor. *He'd probably be pretty hot if you could see past the cockiness.*

Her attitude didn't faze him in the least, and he continued to follow her to two other machines as she finished up her abdominal workout. She started to head to the women's locker room and turned toward Daryn. "See you around," she said, with a half smile.

"You can count on that." Daryn winked and walked away.

After doing the dinner dishes, the girls made their way into Sophie's living room and settled in on the leather couches, chatting and laughing when David Michael and Zach ran into the house shouting "Mom" simultaneously. Sophie and Nikki both looked up, obviously recognizing the voices of each of their sons. Sophie was the first to stand up and try and intercept them. "We're in the family room," she yelled. The sound of their feet could be heard pounding down the hall. Zach reached them first. "Mom, you've got to come see what Jake's doing," he said, his eyes wide with excitement.

Lacey stood up at the mention of Jake's name.

"It's totally awesome. He's trying to do this skateboard trick with my new ramp and there's cars lined up to see it."

"What do you mean 'there's cars lined up'?" Sophie asked, her puzzled expression reaching Lacey.

"Well, he can't have the cars driving back and forth while he's doing this, so I just kind of went along and told the oncoming cars that if they wait, they can see a really neat trick. So now there's a whole bunch of cars waiting to see if he'll do it. It's so cool, Mom. I betcha he does it, too."

"It looks pretty hard, though," David Michael added.

Susie and Nikki got up and joined them. "Well, let's check it out," Nikki said, her enthusiasm matching the boys'.

The girls followed David Michael and Zach as they ran outside. "I'll be darned," Nikki exclaimed, looking first to the left and then to the right. "There really is traffic waiting to see this."

"Yeah," Susie said, noticing the people gathering on the curbside on both sides of the street.

Nikki turned to David Michael, and putting her hand on his shoulder, she asked him, "So what the heck is Jake gonna do?"

David Michael pointed to Lacey's car, and Lacey followed the direction of his finger. Her mouth dropped as she realized that her car had been pushed forward from where she had originally parked, and it was now directly in front of Sophie's driveway. Before she could say anything, David Michael continued with his excited narration of what Jake was going to do. "He's gonna skate from back there"—he pointed again to the section of the driveway that was in the back yard—"to that ramp"—he indicated—"and over the top of the car," he finished emphatically.

As if on cue, the girls looked in the direction of the back yard, and sure enough, Jake was there, one foot on the ground and one foot on the skateboard, ready for takeoff. Adam was standing beside him and giving him a pep talk. Lacey bit back the urge to stop him and send the cars on their way, but something told her not to steal his thunder. All that conflicted with her not wanting him to get hurt. "Talk about dilemma," she whispered.

Sensing her hesitation, Susie spoke up. "Come on, Lacey. Let him try it. Besides, I want to see if he can do it," she added loud enough for Jake to hear. He held up his arm in a wave and smiled. Susie gave him a thumbs-up.

"I say you let him try it," challenged Nikki. "But pray like heck he doesn't hurt himself or hit one of these oncoming cars."

"Oh, thanks a lot," Lacey wailed.

Sophie walked over to Jake. Adam stepped aside as she reached for Jake's head and brought his ear close to her. Whatever she said brought a smile to his face, and he got himself in position again. She came back to the group. "Who wants to be the counter?"

Zach jumped up. "I do. I do."

"Okay. You're it. Count to three and he goes." Sophie turned toward Jake and gave him a thumbs-up and said loud enough for Jake to hear, "When Zach counts to three, you go, okay?"

Jake held his hand up in response.

Lacey held her breath as Zach counted to three and Jake came whizzing by, calm and balanced as he hit the ramp and went up, and *bam*, down right in front of the car, but not over it. Everyone groaned at the same time, and this time Adam yelled out, "Come on, bro. You can do all things through Him who strengthens you. Let's try it one more time."

Lacey was still thinking about what Adam had said when she saw Jake fly past her on his way back to try it again. When he got in position, he gave the sign to begin the countdown, and Zach counted again. "One," he yelled. "Two," he yelled even louder. "Two and a half," he said not quite as loud, "Three." The sound of spinning wheels on concrete rang in Lacey's ears as she watched him fly by again, faster this time, onto the ramp, and up, up, up, and away he went, over her car. Everyone's head moved upward in slow motion, and all eyes followed him into the air and then down to the ground as he executed a safe landing. The pandemonium of horns honking and people screaming and whistling could probably be heard many blocks away, but the thing that would stay in Lacey's memory forever was the look of triumph on her son's face as Adam, Zach, and David Michael ran up to him and gave him high-fives. She didn't know if she was more proud of him for his accomplishment or thankful he hadn't been hurt. She ran and hugged him. "That was awesome, Buddy," she said, her enthusiasm obvious.

"Thanks, Mom."

Sophie came over and gave him a quick hug. "I've got to go thank these cars for waiting now." She giggled. "Hopefully none of them were in a big hurry."

Nikki and Susie joined Lacey and waited their turn to congratulate Jake. By the time all the traffic had left and the onlookers had begun to disperse, it was nearly dark. "So who's the wise guy that moved my car anyway?" she asked with a smile.

All the boys looked at each other and began to laugh. "We all did," they said.

"Figures." Sophie smiled as she playfully hit Zach on the back of the head. "I won't even ask whose idea it was," she added. "Get the ramp moved into the back yard and clean up the cups and stuff, and we'll go in and have some dessert. See you inside."

The girls made their way back into the house. "If I didn't know better," Nikki said, "I'd swear that boy could get a skateboard sponsor."

The girls nodded their agreement and began getting the bowls out to make the banana splits for the boys. Lacey listened to their chatter about Jake. She swallowed the guilt she felt for not confiding in them about her latest discovery about her son and forced herself to change the subject. "Speaking of how much fun it was for Zach, that reminds me, Sophie, can you help me out a couple of days a week while I'm in L. A. on that big case?"

"Actually, it would probably help me out with Zach because he really looks up to Jake. It will be fun for both of them," Sophie agreed.

"Thanks, Sophie. That means a lot." Lacey turned and busied herself with scooping out the ice cream so Sophie wouldn't see the painful guilt in her eyes.

Mixed Messages

"Jake, can you get the door, please?" Lacey shouted out from her bedroom. The only response was the ringing of the doorbell again. Exasperated and frustrated, Lacey put down her book as well as the attempt at some leisure reading and headed downstairs for the door. The doorbell sounded one more time before she made it to the entryway. "Okay. Okay," she yelled, thinking it was probably one of the kids for band practice. She pulled the door open hurriedly. She was in no way prepared for who stood right in front of her, on her doorstep, all bold and brazen.

"What in the heck are you doing here?" Lacey nearly yelled. She stood in the small opening of the door, making it clear she wasn't letting him in. "And how did you know where I live?" she asked incredulously.

"Well, hello to you too," Daryn said with a smirk. "I just wanted to drop by and say hi and thanks for the workout the other day. And as far as knowing where you live, I live a block away, and I see you pull in here all the time."

"But how did you know which condo I lived in?" she countered.

"I didn't. I just thought I'd knock on doors until I found you," he said, the smirk changing to a smile.

Lacey thought about that for a few seconds, and she felt herself smile. "Hasn't anyone ever told you it was rude to stalk girls?" She watched the smile on his face switch hands with sadness, and she almost felt bad.

Clanging cymbals and beating drums reverberated through the walls. Daryn cocked his head. "Is that coming from your garage?"

"Yeah, it's my son and his friends. They're having band practice."

"So how old is your son?" Daryn asked, his confidence front and center again.

"He's fifteen—I mean fourteen. He's almost fifteen." Lacey heard the sound of the garage door opening and brushed past Daryn to see why. She saw Adam walking out of the garage. "Adam, what's going on? Where are you going?"

"I forgot one of the amps so my mom's gonna bring it.

Lacey walked back toward the garage. Daryn joined her. "Jake, you have to make sure there's no music being played when the garage is open."

"We stopped, Mom." Jake motioned with his hands. "Bring it down, guys," he said. "We stopped before it opened."

"Yeah, well, I'm gonna bring it down on you if the association says anything to us. You know how they can be." She suddenly remembered Daryn was right beside her, and almost as an afterthought she turned and introduced him to Jake. "Honey, this is Daryn from the gym. Daryn, this is my son, Jake."

Daryn walked forward and shook Jake's hand. "Nice to meet you, Jake."

Jake shook his hand, and sent Lacey a questioning look.

Lacey shrugged her shoulders, her body language clearly saying, "I don't know."

Jake introduced him to Nikko, Jeremy, Dave, and to Adam who had returned with the amp.

Daryn shook hands with each of them and turned to face them after winking at Lacey. "So do you guys mind if I hang out for a while and listen to you?"

Jake looked as surprised as Lacey did. "Well, we have only a couple of songs ready."

Adam got up from his hunkered-down position. "Hey, Jake, we're gonna need to do a sound check with this second amp." He turned toward Daryn and Lacey. "So give us a couple of minutes."

Daryn looked like he had won a prize. "No problem. I'll just pull up a piece of floor here."

Lacey was about to offer him a beach chair hanging on the wall but stopped when she heard her house phone ringing. "I'll be right back." She walked into the house and grabbed the phone just before it went to voice mail.

"Hello."

"Hey, Lacey, is that you?"

"It's me, but who is this?"

"It's Dan, your bug man." The voice on the other end chuckled.

"Dan. How are you?"

"I'm good; I'm blessed. And you?"

Lacey could almost see his boyish grin through the phone as he gave her his usual "I'm blessed" response, and she couldn't help but smile too. "I'm good."

"And how is Jake doing? Adjusting okay, making lots of new friends?"

Lacey reveled in his genuine concern and felt a tinge of guilt for not having called him since their move to Rancho Cucamonga, especially since he had helped them immensely. "Well, Jake's okay. Not great, but okay. Anyway, that would take too long to go into. So how's the exterminating business?"

"Well, it's hopping, no pun intended." He chuckled. "So what do you say we get together Saturday, you, me and Jake? Let me take you guys out to dinner and maybe a movie or some miniature golf or something."

Lacey didn't hesitate. Dan was like a brother to her. He had been so kind to them after Peter had left, always coming by and checking on them, helping them get their stuff in storage for the move to Doug and Martha's and then again to the condo. "Actually, I think we're both home this Saturday, so that sounds good. We could use a night out. What time?"

They talked for a few minutes more, agreeing on five o'clock before they said their good-byes.

Lacey went back out to the garage. The guys were doing a final sound check. She looked around and saw that Daryn was gone. She tapped Jake on the shoulder and asked him, "So where did he go?"

Jake was adjusting his keyboard pedal on the floor and looked up. "He went to get his son."

"Are you okay with that?"

"Yeah, it's cool. He said he really likes music, so…" He switched his attention back to the keyboard.

Lacey pulled three beach chairs off the hook on the wall and set them several feet back from where the boys were. "I'm going to go fill an ice chest with some sodas and water."

She pulled the ice chest down and went in the house. Within minutes, she had wiped it out, filled it with sodas, bottled water, and ice. She set it on the counter and searched for her pizza coupons, flipped through them quickly and decided on Pizza Hut. She heard the boys start up a song and then stop. She grabbed the ice chest and went back out to the garage. Daryn was introducing his son to the boys. Lacey set the ice chest down when she saw Daryn walk toward her, his son right behind him.

"And this is Lacey, the one I've been telling you about from the gym." His son walked up beside him and held his hand out to her as Daryn introduced them. "Lacey, this is Daryk."

Lacey looked at Daryn and then lowered her gaze to Daryk. He looked a lot like his dad, she noticed. "It's nice to meet you, Daryk. I've got some sodas in the ice chest if you want one."

"It's nice to meet you, too." He turned around and walked over to the ice chest and grabbed a soda.

While Jake pressed the garage door button to close it, Lacey, Daryn and Daryk went and sat down.

Adam got up and made a couple of jokes before introducing them to the band. Jake counted out, "A one, two. A one two three," and the music began. They started and stopped a few times but then worked it out and went all the way through two songs without missing a beat.

The music stopped, and Lacey stood up and did her famous loud whistle, clapping like a proud mom. "That was actually pretty good, guys."

Daryn and Daryk had stood up too and were clapping, and Daryk went up and gave them all a high-five.

Lacey observed that Daryk was definitely not confident or cocky like his father. In fact, there seemed to be a need to fit in and belong, a vulnerable edge around him much like Jake's. "I'm going to go order the pizza now. You all okay with pepperoni and sausage?"

They all voiced their approval, and Lacey walked to the door. Daryn intercepted it for her, standing almost in front of her. His green eyes bore into hers. He pushed the door opened and motioned with his arm. "Allow me."

She walked inside, and he followed. Lacey went to the phone and dialed the number for Pizza Hut. She could feel Daryn staring at her from across the counter where he was standing. She made the mistake of looking up, and he smiled as if to disarm her. She shook her head at him. "What are you—" the voice on the other end interrupted her. She gave the lady on the phone her pizza order, informed her that she had the coupon, and when the lady had given her the total and time estimate for the pizza delivery, Lacey hung up.

Daryn walked around the counter and toward her. "So what were you going to say?" He came to a stop inches from her.

Lacey felt her pulse suddenly pick up speed, and she stood up to try and create a little distance.

He moved a step closer.

She became unnerved by the look in his eyes that contradicted his attire of arrogance. He was directly in front of her now, so close she feared he would hear her heart beating. She moved to her right. "I was just going to ask you what you were smiling at."

He stayed where he was, leaning on the counter, his eyes never leaving her. "You."

Lacey cocked her head, somewhat puzzled by his response. There was something about him that brought her guard up. *Is it something in me or is it his cocky confidence?* She tried to stare past him. He was... *Yeah, that's it,* she smiled at the revelation. *He was intriguing.*

"Now what are you smiling at?" He stood up straight and walked toward her again.

"Just thinking to myself," she said. "I'm going to let the boys know that the pizza's on its way."

He was at the door before her and opened it. "Shall we?"

Lacey walked into the garage and saw that the boys were talking to Daryk, just as if he'd been a part of their group for a long time. "Hey, guys, pizza's on its way."

Jake looked up and smiled. "Thanks, Mom."

"I'm going to go inside and work on a transcript. I'll let you know when it's here." She made her way to the door and away from Daryn and then remembered she needed to let Jake know about Saturday and turned back around. "Jake?"

He looked up to acknowledge that he heard her.

"Do you remember Dan from Hesperia?"

Jake played a few chords on the keyboard, and he hit one last chord harder coinciding with the recognition on his face. "You mean the exterminator guy?"

"Uh-huh."

"How is that little *bugger*?" Jake laughed at his own joke, and Nikko did a three-beat ditty on his drums.

Lacey joined in their laughter. "You don't have any plans this Saturday, do you?"

Jake tilted his head to the side and looked as if he was in deep thought. "No, I don't think so."

"Well, Dan would like to take us out this Saturday for dinner and a movie or miniature golf or something."

Jake had gone back to working out some chords on the keyboard, and Lacey wondered if he heard her. She was about to repeat it, but suddenly the moment felt awkward and she didn't know whether to just go back in the house and let the question go unanswered until later or re-ask it now. She looked around at everyone, and they all seemed to be waiting for Jake to answer, including Daryn who was standing with his arms crossed. She walked past him to get to Jake. "Jake, did you hear me?"

Jake looked up, his expression pensive, and then put his head down again, looking at the keys on the keyboard. "Sorry, Mom; I've got some notes in my head I'm trying to work out. Yeah, that's cool. What time?"

"He'll be here about five o'clock."

"Cool."

Lacey walked past Daryn toward the door. She opened it and turned around one last time to see Daryn's green eyes piercing through her defenses. She tore her eyes from his and looked toward the boys. "I'll let you guys know when the pizza's here."

Lacey went into her office, her mind already on the next thing to do while the guys had their jam session and waited for the pizza.

"Madam Court Reporter, could you read that last question and answer back, please."

Lacey was caught off guard by Danny's request. She'd broken one of her own rules in court reporting, which was to not get emotionally involved in the case she was reporting. That was definitely a lost cause in this case. This was the fourth day of the case, and each day was an emotional roller coaster more thought-provoking and gut-wrenching than the day before. She had listened to the testimonies from two of the seven homeless people that were taken advantage of by these slumlords, now defendants in the lawsuit.

Today they were deposing the third homeless plaintiff in the case, a thirty-five-year-old female, aka Melanie. For ten months, she had been at the beck and call of the slumlord and his manager of the mobile home park. She worked six to seven days a week, nine to ten hours a day just for a roof over her head and a buck fifty a day; the same wages the previous deponents had been paid. *Oh, I hope these slumlords get it good!* Lacey struggled to keep her anger from showing.

Melanie went on to testify about the living conditions of the so-called roof over her head, like no running water so she'd have to walk across the street to the gas station in order to use the restroom. The space she'd been given to live in had no electricity, so she kept candles burning once the sun went down.

Lacey cringed as she listened to Melanie explain about the rats and cockroaches amok in the mobile home. To make matters worse, she had an eleven-year-old daughter who lived with her. Danny must not have liked hearing about it either, because he changed his line of questioning to delve into Melanie's past. Her own testimony proved that she had a shady past, which would affect her credibility, but Lacey knew she was telling the truth about the way these slumlords had treated her. *Two wrongs don't make a right*, Lacey thought.

It was a vicious continuous cycle. They were victims of their own circumstances, caught in this entangled web they kept weaving by thinking they deserved nothing better.

Lacey looked up when she was finished with the read-back and caught the wink in Danny's eye as he said "thank you" to her and instructed the witness to answer the pending question. She put her skill on automatic and wrote what she heard, simultaneously remembering the testimony of the first two plaintiffs, which was more of the same stuff but from a different perspective.

When Lacey heard the words "So stipulated," she let out a sigh of relief. She turned her machine off and put it in the corner, thankful that she didn't have to pack up anything but her laptop. She looked at the bottom left-hand corner of her screen. The transcript was 225 pages. *Wow!* Lacey marveled. *That's a thousand-dollar day.* She went to the beginning of the transcript and began going through and fixing the un-translated words to make it easier when she began the editing process.

"Can I give you a lift to the train station, Lacey?"

Lacey looked up to see Danny standing just a couple of feet from her with his briefcase on the table. She stole a peek at the clock on the wall and was surprised to see that she'd been working on her transcript for almost fifteen minutes already. "Sure. That'd be great," she stammered. She quickly turned off her laptop and went to unplug the cord, but Danny had already done it and was reaching out his arm to hand it to her.

"Thank you."

"Sure. So what do you think so far?"

"You mean what do I think of the case, or your client?"

"I object; that's compound," Danny joked.

Lacey looked up from packing her laptop and laughed. "I guess it is compound," she admitted, "but then again, to me, the case and your client are two different animals, so…"

"Well, that's a good point. So let's start with my client."

"Well, your client gives new meaning to the term 'slumlord,' and co-counsel's client does as well."

Danny bent over to indicate he'd been punched in the gut and then stood up. "Ouch! That hurt." He smiled.

"But as far as your case," Lacey continued, "somehow I get the feeling that you'll defend it well and minimize the damages, judging by your questioning in these first three depositions."

Danny smiled like a young boy who'd been given an A on a paper. "Why, thank you, Madam Court Reporter. You ready to go?"

Danny watched Lacey grab her laptop out of the backseat. "Thanks, Danny. Have a great weekend."

He caught her gaze for a quick moment and was tempted to ask her what she was doing this weekend but lost his nerve. "Yeah, you too, Lacey. See you Monday."

Lacey stepped onto the train and set her laptop and purse down and then plopped into the seat next to it. She leaned her head into the window and stared out to the platform, watching the hustle and bustle of the people going to and from their trains.

Her thoughts returned to the case. She smiled as she remembered walking in the first day and seeing Danny there. As soon as she saw his face, the mystery of which attorney it was that was requesting her disappeared. He was the attorney she had worked with in Orange County a few months ago, the one that had asked her to use his first name and had been really great to work with. Well, they were definitely on a first-name basis now, that is, when he wasn't calling her Madam Court Reporter.

Lacey let out a sigh and reached for her laptop. The ringing of her cell phone interrupted her. She debated with ignoring it or answering it. The latter won out when she saw that it was Susie. "Hey, Susie, what's up?"

"Not much, but I did call to give you a heads-up."

Lacey leaned back in her seat and took the liberty of putting her feet up in the seat in front of her. "Give me a heads-up for what?"

"We've got your birthday bash planned, and I wanted to give you the date so you could mark it on your calendar."

"Susie, my birthday's not for two months."

"Actually, it's just six weeks away, but who's counting?" She giggled and then her voice grew serious. "Besides, I've got to start telling *you know who* now that I'll be gone that night so he can't accuse me of just springing it on him."

"Good point. So what's the date exactly? I know we're going to my sister's in San Diego in a few weeks. I just want to make sure it doesn't conflict with that."

"It's six weeks from this Saturday," Susie recited the date from memory.

"Well, don't forget we have to go to Fresh Peaches three weeks from this Saturday to get my bathing suit picked out for the contest." They talked a few more minutes and said good-bye just as the train started to leave Union Station. Lacey leaned forward, taking her feet off the seat in front of her, but only for a minute while she reached for her laptop again. She leaned back and got comfortable again, glad to escape having to make chit-chat with train neighbors, and began editing the day's job so she'd be less distracted when she got home, more available for whatever the evening would bring with Jake.

"Jake, are you about ready? Dan will be here any minute," Lacey yelled.

Jake stuck his head out of the bathroom door. "Yeah, I'll be down in a minute, Mom."

Lacey turned to walk into her office when Jake's voice came from the top of the stairs.

"Hey, Mom, which Dan is this again?" he asked with a smirk. "Is it Dan the attorney or Dan the exterminator? And isn't your counselor named Dan, too?"

Lacey caught his attempt at humor. "Yeah, but Dan, this Dan, is more like a brother."

"Uh-huh, right. By the way, whatever happened to Seth?"

The ring of the doorbell collided with her heart that nearly stopped at the sound of Seth's name. "He's been real busy." She turned as the doorbell rang again, hoping that Jake hadn't seen the pain in her eyes. She threw open the door, ready to give Dan a big hug and stopped short at the sight of Daryn. "This question's beginning to sound like a broken record, but what are you doing here?"

"Would you believe I was in the area again?" He chuckled at himself. When the only response she gave him was a glare, he continued, "Actually, I wanted to see if you were going to work out tomorrow, see if we could work out together."

"I take Sundays off."

"What about Monday?"

Lacey saw Dan go driving by, motivating her to say good-bye to Daryn. "I am not sure what time I'm going to go to the gym on Monday. I have to work."

Daryn stood there as if glued to the cement. "Then just give me your number and I'll call you." He pulled out a card and pen, ready to scribble down her number on the back.

Exasperated, she recited her cell phone number in hopes of getting rid of him quicker.

He wrote down the number, tore the card in half and scribbled his own number down. He took her hand and put the piece of card in it and then kissed her hand closed and turned to walk away, barely missing Dan as he made his way to her porch. Time seemed to stand still as the two men had a stare-off for a long minute, and then Daryn stretched out his hand. "You must be Dan. I'm Daryn, a friend of Lacey's."

Lacey watched as Dan shook Daryn's hand without saying a word, obviously taken off guard.

"Daryn, this is my good friend, Dan, and, Dan, this is Daryn, a friend from the gym, and he was just leaving."

Daryn took his cue and said good-bye and Dan and Lacey went inside.

"That was weird, and so was he," Dan said.

Lacey was taken aback by Dan's sudden boldness. "He definitely marches to his own drum," she said, looking up to see Jake walking downstairs.

When Jake made it all the way down, Dan grabbed him in a guy-like hug, truly happy to see him. Lacey looked on and, with a twinge, noticed that Jake not only received Dan's affection but returned it as well. "I'll meet you guys out in the car. I'm going to get my sweater and purse and lock up."

Lacey got ready for bed and knocked on Jake's door. His stereo was playing, and Lacey could barely hear his voice when he told her to come in.

She walked in and noticed he was already lying in bed. "Hey, buddy. I just wanted to say good night." She sat down on the edge of his bed and looked at him. He was lying face up with his hands behind his head. She marveled at how he looked so grown up lying there like that. "Did you have a good time tonight?"

"Yeah, it was okay."

Lacey picked up on his somberness right away. "So why do I get the feeling something's wrong, honey?"

"I thought you said he was like a brother to you."

Lacey was taken off guard with his directness. "I did say that, and I meant it."

Lacey watched the different emotions run across his face. She scooted closer to him. "What just went through your head right now?" She watched his eyes as they filled up and changed to the color of a melting honey pot.

"Why do you think my dad's not even calling me?"

Lacey was careful as she thought of a response. Though she was angry with Jake's dad, she didn't want to bad-mouth him and risk them never having a good father and son relationship. "I've been wondering the same thing actually. I was contemplating giving him a call to ask him that very question. I'll see what I can find out, okay?" She took his hand in hers and held it, and with her other hand, gently wiped his tears away. On the inside, she was seething. *How could he do this to our son?*

She changed the subject to lighten the tension for both of them. "So did you have fun tonight?" she asked again.

He looked up at Lacey and gave her a small smile. "Uh-huh. K-1 was fun."

"Yeah, it was fun to watch you," Lacey agreed. "That was nice of Dan to take us out like that."

"Yeah, he's nice."

"I feel a 'but' coming."

Jake laughed. "But I'm telling you, Mom, he doesn't think of you like a sister, no way."

"You are such a perceptive kid, Jake. As a matter of fact, he admitted that tonight while you were speeding around that track." Lacey smiled at the memory of seeing Jake happy and carefree as he sped around the track at the K-1 Indoor Racetrack.

"He admitted what?"

"That he cares for me a great deal, and for you, and that he'd like to be more than friends. I told him I couldn't offer him anything more than friendship."

"See, I told you." Jake sat up in his bed. "Are you sad?"

"No, not sad, I just hope we don't lose him as a friend." She watched his expression as the words reached him. "He also said that Peter was a fool for letting us go."

"Peter was a wimp, Mom."

Lacey searched his face and saw that the tears had been replaced with a look of youthful anger, and she was unsure how to respond to it. "I think it's going to be just you and me for a long time, Jake." She was rewarded with a smile, and she leaned toward him and hugged him to her, distracted by the thoughts of Dan's admission of his feelings for her. "Good night, Buddy."

Jake hugged her back.

She got up and walked to his bedroom door. "I love you more—" She was about to finish it when Jake beat her to it.

"Most." His boyish laugh echoed as she shut his door.

Lacey stood up when she heard him coming down the hall with another client. She was looking forward to her session with the counselor, but she didn't really know why. If anything, coming here was raising more questions within her, but maybe it was the need-to-know sense that brought her back week after week. The door opened; a woman walked out and Daniel remained at the door.

"Come on back."

Lacey followed him as he turned and walked down the hall.

"So what did you do this past weekend?"

Lacey chose her normal spot on the couch and got comfortable. "Not much. I hung out with Jake on Friday night. I'm trying to make it an every-Friday thing where we have dinner and a movie, just the two of us."

Daniel sat in his usual chair, just a few feet in front of Lacey. "That sounds like a good plan." He reached for his writing tablet and smiled.

Lacey continued, "And then Saturday was the usual housecleaning, laundry, training at the gym, grocery shopping, and then an old friend of mine took us out."

Daniel looked genuinely interested. "Who's the 'old friend'?"

"Oh, he used to be my bug guy when we lived in Hesperia. We call him Dan the Bug Man." Lacey smiled.

"And who's the 'us' that this bug man took out?"

"Me and Jake."

Daniel didn't hide the surprise on his face. "So what was that like?"

Lacey started to recount from the point when Dan had walked up and Daryn was still there.

Daniel stopped her. "So who's this Daryn guy?"

"He's just a guy from the gym who keeps coming around, and now his son and Jake have become friends. To tell you the truth, I don't really know too much about him, though I'm getting to know his son a lot more."

"Is he the same age as Jake?"

"Actually, I think he's almost two years younger, but he doesn't look it, nor does he act like it. Anyways, I met Daryn a little over a month ago at the gym." Lacey watched Daniel scribble on his note pad and she waited for him to finish.

Daniel looked up. "Go ahead."

Lacey went on to tell Daniel about the rest of the evening, how Jake seemed really happy to see Dan; that Dan had taken them out to California Pizza Kitchen and to K-1 afterwards.

"So did you each drive a car?"

Lacey shook her head. "No, no, just Jake."

There was a different tone in her voice now. "So what did you guys do while Jake did his laps around the track?"

"We talked. Well, he talked." Lacey relayed what Dan had told her and that she had told him she only wanted to be friends. "I really hope I don't lose his friendship." Her sadness poked through as she repeated her conversation with Jake.

"Let's explore this a little bit, Lacey, because it's a bit confusing, all the men in your life, or should I say in and out of your life. You see, you're giving double messages, first of all, to the boy in your life, meaning your son."

Lacey sat up to the edge of the couch, not sure she heard him right. "What do you mean, 'the men in and out of my life'?"

Well, let's take today's session, for example. So far I've heard about Daryn the new friend and Dan the old friend, and then of course there's your son, Jake, who you assure with your words that it's going to be just you and him for a long time…but could your actions be saying something different? Could your son be receiving a different message? He didn't wait for her answer. "Have you had other guy friends over?"

Lacey listened to his tone, watched his demeanor, read nothing critical in his body language, nothing accusatory, so she struggled to try and understand what he was saying. "I guess I don't get it. I mean, I don't see anything wrong with having guy friends."

Daniel called her on her own statement. "So when's the last time you were able to have just a friendship, a platonic relationship with a guy?"

That question stabbed her rationalization right into pieces. She stared at the clock on the wall, willing the time to go quicker because this was starting to get very uncomfortable.

Daniel continued ripping at more of her rationalizations. "And is it possible that Jake maybe saw something from either one of these guys that makes your statement of not allowing another man in your lives look flimsy? Or could he also have maybe seen *you* behave in a way that contradicts your spoken word? I wasn't there, Lacey, but I can give you one of your mixed messages, that is, if you'd like to hear it?"

Lacey hung her head down and muttered her permission.

"For starters, you admitted that you don't know this Daryn guy very well and yet you gave him your phone number. You then go on to justify it by saying you just wanted to get rid of him and he's just a friend, and yet it's obvious that he's pursuing you. That is definitely a double message."

Lacey let the words penetrate into her mind. "I guess I didn't look at it like that." She cringed when she heard how clumsy she sounded.

"I sense, given your past history, that there's a piece of you, Lacey, that does not feel whole unless there's a man in your life, but we'll explore that more each time you come in here."

Lacey reached for another Kleenex and dabbed at the tears falling down her cheeks. She looked at the clock. *Thank God! Time's up.*

Daniel followed her gaze and noticed the time too. "Lacey, before we end, I just want to give you a little homework assignment to complete before our next session."

Again, his gentle firmness pulled at her, and she brought her gaze to rest on him. "What's that?"

"I want you to take some time and describe an instance, if there is one, where you can truly say that you acted on the message, the signal, that was consistent with your behavior, and then, since you journal anyway, you can write it down."

"I'm not sure I understand what you mean by acting on the message that…" She allowed herself to trail off.

"Meaning is the signal you send out to other people, specifically men, echoed in your behavior? In other words, they don't contradict one another."

"Okay."

"So when we meet again, that's where we'll start. Can you do that?"

Lacey dabbed at her eyes again and nodded her head in agreement.

"Great. Then that's where we'll start next week."

Lacey waited as he scooted his chair closer to her and put his hand on her shoulder and bowed his head to pray with her and for her. Usually Lacey paid attention to what he said, but today, all she could think about was the homework assignment he had given her. She already knew what she was going to write about, but she wasn't sure if her actions really matched her signal that she gave to Seth that night. Maybe, just maybe, her counselor could help her figure it out.

There was a crowd gathered around the Roman chair in the abdominal machine section. Seth strained to see what was going on. All he could see were people gathered in a quasi-circle, three or four people thick all the way around. He came to the growing crowd of people and inched his way in, one of the few times he was grateful for his lack of height.

He stopped as though he had been pulled back, stunned when he saw them. Harrison was doing a resistance abdominal exercise with Lacey, and the sight of her twisted his insides. Seth could see that her hard work was paying off as he looked at her abdominal six-pack and her obliques. Her shoulder and arm definition were obvious as she gripped the handles to hold herself up on the chair as Harrison pushed her legs down, and she had to resist his push. *He must have started her on her carb depletion diet,* Seth concluded. He turned to walk away, but before he turned completely away, he risked another glance at her just as she was bringing her head up. Everything seemed to stop for him as she froze in the upright position, her eyes on him. He counted to himself, *One thousand one, one thousand two… I've got to get out of here.* He pulled himself away, and he heard the crowd resume their commands for Harrison to continue his torture/training with Lacey. There was no need to get sucked in by his emotions only to collide with her broken heart and lose his footing, at the very least, or wind up with a broken heart himself.

Lacey pulled back the covers and moved all her extra pillows down the right side of the bed in a semi-straight line to fill the void on the other side of the bed. Sometimes, in the middle of the night, when she would toss and turn, the pillows would feel as though a body were next to her. She plumped her own two pillows up and was about to turn off her light and get into bed when the phone rang. She reached for it and looked on the caller ID.

When she saw who it was, she made herself comfortable sitting up in bed. "Hey, Sophie, is everything all right?"

"Well, hello to you, too."

"I'm sorry. It's just that you don't normally call this late." Lacey looked at her clock. "It's almost ten thirty." There was a long silence. "Sophie, are you there?"

"Yeah, I'm here. Look, I don't know how to tell you this, but I think you should know."

Lacey sat up, recognizing the seriousness in Sophie's voice. "Is Zach okay?"

"Yeah, Zach's fine, but I don't know about Jake."

Fear gripped at Lacey's stomach, and she hunched over fearing the worst. *She's found out about Jake smoking pot. What if he smoked it over there?* "What do you mean?" she asked, trying to quiet her own thoughts.

"Well, apparently he's been talking to Zach and telling him how depressed he is because his dad isn't calling him again or seeing him. Anyways, Zach is really worried about him."

Lacey was silent.

It was Sophie's turn to ask if Lacey was okay.

Lacey sniffled lightly. "Yeah, I'm okay. It's just that this single-parenting thing really inhales vigorously most of the time."

"I know what you mean. I don't know what's worse, having a comatose dad or a deadbeat dad."

They giggled at their attempts of humor over their predicaments, and then Lacey steered the conversation back on course. "I've tried calling his dad; I've left messages, but so far, I haven't heard from him. Anyway, that's really sweet of Zach to be worried about Jake."

"Yeah, Zach's a pretty sensitive kid. By the way, who's Daryk? Zach keeps talking about him and says he's a friend of Jake's. Do you know who he's talking about?"

"Oh, it's Daryn's son, you know, that guy from the gym I told you about."

"So what's his story?"

"What do you mean?"

"Well, it's obviously developing into something more than friendship if you're meeting his son."

Sophie's tone reminded Lacey of her counselor's, neither critical nor condemning, which made her think of her writing assignment. She'd completed it, but since then, she had pushed the last counseling session to the back of her mind, compartmentalizing it until she would see her counselor again.

"Are you there, Lacey?"

"Yeah, I'm here. I was just thinking about something you said. You sounded like my counselor."

"How's that going, by the way?"

"Pretty good, I guess. I mean, I haven't gone for a couple of weeks because of this job in Los Angeles, but the last session was kind of brutal."

"What do you mean 'brutal'?"

Lacey noticed the protectiveness in Sophie's voice. "Well, maybe that's the wrong word. It's just some things he said really made me dig deep into the past and…" She left the sentence unfinished.

"It's never easy to talk about the past when it includes a painful childhood," Sophie empathized with her. "So what exactly did you guys talk about?"

"We were talking about the men in and out of my life, as he puts it, and he said that I'm not only giving Jake mixed signals, but Daryn, too."

"Mixed signals in what way?"

"He gave me a couple examples, but he's also making the correlation between my childhood and the men in and out of my life." Lacey hesitated. "I'm still trying to understand it all." She paused. "Seriously, Sophie, we're just friends, me and Daryn that is. I mean, he keeps showing up uninvited, just like he did when you and Nikki were over the other day. On one hand, he's annoying, and on the other, he's not so bad to hang out with."

Sophie went along with the switch in subjects. "He may be annoying, but he's definitely good-looking, and at least you don't have to bend over to hug him." Her laughter reached Lacey through the phone.

Lacey felt a stab in her heart at the joke. She knew Sophie's intent was to make her laugh, not to make her mad, but it had bumped into the wound that was still there named Seth. "That so wasn't funny, Sophie." Her tone was somber now.

"I'm sorry. You know I was just trying to make you laugh."

"I do know that. I guess the wound is still pretty raw."

"Well, anyway, Zach also asked if Daryk could come over this week and hang out with them, but I wanted to run it by you. What do you think?"

Lacey hesitated a moment. "Well, I guess so. I mean he seems like a pretty good kid, but it's your house. I don't want you to be put out or overwhelmed with it all."

"I can handle it, girl. I just wanted to check with you first."

"I really appreciate it, Sophie, and all you're doing to help me."

"Don't mention it. Hey, I almost forgot to ask you. Did Susie get a hold of you about the birthday thing we're planning for you?"

"Yeah, she did. At first when she told me the date, I thought it was the same weekend that we were going to San Diego to see my sister and my niece, but that's two weekends before."

"Yeah, Jake mentioned something about you guys going up there for a visit. I think he's looking forward to it."

"It will be good to get away, just him and me."

Sophie yawned into the phone. "Sorry about that. So how's the case going?"

Lacey caught the yawn and reciprocated it. "It's good. I'll tell you all about it later. I think we'd better get to sleep."

"You're probably right. I'll see you tomorrow."

Daniel closed the door behind him and Lacey. "So I thought maybe you weren't going to come back after our last session."

Lacey sat down on the couch before she responded. "No, it really wasn't the last session that kept me from coming these last two weeks. It's been difficult because I'm on this case in Los Angeles, and many nights, I don't get home until after six or six thirty, and there's Jake, his depression, his homework, his music, my own training, transcripts, house stuff. I mean, the list is pretty long."

Daniel nodded his head in understanding. "And then last, but not least, there's you and your emotional health, huh?"

Lacey brought her head up and appreciated his warm smile. "Well, I won't lie. The last session was pretty…"

"Pretty what?"

"Well, it was tough, some of the things you said. But I did do my homework assignment." She reached in her purse and brought out her piece of paper she had typed from the notes she wrote in her journal. "Here you go." She handed him her assignment like a proud child eager to please, waiting expectantly for her grade. She listened to the ticking of the secondhand on the clock just behind him. One minute, two minutes, three minutes and thirty seconds, thirty-five seconds, forty-five… Finally, Daniel cleared his throat.

"So before we ended last time, I asked you to describe when the last time was that your behavior matched the message or the signals you were sending out. As I read what you wrote, Lacey, I sense that you have a definite person in mind, that being this Seth guy, but that you are yourself still confused about whether your signal matched your behavior. Am I right so far?"

Lacey nodded her head in agreement.

Daniel continued. I can also glean from what you have written here that you are ashamed for sharing that night with Seth?"

Daniel watched Lacey fidget with the tissue in her hand and listened to the rapid tap of her foot going up and down. "What are you thinking right this moment, Lacey?"

His tone was gentle, but Lacey was unable to speak, her thoughts practically paralyzing her. She was remembering the last time she saw Seth in the gym.

Daniel sat and waited.

The ticking of the clock seemed louder, and, finally, Lacey couldn't hold it in anymore. "I just don't understand why it all changed, like it blew up in my face. I don't understand why he had to go away. He was like a best friend to me. We did so much together." She stopped, silenced by her confessions, and then as if rekindled, began again. "I mean every time I think about that night, I cringe outwardly knowing I called him Peter, but even worse than that, I cringe inwardly, wondering how something so wrong could feel so…" Lacey couldn't finish her thought.

"Feel so good, you mean?"

All Lacey could do was hang her head and let the tears flow as she wallowed in her shame.

Daniel handed her some more Kleenex. "Lacey, first of all, God intended for sex to be incredible, inside of marriage."

His last words stung her. "So is that why I'm having so much trouble with my son, because He's punishing me?"

"No, no, no, He doesn't work that way. He doesn't condemn because condemnation pushes us away; He desires to draw us nearer to Him, but your shame goes much deeper, I'm afraid."

Lacey wiped more tears from her face, letting his words sink in. "Deeper? I don't understand."

"Your shame doesn't start with your moral convictions; it goes much deeper than that. See, Lacey, your shame is rooted in your molestation." He saw the question in her eyes and continued, "You were right to use this Seth guy as an example of your behavior that matched the signals you'd given out. When you think about what it was like outside the bedroom, all that you shared, and then acknowledging that you thought he had feelings for you, all of that was real. But then the sex happens, and you run, run, run, because you were too ashamed to admit that it felt good, or that it was amazing or that you were intimately satisfied and you enjoyed making him feel equally cared for. That would mean, to you, from your perception, that you enjoyed the molestation; that you were prostitute-like, when in actuality, you just wanted to be loved freely and love freely."

Lacey listened and took his words in, processing them, digesting them.

Daniel continued, "A God-given desire is to be valued, unafraid and unashamed. But what your stepfather did has interfered with that. Lacey, what you must understand is that it was his choice to make it shameful and dirty, not yours."

Daniel watched her grab at her sides as she threw herself forward and her sobs echoed in his small office. He got up from his chair to sit beside her on the couch, putting his arm around her, letting her know she was safe and well on her way in this painful process of discovery and healing.

Lacey dialed Clint's number, trying to remember what she'd rehearsed in her mind over and over again. The rehearsing stopped when she heard the voice on the other end. "Jenna, is that you?"

"This is Jenna. Who's this?"

"It's me, Lacey."

"Oh, I'm sorry. I didn't recognize your voice. Is everything okay with Jake?"

"Yeah," she stammered and then checked herself. "Well, actually, no, not really. I mean he's okay physically. It's his emotional state I'm worried about. That's why I'm calling. I really need to talk to Clint."

Jenna paused before responding. "Well, I can tell him you called."

Lacey picked up on her hesitation. "Is he not home?"

"He's home, but he's sleeping." Jenna let out a sigh. "That's all he seems to do these days."

Lacey picked up on her sad tone and at once felt empathy for her. "Is he sick?" As soon as she had said the words, Lacey regretted them. "I'm sorry. That's a dumb question."

"That's all right," Jenna offered. "You get used to Freudian slips like that with this disease. It's just part of the territory because too many people don't understand what it does to the body, let alone what it does to the person's emotional well-being."

Lacey picked up on the sincerity of Jenna's explanation. There was no anger in it at all, just wistfulness. Lacey chose to ignore her own pent-up questions and anger she'd been holding inside for this woman ever since she had learned that Jake's dad had contracted the HIV virus from her. "So he's been depressed, huh?"

"Definitely," Jenna confirmed. "It's another one of the side effects of this disease so I'm trying to get him to go to a psychiatrist so they can prescribe him an antidepressant, but he's refusing to go."

Lacey didn't know what to say to encourage Jenna. She didn't dare tell her what Clint had said years ago about going to a psychologist or a psychiatrist when she had begged him to get help with his drug addiction. He had adamantly refused, saying that he didn't need a shrink to fix what was wrong with him. *His pride had definitely caused him to fall*, she thought. "Well, I hope he changes his mind. I know from experience that going to a psychologist can be a good thing."

Jenna didn't hide her surprise. "So are *you* going to a psychiatrist?"

"I think he's a psychologist."

"So how long have you been going?"

"Well, I started about six weeks ago because of..." She stopped herself when she remembered who she was talking to. *I can't tell her about Clint getting high with his son... Or can I?*

"Are you there, Lacey?" Jenna asked.

"Sorry about that. I just wanted to make sure my bedroom door was closed. Anyways, as I was saying, I started going because of Jake and his depression and all, but actually, we haven't delved too much into that yet. We're kind of going backwards, into my childhood, and sometimes he switches the conversation to the present. Inevitably, we seem to wind up talking about the men in my life, or as he says, the men in and out of my life."

"So your counselor is a male?"

"Uh-huh. I thought that was going to be a problem at first, but I actually like him. He's safe." She thought about the way he had assured her in their last session that though she was in the beginning stages of the process, she'd appreciate it later on, especially when it came to future relationships.

Jenna interrupted her thoughts. "Yeah, my counselor's a guy, and I also thought it would be weird, but then again, women can be so catty and I've always communicated better with guys."

Lacey smiled. "I know what you mean. The funny thing is I used to go in there with a preconceived idea of what we were going to talk about, all the questions running around in my head that I wanted to ask him, you know, like my own agenda, but I've learned I can't do that. I have to let him lead, ask the questions, and it always flows from there. You know what I mean?"

"That's so true."

"Okay. That's enough about me. I just hope Clint changes his mind about going and seeing someone. Besides, I would think that being with Jake would be more important than ever, give him a reason to want to beat this thing."

"That's what I keep telling him, Lacey. When he gets up, I'll try to get him to at least call Jake."

"Thanks, Jenna. Could you tell him that his son really misses him?"

"I will. I know how hard that is because I see Courtney go through that a lot, that depression because of her dad being gone. At least Jake's dad is still here and not gone forever," she reminded Lacey. "And I agree with you; he does need to be a presence in Jake's life."

Lacey was touched by her words. "Thank you for that, Jenna." She steered the conversation back on track. "And how's Courtney doing with all of this, Jenna?"

Jenna was quiet for a few seconds.

"Jenna?"

"I'm here. She's having a hard time, too. I'm trying to be strong for all of us."

Lacey didn't know what to say, couldn't even begin to imagine what it must be like to be Jenna. "Well, tell her Jake keeps asking about her."

"I will. Thanks, Lacey."

"Hey, Mom. I've invited Daryk over."

Lacey was bent over the dishwasher. She stood up and took the last glass Jake handed her. She realized that that meant Daryn would be coming too; how else would Daryk get here? When Daryk stayed with his mom, he rarely got to go anywhere because she wasn't always able to drive due to her fibromyalgia. Lacey wasn't irritated about Daryk coming over. In fact, she was really beginning to like him. He seemed like a sweet enough kid. It was his dad who unnerved her with his long stares and unasked questions as if he could figure her out and put her in a box. "Well, thanks for letting me know." Her tone sounded irritated even to her own ears.

"I thought you liked him," Jake countered.

"I do. It's his dad who annoys me."

Jake looked at her with a puzzled look on his face. "Mom, he totally likes you; otherwise he wouldn't try to annoy you so much."

"Since when did you get so wise?"

"Even Daryk says his dad likes you."

Lacey filled up the dishwasher's soap dispenser, closed it and pressed the start button. "So what time will he be here?"

"He said his dad's picking him up about six. So"—he looked at the clock on the stove—"any minute. It's almost six thirty now."

"Did you have any homework that needs to be done for Monday? I don't want you waiting until the last minute, Jake."

"I had some math to do, but Adam helped me get it done so I'm good."

Lacey handed him the last coffee cup to put away and began wiping the counters. "Thanks for helping, Jake."

"You're welcome." He shut the cabinet door and turned around to face her again. "Guess who called me today?"

Lacey hoped with all of her being that it was Clint that had called him, but that would be two times this week, and she didn't want to add salt to his wound if it wasn't his dad. She pretended not to know. "I give up; tell me."

Jake tried to act nonchalant but his enthusiasm won out. "My dad did. That makes two times this week. Can you believe it?"

"How is he?"

"He seemed okay. He asked if he could come down in a couple of weeks and stay the night, and then he's gonna catch the train to go back."

Lacey had been leaning on the counter and now stood up straight. "Stay the night where?"

"I don't know. I think he said here but you'll have to ask him. He said for you to call him when you got a chance."

They both heard the sound of a motorcycle coming closer and closer, and then it stopped. Lacey rolled her eyes. "I guess we'll finish talking about this later."

"Okay." Jake turned and walked out the front door to go and greet Daryk.

Lacey leaned into the counter and stared down, suddenly a bit anxious, uncomfortable in her own skin. The grout on her tile counters seemed to shout for a cleaning so she pulled out her Clorox cleaner and a toothbrush and began the mindless task of cleaning.

Minutes later, Lacey heard the front door open. "Mom, Daryn's here," Jake yelled from the doorway.

Lacey looked up to see Daryn walking toward her. Despite the fact that they had spent more time together over the last several weeks, Lacey was still somewhat unnerved around him, and it took a lot of effort to hide it. She put her head down and concentrated on cleaning the grout. "Hey, how are you?"

"From the look on your face, I'd say I'm probably better than you."

Lacey's head shot up. "Why do you always act like you know me and what I'm thinking?" She grabbed the spray bottle in frustration.

Daryn walked toward her and took the bottle from her hands, set it on the counter, and turned her toward him. "Maybe it's my way of trying to get to know you and understand what you're thinking."

Lacey was taken off guard both by his nearness and his admission. He was standing so close to her that she could see a small dark freckle on his upper lip, She looked up to find him staring at her but didn't accept the invitation in his green eyes beckoning her closer. She took a couple steps back and put her focus back on the cleaning task instead of the chemistry between them. She cleared her throat and swallowed her pride.

When she had created a comfortable space between them, she lifted her head up and slowly let her eyes lift until they met his again. "I'm sorry. I guess I'm just not used to someone trying to figure me out like I'm some set of instructions written in a foreign language."

Daryn threw his head back and started to laugh.

Lacey stared at him in shock, her defensive wall rising higher as she realized he may be laughing at her. "What's so funny?"

His laughter stopped and the smile in his eyes was gone. His usual emerald green eyes turned dark, a contrast to his usual self-control. "Why are you always so critical, Lacey?"

"Critical? How am I critical?"

"Can't you just let someone be nice to you without thinking they want something? From what I've seen, you're always doing for others; isn't it time that someone does something for you?"

Again, Lacey was rendered defenseless, but not speechless. *Is this what the counselor's talking about?* "I don't need anything. Besides, I've learned that men always have an agenda. I've never met a man yet with a pure motive."

Daryn didn't bite at the bait. Instead, he switched gears. "Look, what do you say we go for a motorcycle ride? The fresh air will probably do you good; it will be fun. I promise."

"I don't have a helmet."

"You can use Daryk's. Come on." He reached for her hand, and Lacey didn't have the emotional strength to fight him off. *Don't kid yourself, girl. You know a ride on his Harley sounds a heck of a lot better than scrubbing the grout on the countertops.* They reached the door and Lacey gave one more attempt at resisting. "What about the boys?"

Daryn let go of her hand and reached for the door. "What about them?"

Lacey couldn't think of an answer.

"They'll be fine. We won't be gone that long." He held the door open for her and she walked outside. Lacey noticed that the sun was still out, but barely. She could see dusk in the horizon. She breathed in the warm air made fresh with the slight breeze. It really was a nice night for a motorcycle ride. She could hear

Jake and Daryk by the garage so she walked toward them. They were standing by Daryn's bike. "Hey, guys." She gave Daryk a hug. "Jake, Daryn's gonna take me for a motorcycle ride, but we won't be long."

Daryn put his hand on Daryk's shoulder. "We'll be about a half hour." He looked over at Jake and smiled then turned to Lacey. "The weather's been warm enough lately. Can they go swimming?"

The boys came to life at the suggestion.

"But they have to have an adult with them." Lacey reminded Jake, and she watched his shoulders slump slowly. "Hey, what do you say you guys hang out here while we go for a quick ride, and then when we get back, we'll go down and hang out for a while so you can swim?"

"Won't it be too late?" Jake asked.

Lacey looked at her watch. "No. The pool's closed at nine, and since it's only six thirty now, I think it will be okay."

"We better get going before it gets dark. I don't want you freaking out on the bike," Daryn joked.

"Let me run upstairs and get a light jacket. I'll be right back." She ran in the house and upstairs. She reached for her Roxy cream-colored sweatshirt and put it on. When she went back outside, Daryn was doing some coin trick with the boys.

When he saw her shadow, he looked up and handed the coin to Daryk. "See if you can finish it, Son." He took Daryk's helmet off the back and handed it to Lacey, grabbed his own, and began putting it on.

Lacey felt a little awkward at first. She tried to put hers on while watching him put his on, but before she could get hers completely situated on her head, he already had his on and buckled. He reached over to help her, and Lacey didn't stop him. When he had buckled the strap securely, she looked to her right and Jake gave her a thumbs-up sign as he mouthed the words "Be careful."

She smiled and blew him a kiss and then hopped up on the bike behind Daryn. The sound of the pipes reverberated in her ears and vibrated against her thighs. A childhood memory reminded her to gauge the position of her feet to the pipes to avoid getting burned. She pulled her head back up when she felt Daryn turn around toward her.

He grabbed both her hands and put them around his waist. "Hold on tight," he yelled. The bike jumped forward, and Lacey squealed nervously. She felt his hand on her hands and thought about pulling away, but dismissed the thought as Daryn headed up the main boulevard toward the hills. Keeping her hands around his waist, she leaned back to enjoy the ride.

Jake looked at Daryk. "So what do you want to do while they're gone?"

"Do you want to jam for a while?" Daryk's tone was eager.

"Not really. I don't feel like playing music right now. Besides, what can you play?"

"I'm starting to learn how to play the bass guitar, but I was thinking maybe you could show me a few things on the acoustic. How did you learn to play the keyboard and the guitar, anyway?"

Jake looked at his new friend. He held up his hand and pounded his heart. "It's in here, dude; it's in here."

Daryk nodded his head as if he understood.

"Lets play bowling on the Wii."

"That's cool."

Jake liked that about Daryk—he seemed to be so easygoing. They went into the living room, and Jake pulled the Wii and both controllers out. "So have you bowled on the Wii before?"

"I've played it on the Super Nintendo, but not the Wii."

Jake went on to show Daryk how the controller worked and then set the game to start.

"Thanks, brother."

Jake turned abruptly to face Daryk. "Dude, don't call me that, okay?" His tone was a notch above irritated.

"Sorry. It's just what we say at school when we like chillin' with someone. I didn't mean to piss you off, man."

Jake looked down at Daryk who looked as though he might cry any minute. "I'm sorry. I didn't mean to scare you." He pressed the start button, and they played their first game in near silence, Daryk concentrating on his game, and Jake thinking about the way he had reacted to Daryk calling him brother. Jake liked having Daryk around as his friend, but that was the limit. He didn't want him as a stepbrother, and he needed to make sure that Daryn knew that, especially after he'd seen the way that he had been looking at his mom.

They played six games, and Jake won four out of seven, but it hadn't been easy. Daryk had proved to be a good bowler. "Good games," Jake offered.

"Thanks. Me and my dad bowl a lot."

"That's cool. Want some ice cream?"

"Sure," Daryk agreed.

They helped themselves to some ice cream and went to sit down on the couch to watch TV.

"I think I hear my dad's motorcycle."

Jake stopped and looked at the clock. "It's seven fifteen. We better get ready; otherwise there's not going to be any swimming time left." They put their bowls of ice cream in the freezer for later.

Daryn got up from the couch and walked over to the stairs. "Hey, Daryk, we'd better get going. No use in wearing out our welcome."

"Okay, Dad."

Lacey was in the kitchen putting the dessert dishes in the dishwasher. She heard the pounding of feet running down the stairs, and then the front door opened and closed. She reached for the dishtowel to wipe her hands dry and hurried toward the front door to go and say good-bye to Daryk and Daryn.

"Where are you going so fast?" Daryn's voice stopped her inches before she ran right into him.

Lacey squealed in shock. "You scared me."

Daryn said nothing verbally, but Lacey could tell he was trying to say something with his eyes.

"I thought you were all outside already, I was coming to say good-bye."

"The boys went outside. I was coming to say good-bye to you." He smiled as he reached for her and pulled her close to him. Before she could get away, he brought his mouth down on hers, gentle at first, and then more forceful as his tongue danced with hers; and then just as quick as he had initiated it, he stopped. He pulled his face away from hers just a few inches and then with his right hand, he lifted her chin up until she was staring into his eyes. "I'll just say good night, but I don't plan on saying good-bye anytime soon, Lacey girl."

With that, he let her go and walked out.

Losing Control

"Now that's what I call front-row parking, Peanut," Nikki exclaimed. She took her seat belt off, opened her door, and stepped out. Susie and Sophie followed from the back seat quickly when they heard Nikki burst out laughing.

When Susie stepped out of the car, she looked in the direction that Nikki was pointing and saw what she was laughing about. She turned Lacey toward the two mannequins, and Nikki walked over and joined Sophie and Susie who were both laughing. "Check it out. There's Lacey's contest bikini."

Susie came up beside Lacey. "Which one do you like, Lacey, the one- or two-piece?" The rest of the girls gathered around Lacey, giggling like high-school girls and pointing to the models. One was wearing what looked like a Band-Aid held together by strings, which was supposed to be a one-piece. The other mannequin was wearing a loin cloth and two Band-Aids held together by strings, apparently a two-piece bathing suit.

Lacey turned to the girls shaking her head. "I can't wear anything like that."

"Oh, yes you can," Sophie assured her.

"But…" Lacey stammered.

"Come on, Peanut. I bet they even have inflatable tops."

Even Lacey had to laugh at Nikki's humor.

Susie was the first to stop laughing. "We better get in there or you're going to be late for your appointment."

The lady looked up when she heard the bell ring and saw three girls gently pushing Lacey forward. "Hi, may I help you?"

"Yes. This is Lacey Thorton." Susie tugged at Lacey to bring her in front of them. "She has an appointment to pick out a bathing suit and a costume for the Ms. Fitness contest."

The lady came from behind the counter and extended her hand. "I'm Sylvia. Welcome to Fresh Peaches. Why don't you all come on back, and we'll begin the design process." They followed Sylvia into her office, and she got them each a chair.

"Can I get you anything to drink?"

Sophie and Lacey asked for water, and Susie and Nikki declined.

"While I'm getting your water, here's a form to fill out and a catalogue you can begin to look through to get some ideas. I'll be back in a couple of minutes."

When she had walked out of her office, Nikki was the first to speak. "I thought my office was a mess. How does this woman get anything done here?"

"No kidding. This even makes my office look organized," Susie agreed.

Lacey was busy looking over the form. "I didn't realize this was so involved.

Sophie leaned toward Lacey and looked at the form. "I don't think you fill in that section. She has to take all of your measurements first, and then she probably fills that in for you. She pointed to another question. "Have you decided on a costume for your routine yet?"

"Not yet. I think I want to do some sort of business-type dress that has Velcro all the way up the front, so I can rip it off easier."

Sophie nodded in silent approval.

Nikki's eyebrows shot up. "I'm sorry. I'm just checking out all this chaos." She pointed to the different bolts of fabrics that were scattered everywhere and to the desk that had papers strewn all over it and on the floor around it. "So what were you saying about your routine?"

Susie intercepted the question. "What she was saying is she's going to do a strip-tease for her routine." She looked over at Lacey whose expression made it clear that she wasn't finding what Susie had said in the least bit funny. "I was just kidding, Lacey. Tell them what you're going to do."

"I want to start the routine off to the right of the stage, posed like I'm court-reporting, and the voice will come over the speaker and say something like, 'That concludes the record for today.' Then the music will start really loud and I'll turn to face the audience and rip my work clothes off and have my shorts and sports bra top on underneath."

Nikki had her hand over her heart and was nodding her head as if she could see what Lacey was explaining. "You had me going for a second there, Peanut."

"Me, too," Sophie agreed. "I think that sounds really cool, though. Have you worked on your routine yet?"

"Not yet. I just found a choreographer, and I've actually got an appointment with her in L. A. She was the one who doubled for that girl who did that incredible dancing in that crazy movie…" Lacey faded out because she couldn't remember the name of the movie.

Nikki and Sophie spoke up simultaneously. "Who starred in it?" Lacey looked at them and laughed. "You two movie buffs crack me up." She paused. "I think it was Jim Carey."

"Oh, *The Mask*," Nikki said.

"Yeah, that movie," Lacey agreed. "But I have an appointment in a week or so with the dancer who was spinning up in the air and all over the room."

"She must cost a fortune," Nikki exclaimed.

"Not too bad. I think she's like seventy-five dollars an hour, something like that, and I'm only going to spend five or six hours with her."

"What exactly is she going to do for you? She doesn't guarantee that you'll be dancing like her, does she? If she does, sign me up, but then again, fat chicks don't dance." Nikki laughed at herself.

Susie contradicted her. "Hey, if you can run, you can dance."

"Yeah, that's true." Nikki laughed.

Lacey answered Nikki's question. "Well, the first appointment is where we'll meet and she'll figure out what I can and can't do as far as strength moves, gymnastics, which I've never done, but that way she can choreograph the routine. Then I'll meet with her however many times it takes to learn the routine."

"That's actually not bad," Sophie said. She looked up and saw Susie grab a bolt of fabric and begin to wrap it around the mannequin that was standing in the corner. "Susie, what are you doing?"

"I'm tired of looking at her perfect body. I mean, come on, what naked body looks flawless like this with no cellulite or flab anywhere? She's making me feel a bit self-conscious," she sputtered through fits of giggles that were contagious, and when Sylvia walked in, they were all laughing. Susie propped the bolt of fabric up against the mannequin and nearly ran for her chair as if she were a child caught doing something wrong. Sylvia looked at the now fabric-draped mannequin and saw what they were laughing about and let out a giggle. "That doesn't look half bad."

The next hour flew by as the girls helped Lacey look through the catalogues at countless bathing suits, dance and gymnastic wear, as well as fabric. Lacey finally decided on a bright coral velour fabric for the "Brazilian beauty bikini." Sylvia drew the bikini showing the bottoms with bold and very high-cut legs, which she described as the Brazilian cut. The top was simple but classy in a petal style, which was popular for the not-so-endowed girl, and it had thicker straps. "And for a finishing touch, we'll add some sequins like this." Sylvia drew a row of diamond shapes along the ridge of the bikini bottoms and then around the edge of the bikini top.

Sophia looked up from the drawing and got Lacey's attention. "That definitely adds to it. Do you like it, Lacey?"

"Oh, I like it. Now I need to work hard so I look good in it."

Nikki's startled laughter made them all look up at her. "I couldn't even put my big toe in the leg of that bikini bottom, and you want to know if you're gonna look good?" She put her hand over her forehead dramatically, leaned back and muttered one of her favorite Italian sayings, "Oh, Madonna. You're killing me."

"Yeah, no kidding," Susie chimed in. "Maybe I should do a Ms. Fitness show so I can get rid of my baby fat."

"I'd join you, Susie," Nikki said, "but I'm afraid I'd have a heart attack if I did any exercise."

Sylvia put her hand on Lacey's shoulder. "What a great support system you have here." She stood up and asked Lacey what she thought about the style they had chosen.

Lacey was overwhelmed and getting hungry as well. "I'm sure it will be fine. I'm just not used to showing so much skin, that's all. This will be the first bikini I've worn since I was in high school."

"Well, I've been doing this for years, and I think this is going to be an incredibly flattering suit for you. Let me get some measurements. And, girls, while I'm doing that, look through this book for ideas for her routine outfit and then we'll finish up the paperwork so you can get out of here and go have lunch."

Less than an hour later, Lacey's measurements were done, and they had designed a two piece outfit that would go underneath a simple black dress that would Velcro straight up the middle. The cost was staggering. Lacey was overwhelmed as she wrote a two hundred dollar deposit. She had never spent so much on a bathing suit, but as Nikki had reminded her, she'd never competed in a Ms. Fitness contest either.

While they were waiting to be seated in Mimi's Cafe, they talked about their upcoming trip to Knott's Berry Farm with the kids for Friday's Jubilee night. Lacey remembered that Susie still hadn't told them if she could go or not. "Susie, so do you think you can come?"

"We'll see. It all depends on work."

"I know my David Michael would be thrilled," Nikki added.

"We'll have to figure out who's driving because so far we have Nikki and David Michael, Sophie and Zach, me, Jake and Daryk, and hopefully you, Susie."

"Daryk, as in the son of Daryn?" Nikki asked.

Lacey smiled. "Nikki, not so loud. Yes, I mean Daryn's son, Daryk. Really, I think it would be more fun if we could all go in one car." As soon as she said that, a thought came to her. "I could ask Daryn if I could use his Excursion."

"Wait a minute," Sophie grinned. "Isn't it Seth who has the Excursion?"

"Oops, I guess I'm getting the men in and out of my life confused." Lacey's smile came from the inside out as she realized she was able to hear his name without flinching or tearing up.

"Oh, yeah, that ought to go over well," Sophie said. "Don't invite either one of them but ask them to borrow their SUV."

"Yeah, I guess that wouldn't be too cool, huh?"

The girls were laughing when the hostess came to seat them, and by the time the waiter had taken their orders and brought their drinks, Lacey had finished telling them about Daryn and his kiss. "Which I hate to admit, but it was actually pretty good," she confessed.

Nikki put her arm over her forehead. "Oh my God, you've kissed more men in the last six months than I have in my whole lifetime."

Lacey laughed when she saw the open exasperation on Nikki's face.

Sophie leaned into the table toward Lacey. "So did Jake see him kiss you?"

"No. He was outside with Daryk, thank God."

"So he just planted one on you and left?" Nikki didn't wait for Lacey to answer. "Have you seen him since then?"

"A few times, uh-huh. I mean, he hasn't taken me out on a date or anything like that. He's perfectly content with just popping over with Daryk and hanging out."

"And has he kissed you again?" Sophie's disapproval was obvious.

"That's a negative," Susie answered for Lacey and got up from the table. "I'm going to the ladies' room."

"Don't you want to hear about daring Daryn?" Nikki asked.

"I've already heard about him." She turned around and walked toward the restroom.

Sophie and Nikki looked to Lacey for an explanation. Sophie was the first to ask. "So what's her deal? She seemed a bit perturbed."

"Actually, I've been talking to her almost every day and things seem to be really heating up between her and Jimmy."

"And it's probably not easy to hear about all the men in and out of your life, Lacey," Sophie added.

Lacey picked her head up, startled by her statement.

Sophie reached her arm across the table for Lacey. "No, no, don't misunderstand me. I'm not saying that to be critical." She squeezed her hand. "All I'm saying is that it can't be easy for her to hear about our love lives—"

Nikki interrupted her. "Or lack thereof."

They giggled at her interjection.

"Right, or lack thereof," Sophie repeated. "She's not in a happy place right now, and I think we should be sensitive to that." She looked up to make sure Susie was not walking back to the table.

"So I guess I won't be talking about the new guy I've met, at least not today."

Nikki and Lacey sat up in the booth and looked at each other and then at Sophie. "That's not fair," Lacey whined. "Besides, Susie wouldn't mind."

"I wouldn't mind what?" Susie sat down.

Sophie shot Lacey a look that could paralyze, which Lacey disregarded. "It's okay," she mouthed quietly across to Sophie. She turned to Susie. "Sophie has some exciting news, but she thought she should wait to share it."

Susie turned in the booth, so she could look directly at Sophie. "Why would you wait to share it?"

Sophie started to speak and Lacey interrupted her. "It's because of your situation with Jimmy. I was starting to explain to her that you were getting closer and closer to getting out of it and that you would be happy for her."

Nikki's optimism stepped in. "Well, when you kick that idiot to the curb, Susie, I will go out on the town, huh?"

Before Susie could answer, the waiter was there with their entrees. He served them and left their table, and Lacey restarted the conversation, purposely steering it away from men. "Sophie, by the way, I took your advice and checked on line for a car. I think I may have found one, but it's in San Diego."

"Well, aren't you going there in a couple weeks?"

"Yeah, I am. I've been working with this Chrysler dealer out there. They have this way cute red convertible Solara, and if the guy comes down just a little bit more on the price, I think I'm going to lease it. But that means I'll have to rent a car to get to San Diego, drop it off down there, and have the car rental place take me to the dealership."

"What are you going to do with your other car, Peanut?"

"The lease is up and I'm going to turn it back in."

"That's perfect timing," Nikki said.

"And it's your last tie to Peter," Susie chimed in. "Then you'll be completely free from anything having to do with him."

"Here's to being free from any unwanted ties," Sophie added. She looked right into Susie's eyes and winked.

"Jake, come on. You're gonna be late."

He appeared at the top of the stairs, sloppily dressed and missing his socks and shoes. "I don't feel so good, Mom."

"What's wrong? What do you mean you don't feel good?"

"My stomach hurts."

"Like what kind of hurt?"

Jake let out a loud, frustrated groan. "Like, it just hurts. I don't know how to describe it."

Lacey stood at the bottom of the stairs paralyzed by the loss of control she felt. *Now what do I do?* "Jake, it's too late for me to call in sick. They'll never get someone there in time to cover me."

"Just let me stay home then."

Lacey's intuition kicked in. "You know I can't let you do that; now wash your face, brush your teeth. You can put your socks and shoes on in the car. If you still feel that way after first period, you can go to the nurse's office, and Sophie can come and get you."

The bathroom door slammed in response, and Lacey heard the sound of running water. She spent a few minutes tidying up the kitchen and getting her laptop and gym bag in the car, hoping and praying that the rest of the morning would go smoothly. Less than five minutes later, she heard his feet treading heavily on the stairs so she went out and started the car and waited. Finally, he got in and Lacey noticed that he didn't have his backpack. She got out and went back inside, grabbed it and went back out to the car, the frustration oozing out of her pores. By the time she pulled out, he had hunkered down for his usual on-the-way-to-school nap.

They pulled up in front of the school, and the bell was ring-ing. Jake popped his head up. "Can I have some lunch money?"

Lacey bit her tongue so she wouldn't rip his head off and reached into her purse, handed him a five-dollar bill and gave him a quick kiss. "Have a great day. I'll see you at Sophie's after work."

Lacey closed her laptop and rubbed her temples. She was glad that Jake was spending the night with Adam, something she didn't ordinarily let him do on a school night. Martha had insisted it would be okay, especially since Jake hadn't been there overnight for a while. Lacey missed him, but the break also felt good. It had been an emotional three days at work. The heat was turning up on the case, and the testimony was more and more incriminating to Danny's clients. He was doing a good job, and Lacey didn't mind telling him so over lunch. She was getting more comfortable working with him, and he was pretty easy to talk to. *Which should make going out to dinner less nerve-racking,* she thought.

She reached for her daily to-do list. "I am definitely look-ing forward to getting away this weekend," she mumbled. Number ten on the list: pay bills. She reached for her stack of bills and her checkbook. Ten minutes later, she wrote the last check, subtracted it from her register and let out a sigh. Every bill was paid, and she still had some play money for the week-end. She glanced at her balance and ran her eyes over the last couple of week's entries doing a mental adding up of what she had spent lately. There was the entry for the new shoes for Jake, and they couldn't be just regular tennis shoes because he *had* to have skater shoes at a hundred dollars a pop. And they had gone to Knott's Berry Farm the week before. That had cost a couple of hundred. And then of course there was the mortgage, utilities, a couple of shirts for Jake, groceries, car insurance, professional liability insurance, the cell phone, and more groceries. Jake could really eat.

She was going to have to tighten up a bit on her budget in order to comfortably afford the car she was thinking of leasing. The down payment would have to come out of her savings, no matter what car she got, and Lacey knew it would be a couple of thousand at least. She closed her checkbook and checked off "pay bills" from her list. She still needed to call her sister to confirm their arrangements for this coming weekend, just the day after tomorrow, and get directions, but she couldn't do that until she heard from Marcus, the car salesman in San Diego.

She looked at the clock. It was a few minutes before nine. She remembered he had said that he usually worked until nine. "Hopefully I can still catch him." The phone was picked up on the second ring.

"This is Marcus."

"Hey, Marcus. It's Lacey, from Rancho Cucamonga."

"Hi, Lacey. You must be able to read minds. I was just going to call you."

"No, just trying to plan my weekend. So what's the verdict? Did your manager come down on the price?"

"You don't beat around the bush, do you?" He didn't wait for her to answer. "I just walked out of his office and the bad news is he won't come down the fifteen hundred, but the good news is he came down a thousand."

Lacey was quietly thinking about the numbers.

"So what do you think?"

"I think I've spent enough time looking and I'm running out of time, so…" She faded off and then came back. "I really like the car…" She trailed off again, toying with the idea of her first convertible, liking it more and more.

"That extra five hundred will only cost you a couple more bucks a month."

I can afford a couple of bucks, can't I? "Okay. I'll be there on Sunday afternoon." She smiled, realizing she was going to get her very first convertible in a matter of days. It took Marcus only a few minutes to get the rest of her financial information down on the application. Before they hung up, he told her the down payment was twenty-one hundred dollars and that she would need to fax a copy of her latest two paychecks to him.

She was so excited to be getting a new car, she had to tell someone, but she wasn't going to tell Jake until they were down there. This was going to be a surprise for him.

She started to call Sophie and then thought about her big sister Elaine who complained that Lacey rarely told her about anything that was going on in her life. She smiled as she saw her sister's face in her mind. Out of the five siblings they were the only two who tried to stay in some sort of contact with each other. Because they had grown up in the foster-care system separate and apart, they had each taken different paths.

Lacey smiled as she thought of her youngest brother, Luke, his sweet wife, and their two-year-old daughter. They had just moved to Vegas because of his job. He was such a gentle soul, and she really liked him as a person.

She grew somber thinking about her other brother, Robert, not such a gentle soul and one year her junior. Lacey let out a sad sigh. They used to be so close, but being under the foster care system had ripped them apart. His life seemed to be going just the way he wanted it to, though. He was married, had two boys and had just retired from the military after obtaining his master's degree. He was settling down with his wife and family in the state of Washington, earning a six-figure income as well as collecting his military retirement.

Then there was her sister Jo-Anne who was two years older than her, the one she used to be really close to, especially when they were in the foster home together. But after two years, she had run away. Since then, there had been very little contact. Jo

Anne had two daughters and Lacey had never met them. The father, with the help of his mom, had kidnapped them and taken them overseas. That was over four years ago and Jo Anne hadn't fought very hard to get them back. Lacey shook her head in frustration as she realized that her sister, unfortunately, was repeating their mother's history of hiding behind the bottle.

Elaine was the oldest of the five of them, and in some respects, she was like a hero to Lacey. She had been the one who had helped them get out of the abusive situation with their stepfather and their mom, but it hadn't been easy. In fact, it had cost her dearly, especially when she discovered she had gonorrhea before getting married the first time. She had caught it from their stepfather and his friends. Lacey shook her head in disgust remembering the times Elaine would tell her about him and his friends taking her up on the mountain and doing their thing with her. It had really scarred Elaine for life. No wonder she had chosen to live a gay lifestyle, having been so used and abused by men. She had tried marriage, twice, both times unsuccessfully, and had finally given up, four children later.

No, Lacey couldn't speak for the rest of them, but for her, seeing all of them represented too much pain, like going backwards in time, so for the most part, she rarely bothered.

She stared at the phone, and her sister's number kept coming to the forefront of her mind. *This is a first, telling my sister something before I tell my friends.* She smiled at the realization and dialed her sister's number.

Danny looked up at Lacey. "Let's go off the record for a minute."

Lacey relaxed her hands and sat back in her chair.

"So we'll not be in session tomorrow but we'll resume Monday morning at ten o'clock." Danny turned to Plaintiffs' counsel. "Will that be all right with you, Counsel?"

"Sure."

Danny looked at Lacey. "You ready to put the stipulation on the record?"

Lacey nodded her head in silent agreement and listened as Danny recited almost word for word the same stipulation he'd been reciting for the previous depositions. When they had agreed to his stipulation, Lacey looked up and turned her machine off. Danny quickly excused himself for a restroom break, and she let out a big exhausted sigh.

Plaintiffs' counsel looked up and smiled. "Tired, huh?"

Lacey had the professionalism to look embarrassed. "Yeah, I guess I am." She liked working with Julie. She was from a prestigious law firm that had offices in Los Angeles, the Inland Empire, San Diego, and San Francisco. Her demeanor was two-edged; gentle and kind when interacting with her clients, but a lioness when it came to protecting them during the deposition process and dealing with the opposition. Lacey really appreciated the fact that she was mindful of keeping a good record by trying to not interrupt either the witness or the other attorney when they were talking, and often helped Lacey by stopping the witness from answering before the complete question was out. It definitely made her job easier.

Julie interrupted her thoughts. "So do you have any exciting plans this weekend, especially since you have tomorrow off?"

"As a matter of fact, my son and I are going to San Diego to see my sister who has a part in a musical, and on the way home on Sunday, we're stopping by and picking up my new car."

Julie's delight was genuine. "Good for you. How exciting. What are you getting?"

Lacey went on to tell her about the car, and they were still talking when they heard a throat clear. They both looked up. "Lacey was just telling me about her new car she's getting this weekend.

Danny looked surprised.

Julie stood up. "Anyway, have a great time with your son at your sister's play, and congratulations on the new car. See you on Monday."

Julie had barely made it out of the door when Danny turned to face Lacey. "Did you forget about Saturday, dinner in Pasadena?"

Lacey felt her cheeks get hot as soon as the words came out of his mouth.

"I can tell by the look on your face that you did."

Lacey didn't miss his slightly irritated tone. "Danny, I'm so sorry. I got my weekends mixed up. I was thinking we were going to San Diego last weekend. There's just so much going on right now that the days sometimes blur together." She tried to gauge his acceptance of her apology, but he was busying himself with putting his stuff away, so she finished packing up her stuff. When he didn't respond, she cleared her throat, hoping that would get his attention. He stood up and looked at her but said nothing. The moment was awkward, and then they both started to speak at once.

"No, you go ahead," Danny offered.

"I was just going to suggest, what about next Saturday?"

"That might work," he countered, "but I'll let you know on Monday, okay?"

"Sure."

Danny relaxed his guarded posture and smiled. "So what's this about you getting a new car?"

Lacey forgot about the tension and began to tell him about her online shopping experience and the great deal she had gotten. "So far, it's been the easiest car-buying experience I've ever had," she added.

Danny reached for his briefcase. "I'll have to remember that the next time I want to get a new car. Come on. Let me take you to the train station."

Lacey watched Jake walk towards his class and breathed a sigh of relief. They had made it through another week without too many arguments, and Clint's phone calls were going a long way in easing Jake's depression. Only a couple weeks of school left.

She pulled away from the curb and began to plan her busy day. First there was training and then she needed to pack for the weekend, finish a transcript and then drop it off at the post office on the way to counseling. After counseling, she planned to go to Staples for some supplies, and then if there was enough time, she'd stop in at Macy's for a new outfit, maybe some shoes, too. After that, she had a nail appointment and then it would be time to pick up Jake. They were planning to pack his stuff, then get Chinese take-out and watch a movie. Tomorrow morning, they would be on their way to San Diego.

Lacey opened up the sunroof and welcomed the rapid, semi-warm breeze as it ran its fingers through her hair and filled her with a sense of giddiness she hadn't remembered feeling in a long time.

"I'll see you Monday, Harrison."

"Just remember, this is your last weekend off from training until after the show."

"Okay, Mr. Grumpy Bear."

Harrison smiled in response.

Lacey turned to walk out the door and nearly ran into Daryn.

"There you go crashing into me again." His tone was sultry and teasing. "Are you already done with your workout?"

"Uh-huh. I've got an appointment this morning, so I needed to train earlier. I should get going."

He obviously wasn't ready for her to go. "So are you going to be home later?"

"No. As soon as I get Jake from school and he gets packed, we're leaving for San Diego."

"Oh, that's right." He smiled. "Be safe, and have a good time with your sister." He winked at her and walked into the gym.

Lacey was a little surprised to hear his seemingly genuine statement. She walked to her car confessing under her breath, "God, please forgive me for that little lie about not being home later. I just don't want him interrupting my time with Jake."

The door leading down the hall into Daniel's office was open so she walked down the hall. His voice startled her.

"I was just coming to see if you were out there." Daniel smiled.

"The door was open, so I thought that was a green light to come on back."

"Well, come on in. Make yourself comfortable, and I'm going to go close that front door."

Lacey did as Daniel suggested and was sitting in her usual spot when he returned.

"So how are things?" Daniel made himself comfortable in his chair in front of her.

Lacey stayed in her head for a few seconds, thinking of where she wanted to start, which was with Jake. She had come in today determined to stay focused on some questions about Jake and her parenting, and not on her relationships and/or her childhood. She began with small talk, telling him that Jake's dad was calling again. "I think the reason he hasn't been calling is he's been depressed, coping with his HIV, or maybe not coping. I'm not sure. But I'm just glad he's calling his son again."

Daniel was taking notes and looked up when she paused. "So what's really on your mind?"

How does he do that? she wondered. She brought up the subject of the note she had found under Jake's pillow again. "So what do I do? Do I let Jake know that I know, or do I tell his dad that I know? I mean, I feel bad for his dad and all, but come on, getting high with your son? That's just unacceptable. "

227

Daniel looked up from his notes. "You obviously feel there's some sort of dilemma in telling Jake that you found this note, so let me ask you, what are you afraid of, Lacey?"

Lacey pondered the question and answered Daniel honestly. "I don't really know what I'm afraid of. "

Daniel scribbled a note on his pad. "I think that it's more your natural disposition to avoid making anyone unhappy, because, in your mind, to make someone unhappy feeds your fear. But what do you think that fear is all about, Lacey? Or better yet, where do you think it comes from?"

Lacey could hear the ticking of the secondhand of the clock on the wall, or was that her heartbeat? "I dunno," she mumbled. *Isn't that why I'm here?* Lacey had to refrain from asking.

Daniel finally spoke. "Your fear is rooted in your own issue of abandonment, first by your father, and then by your mother, and thereafter by Jake's dad and then finally Peter. So to confront Jake and or his dad would feed the fear of being abandoned because you either fear your son will do that to you or even more likely, you fear that your son will feel you're doing that to him."

Lacey gasped at the sense he was making.

Daniel continued, not pulling any punches. "So you live in projective identification, anticipating—"

"What the heck is that?" Lacey interrupted.

"That's reading minds," he answered without skipping a beat, "about someone's experience of life or reaction because of an action you will take. You can't bear to be guilty of causing some-one the same types of feelings you have had in your past.

Lacey felt the tears trickle down her cheeks as the truth crashed into her senses. She took the tissue that Daniel handed her.

"But, Lacey, what you need to see is this way of thinking is only handicapping you from truly being, especially if unhappi-ness or anger or aloneness will be the result."

"I don't think I get that. What do you mean by 'handicapping me from truly being'?"

"Well, first of all—and this is one of those symptoms, if you will, of child abuse and child sexual abuse—you think you can control much more than you really can, so consequently, you have no practice of decision making; therefore, you reaction-manage, not pro-active manage, and reaction-managing is a form of control."

Lacey sat there shaking her head in silence.

"Why are you shaking your head?" Daniel's tone was gentle.

"Because this picture you've described is so ugly. I've never really liked myself, and now..." Lacey's confession brought another wave of tears and she couldn't stop the open sobbing. "I thought," she caught her breath and continued, "that counseling was supposed"—she gasped for more air—"to help," she finally finished.

Daniel sat forward in his chair and spoke even more gently. "But it does, Lacey. Counseling is not a Band-Aid; it's a tool that we use to peel back the layers, reveal hidden things, such as the root of your fears, resentments and your need to be in control, and then true healing can take place."

"Well, if this is what healing takes..." She let the rest of her sentence go unfinished, not sure she meant what she didn't say.

Daniel went on to explain that the beginning of counseling was comparative to a cup of dirt. Each session represented a dose of water, and as the water mixed with the dirt, it became mud. "But," he finished, "the more you come back, the more water goes in the cup and the less mud you have. In other words, the clearer everything looks." He smiled at the recognition on her face and looked up at the clock. "I think that's enough for one session."

Lacey didn't have the emotional wherewithal to disagree.

He reached out his hand and put it on her shoulder and bowed his head.

"I'll tell her. Bye, Dad. See you in a couple weeks." Jake flipped the phone closed, put it in the cup holder and turned up the volume on the stereo.

Lacey reached over and turned it back down. "You'll tell me what?"

"My dad wants to come over next weekend and spend the night at our house, and he needs you to pick him up at the train station."

"Why's he taking a train down here? What happened to his car?"

"I don't know. Maybe you should call and ask him."

"You know what? I think I'll do that right now. Hand me my ear piece." She turned the volume down even more on the stereo. "Go ahead and hit the redial button, honey."

"Hello."

"Hey. Jake just told me you want to come down next weekend, but you're coming into the train station. What's going on?" she asked, getting right to the point. She listened as he explained to her he was on several medications and that he couldn't drive because of them. *So he'd finally gone to the doctor, huh?*

"And I didn't tell Jake," he finished.

"Why?" She sounded badgering, even to her own ears.

Lacey strained to hear his answer, but he wasn't talking so she asked it differently, more gently. "I don't understand. Why wouldn't you tell him?" As soon as she said it, she looked to see if Jake had heard her, and by the look on his face, she could tell he had. *Dang it, now I'm going to have to do damage control for his dad, again!* "I mean, why wouldn't you want to say anything?"

"Is he right there?"

"Yeah, we're driving to San Diego to see my sister."

"Come on, Lacey. I'm having a hard enough time understanding all there is to know about this HIV and the symptoms, let alone accepting it. I don't want to tell him about this. Can't you understand that?"

"I'm sorry, Clint." She changed the subject quickly. "So when are you coming down, then?"

"Next week," he answered, willingly following the change of subject. "I've got to check into the train schedule, so as soon as I figure it out, I'll let you know. Jake's told me you've been working Fridays so I thought I'd come in on Saturday morning and then go back Sunday night."

"That should work. Just give me a call as soon as you know, and we'll work it out."

"Did Jake tell you I'm going to need to stay at your place?"

"Yeah, he did. That's fine," she added. "You can either sleep in his room or on the couch. We'll figure something out."

"Thanks. I'll be in touch."

Lacey took the earpiece out of her ear.

"So what didn't he tell me?" Jake asked.

The counselor's words suddenly came to mind, and Lacey was caught in the struggle between reactively managing this situation and proactively handling this situation. *Here goes,* she thought. "Well, he didn't want to tell you, but your dad has just started his medications for his HIV, and they keep him pretty tired, so that's why he's taking the train down." She tried to concentrate on her driving, glancing at him every few seconds to gauge his reaction to her honesty. "You okay?"

"I guess so." He was quiet for a few seconds, tapping his hand on his leg to the beat of the music. He reached for the volume knob and turned it up.

Lacey turned it back down. "Jake, I think we should talk about this. I mean, this is for real and we can't just pretend it's not happening."

"I'm not trying to pretend it's not happening."

Lacey heard the anger in his tone.

"I just want to know, is he…" He trailed off as the tears fell down his face.

"Is he what, honey?"

"Is he going to die?"

Lacey thought his question came out like a pop of a balloon, and he looked almost relieved to have asked it. She choked back her own threatening emotions. She wished she could kiss his tears away and assure him that he'd never have to cry again over his dad's condition. She wiped her own eyes and then glanced at him and reached down deep to gather some optimism. She was quiet for a few seconds, concentrating on keeping her eyes on the road, but glancing at him every now and then said, "I really think he's going to be around for a long, long time, Jake. Honestly, they've really come far with AIDS and the HIV virus as far as finding a way to keep it from progressing."

Jake looked up, his eyes shining with hope. "Really?"

"Really, and I'm not just saying it either."

"How did you know I was going to ask you that, Mom?"

"Because you're my son and I think I know you pretty well, kiddo." Lacey reached across and tousled his hair. Now what's the next street I'm looking for? We don't want to tell her we got lost."

A half hour later, they arrived at Elaine's. Lacey put it in park and saw her niece come running out. "Oh, look, there's Alexandria. She must have been watching out for us."

Jake got out of the car and hugged his cousin. Lacey smiled at their excitement of seeing each other again. It had been almost six months, but then again, they talked on the phone quite often, a lot more than she and Elaine did. Both Alex and Jake had had their share of premature emotional pain as a result of their parents' choices. Two years ago, Alex had learned that her mom was a lesbian. Shortly after that, Jake had to endure the announcement that his dad was HIV and then yet again, still more pain when his mom's second marriage had ended in another divorce. All of the pain had brought the two cousins closer, unlike what it had done to Lacey and Elaine.

Alex came around and hugged Lacey. "Hi, Auntie, I'm so excited that you guys are finally here."

Lacey hugged her close. "You are getting just too darned pretty, young lady," Lacey teased. She looked up to see Elaine smiling at the two of them.

"I know. Doesn't she remind you of grandma?"

Lacey pulled Alex a couple inches away from her and really looked at her. She was almost two years younger than Jake, and already almost as tall as Lacey with quite a little shape on her, not skinny, but shapely. Her blond hair was long and wavy and Lacey noticed that it came to the middle of her back. Her eyes were an icy blue, and she had round cheeks with a dimple on each side. Lacey reached up and gently squeezed her right cheek. "As a matter of fact, she is a beautiful, young version of Grandma." She reached for her sister. "And how are you, sis?"

Elaine hugged her firmly. "I'm excited you're here, too. Let's get your stuff and go in, and you can say hi to our new kitty."

The three of them sat in the third row from the front waiting for the play to start. Jake and Alex were making up songs, laughing and carrying on and entertaining Lacey in the process. The lights went on and off three times and she leaned over to toward them. "Shhh, you guys. You don't want to get us kicked out before the play even starts." The announcer introduced the play, and the music began. It was curtain time.

An hour and a half later, the final curtain came down, and the three of them made their way to the side where the cast would be waiting. When Lacey saw Elaine surrounded by a lot of people, she felt a sense of pride. Her sister's vocal talent never ceased to amaze her. She was glad that she was finally doing something with it. The play had been really entertaining, surprisingly much more than Lacey had anticipated. When she finally got her turn to talk to Elaine, she grabbed her in a big hug. "I was so proud of you, sis. You did great. I especially loved that part where you made everyone laugh."

Elaine pulled away. "Really?"

"Why are you so surprised? Yes, really. You did a great job." Lacey was about to tell her she'd come to any play she was in, but Elaine began introducing her to a few of the other cast members. They spent a while there, talking and laughing comfortably and then Elaine got the group's attention. "Hey, everybody, let's go out to drunch at El Torito."

"What's 'drunch'?" Lacey asked.

"Dinner/lunch," Alex and Elaine said in unison, giggling at their newly coined word.

Lacey checked her watch. It was just a little after one o'clock. Her growling stomach reminded her that she was hungry. "Sure. I just have to be at the dealership before three o'clock." She looked at Elaine. "Can you still follow me over to the car rental place and then take me to the dealership?"

"Yeah. Let's go eat."

"Here are the keys. She's all yours." Marcus handed Lacey the keys and congratulated her. She walked toward her new car somewhat in a daze from all the excitement. They had put the top down, and Elaine and Alex were sitting in the backseat and Jake was already settled in the front playing with the stereo and pre-setting his favorite channels. Lacey got to the car, and they all got out so they could say good-bye.

"Thanks again for coming, Lacey. It really meant a lot." Her sister hugged her tight.

Lacey hugged her back. "I'm so glad we did it. The play was so good, and you were awesome. Don't forget to let me know when you're in another play, and we'll make sure we're here." She reached for Alex and hugged her close. "I'll see you soon, sweetheart. Keep practicing for your cheer try-outs. You'll make it; I know you will." She looked over at Jake. "I'm gonna check out our new ride while you say good-bye." She got in the car and began adjusting the side mirrors and the rearview mirror. She looked around into the backseat and then up front again, enjoying the scent of the new leather. She ran her hand along the wood-grain dash and center console, checking out all the neat little storage compartments as well as a roomy glove compartment. She looked up when Jake got in front with her. She started the engine, surprised at how quiet it was. "Fasten your seat belt, buddy." They each raised a hand up in the air and waved good-bye to them as she pulled away.

"So how is the routine coming?" Harrison asked, taking the bar from her.

"It's coming, I guess." Lacey stretched out her arms relieving the tightness in her biceps.

"You don't sound very confident."

"I really like the routine she choreographed; it's just there's one move in it that I still haven't mastered, and I'm getting kind of frustrated."

"Well, how many times have you met with her?"

"Three, and I think we have just three more set up between now and the contest."

Harrison nodded his head. "Okay. So what's the move that has you so frustrated?"

"It's too hard to explain. I'd have to show you."

"Well, let's go in the aerobic room."

Lacey followed him into the room. She sat down on the ground and pulled her shoes off. "It's that move where you put your legs out, like a wide V-like position, and then your arms are right in front of you and you lift yourself up."

"The planche maneuver?" He sat down and did exactly as Lacey described.

Lacey's mouth dropped open as she saw how far off the ground he lifted himself. "How in the heck did you do that?" she nearly yelled. "You must have gotten six inches off the ground."

Harrison laughed at her exaggeration. "Let me see you do it now."

Lacey gave him a frustrated look.

"Come on. You can do this, Lacey. You have incredible upper-body strength and abdominals, which is what this move takes."

"I thought it was all upper body strength."

"No, watch me." He spread his legs into the V position again, sat up straight, and Lacey watched as he tightened his core and then lifted off the ground.

"Let me try." She did exactly as she had watched him do. First she put her legs in a V-like position, pointed her toes and put her hands inside the V-opening. She sat up straight and then sucked in her core and lifted. "Wait a minute. I'm up!" Lacey felt her arms start to shake, and she let herself down, though her emotions were still up. "I did it!" she exclaimed, more dazed than excited.

Harrison stood to his feet and pulled her up. "You sure did, Lacey, and I had no doubts. Keep practicing, and by the time the contest comes, you'll look as though you've been doing it forever."

"You sure you don't mind Jake having a friend over?" Lacey asked Clint.

"It's fine. He seems like a nice enough kid. We'll be fine," Clint assured her.

Lacey was internally grateful that Daryk had come over. In fact, it had seemed the perfect solution to an awkward situation. *He wouldn't dare try and get high with his son while his son's friend is here,* Lacey thought.

"So where are you off to again?" Clint asked. "I forgot."

"I have a business dinner in Pasadena"—*Why did I call it a business dinner?*—"with a client that I'm working with on a big case in L. A.," she added. *I mean, it's not like I owe him any explanations.*

"Oh, is the agency owner going to be there, too?"

Lacey was quick to answer in the negative as she observed Clint's grin which for some reason grated on her last nerve.

"Then it's not a business dinner." He chuckled. "Don't worry about me and the boys. We'll probably be on the Wii most of the time. That's about all I have the energy for anyway."

Jake and Daryk walked in from outside. "Hey, Dad, you want to come hear me and Daryk's new song?"

"Sure." He stood up to walk out to the garage.

Lacey glanced at the clock. I'd better get going. Come give me a hug, Jake."

Both Jake and Daryk came over and hugged Lacey good-bye. "Have fun, Mom."

"You guys have fun, too. And go easy on your dad on that Wii. Don't kick his butt too hard." She smiled at them before walking out the door to her new car. She started it up and debated on letting the top down and then decided against it, not wanting to show up at the restaurant with wind-blown hair when she had taken extra time on not just her hair, but her makeup too. She keyed the restaurant's address into her GPS, put her car in drive and headed out of the complex.

She let out a sigh of relief when she got on the freeway. It felt good to be out of the house. It had been weird all day, having Jake's dad there, but Jake had sure been happy. She turned up her stereo when she heard a familiar song come on the radio and realized that now that she was on her way, she was looking forward to dinner with Danny more than she realized.

Lacey walked into California Pizza Kitchen and saw him immediately. He was waving his hand up in the air. She walked by the hostess toward him. He stood to greet her and gave her a gentle hug and pulled her chair out for her. There was already a glass of water with lemon in front of her, and she reached for it and took a sip. "Thanks. I was thirsty." She smiled at the sweet gesture, impressed that he remembered that she liked lemon with her water just from the few times they had had lunch together.

He held up his glass of wine and took a sip. "I was going to order you a glass of wine, but I wasn't sure if you liked red or white."

"Well, as a matter of fact, I happen to like red, like a good Merlot or a Shiraz is nice."

"Ahh, a girl after my own heart." He smiled. "Here, try this. This is actually a Mondavi Merlot."

Lacey took a sip and let it sit in her mouth for a few seconds, absorbing the taste on her tongue so she could truly appreciate it. "That's actually pretty good. I'll have what you're having."

They talked comfortably nonstop until the waiter came to take their order. Lacey realized she hadn't even looked at the menu yet. Danny took charge and gave him the order for both of them, a medium three-cheese pizza and a large antipasto salad. The waiter took their menus. "And she'll have a glass of the Mondavi Merlot, as well," Danny added. The waiter returned within minutes with Lacey's wine, and left again, and they continued talking in between sips of wine. When the salad came, Danny served both of them as Lacey told him about her training schedule.

"So is all of this really bad for your training diet, then?" Danny asked.

"Not too bad." Lacey smiled. "Although I'm sure my trainer would have a fit about the wine."

Danny pretended to look sorry and then smiled. "Oops. Just don't tell him."

"The real contest diet hasn't even begun yet. When that starts, then I won't be able to get away with it." Lacey took another sip of her wine. "And what about you, Danny, what do you do for fun?"

Danny got a serious look on his face.

"I mean when you're not preparing for depositions of homeless people," Lacey kidded him.

Danny chuckled. "Well, I like to play racquetball, go bikeriding. I don't really get to do very much of that when I'm on a big case, though, and besides..." His tone got quiet, and Lacey looked up.

"Besides what?" she prodded.

"Well, it's always more fun when you have someone to enjoy those things with, you know what I mean?"

Lacey nodded her head in definite agreement, internally grateful for the girls. "Oh, come on, Danny. You have friends; I know you do."

Danny helped himself to the pizza that had come. "Yeah, I have a few, but they're all married. I'm talking about a significant other." He handed her a plate with a piece of pizza on it.

She took a bite of her pizza, thankful to have a diversion from his last comment. "This is awesome. You know, I've never been here, and I very rarely have pizza. Good choice."

"Thank you. As I was saying, the kinds of hobbies I have are better with a partner."

Lacey decided to quit running from the subject. "So have you ever been married, Danny?"

"As a matter of fact, I was, for almost eight years."

Lacey didn't miss the bitterness in his last words. "What happened?" She watched as he hesitated. "That is if you want to talk about it. You can tell me if I'm being too nosey."

"No, no, it's okay." He went on to share with her his horrific experience of his wife leaving him for his college buddy and how they had tried to work it out afterwards but he just couldn't let himself trust her anymore.

Lacey listened to his story, touched by the similarities of her own story with Peter. When the waiter came over and asked if they had saved room for dessert, Danny looked to her and she shook her head. "How about another glass of wine," he asked.

Lacey hesitated. "I'm driving, so…"

"We'll take a walk after dinner." He turned to the waiter. "No dessert, but we'll take another glass of Merlot."

They continued talking and comparing love and war stories as they sipped their wine, and the time passed quickly. When Danny had paid the bill, he stood up and helped her out of her chair and into her sweater. "Let's take a little after-dinner walk," he urged, "and then if your trainer does find out about the wine, at least I can defend myself by saying we exercised." He put his arm on the small of her back and led her out of the restaurant.

Lacey put her key in the side door to unlock it and realized it was already unlocked. "Nice to know my son's safe and sound with such a responsible adult here," she muttered to herself as she pushed the door open. The sound of the TV beckoned her to the living room where Clint was sprawled out on the couch, fast asleep. He looked like a little boy sprawled out, not like a person who was HIV positive. Lacey continued to stare at him and reflect back on her season with him. They had both been so young, so happy in the beginning, but when Lacey had discovered his crystal meth habit, her world had come crashing down, ripping her dream of being a family apart. She begged him to get help; he said he would but never did, and she had finally tossed him out. She had wanted to hang on, but his addiction was beyond her comprehension and her love wasn't enough to change him, and neither was having a son.

His movement on the couch startled her, and she stood completely still. He had rolled over onto his side and was facing the couch. His breathing was even, and Lacey could see that he was still sleeping. A familiar feeling tugged at her, almost embraced her. It was guilt, so heavy and suffocating. She continued to stare at him. *If only she had tried harder, not thrown him out like a piece of trash; then he wouldn't have met Jenna and he wouldn't be HIV positive.* Lacey put her hand on the counter to steady herself and push away from the suffocating blanket of guilt. She walked upstairs wondering how one could experience so many emotional highs and lows in a matter of a couple of hours. She turned her thoughts away from Clint and brought them back to the present, her date with Danny. She got ready for bed and reached for her journal so she could write about the highs and lows of the day.

Lacey sat up in her bed, startled. *I must have had a dream*, she thought. She caught her breath when she heard it again, the sound of her doorbell ringing. She looked at her clock on the night-stand. 5:33 a.m. "Am I dreaming?" she asked herself aloud. She threw her covers off and ran downstairs, her adrenalin pumping. Clint was still sprawled out on the couch, oblivious to the ringing bell. She looked through the peephole of her door. "What in the heck..." She trailed off as she opened the door.

There on her front porch stood two police officers, one male and one female. "Can I help you?" Lacey managed to stammer.

The male police officer cleared his throat. "Do you have a son by the name of Jake Thorton, ma'am?"

Lacey's blood turned to ice. "Is he okay? What's going on?" she said, her voice raising with each question.

The female officer stepped forward, her voice gentle with compassion. "He's fine. So then Jake is your son?"

"Yes." Lacey started to hyperventilate.

The male officer spoke again. "Do you happen to know where he is?"

Lacey didn't need to hesitate before answering. "He's in bed."

"Are you sure about that?"

"Hold on. I'll be right back." She left the door slightly ajar and ran up the stairs to Jake's room. She threw open his door to confirm for her own peace of mind that her son was in his bed still sleeping. She turned on the light and gasped at what she saw. His bed was empty, and Daryk's covers were askew on the floor. They were both gone!

T. M. I.

Lacey felt as though the wind had been knocked out of her as she stared at Jake's empty bed and what was Daryk's makeshift bed on the floor. Clint's voice reminded her to breathe again. "Lacey, are you up there? The officers want to talk to you."

Lacey came running downstairs so fast, she barely felt the steps beneath her feet. Clint was standing in the door, and Lacey walked up just as she heard him say, "No, I don't live here. I was actually just down overnight to visit my son."

Officer Joe noticed Lacey had made it back. "I didn't get to finish telling you that we actually have him and his friend in the backseat of our police car." Lacey slumped against the door to keep from collapsing. "They're okay," he continued, "but unfortunately, the car isn't."

"Wha-what car?" Lacey stammered. She looked up when Officer Pam cleared her throat and she could visibly see compassion in her eyes.

"Do you own a brand new red Solara? A convertible?" she added.

Lacey nodded her head in agreement, not fully comprehending where this was all going.

"Well, I'm afraid there's been an accident—"

Lacey nearly fell this time, and Clint leaned over to steady her.

Officer Joe continued, "The good news is no one else was involved, and Jake and Daryk weren't hurt."

And that's supposed to make me feel better? Lacey wondered.

As if he could read her mind, Officer Joe continued, "The bad news is we're pretty sure your car is totaled." He handed her a card with a phone number and a police report number. "Here you go. This is where your car's been towed to, so you can call your insurance company and give them that information, and this," he said, pointing to the long number on the card, "is the police report number."

Lacey took the card and mumbled a thank you.

Officer Joe cleared his throat. "Now, unfortunately, we had to cite your son for reckless driving, driving without a license, and we did give both him and his buddy a breathalyzer test."

Lacey's insides twisted.

"Jake blew a .04 and the other boy a .05."

Lacey glared at Clint and then looked back to both officers.

"There was also some damage done to a fire hydrant, so you'll be getting a letter and a bill from the city asking for full payment for that as well as the city's fire engine that had to drive out to the scene."

Lacey's eyes welled up, and Officer Pam pulled a tissue out of her pocket and handed it to her.

The officers explained a couple more details and then suggested that Clint come with them to get Jake out of the car so they could take Daryk home to his mom. Lacey didn't argue. She wanted to slam the door with all her might but exerted some self-control. She went into the living room and sat down, put her face in her hands, and sobbed. She didn't stop until she heard them come in, and even then, she made no attempt to hide her tears. She had no idea what to say, but one thing was for certain, this was definitely an open door for the secret she'd kept buried to come out. The coincidence of Clint being here and this happening didn't go unnoticed by her either. She debated between confronting them both together and dealing with Clint first. Her gut told her that the latter would be better, and when Clint spoke up and asked Jake to go to his room, she knew that was her answer.

She heard Jake's door close, and her adrenalin started pumping. She was ready to lay into him but good.

"So what do you think we should do?" Clint asked.

His calm tone and his steady demeanor added to the already-blazing fire. She got up from the couch. "What are *we* going to do? What do you mean 'we'?"

"Well, he's my son, too."

"Is that why you got high with him a couple months ago, because he's your son?" Lacey was so angry, she could feel her veins popping out of her neck. When Clint didn't respond, she continued, only louder. "Don't look so surprised, Clint. And don't even try to lie to me about it, either. I was married to you, remember?"

"It was only one time."

"Are you going to tell me you had nothing to do with Jake and Daryk getting alcohol last night?"

His head shot up and his eyes boiled with anger. "Don't you put that on me, Lacey. I didn't think they would drink the beer I put in the fridge. I thought they had gone to bed and I passed out on the couch."

She slumped back down into the couch. "If only you knew how badly I want to believe that, but even if that were the case, you had no right, no business even getting high with your son one time." Lacey didn't even try to stop the tears from coming.

He came and sat down on the opposite end of the couch. "I know you're not going to understand this, Lacey, but I knew he'd want to experiment, and I didn't want him to experiment with his friends, especially since…" He trailed off.

"'Especially since' what?"

"Since I probably won't be around when he's older."

Lacey glared at him, her eyes pooling over.

"And that's not a cop-out, either," he said.

"It may not be a cop-out, but it's a crutch. You can't use this HIV diagnosis as an excuse to do whatever the heck you want to do in life that you feel you never got to do. Is that the kind of legacy you want to leave for your son? And besides, they didn't hand you a death sentence; you're getting a warning, Clint, a chance to do things right in your life."

He stared at her seemingly unmoved by her words.

"Hello. Is there anybody home in there, Clint?"

"I'm listening," he mumbled.

"All I'm saying is none of us are guaranteed tomorrow, so we've got to make the most of today, and I get the feeling that you've already thrown in the towel."

Clint put his head down in admission and picked it back up to stare at nothing in particular.

He changed the subject. "So what do you think his punishment should be?"

Lacey shook her head. She was totally at a loss for words. "I don't know."

Clint stood up and began pacing the living room floor. "Well, I think he shouldn't be allowed to have band practice here for a while."

Lacey didn't agree and told him so.

"But he has to lose something valuable so he thinks about what he's done. Then hopefully, he won't do it again."

"I get that, Clint, but music is his outlet."

"He can still play his music, just not in a band setting. And I think his Wii needs to be taken away also."

"Yeah, make him completely miserable is easy for you to say because you don't have to live with him."

Clint stopped pacing and stared at her. "That was a cheap shot, Lacey."

"I'm sorry. I shouldn't have said that. Okay. So no band practice here for a month, but he can play his music on his own, and no playing the Wii. But I think there has to be something to make him think about the financial aspect of this. I mean, if they total this car, my down payment of twenty-seven hundred dollars is out the window." Lacey put her head in her hands and sat there with all kinds of "what-ifs" swimming in her head while tears threatened to take her under.

Clint sat down again. "It's time he was given things to do around here to help you."

Lacey brought her head up and nodded in agreement. "Let's put some things on paper in the form of a contract." She got up and went to her office and grabbed some paper and a pen and came back to the living room. For the next half hour, they brainstormed in a way that they never did while they were married. When they had agreed on his punishment, Lacey went into her office and quickly typed it out. When she returned to the living room, Jake was sitting next to Clint.

"Did you finish typing the contract?" he asked.

Lacey handed it to him and stared at Jake.

"This is what your mom and I came up with, and I want you to know I'll be checking with your mom to make sure you're abiding by this. You need to understand the seriousness of what you've done, Jake. Take a look at it."

Jake looked it over somberly and handed it back to his dad.

"You're going to start participating a lot more around here by helping your mom out." He read the list of daily and weekly chores that were his for the next six weeks.

Lacey saw Jake roll his eyes as Clint read the list. "No, you did not just do that, Jake."

"What are you talking about?"

His tone sent Lacey's anger to a higher level. "You know exactly what I'm talking about. I saw you roll your eyes. I'm sorry if you don't like it. I don't like the fact that you took my car and totaled it."

Clint put the lid on Lacey's boiling anger. "And these are the things you are no longer allowed to do for the next month, no more band practice for a month, no more Wii, no friends over, and no spending the night with friends. And finally, if any of your grades are below a C, this contract will continue indefinitely." He handed it to him and turned to Lacey. "Do you have a pen for him?"

Lacey walked to her office and came back with a pen and handed it to Jake.

He took it and signed it. He handed both the pen and contract to Lacey without looking at her.

She bent down to sign it in front of Jake and then stood up. Before she turned to walk back to her office she could have sworn she saw Clint wink at Jake.

"Mom, telephone's for you," Jake yelled up the stairs.

She picked up the receiver on her nightstand. "Hello."

The voice on the other end introduced himself as James, the adjustor for her insurance claim. "I need to ask you a few questions about your claim, tell you what information I already have, and then we'll go from there. Do you have a few minutes?"

"Yeah, I guess so."

He took a few minutes to get her general contact information and asked if she had the purchase contract for the car in front of her.

"Yes, I have it right here."

He asked her for the date of purchase, how much she paid for it, the vehicle identification number and the equipment on the car. "So you just got this car a few weeks ago, right?"

The reminder punched her in the gut. "Yeah."

"That's too bad. Let me take a look at your policy here and see…"

A warning bell went off in her head. "Is there a problem?"

"How old is your son?"

"He's almost fifteen."

"Well, we may have a problem then, Ms. Thorton."

Lacey walked to her chair in her office and sat. "And what's that?"

"I'm going to have to research this to see if there's any way around it, but from a first glance at your policy, it appears that the only way that we can cover this accident for you is for you to press charges against your son."

"What's for dinner, Mom?"

Lacey ignored him as she carried their plates to the table and sat down. She decided against telling him about what the insurance guy had said because she knew in her heart that it would do more damage than good. "Do you want to bless the food, or do you want me to?"

"I'll do it." Jake bowed his head and blessed the food. When he finished, he looked up at her. He shrugged his shoulders and began eating.

"So let's talk about what you're doing right." She tried to smile.

Jake had a mouthful of food but nodded his head in agreement.

"Like the great job you're doing on keeping your end of the contract."

Jake looked like he'd won a prize. "Thanks."

Lacey pushed her food back and forth on her plate. "I just want to remind you that even when school's out, this contract is still in effect, Jake." She put a bite of food in her mouth to shut herself up.

"Mom, you look like you could use some good news."

Lacey let her guard down a little and smiled. "I look that bad, huh?"

"No, no, you don't look bad." Jake said. "I just know you're a little edgy and thought you'd want to know that I have three A's, two B's and..." He stopped as if he had reached the edge of a cliff.

"And..."

"And one D-plus," he gushed out. "But I should be able to bring it up to a C by next week."

"Math?"

He gave her his innocent look, and flashed his dimpled smile.

Lacey wasn't amused. "I don't see what's so funny. Just bring it up, Jake, please." She got up and washed her uneaten food down the garbage disposal, wishing she could send her life's problems down with it.

Lacey stopped by the ATM on her way to the train station, withdrew forty dollars from her checking account and requested a balance on her savings. She grabbed the receipt and stared at it quickly on the way back to her rental car. She stopped when she saw the balance. *Shouldn't there be about twelve hundred more?* She stuffed it in her wallet. "I can't deal with this right now," she muttered and got in the car and headed to the train station. As soon as she parked and got out, the sound of the train coming down the track sent her running to the machine to validate her ticket. The machine spit out her ticket just as the train pulled up. She climbed up the stairs into the train and sat in her usual seat. "That was a God moment," she said under her breath as she pulled her laptop out to work on the way into L.A. By the time the train stopped in Union Station, Lacey had finished editing the transcript from three days prior and was ready for the day's deposition.

"Good morning, Lacey." Danny's cheerfulness soothed her weary heart.

Lacey took her laptop out and began hooking it up to her court reporting machine. "Good morning, Danny."

"You don't sound so good. Is everything okay?"

"I'll tell you at lunch. If I talk about it now, I'm going to lose it."

"Then we'll go to the French Bakery. Does that sound all right?"

"The company does; the food doesn't."

"Would you rather go somewhere else?"

Lacey looked up and smiled. "No, no, that's all right. I'm just saying I don't have much of an appetite, no matter where we go." She turned toward the door as she saw Julie walk in. "Good morning, Julie."

"Good morning, Lacey, Danny." She set her briefcase down. "Has my witness shown up yet?"

Lacey shook her head no. Danny told her he hadn't seen anyone come in, but he hadn't checked the lobby since he'd come in earlier. "You might want to check with our receptionist," he offered.

She grabbed her phone from her purse. "Let me give her a call and see where she is. I'll be right back."

Lacey sat down after getting her machine hooked up to her laptop. Danny reached over and put his hand over hers and squeezed it. Lacey looked up, pleasantly startled by his touch, and smiled.

He smiled back. "It's gonna be okay," he assured her.

She gently pulled her hand away so she could begin writing in her deposition book. "Thanks, Danny." She gave him a warm smile, all the while trying to push her personal life out the door of the conference room so she could focus on the job.

At twelve thirty, they broke for lunch. Lacey reached for her purse and stood by her machine, suddenly a little uncertain about having lunch with Danny. They'd had lunch together a couple of times, but the other occasions were more accidental coincidence. Dinner together last weekend had definitely changed the dynamics of their relationship, and his reassuring touch earlier had just turned things up another degree. She noticed Danny was still talking to Julie so she decided to play it cool and walk out of the conference room. She was almost to the door, and the next thing she saw was Danny's hand reaching to open it. They both walked out and Lacey felt his hand on her elbow.

"Where are you going? I thought we were having lunch at the French Bakery."

"I'm just going to use the ladies' room. I'll be right back."

Danny smiled. "Well, I've got to talk to Julie for a couple of minutes, so I'll meet you there. Besides, I don't want her to think there's anything going on."

"Sure." Lacey understood the importance of the civil code that governed court reporters. It required that they were to remain unbiased. The two of them leaving for lunch together would definitely not look appropriate. "Do you want me to order for you?"

"Just order me an iced tea, and by the time it gets there, I'll be right behind it."

She walked away, baffled at the butterflies in her stomach.

Lacey found the phone and headed for her oversized chair in her office. She was overwhelmed by with the need to hear her mom's gentle voice and wise words that always pointed her in the right direction. When she answered, Lacey heard her weariness right away and decided against burdening her with her own concerns and suspicions.

"So how's Dad doing?"

Mom hesitated before she answered. "Well, he's doing a lot better than we thought he'd do with the treatment. So we're thinking of taking a little trip up to the Eldorado National Forest. The fresh air will probably do him good, and you know how we love to drive."

"Do you think that it's okay for you guys to travel though?"

"Well, he has a break in the chemo the week after next, so we're thinking about doing it then, but I'll talk to the doctor and if he gives us the go-ahead, then we're going to do it. Enough about me, have you heard anything from the insurance company yet?"

"No, I haven't." Lacey sighed.

"And what about Jake, is he on his best behavior and abiding by the contract?"

"He seems to be."

Mom chuckled. "You don't sound very convincing."

"No, he's actually keeping up with the contract and his grades. I'm just tired. Working in L. A. makes for a really long day. I spend a lot of time feeling guilty for being gone so much."

"Lacey, there's no one else that's going to take care of the two of you, so don't let guilt guide you in how you parent Jake. Remember, honey, he needs a mom, not a friend."

Why can't I be both? Lacey swallowed her response and switched subjects. "So this case is really interesting and so is the guy we're working for."

They talked about the case for a few minutes, and then Lacey told her about the lunches and dinner in Pasadena with Danny.

"All I can say is I'm not surprised."

Lacey could hear Mom's chuckle in her throat. "Surprised about what?"

"His attraction to you doesn't surprise me because you have this ability to turn a stranger into a friend. So certainly after working with the same attorney for a while, the minimum level of friendship is bound to happen with you. You've just got to be careful to protect that professional relationship, Lacey." She paused for a second. "And your heart," she added. "I would hate to see the same thing happen as—"

"I know, Mom," Lacey interrupted her, not knowing if she was referring to Peter or Seth or both.

"What's this attorney's last name anyway? Sometimes you can tell a lot about by a person's last name, you know."

Lacey smiled. "I'm so tired, I can't for the life of me remember right now. Let me get his card." She reached for her purse and pulled her wallet out to get his card and the savings account receipt she'd gotten a few mornings ago fell out. "Oh, darn it. I forgot to check into this," she said unintentionally.

"You forgot to check into what?" Mom asked.

Lacey refrained from sharing her suspicion. The thought of Jake stealing money out of her savings account was just too much to bear right now. "It's nothing. I just need to go to the bank and check on my savings balance." She looked at Danny's card. "Anyways, his last name is Kuzak."

"Well, in all my years, I don't think I've ever run across a 'Kuzak.' Is he a big guy?"

Lacey didn't hold back her surprise. "Yes, as a matter of fact, he is. He's about six two, stocky, like a big teddy bear, sand-colored hair, and light blue eyes. He's okay looking, but he has a great smile. And he's definitely a good attorney."

"And you're a good court reporter, so be careful."

Her compliment and warning warmed Lacey's heart, and she laughed. "Well, I'm enjoying the job and it is kind of exciting working with someone you look forward to seeing."

"Well, you know I can understand that. Your dad and I worked together most of our working years."

Lacey heard the smile in her voice.

"Speaking of Dad, I better go. He's calling me."

"Okay. I love you, Mom. Give Dad my love, too, please."

"I will. Love you, too. I'll talk to you tomorrow, honey."

Lacey parked in the church parking lot and got out. Jake looked at her, obviously surprised. "What are you doing?" he asked.

"Well, I keep getting invited by Bruce's wife, so I just thought I'd check out the midweek service and start feeding my faith. You okay with that?" She looked up to see Shellie walking toward Jake.

Jake apparently noticed too and forgot to answer her.

Lacey watched them hug each other. *Okay, that's long enough.* "Hey, Shellie, how are you?"

She pulled away from Jake, her face beaming with happiness. "I'm good. How are you?"

"I'm okay."

"So are you staying for the service?" she asked innocently.

"Yeah, I think so." Lacey switched her gaze to Jake. "So I guess I'll just meet you right out here, okay?"

Jake came forward and gave her a hug. "I'll see you out here, little Mama. Go feed your faith." She made a mental note to talk to the youth pastor

Lacey watched them begin to walk toward the youth room and saw Jake reach for Shellie's hand. *I thought public displays of affection weren't allowed.* She watched them until they turned the corner, and then walked into the sanctuary. The pastor standing up front with a girl that looked to be a little younger than Lacey. He had his hand on her shoulder and his head was bowed. Lacey scanned over the audience and saw that everyone's head was down so she waited before going inside. She saw the pastor lift his head and begin to speak. She opened the door ever so gently and walked in. Picking an end seat in the very last row, she sat down just as he finished introducing the speaker.

Everyone began to clap, and Lacey followed suit. She sat back as the girl pointed to the overhead screens to introduce her topic.

Lacey scanned each of the screens to see if they all said the same thing. They did. The words seemed to pull her to the edge of her seat: Relationships the Right Way, part one. "This ought to be great," she muttered under her breath. She looked all around and saw that the entire audience was female. Lacey looked up at the speaker when she heard laughing, and pushed away her negative thoughts.

"So the only reason I am here with you tonight is because of *all* of my experience in doing relationships the *wrong* way. I have all sorts of credentials in this area. In the way of history, when I was eighteen, I met, befriended, fell in love, and married my son's father. Yes, I had all the classical signs of the L-word"—she paused for a second—"I still don't know if it was lust or love."

Lacey joined in the rampant laughter this time.

"Yes, I got bit pretty hard with the 'love bug,' but it felt good, so I told myself it had to be right. Isn't that the way it goes with a lot of things; if it feels good, it must be right, huh?"

The audience nodded their agreement and she continued.

"So here were are, married, and five years later, we have a son. We were complete, a real family, and we even started to do the church thing."

Lacey sat mesmerized by the similarities she shared with this stranger.

"Well, it was the 'church thing' and hearing messages from the Bible that started to expose me and my damage, which was in my unpacked baggage, but I still wasn't really getting it." She stood there for a minute and looked out into the audience. Lacey could have sworn that she locked eyes with her.

"From Mondays to Saturdays, I was still trying to fix the people in my world, especially my husband, but I spent no time trying to fix myself. Now when I say the word 'fix,' I want you all to know that I use that interchangeably with the word 'control.' Actually, I think the word control should be a synonym for 'delusional' because that's exactly what we are if we think we can control anything or anyone but ourselves.

"The funny thing about me trying to fix and control my husband was that the more I tried to control him, the more apparent his flaws became, and soon his biggest flaw surfaced, which was his addiction to cocaine."

Lacey gasped. It was like she had been reading her journals.

"Well, he refused to get help and to make that long story short, 'happily ever after' ended. I sought counseling from the staff at the church we had gone to occasionally. I learned that the nurturing that I had not been given as a child was the driving force in all of my relationships, especially my romantic ones, which caused me to put unrealistic expectations on them that were entirely unfair and impossible for them to meet. So my process was just beginning, but I thought I was well on my way.

"How many of you have ever seen that 'footprints' poem?"

Lacey raised her hand without hesitating.

"Now, the next three years were definitely a 'footprints' season for me, you know, a season where the only explanation for my survival were His arms that carried me."

So that's what that means?

"I worked my way through law school as an independent contractor doing sales and recruiting for a large company. I became successful in the world's eyes. As a way of guilt management, my time with my son became quality versus quantity. I had to hire a full-time nanny to help me juggle it all and my motivation was my desire to provide for my son in a way that I had never been provided for."

Lacey reached for some tissue in her purse. *This is way too weird. So how does our story end, huh?*

"And then, victim number two." Everyone laughed.

"He was a nice guy, kind of quiet with a calm spirit, and he didn't believe in 'organized religion,' but of course, I persuaded him to give the 'church thing' a try." She looked up and out into the audience, and Lacey squirmed as the speaker's eyes seemed to connect with her again, and then she continued, "So as you can tell, I still had not dealt with my own control issues." She was nodding her own head up and down. "You know, ladies, we already have so many hats we need to wear to function in our various roles. We don't need to put the hats of control, fixer, and/or salesperson on top of our wife and/or mother hats."

Lacey joined the women as they laughed with the speaker.

"Well, I convinced him all right, so much so that he proposed to me a few months later, on Easter Sunday, after the 'church thing,' of course."

"Well, two years into the marriage, I realized I had made a mistake. By this time I was actually talking to God on a fairly regular basis, and I yelled out to Him, 'Now what do I do'? And I heard, 'Work on you; I'll work on him.'"

Lacey's eyebrows rose. *So she hears the Voice too?*

"So I did, but it still didn't work. He left me for another woman."

What a scumbag. Maybe he and my ex should start the Scumbag Club. Lacey wished she could catch her gaze now and offer comfort, knowing she wasn't the only one to have gone through that humiliating experience.

"But when I review my mistakes in my relationships, I am humbled, yet incredibly repulsed. I am also incredibly grateful that God never gave up on me, despite my desire to control my world and everything and everyone in it, a desire that began when I was five, and was pounded in me every time I saw my stepfather beat my mother to a pulp, vowing that no man would be stronger than me. Now, that's not an excuse, but when we understand our past, it brings clarity to the picture, and clarity illuminates better choices so we don't keep making the same mistakes. Something cool about God is He uses your past mistakes to positively affect your present and future, if you let Him.

"I began playing the dating game with a vengeance, and my son and I counted that in one year, I had dated twenty-six guys, all simultaneously." She looked out into the audience. "Don't get me wrong. I never deceived them into thinking I was dating only them; I just didn't make a big deal about it."

Lacey felt herself exhale. She smiled at the thought of dating twenty-six guys in a year.

"The dating game came to an abrupt halt when I put myself in a situation of date rape."

Lacey gasped with the rest of the audience.

"The next ten years that followed were filled with provision and revelations for my life, and they were some of the most painful, yet sweetest years. You've heard the expression, 'No pain, no gain.' Well, I'm here to tell you that pain is really growth inside out."

Lacey wiped at her eyes with her tissue.

"Now, I want to introduce you to someone."

Everyone shifted in their seats as she left the stage and came back holding a six-foot tall cardboard sculpture of Jesus, but He was dressed in some pretty trendy jeans, a cool shirt, and shoes. She set him down beside her and the audience laughed with her as she looked him over from head to toe.

"Ladies, I'd like to introduce you to my constant companion, my guide, my counselor and mentor, my provider and my financial advisor, my first love who will never leave me nor forsake me, whose plans are to offer me a hope and a future, to build me up, not let me down." She put her arm around the cardboard statute. "This is J. C." She removed her arm and stood facing the audience again.

The audience broke out with thunderous applause, and Lacey sat there a bit baffled, chills running up her arms.

"He's kinda cute, huh?" She giggled and took a sip of water. "Now there's not enough time to go into the ten years worth of lessons, so let me just highlight a few. I've learned that God's love and nurturing are what we need to make us complete. To expect that need to be fulfilled by any person here on earth is a setup for failure." She looked out into the audience again. "How many of you out there are single?"

Lacey scanned the sanctuary and saw several hands go up. She put hers up too.

"Okay, several of you. Then know this: He uses your season of singleness to prepare you for whom *He* has for you, so a lot of times how long it takes is up to us. Another thing I've learned and am grateful for is that He forgives impurity; He just doesn't bless it. And lastly, I know that His love is available twenty-four/seven to guide us in any and all circumstances. He never has voice mail on, or a secretary to take our prayers. He never grows weary in comforting us. Those are all facts." She paused for a few seconds. "As we close in prayer, remember, this is part one, and part two will be same time, same place next week. I hope you'll come back."

Lacey watched as everyone bowed their heads. The last thing she wanted to do was be still. This girl's words had been like darts into the core of her being. She had to get out. She got up quietly and tiptoed out the double doors and headed outside for her car.

"Okay. We'll be in recess until one thirty."

Julie and her client left the conference room. "Do you want to grab some lunch?" Danny asked.

"I'd love to, but I've got to run over to the credit union and take care of something."

"Well, how about if I pick you up a sandwich and have it for you when you get back?"

"That's really sweet, Danny. I don't know how long this will take, so…" She let her sentence trail off.

"Then I'll see you back here before one thirty."

Lacey walked out the door and headed to the credit union. Within ten minutes, she was standing in front of the teller.

"Can I help you?"

"Yes. I was wondering if you could print me a two-month history for my savings account."

The teller looked annoyed by her request. "Are you looking for something in particular?"

"Well, my balance is a thousand dollars less than what I think should be in there. So I just wanted a history so I can match it with my records."

The teller let out an irritated sigh. "I'll be right back."

Lacey stood away from the counter, offended. "I can see you love your job," she muttered under her breath.

The teller came back with a printout. "Is there anything else I can do for you, Ms. Thorton?" She glared at Lacey.

Yeah, try smiling a little. "No." Lacey looked right at her. "Thank you for your patience. You have a nice day." She grabbed the printout and walked out. When she got within a block of Danny's office, she stopped to sit on a bench at a bus stop so she could look at the printout. Her eyes scanned page after page after page of withdrawals. "What in the world…?" The rest of the words got caught in her throat. Over the last six weeks, there had been withdrawals almost every night. The first few were twenty dollars; then they grew to forty, sixty, and the last five had been one hundred and twenty each. Lacey watched her tears spill onto the printout. Anger replaced her tears. Her eyes widened when she saw some of the times of the withdrawals. *Three o'clock in the morning! My son is out on the streets at three a.m. Who is he? How could he do this?* She set the printout aside again and sat there unable to formulate a complete thought, totally at a loss at what to do. "I've got to get back to work," she told herself.

She lit a cigarette and got up and began walking. She needed to talk to someone. She decided to call Clint. She was relieved when he picked up the phone. She started crying and talking at the same time until Clint stopped her and told her to calm down so he could understand her. She took a deep breath and relayed the news of the withdrawals, including the times.

"Damn it. What has gotten into him?"

"That's the million-dollar question."

"I just don't know why he would do this," Clint repeated. "That's one thing I've never done, is steal from my own mother. I'm going to check into some things, Lacey, and I'll get back to you. But I think we need to get him some help. He needs his butt kicked is what he needs." Silence filled the air. "I'll call you back."

"Clint, don't…" He had already hung up. The discovery had zapped her energy, and the only thing she wanted was a rock to hide under. She walked the rest of the way to Danny's office and lit another cigarette. Her thoughts were racing as she stood there, and then she remembered her counseling appointment. *Crap; I've got to cancel it.* She dialed Daniel's number and took two more deep puffs while waiting for him or his voice mail to pick up. She could barely hear the ringing on the other end because of all the traffic. His voice mail finally picked up. "Hey, Daniel, it's Lacey. I'm down in L. A. on that case, and it looks like we're going to be going later than usual today, so I can't make it this evening. Give me a call so we can reschedule for next week. I really need to talk to you." She hung up and dialed Sophie and explained the same thing to her.

"Don't worry. He'll be fine here," Sophie assured her.

"Can you make sure he does his homework? And tell him that…"

"Tell him what?"

That I'm going to wring his stinking neck. "Never mind, just tell him I'll get home as soon as I can."

"I've got it covered. Have a good rest of the day. I'll see you when you get here."

"Thanks, Sophie. I'll call you when I'm on the train." She put her cigarette in the outdoor ashtray, reached in her purse for her hand lotion and poured a generous amount out to smooth over on her arms and hands. "I can still smell those nasty things," she muttered under her breath. She took her perfume out and dosed herself with a couple of squirts. *That's better.* Satisfied that she didn't smell like an ashtray, she went back to work.

Lacey leaned forward and began editing the transcript. The deposition had ended much quicker than they had all thought. She listened with half an ear as Danny and Julie talked about the plaintiff's explanation for not wanting to divulge his address on the record. He had been beaten nearly to death twice and he suspected the defendants, so they were discussing how to handle the transcript. Lacey shook her head and turned her complete attention to her editing and her own problems, namely the newest development with Jake. Danny's voice moved her thoughts to the back of her mind.

"You ready, Lacey?"

"Sure."

"We're back on the record."

Lacey reported verbatim their agreed-upon stipulation, then saved the file and shut down her computer. She began packing up, wasting no time so she could catch the 4:40 train. *I'll still get home by six, plenty of time to have a picnic dinner at the park, or eat out on the back patio, then I can catch him off guard and let him know I found out about him stealing money and sneaking out at all hours of the night.*

"See you tomorrow, Lacey."

Lacey pulled herself out of her head. "See you tomorrow, Julie." She finished zipping up her laptop bag as the conference room door closed.

"How about I take you out for a nice dinner?" Danny asked.

Lacey hesitated.

"Come on. You deserve to relax, and then I'll take you to the train station afterwards."

Lacey stood there in a mental tug of war between her own wants and her responsibilities. "Well, I did call my girlfriend and tell her we were going to be working later tonight."

Danny tugged at her selfish side. "Then it's already set up. They're not expecting you anyway. You can't be all work and no play all the time, 'Ms. Court Reporter.'"

Lacey smiled and walked out the door that he held open for her.

He led her to his car and took her laptop and put it in the backseat and then opened her door. Lacey watched him as he walked around. *A BMW 745, nice!* He got in, and suddenly Lacey was keenly aware of just how close he was. They hadn't even sat this close at dinner in Pasadena, and he'd been a perfect gentleman, ending their date with just a little peck on the cheek. Looking at him now, Lacey knew in her gut that that was going to change. "I like your car." *Oh that was lame.*

Danny smiled and started it up. "It's a great car—fast, dependable, and good looking." He looked right at her and then began to back up.

That's probably just the way you like your women, too. "I've always wanted a Beamer; maybe someday."

"Maybe that's the car you should get to replace your Solara."

"We'll see." *Not!*

They rode the short distance to the restaurant in comfortable silence, and when he pulled up to the Bonaventure Hotel valet parking, Lacey tried to hide her excitement. A valet attendant opened her door, and she got out as if she'd frequented the hotel every other day of her life. Danny led them up a never-ending escalator and to a small table in the famous BonaVista revolving cocktail lounge. When the waiter had come and taken their drink orders, Lacey exclaimed how beautiful the view was.

Danny smiled knowingly. "Haven't you ever been here before?"

Lacey shook her head. "No, but I've heard about it, of course." She looked out and was mesmerized by the panoramic view of the city. She barely noticed the waiter who brought their wine and quietly slipped away.

They began talking about the case and another waiter came over to them and told Danny that their dining table was ready. They got up, and Lacey followed the waiter. Danny was right behind her with their glasses of wine. She felt giddy with it all. Just an hour ago, she was making plans to go home and deal with Jake. Now, here she was being escorted into the famous Prime Steakhouse for dinner, and with a well-known attorney no less. *Please don't let me trip.* The waiter guided them to their table, and Lacey caught her breath as she took in another spectacular view. Danny set down their wine glasses and reached over and pulled her chair out for her.

They were sipping their wine, enjoying easy conversation when a waiter returned for their order. They both laughed and admitted they hadn't even looked at the menu. Danny asked the waiter to give them just a couple minutes.

"What do you feel like having?" he asked.

Lacey set her wine down and realized she wasn't that hungry. The view, the wine and his company were more than enough to fill her up. She looked over the menu. "I'm really not that hungry, so maybe something light. What would you suggest?" She looked across the table at him. He was engrossed in the menu, and Lacey took advantage of the moment. He wasn't great looking, but he was handsome. His sandy brown hair lay just above his ears and was parted to the side and gave him a sort of clean-cut look. His eyes were like a hazel green, almost dull, that is, until he smiled. He was tall and stocky, not fat by any means. Suddenly he looked up, as if he could feel her eyes on him. Lacey thought about putting her head down but couldn't. She continued to look into his eyes, charging the current between them until she was locked in his gaze.

Danny interrupted the electrifying flow. "Would you be offended if I ordered for you?"

Lacey reached for her wine and took a sip. "No, not at all." The view held her in a state of relaxation and she was only half-listening to Danny when he gave the waiter their order. Their conversation continued to be easy and comfortable through dinner. "That salmon was absolutely delicious, Danny. Good choice."

"Why thank you." The waiter had taken their dinner plates away and was bringing them another glass of wine. Danny brought his chair closer to hers and took her hand. "Look," he whispered in her ear.

Lacey looked up in the direction he was pointing and gasped. The sun was setting and the picture it painted up there on the thirty-fourth floor was absolutely beautiful. Lacey realized it had to be the most romantic thing she had ever experienced. "I've traveled a lot of places and seen a lot of things," she said, "but I don't think I've ever seen a view quite so beautiful." She turned to tell him thank you and he was right there. He kissed her then, just a simple, short kiss on the lips. It was an incredibly sweet moment. She pulled away, just an inch or two. "Thank you," she whispered.

"You're welcome. Now let's get you to your car."

Lacey started to object and tell him there was still one more train but he interrupted her by placing his index finger over her lip. "I'm not about to put you on a train in L. A. at this hour."

"Okay. I'll call Sophie and tell her I'm on my way."

"Jake, are you finished with your room?" He was standing in the door of the refrigerator with his back to her. He reached in the crisper and began pulling out all the salad stuff, and when he closed the refrigerator, he finally answered her.

"Kind of," he said. He reached for a cucumber and grabbed the peeler and began to peel it.

Her frustration over what she'd discovered was mounting, but she was waiting until she'd done all her homework before telling him that she knew he'd been sneaking out at night and stealing money from her account. Now she was locking up her purse at night and using a new code on the alarm, and all she'd told him was she was trying some new company out so she wasn't allowed to give it to him. At least he hadn't gotten out since.

Lacey stared at him standing at the counter as if seeing him for the first time in weeks. She smiled and shook her head, perplexed at how tall he'd gotten in the past two weeks. She sat down on one of the barstools and watched him create his pre-lunch snack.

"What are you smiling at, little Mama?"

Lacey reveled in moments like this, when he was so approachable and light-hearted. "I'm just wondering when you grew the extra six or so inches. You look so tall all of a sudden."

Jake finished cutting up the peeled cucumber and scattered the slices in his bowl of baby greens. "So maybe that's why my shoes don't fit."

Lacey caught the twinkle in his eyes. "Jake, you're not trying to tell me you already have a hole in your skate shoes, are you?"

"Well, yeah, but maybe the hole's because my feet are growing too." He put his head down, pretending to be concentrating on his salad as he tossed tomatoes, olives, sunflower seeds, and croutons in.

Lacey didn't bother to argue with him about the fact that his shoes weren't even two months old, that he should be taking better care of them, and that she had to work hard for the money that paid for those shoes. When he was so adorable like this, she felt like she would do anything for him. "Well, make them last at least until next weekend, okay?"

Jake had a mouthful of salad so he gave her a thumbs-up sign.

"So while you clean your room, I'll go get some groceries, and then I was thinking we'd go over to Adam's so you can hang out with him and I can visit with Martha and Doug. Sound good?"

Jake swallowed another bite of salad and nodded his head yes at the same time.

"Okay. We'll leave in an hour then, but only if you get your room done."

Lacey let herself into the condo. It was quiet. She looked around and let out a deep sigh, enjoying the silence. It had been good to see Martha and Doug. Jake and Adam were still inseparable as ever, and they convinced Lacey and Martha that Jake needed to spend the night because he hadn't been over since being on restriction. "I might as well take advantage of this time and get some work done." She headed to her office. The shrill of the phone turned her around.

"Hello."

The static on the other end was loud.

"Hello," Lacey repeated.

"Lacey, it's Danny."

"Hi, Danny, how are you?"

"Well, I was actually getting ready to go to the Cabazon Outlet Mall for some shopping, which means I'll be passing by your place on my way. Would you like to join me?"

Lacey hesitated.

"Come on, you can't let a guy go shopping alone. No telling what I'll wind up with."

Lacey laughed at his logic. She gave him directions and hung up the phone. She stood still for a minute, thinking about the change in their relationship. The pace was picking up speed at a good rate, not too slow and not too fast. She looked at the clock and moved into supersonic speed. One and a half hours later, her entire house had been vacuumed, and the downstairs had been cleaned. Now she stood in her kitchen, showered and dressed, sipping a glass of iced tea.

The doorbell rang and halted her thoughts. She set her glass down on the counter and headed for the door. Her steps were slow, but her heart was racing.

"Well, don't you look adorable," he greeted.

Lacey blushed. "Thanks. You look great yourself. Would you like to come in for a minute?"

He walked toward her, and she shut the door. He pulled her to him, nearly lifting her off her feet.

His strong embrace surprised Lacey, and as he began to nuzzle her neck, she became a little uncomfortable. She turned to look at him, but because he was so much taller, her eyes landed on his chest. She smelled his cologne, which was intoxicating. She lifted her gaze to break the trance, and his mouth came down on hers, gentle at first and then more passionate. She could feel the pulse from his chest reverberating on hers, matching the rhythm of their long and fervent kiss, which was sending sparks down her body.

He brought their kiss to a slow halt, and Lacey burrowed her face in his chest, a little dizzy from it all. "Whew, that was some hello," she admitted breathlessly.

Danny laughed as he guided her to the ground. "Yeah, tell me about it." He winked.

"Would you like some iced tea?"

"That sounds great."

He followed her to the kitchen and stood at the bar and watched her. "Nice place. I really like how you decorated it."

"Thanks. It's been fun. I think what's made it even better is it's mine. I don't have to worry about asking someone's permission to do things." She handed him his glass of tea and refilled hers.

"So where's Jake?"

"He's at his best friend's house actually, something he hasn't done for a while because of being on restriction and all. As a matter of fact, I had just gotten home when you called me."

Danny put his glass down and walked around the counter, toward her. "Well, that was perfect timing, then."

There was no mistaken his sultry tone, and Lacey could see the heat in his eyes as he came closer. She reached for his hand as a way of distraction. "Come on. Let me show you around." She took him into the formal dining and living area.

"Who plays the piano?"

"Jake." She let go of his hand and walked down the hall so she could show him the photos on the wall.

He looked at the photos somewhat obligatorily and then took her hand and turned her so that her back was to the wall, and he was directly in front of her. "So are you going to show me the upstairs?" His voice was just above a whisper.

Before she could protest, his mouth came down on hers again, his hands reaching under her arms and sliding her ever so gently up the wall. Her feet were a few inches from the ground, making it easier for his body to press into hers. The kiss lingered, and Lacey felt him beneath her. The Voice pulled her gently from her senses. *Resist him and he will flee from you.* The words were like cold water splashed in her face. Lacey pulled away and pushed her way down.

"What's wrong?" Danny asked.

Lacey was still leaning against the wall, her head tilted up to see if she could detect the anger on his face that she thought she heard in his voice. His eyes were dark, not dull. She ducked under his arm to put some distance between them. "Nothing's wrong. I just don't think it would be a good idea to go any further."

"Well, that's not what your kiss was saying."

Lacey felt the flame of embarrassment on her cheeks. "I'm sorry. I sometimes lose myself in a kiss."

Danny straightened his rumpled shirt and stood straight. "Yeah, well, when you find yourself, give me a call."

Lacey stood there in shock and only moved when she heard her front door close. "Did I just find a boundary and clear up my signal?" she needed to hear herself think. *It feels good, but oh, the cost,* she thought, as she remembered his parting words. She locked her front door, resolving to have a nice evening despite what had just happened. She picked up her phone and called the girls to see if they could get together, feeling better after confirming dinner plans and a movie with all three of them. "Who says I need a man to find myself?"

Harrison picked up on her mood right away. "Okay. Let it out. What's going on?"

Lacey laid down on the bench for the chest press and positioned her hands on the bar. "Not now," she muttered. She indicated she was ready for him to spot her, and he stepped up onto the platform.

He was about to inform her of the amount of weight that he had put on, but she took the bar off the rack and went for it. He positioned his hands underneath and in between hers and counted each one. "Come on, Lacey, two more. You can do it. Blow it out so you can push it up."

Lacey did what he said, taking her frustration and anger out with each press until she had nothing left. She sat up and reached for her water, drying the sweat from her forehead.

"Wow. Do you realize how much weight that was?"

"No, and don't tell me until I do my last two sets." She lay back down and pumped out another set almost as strong as the first one, and then finished her third with just a little help from Harrison.

"That was incredible, Lacey. Now I'll tell you what the weight was. These"—he pointed to the plates on the bar—"are forty-five pounds each, and then the bar is thirty-five, so that means you're lifting your entire body weight!" He reached for her hand to help her up. "So where did you get all that energy from?"

Lacey started talking. "I thought I caught a real winner from the sea of men. You know that attorney I've been telling you about?"

Harrison nodded his head.

"Well, he tried to bite more than the bait, let's just say, and I wasn't handing it over, so…"

"Then let him go. If he comes back, that means he's willing to respect your needs ahead of his own, which will be more than a physical relationship."

"Exactly," Lacey agreed.

"Come on. Let's go in the aerobic room and do some push-ups, and then I want to see your routine."

"Hey, Flo, what's up? Why are you calling me on a Sunday?"

"Well, I don't know what happened, but Danny Kuzac called and asked that you be taken off the case in Los Angeles."

Lacey stopped walking. "What? Did he say why?"

"No. I was hoping you could tell me something."

What am I supposed to say? Lacey thought. Norm didn't have a problem with the reporters dating the attorneys, but she hadn't told him anything about her and Danny. Then again, there hadn't been a lot to tell until now.

"Lacey, are you there?"

"I'm sorry. I was just walking to my car and you caught me off guard."

"Do you want to call me back?"

"No, it's okay. I'm just shocked. I just never pegged him to be a guy like that."

"Pegged him to be a guy like what?" Flo asked.

Lacey gave Flo a condensed version of the events leading up to his leaving her house Saturday afternoon. "So I guess because I won't put out, he wants me to get out."

"Don't worry, Lacey. There's plenty of work," Flo assured her.

"Yeah, but I would love to be a fly on the wall when he's telling Norm about this. Do you think Norm will tell you to stop giving me jobs?"

"He's smarter than that, Lacey. As much as Norm annoys me, I can still give him credit for doing the right thing when it comes to things like this. Just don't worry about it. Take Monday off, and call me for Tuesday."

Lacey dropped Jake off at school, and they had actually made it with four minutes to spare. "Don't forget, I'm not working today, so I'll be here to pick you up." She reached over and gave him a hug. She hadn't told him that she was no longer on the L. A. job because she didn't know how to tell him without telling him the truth, and she didn't want to give him any more ammunition to self-destruct. He would be out of school in a week, so maybe this was a mixed blessing after all. She squeezed him close to her as she thought about the stolen money and her letter of inquiry to the Job Corps requesting information and possible placement for Jake in their program.

"See you later, Mom."

Lacey watched him walk toward the school entrance and was surprised when he turned around and smiled and waved. She waved back and pulled away, already focusing on her day and the things she wanted to accomplish.

She went to the gym first, and after her workout, she went to check in with Harrison to let him know what she'd done, and she saw Daryn walking toward her. She waved to him, trying to look nonchalant but too busy for chitchat. Her attempt failed. He blocked her path toward Harrison.

"So, how are you?" he asked.

"I'm okay. How's Daryk?"

"He's going to be fine. He really misses you. His mom and I still have him on restriction, and we're keeping a close eye on him. Even his stepdad is working with us instead of against us, so I guess you could say there's been some good that's come out of it all."

Lacey took a sip of her water. "That's a good way of looking at it. Well, I better get going. I have a full day ahead of me." She started to walk forward and he moved with her.

"There is one thing I'd like to know."

"What's that, Daryn?"

"Why'd you end it with me?"

Lacey was looking at everything and everyone but him. He reached over and waved his hand close to her face. "Can't you at least give me that, Lacey?"

"I just don't think our boys were good for each other, and I need to be more attentive to Jake's needs than my own right now." *Besides, you make me uncomfortable.* She smiled to lessen the blow and erase her unspoken thought.

He shortened the space between them. "Well, I want you to know that I miss hanging out with you."

Lacey was caught off guard by his obvious sadness. "Thanks, Daryn. I've got to go." This time when she went to move forward, he didn't stop her. She passed by Harrison's office and saw that he was with a client so she stuck her head in and waved.

Harrison excused himself from his client and hurried toward her. "You're here early today. Is everything okay?"

She swallowed the many mixed emotions that were threatening to surface, determined to not wear them on her face. "Yeah, I just got a day off, so I thought I'd come in and finish my training early. I need to be available for Jake later."

"Great. I was going to call you and let you know that starting Saturday, you have to increase your cardio from thirty minutes twice a day to forty-five minutes. And that's six days a week, by the way."

Lacey made a face and groaned her disapproval. "And here I thought you just wanted to say 'hi.'"

Harrison smiled and squeezed her shoulder. "I gotta run. See you Wednesday night."

"Wait, could we make that Thursday? I'm doing something on Wednesday nights now."

Harrison turned and nodded yes. "Just give me a call later so we can schedule it."

Lacey thanked him and headed out of the gym and toward the rest of her day. She went over her mental checklist: grocery shopping, dry cleaners, Starbucks, and then home to make the call to Job Corps. The call loomed over her like a stormy cloud as she sped out of the gym parking lot and toward the grocery store.

Lacey stared at the faxed information from the Job Corps. The phone rang and she picked it up, her hand feeling almost as heavy as her heart. "Hello."

"Hi, this is James from Mercury Insurance."

Her stomach dropped. "Hi, James, how are you?"

"I'm great. Thanks for asking, but I won't waste your time. I know you're a busy lady. I just wanted to let you know that I've found a way around this dilemma with your son."

"You have?"

"Yes, I believe so. All it's going to take is you signing an exclusion form for the life of your policy with us."

"What does that mean?"

"The form just states that Jake will be excluded from your policy, which means he will not be allowed to drive any of your future cars until he reaches the age of eighteen, and if he is caught driving and something happens, Mercury will not be liable for the damages.

Lacey's heart soared for the first time in weeks. "And then that's it; this will be all over?"

"Yep, that's it, and then Mercury will be paying off your car and issuing you a check for twenty-two hundred dollars."

That's almost the entire down payment! Lacey breathed a sigh of relief and started to cry. "Thank you, James. Thank you so much."

"My pleasure, Lacey. Oh, and one more thing; you'll have just a few days from the day you receive this final check to turn the rental in and get yourself another car, so you might want to start shopping."

One Leg out of the Nest

Lacey pulled into the parking lot of Red Hill Park.

"Why are we coming here, Mom?" Jake asked.

Lacey parked the car and struggled to keep her voice as calm as possible. "Because we need to talk." They got out and Lacey led the way to an empty spot just over the rise of a hill. Her heart was heavy, and she was still apprehensive about how to start this much-needed confrontation. She had intentionally waited until his last day of school, and now she knew in her gut that she couldn't put it off any longer. She stopped under a huge elm tree and bent down to feel the grass. It was dry. "Pull up a seat." She tried to smile. She sat down and took in a breath of fresh air. She looked up and saw Jake standing there and patted a spot across from her.

Jake sat close to the spot she indicated.

Lacey let out a big sigh. She decided to change gears for a minute before plunging in. "So it looks like I'm going to be getting another car soon."

Jake pulled at some grass. "Have you even been shopping?"

Évinda Lepins

"Well, sort of."

Jake looked puzzled.

Lacey went on to explain. "A client from the agency recommended a broker who shops for you and buys the car you want from the dealer. Then he sells it to you for a few hundred bucks over invoice. So I don't have to hassle with any of the negotiations or anything."

"That's cool."

"So it will be even quicker than when we got the convertible," she added. *Was that a flicker of pain or guilt I just saw go running across his face?* She wondered. Lacey leaned back, refreshed by the breeze, but the tension mounted. "Anyway, I'm hoping to have a new car within a couple weeks so I can turn in this rental."

Lacey looked at him, and his head was down. He was sitting with his legs out to the side, one arm holding him up while the other hand was free to pull at the grass. "So the reason I brought you here is this." She pulled the printout from her purse and handed it to him.

Jake sat up and took it. "What's this?"

"It's a printout for my savings account."

The color drained from his face, and he put his head back down and his eyes on the paper.

She sat there listening to the sound of children's laughter, birds singing and the breeze rustling the leaves in the trees. Those sounds normally calmed her, made her smile, but not today. Today it felt like those sounds were from another world, a faraway world because they represented happiness and contentment, and right now, Lacey was anything but happy.

"Why, Jake?" Lacey stared at him intently, looking for signs of remorse, admission, something.

He looked up and gave her a blank stare.

She put her head down and visualized her own mental tug of war between calmness and anger. Part of her wanted to really let him have it, and part of her wrestled with seeing him struggle.

She wasn't about to make it easy for him. She reached for the printout and took it back. "I don't get it, Jake. Not only have you been stealing from me, but you've been doing it at all hours of the night."

Jake popped his head up and stared past Lacey and mumbled something incoherent.

"What did you say?"

He glared at her. "I said that was a long time ago."

"Jake, the last time was just a couple of weeks ago, and it went on for weeks prior to that. The only reason it hasn't happened in the last two weeks is because I changed the alarm code on you."

He picked his head up again and glared at her.

"So what did you do with my money, Jake? And I want the truth."

The children's laughter sounded louder, the birds' singing more uninhibited in the silence between them. Finally he spoke.

"I used it for pot for me and my friends," he blurted out.

Lacey was speechless, reeling from the sucker-punch. She was trying to grasp the realization that her money had been used for his self-destruction and others' too. The bitter taste of betrayal rose from her soul and stayed in her mouth, threatening to mix with her words and make them ugly. The taste was familiar, and as she sat there in silence, the memory of a final confrontation with Jake's dad because of his self-destruction with drugs shook her. She forced herself to swallow the bitter truth and her mom's words wiggled to the surface: *He needs a parent first, not a friend.* "So who are these so-called friends?"

Jake shrugged his shoulders, obviously reluctant to divulge any names, "Just friends from our old house and then a couple friends from school." He sort of faded off and then added, "And Courtney."

"You mean Jenna's daughter, Courtney?"

"No, a friend from school."

Lacey was so shocked she didn't even think to ask where Courtney lived. She kept her voice calm but her words were sharp. "What kind of friends are they that you have to buy them with pot bought with *my* money?"

Jake put his elbows on his knees and dropped his head. The silence between them got louder.

"Well, I've told your dad about this, and he thinks we need to find you some help."

"What's that supposed to mean?" Jake grumbled.

"It means just what I said, Jake. You need help. You keep choosing to head down the wrong path, and I don't know how to help you."

"Then send me to my dad's."

Lacey looked up, feeling like she had gotten the wind knocked out of her and her heart stomped on at the same time. "I don't think that's a good idea, Jake."

"You used to say I was just like him, so why don't you let me go live with him?"

Lacey was stunned by his accusation. "Look at me, Jake."

He kept his head down.

"Jake, please," Lacey prodded gently.

He looked up slowly.

"Do you believe that I want the best for you?"

He shrugged his shoulders and dropped his head again.

She reached across and put her first two fingers under his chin to bring his eyes level with hers. "Jake, I don't know how to fix this." She dropped her hold under his chin but not her stare. *Just like I couldn't fix your father.* She shook her head to ward off the thoughts. Tears spilled down his cheeks, and she pulled him to her.

"I'm sorry." He sobbed. "I'm sorry."

Time stood still while Lacey held him as he cried, her own tears streaming silently down her face until he pulled away, completely cried out and at a loss for words.

"Do you really want to go live with your dad?" Lacey could see so many emotions running across his face, and his eyes started to fill again. She continued to watch him, and then she saw it, a twinge of hope that clashed with a speck of fear. She stood up and held her hand out to him to help him up. "Come on. We both have a lot to think about."

"Jake, it's time for dinner," Lacey yelled from the kitchen. When she heard his steps on the stairs, she dished out his chicken and rice. "Here you go, and the salad's on the counter. I thought we'd eat outside tonight."

Jake put salad on a separate plate, grabbed some silverware, and went outside. Lacey put a couple bites on her plate, got a soda out of the refrigerator for Jake and a bottle of water for herself, and joined him outside. Lacey noticed he had waited for her. This time she said the blessing.

"Amen," Jake said. He looked at her plate. "Gee, Mom, birds eat more than you do."

Lacey recognized his attempt to tease her and wondered if he was being manipulative. "Chirp, chirp," she bantered back. She wasn't one to eat when she was stressed or unhappy, and tonight was no exception. She had talked to Clint when they had come home from the park and they had argued for a long time. He wanted Jake to come live with him, but Lacey didn't trust him. It was as simple as that. "So I talked with your dad earlier."

Jake stopped his fork in midair. "And what happened?"

"Well, there's been no decision yet. I need some time to think about it and research a couple of other options."

He finished taking his bite. "Okay. Could we change the subject now?"

"Yeah, let's change the subject. So how's Shellie?"

"She's good. She's been ticked off at me for a couple of days, though."

"Why?"

"I told her what I did."

Lacey was enjoying his blunt but innocent honesty. "Didn't she know you were doing it?"

"She sort of knew it."

It was Lacey's turn to be confused.

"I'd tell her I was sneaking out, but not what I did or how I did it, or who I went and saw," he added.

"Oh, so you didn't tell her about going and seeing Courtney?"

Jake shook his head.

"And so what did she say when you told her about sneaking out?"

"Well, she made me promise never to do any of it again." Jake took a huge bite of his salad.

I think I like this girl Shellie. "Well, you need to be around as many positive influences as you can. If you hang around people that do crappy things, then you're gonna start smelling too." Her tone sounded sharp even to her own ears. "Hey, we were supposed to change the subject."

Jake smiled. "So Ollie's Board Shop might sponsor me."

Lacey put her fork down. "Jake, that's awesome. You have gotten pretty good on that thing."

Jake accepted the compliment with a smile and put the last bite of salad in his mouth.

Lacey let out a sigh, grateful for the reprieve in the tension. "So what do you say you show me some of those skateboard moves after dinner?"

The week had gone by slowly. In between jobs, Lacey was searching online for some sort of help for Jake. It was overwhelming to see all the different programs and frustrating at the same time because not one of them was a fit. They were either too expensive, too far away, or he was too young. There had been a couple of Christian programs that were fairly close, but they were filled up so they had put Jake on a waiting list and told Lacey to keep checking back. She had gotten the information from the Job Corps, but the required age was sixteen years old, so that had been crossed off her list with a silent prayer that by the time he reached sixteen, this would be behind them.

She was also juggling spending time with him without making it look so obvious that she was watching him like a hawk. She had him go with her on her usual errands, to the bank, grocery shopping, and they made a couple trips to Best Buy where he looked at CDs while she shopped for court reporting supplies. She had even thought of taking him to counseling with her, but then decided against it. Instead, she cancelled her last two appointments because she didn't have the energy. He was on his best behavior, keeping up with the terms of the contract, which now included him not being allowed to hang out with anybody or have anyone over unless she knew about it. Adam, Shellie, Zach, and David Michael were allowed to come over, but that was only when she was home. It was tough to entertain a teenager, but in some respects, she was enjoying being with him.

Lacey let out a heavy sigh and reached for the phone to dial her office. "Hi, Flo, I'm calling for my job assignment for tomorrow."

"Well, as a matter of fact, we had a new client call and request you tomorrow. She's house counsel for All State Insurance."

"Get out." Lacey interrupted her. "Are you talking about Jillian?"

"Let me check the notice. Hold on."

Lacey began dusting her desk while she waited for Flo to come back.

"You're right. Her name is Jillian."

"That's great. She must have gotten us approved. She was a client of mine when I owned my own agency, and we became friends. I haven't talked to her for a while, though."

"I keep forgetting that you had your own agency before. Anyway, the job starts at ten and then there's a one o'clock also."

"Great." Lacey quickly wrote the information down and her curiosity got the best of her. "So has there been any word from Danny? Did you get his job covered?"

"Well, we've sent a couple different reporters out to him, and they've both come back complaining he's too hard to work with, so we're still trying to find a reporter that will stay on the job."

Lacey smiled. *Serves you right, sucker.*

"But don't worry. It will be fine," Flo assured her.

"Thanks, Flo, and thanks for keeping me working."

Lacey hung up the phone and went upstairs to tell Jake she was headed for the gym.

Lacey turned her computer on, and logged into her AOL account. She clicked the icon for the "Thirty-something single parent chat room." Almost every night for the last two weeks, Lacey had been visiting the site, and it gave her something to look forward to. She had joined it unintentionally when she was trying to Google information about another potential program for Jake and saw a pop-up Ad for it. Now it had become somewhat of an addiction. It was fun, uninhibiting, and safe. The first time had been a little awkward but within thirty minutes, she had been pulled into the conversation by many of the chatters. Since then, she had chatted with innumerable single parents about the ups and downs of parenting, dead-beat dads, and even about dating.

Out of the many people that came to the chat room, there were just a few that she really connected with, two of which were single moms. One of them lived in Nevada and had a ten-year-old son, and the other lived just a couple hours away in Long Beach and had a fifteen-year-old daughter. There was also a single dad of two toddlers who lived in Canada that joined them a couple times a week, a sort of shy guy who didn't say too much, but when he put his comments out there, everyone responded. Recently an engineer for Nokia who lived in Colorado had joined their chat room. He didn't have any kids, but he said he was single. Lacey couldn't figure out at first why he had joined their chat room because the common denominator was kids, but after several chat sessions, he revealed that the girl he had recently broken up with had a teenaged boy and he actually had some good things to offer about teenagers every now and then.

Lacey was fascinated with the concept of talking with people through a keyboard, especially since she made a living producing a record from her court reporting keyboard. She loved to type what she really felt and then press the send button, wondering who would respond out there in the cyber world. She was uninhibited when it came to sharing her frustrations and completely at ease to offer opinions when asked. It was amazing how much better she felt every time she logged off, knowing she wasn't the only struggling single parent out there.

She signed in. "Hey, everyone. How was your day?" She got comfortable in her chair and sorted through her mail while she waited for a response. She didn't have long to wait. She looked up and several of them had welcomed her in. The single mom in Nevada asked how Jake was doing, and Lacey filled them in on the latest endeavors to try to find a program that would help him. Surprisingly, the Nokia engineer from Colorado jumped in and asked if she had tried the Job Corps, and Lacey wrote back that she actually had but he wasn't old enough yet. Lacey asked each of them about their kids; then, as not to leave the Nokia guy out, she asked him about his job.

Before she knew it, it was after eleven. Lacey told everyone she needed to sign off and said good night. She was just about to sign off when she received another message from the Nokia engineer. "Would you mind if we exchanged e-mail addresses? I'd like to talk with you more outside of this chat room."

Lacey stared at the words on the screen. "What could be the harm in that?" she asked aloud. "It's not like he knows where

I live." She responded back with her e-mail address and said good night.

He obviously liked to have the last word because he sent her a smiley face back with a "ttys." She signed off and went to get ready for bed.

Lacey walked into the quiet house and dropped her laptop on the couch. It had been a long day and she was exhausted, but it had been great to work with Jillian again. They had even gone to lunch and caught up on each of their lives. Jillian had just broken it off with a guy she'd been seeing for about six weeks so she was back to single again, independent as ever and really involved with her horses, her seventeen dogs and twelve cats. Lacey filled her in on what had been going on since they had last seen each other, which was right before she broke it off with Ian. They shared some laughs about the men in and out of their lives, and at the end of the deposition, Jillian invited her and Jake to come horseback riding with her some weekend.

Lacey grabbed a bottle of water from the refrigerator and walked toward the patio. "Jake, I'm home." She strained to listen for signs of him. There was no sound coming from anywhere except the quiet hum of the air conditioning. She opened the window. He wasn't in the backyard. "Hmm, that's strange," Lacey murmured. She walked upstairs to see if he was sleeping. She was so convinced that he was sleeping that she tiptoed down the hall to his room. She opened his room and was surprised to see that he wasn't there. Her eyes scanned the room. There were no clothes on the floor. There were no empty cups or soda cans on the nightstand. In fact, the room looked really good, better than contract condition. She looked over at his neatly made bed and there in the middle of it was an envelope. She stood frozen for a few seconds, and as she walked toward the bed, chills of fearful premonition ran down her spine. She looked at the writing on the outside of the envelope. It just said "Mom." She turned her envelope over. It was sealed. "Where are you, Jake?" she whispered.

She was about to rip open the letter but then remembered that there had been two missed calls from Clint while she'd been working. She ran downstairs and grabbed her cell phone to see what time he had called. One was at 1:40, and the last one was just a little over two hours ago. She hit the call back button, and Clint picked up on the first ring.

"Lacey, is that you?"

"Yes, it's me. What's going on?"

"Where have you been? I've been trying to reach you since one thirty."

"I worked today, Clint, and both times you called, I was on the record."

"Don't you get a lunch break?"

"Yeah, and you called after I'd already taken it." "What's up?" She had changed her mind about asking if he knew where Jake was, at least for the moment.

"I just wanted to give you a heads-up. Jake called me about one fifteen this afternoon, and he was really upset. He said he was going to catch the next train out here because he couldn't take it anymore out there."

"Well, didn't you tell him he couldn't do that?"

"I did, in so many words."

"What in the heck is that supposed to mean?"

"I told him it wouldn't be a good idea; that he needed to wait until you got home and talk to you about it. He was pretty upset, though, and he kept saying he was a screw-up."

The fear returned and trickled down her spine as Lacey looked at the envelope. "Did he say anything specific?"

"I can't really remember how he put it, something about he was tired of screwing up. Did he leave you any note or anything?"

"Well, as a matter of fact, I'm holding a letter addressed to me."

"Did you read it?" Clint asked.

"No, I didn't, not yet."

Clint cut her off. "Wait a minute. So he's really not there?"

Lacey hesitated until she couldn't stretch the silence any more. "I just came home from work and he's not here, but I talked to him as soon as I got out of my depo and told him I was on my way home. He sounded okay," Lacey added, trying to speak to her own fears more than Clint.

"Well maybe the letter will tell us where he is or what's going on."

Lacey stared at it and didn't even have to open it to know whatever was inside wasn't good. She held it up toward the sunlight to see if she could see any of the writing.

"Lacey, are you there?"

"Yeah, I was just—" She stopped midsentence when she heard the front door slam. "I think he just walked in, Clint. I'll call you back." She hung up without waiting for his good-bye. She practically ran out of his room, and by the time she had made it to the landing of the stairs, there he was, just beginning to come up the stairs, heavy-footed and obviously heavy-hearted. "Where have you been?"

He stopped in the middle of the stairs and looked up. "I was going to go to my dad's."

Lacey let herself down on the top step and motioned for him to join her.

Jake made his way up and sat beside her. He extended his hand. "Can I have that letter back?"

"Not right now, but why don't you at least tell me what's in the letter."

"Nothing, it's pretty stupid."

"Jake, if something was bothering you enough to put it in a letter and then leave, it's not stupid."

"I was just telling you I'm sorry and that maybe I should go to my dad's." He paused. "At least I won't be a burden to you anymore," he mumbled and looked away. She stared at him and struggled to see him struggling. His eyes spoke of pain and sadness and Lacey couldn't take it. "You're not a burden, Jake."

He lifted his head up, and his expression clearly said he didn't believe her.

She scooted closer to him and brought her face within inches of his. "You're the most important person in my life."

Jake said nothing and put his head back down.

"So how about if you go visit your dad for the summer?"

Jake's head came up abruptly, and he began to cry openly.

"Jake, what's the matter? I thought that's what you wanted."

He put his head back down and mumbled incoherently.

Lacey put her head down close to his, straining to hear. "I can't hear what you're saying, Jake."

He lifted his head. "I said it is, but I don't want to hurt you." He paused. "And I'm going to miss my friends and…" He faded off.

"And Shellie," Lacey finished for him.

He smiled for the first time but then put his head into his hands, obviously torn.

"Well, it's just a visit; you're not going there to live. It's only for the summer," she assured him while she tried to convince herself. "But you have to come back for my contest. Is that a deal?"

He grabbed her four fingers and put his knuckles to her knuckles, his thumb to her thumb to seal the deal.

"Bruce, can I talk to you for a minute?"

Bruce was hurriedly setting up the chairs for the youth group. "Sure. Just give me a minute to finish this."

Lacey walked over to the pile of chairs and began to help him set them up. They worked quietly and quickly until the last row was complete. Lacey looked at all of the chairs. "Wow, that many kids come here?"

"Usually. The kids keep bringing their friends, so we're really growing. I'm going to go grab Frankie, and we can go into the library. We'll meet you in there.

Lacey walked into the library, and they followed within a couple of minutes. Frankie greeted her with a hug and the two of them sat on the couch, and Bruce sat across from them. Lacey cleared her throat. "I just wanted to say thank you for all of your help with Jake." She had to stop for a few seconds to let the lump in her throat subside. She continued, "There's been a lot going on over the last month or so."

Frankie scooted closer to her and took her hand, and Lacey filled them both in on the events of the last several weeks. "He wants to go stay with his dad, but I'm really thinking that it's not the right place for him to be. I don't know how to explain that to Jake without bad-mouthing his dad, but I've told him that he can go for the summer."

Bruce was the first to speak when she had finished. "Well, first of all, I think it's a good idea that you call it a summer visit." He looked at Frankie and then to Lacey. "He needs his dad, Lacey, because a dad's role in a child's life is the framework, so to speak, and he's been without that for too long. We'll just have to pray that this will be a time of building a good framework for Jake. Maybe you can visit him," he added with a smile. "And make sure you call him often."

What he said made sense to Lacey.

"But don't forget, things go better with prayer. Don't do any of it without praying, Lacey." He looked at his watch. "I've got to get in there; the kids are starting to get pretty loud."

Lacey and Frankie stood up and Frankie hugged Lacey to her. "We'll be praying for you, Lacey, and for Jake."

"Thank you, both of you." Lacey wiped at her eyes. "I'd better get in the sanctuary. I'm already a couple minutes late." Lacey left the library and walked toward the sanctuary definitely more encouraged about her decision to let Jake go to his dad's.

The speaker was already standing up front and the pastor was walking off stage as Lacey tiptoed in and went to the same seat she'd taken the week before.

The speaker scanned the audience and welcomed them back for part two of Relationships the Right Way. "So last week we touched on some important things to remember during our season of singleness, and tonight what I'd like to share with you is the ideal chronology of a relationship. Now the only way to have an ideal chronology in a relationship is to be in a relationship with J. C. here." She walked to the corner of the stage and brought the same cardboard cutout she'd introduced last week. She looked out into the audience. "I see He hasn't changed."

Lacey didn't understand the audience's laughter, but she wasn't the only one.

"For those of you who didn't get that little pun, His availability and love for us never changes, and I'll explain that when I conclude tonight."

Good, Lacey thought.

The speaker looked up from her notes. "So the first step in a relationship is acquaintances, which are people we see every so often, say 'hi' to in passing, but never really engage with, unless we choose to. When and if we choose to, then we move to the second level. That is what we term a 'working' relationship. Two of the most common examples of this type of relationship are coworkers, classmates, et cetera. The significance of the connection here is that we may share personal information because of the amount of time we spend together, but it is limited by how much risk we are willing to take.

"From the working relationship level, we choose our friendships. Now, friendship is real and always honest. We are more willing to take risks, understanding that we are going to hurt each other at times, but in true friendship, we desire to reconcile our differences and we desire to see each other as we *really* are. It is *other* centered and requires the investment of time." She looked out into the audience. "My point is you can't really know someone unless there is time spent with them." She pointed to J. C. "The same applies to Him.

"Now, the fourth level is dating, which I have to be honest with you, should truly be saved for marriage, because that's when dating is really necessary, trust me."

The audience laughed with her.

"See, if you think about it, dating outside of marriage is more like a stage, and a stage is for actors and actresses."

That's an interesting analogy, Lacey thought.

"Let me explain that. What are we typically looking for in dating?" She looked out into the audience. "Anybody have any idea?"

"Romance," somebody shouted out.

"Exactly," the speaker answered. "Romance, everybody wants to date for the romance of it all, but let's think about this. What usually happens in dating is the physical gets involved, and when bodies touch, as in the first kiss, we're pulled right in. Our focus changes to always wanting them happy, which really translates, 'I don't want them unhappy with me.' But when unhappiness rears its ugly head, and trust me, it always does, we don't talk about it in this level of dating. Oftentimes, we use sex as a Band-Aid, and then it's all better, for the time being."

Wow, this woman's blunt, Lacey surmised.

"Another negative about dating is that it is not *other* centered, rather it is driven by our insecurities; in other words, it is emotion driven, not dishonest, but certainly not as honest, and now the relationship is based a lot on feelings, and if you haven't figured it out yet, feelings are *not* to be trusted."

Lacey silently agreed with her.

"Now what happens next is we start listening to those undependable feelings that showed themselves on this stage of dating, and then we jump to the next level in the chronology, which is marriage. The success of marriage hinges on how much friendship we experienced before dating. And if we skipped friendship, then chances are that the foundation is built with very little true honesty and the investment is minimal. Another danger of skipping friendship and going right to dating, which is actually a stage to perform our best behavior, is that when the true behavior comes out during the marriage, that honesty about all that your partner is doing wrong comes out in buckets, and I guarantee you, you're not gonna be spilling out your feelings while dressed in a sexy teddy."

Lacey had to laugh at that.

"Unfortunately, many of us go from acquaintance to marriage *way* too quickly, and when we realize this, we don't have a strong enough foundation to go back and build steps two through four. That is why we all need Him." She pulled J. C. closer to her. "Remember when I said earlier that He's always available, and more importantly, that His love never wavers?"

Lacey nodded her head in silent agreement along with everyone else.

"Well, it's a hard concept to grasp, one that we don't want to take advantage of either, but the truth is He doesn't love you more when you are on your best behavior. His love is *not* based on your actions or inactions, but on His character. I can't really explain it and you won't understand it until you make that leap of faith and accept His love for you. Once you're in His love, then you'll begin to understand it. You need to entwine your heart with His."

What's that supposed to mean? Lacey wondered.

"In closing, let me share what I mean with a poem entitled 'Entwine Your Heart with Mine.' These words are for all of you and as you leave tonight, we have a copy of this for each of you." She looked up and out into the audience and then back at her notes and read them the poem.

Lacey reached for her tissue and saw that she wasn't alone in her tears.

"No matter where you are in your life, whether it's in a season of singleness, in a not-so-happy marriage, or even a happy marriage, there are always happier endings with Him." She pointed to J.C. and looked out to the audience. "I'd like to show you the happy ending to the relationship part of my life which took not one try, not even two tries, but three tries. You've heard the saying, 'Third time's a charm'?"

The audience giggled.

"Can I have you dim the lights and play that clip, please."

Lacey leaned forward in her chair. *Happy endings are for everybody else*, she mimicked in her head. As soon as the lights were dimmed, Lacey got up and left. Before she walked out the door, somebody thrust a scroll of paper in her hands. She walked to her car and glanced at her watch. She still had a few minutes before Jake would be out. She got in, turned the light on, and reached for the little scroll. She unrolled it and began to read the words the speaker had recited:

> Oh, my precious daughter, I'm standing at the door of your heart.
>
> I'm waiting for you to invite me in, and I will never depart.
>
> I know you long to be happy; your search for love is in all the wrong places;
>
> You'll never reach that destination while hiding behind all those faces.
>
> Self-fulfillment, self-control, wanting to fit in and overachieving
>
> Are some of the faces you hide behind that stop your heart from believing
>
> That I do have great plans for you, but they begin with you and Me.

I must be the first love in your heart, but you are the one who holds that key.

Yes, you can trust Me with your heart, for I am gentle and kind;

I will never forsake you, daughter, for you're always on My mind.

How will you or can you recognize the man I've chosen for you

To comfort and accompany you on this journey you are passing through

If you won't accept and experience the love I long to bless you with

Then "happily ever after" will always be just a myth.

So seek Me with your whole heart, and everything will be fine.

I will truly bless you as you entwine your heart with Mine.

Lacey rolled the poem back up, thinking about the words she just read. "Maybe that's my problem," she muttered. "I've given too much of my heart to the wrong people, and I just don't think there's anything left to entwine, but I'm willing to try." She dabbed at her eyes and threw both her tissue and the poem in her purse when she saw Jake walking toward the car, hand in hand with Shellie.

"So how was your trip, Mom?"

"It was wonderful."

Lacey could hear the sob in her throat. "Mom, you okay?"

"Not really. I was just thinking it was probably the last road trip we'll ever take together."

Lacey could hear her blowing her nose and then allowed the silence to linger because there were no words to fill it adequately.

"So anything exciting happen while I was gone?" her mom said, changed the subject stoically.

"No, not really," Lacey lied.

"How come I don't believe you?"

"You know me too well. Are you sure you didn't carry me in your womb?"

She chuckled. "So how's the job going with Danny?"

"Oh, well I guess there has been a little bit of excitement while you were gone." Lacey explained what had happened with him, how he had come over and come on to her and she had pushed him away and he had left. "So now I'm off the case. And from what Flo tells me, he's having a hard time keeping a reporter."

"That serves him right. I'm proud of you. You don't need to work with somebody like that." She paused. "So are they still giving you jobs?"

"Oh, I'm staying pretty busy. As a matter of fact, do you remember our All State client Jillian?"

"Sort of."

"She finally got our agency on her approved list, so she's set a few depos with us and I've already worked with her once."

"Now I remember her. She was a good client. She sure is proving her loyalty."

Lacey agreed.

"God has a way of working something good out of something not so good," Mom reminded her.

Lacey realized the truth in that. "Well, there is something else that's happened."

"Oh, what's that?"

"I've made a decision about Jake."

"And what's that?"

"I'm going to let him go stay with his dad for the summer." Lacey started to cry silently.

"Are you sure it's the right thing to do?"

"No, actually I'm not sure. Some days I feel good about it and some days I'm so scared, but I kind of feel like I have no choice." She decided against telling her about Jake's attempt at running away.

"That's a tough spot to be in, honey, and at this point you have to try to do what's best for him and then what's best for you."

"I'm hoping that his dad will step up to the plate, and it will be good for both him and Jake."

"Then that's all you can do. So when's he leaving, and how is that all going to take place?"

Lacey cleared her throat. "He's actually leaving this Saturday—"

Mom interrupted. "This Saturday, do you mean tomorrow?"

"Yes, tomorrow, and Susie and I are going to drive him up there."

"Well, I'm glad you won't have to do it alone." She changed the subject back to their trip.

"Speaking of the trip, I'm meeting with the girls tonight to let them know what's going on."

"And where's Jake going to be?"

"Martha is letting Adam host a little get-together for Jake, so they can all hang out before he leaves."

"Well, try and have a good time, honey. Call me Saturday after you get back."

"I will, Mom."

They hung up and Lacey went to let Jake know she'd be ready to take him to Adam's in half an hour.

The girls met at Island's for drinks and appetizers. They each had their drink and the waiter had just brought their mini hamburgers with caramelized onions and a plate of cheddar fries to go with them. Lacey's mouth watered as she watched them scoop up the fries. The waiter put the Island salad in front of Lacey and smiled. Lacey put her napkin on her lap and tried not to glare at him. She forced herself to return the smile. "Thank you."

"You're welcome." He winked at her. "Can I get you girls anything else?"

The girls said no simultaneously, and Lacey looked up and giggled. "What I'd really like is a big plate of nachos right now."

The waiter looked flustered.

"I'm just kidding," she told him. "We're good. Thank you."

"Okay. Enjoy and I'll be back to check on you."

"You know, Lacey, I'm proud of you for being so disciplined while we're stuffing our faces with this junk food," Sophie said.

"Well, the contest is just a month away, so…" Lacey faded off.

"So why did you decide to let Jake go to his dad's?" Nikki switched the subject, obviously eager for the answer. "David Michael is so bummed."

"Yeah, so is Zach," Sophie added.

Lacey looked across to Susie. She had confided in her earlier in the week about what was going on and she was glad she had. Susie had offered to make the trip with her when she took Jake to his dad's.

"So what's going on?" Sophie prodded.

Lacey debated how much to tell them. She looked at each of them. They had truly been her support system through thick and thin. The one she was most concerned about was Sophie, because Jake and Zach had gotten close and Lacey didn't want Sophie to start thinking bad about Jake. She heaved a heavy sigh and began to explain all of the recent problems she'd been having with Jake.

"Well, that explains some of his behavior, then," Sophie said, "like the crazy amounts of food he ate sometimes, the depression, and lack of motivation. I just thought it was a teenage thing, but then again, Zach struggles with depression because of his dad being in a coma." Her tone became gentle. "At least Jake still has a dad you can send him to. It might turn out to be good for him."

"Thanks, Sophie."

"That means you're gonna have sort of an empty nest all summer," Nikki exclaimed.

Lacey's eyes filled up at the mention of an empty nest.

"You're going to be okay, Peanut," Nikki assured her.

Lacey was wiping at her eyes and trying to swallow the all too familiar lump in her throat. "It's just for the summer, and I'll just work my butt off while he's gone. Between work and training for the contest, I'll stay pretty busy; and before I know it, he'll be back. He is going to come home for the contest though."

"Speaking of which," Susie interrupted, "I've booked a couple of suites at the Rio Hotel where the contest is. You both are still planning to go, right?" She looked at Nikki first.

"You betcha," Nikki said. "I wouldn't miss this for all the tea in China."

Susie looked at Sophie who was laughing with Nikki.

"Yeah, so far so good," she said. "I've already made arrangements for Zach."

"Well, Jake and Adam will be there. Why don't you let him come," Lacey offered.

"I was going to ask you about that because David Michael would love it."

Lacey noticed that Sophie seemed a little reserved, so she didn't push it.

"What about your birthday, Peanut? Are we still on for that?"

They all looked at Lacey. Her eyes were filling up again. "I just realized Jake won't be here for my birthday."

Susie interrupted. "No, he won't be, but we're going to be with you, and we've got a great night planned for you."

"What are we doing, by the way?" Lacey asked.

"We can't tell you. The only thing we will tell you is that we've hired a limo driver to help us celebrate."

Lacey smiled at Susie, surprised at her assertiveness. "When is that again?"

Susie rolled her eyes pretending to be exasperated. "Just kidding." She laughed. "It's next Saturday."

Nikki looked a little confused. "So it's one week from tonight? I thought it was two weeks away. I'm losing track of time here."

They all began talking about the details of the party, and decided they would meet at Lacey's so the limo driver would only have to go to one house.

"You got that, Lacey?" Susie asked.

"Hey, where did you go, Girl?" Sophie asked.

Lacey shook her head. "I'm sorry," she stammered. She felt like she was looking down on somebody else's life. She was still trying to absorb the fact that she was taking Jake to his dad's in the morning and he'd be gone on her birthday. "I'm still thinking about Jake leaving tomorrow."

"Peanut, keep reminding yourself he's just going for the summer. Come on. Drink up and cheer up." She reached over and gave Lacey's hand an affectionate squeeze and then turned to Sophie. "So I hear there's a new guy in the picture. Come on, spill the beans. What's he like? What does he do? What's in his bank account?

Lacey teased Nikki. "Objection, that was compound, and I instruct the witness not to answer."

Everyone laughed, including Nikki. "She knows I'm only kidding." She grabbed her drink. "Sort of," she said quietly, which sent them into girly giggling again.

Sophie wasn't bothered in the least by Nikki's questions. Her expression totally changed the minute she began talking about her new boyfriend and about some of the dates he'd taken her on, what he did for a living, how she'd met his daughter, and he'd met Zach.

"Sounds like it's getting pretty serious, huh?" Lacey asked.

Sophie looked to be thinking for a moment and nodded. "Yeah, I guess you could say that. Enough about me; what about you guys? Tell me what's happening in your lives." She looked at Susie first.

Susie tried to switch the attention on over to Nikki, but Sophie wasn't about to let her get away with that.

"Okay, okay," Susie exclaimed. "All I'm going to say is get the fork out because I'm almost done."

Lacey watched Nikki's mouth drop open and Sophie's eyebrows raise and gave Susie a reassuring smile.

"So are you going to tell us what you mean by that?" Nikki asked.

Lacey smiled at Nikki's naïve nature. "Duh, she's talking about Jimmy."

They all could see the light go on in Nikki's head, and as if on cue, they all began to laugh.

When Nikki had stopped laughing, she looked over at Susie. "Well, then, I guess we'll soon have another reason to go out on the town to celebrate, or should we combine Lacey's birthday with your freedom?"

Lacey knew Nikki wasn't being pushy, but Susie looked a bit uncomfortable. "The double celebration will be nice, but then again, another night out to celebrate something will be even better, so you just keep us posted, Susie."

Nikki changed the subject and began talking about her recent deposition experience, describing it in a way that only she could, sending them into fits of contagious laughter, so contagious that their waiter came over.

"What are we drinking over here?" he asked.

Sophie was the first to compose and respond to their waiter. "It's not the alcohol. As you can see, we haven't even finished our drinks."

"Oh, don't misunderstand me," he said. "My manager has offered to buy you a round of drinks. He says he likes your zest for laughter, for life."

"Well, in that case," Susie offered, "I'll take another margarita, but make it a strawberry one." She handed him her empty glass.

The waiter took the glass from her and then looked to each of them.

Sophie smiled her sophisticated smile. "I'll take another glass of the Mondavi Merlot."

"Ditto," Lacey said.

"I'll take a glass of water with lemon," Nikki said.

The waiter raised his eyebrows. "Are you sure?"

"Absodarnlutely, one's my limit."

The waiter smiled. "Okay. I'll be back with your drinks."

"Good night, Jake." She turned his light off.

"Love you, Mom."

"Love you, too, more." She started to close his door and heard his last word.

"Most."

"I'm going to miss that all summer," she whispered while the tears fell down her face. She walked downstairs and turned on her computer and put her head down. She brought her arms up and began massaging the knots in her shoulders while waiting for her computer to warm up. This was the first time in three nights that she'd signed on. This past week had been a whirlwind of a week between getting Jake ready for his trip to his dad's, work, training, and just keeping an eye on Jake while meeting life on life's terms. She sat up and logged into her AOL e-mail account first. The AOL messenger's voice startled her, and when she heard, "You've got mail," she smiled. She looked at her inbox of mail. "What the heck...?" She trailed off. She counted the messages from the Nokia guy. "One, two, three—four messages?" She went to the oldest one first, which was three days old.

"Hello there, Smiling CSR. How was your day?" Lacey read aloud. He had signed it Giovanni, aka, the Nokia guy. She opened up the next one, sent the same day but several hours later. "Where are you? I'm looking forward to chatting with you." This time he signed off as Gio. Lacey wondered what he looked like. She opened the next one, which was dated the following day. "Have I said something to offend you?" The final one said, "I get the hint. I hope you're okay." He had signed it The Nokia Guy. Lacey hit the reply button on the final e-mail message and apologized first, and then explained that she was taking her son tomorrow to his dad's for the summer and had just been crazy busy this past week. She signed it Lacey and then added Smiling CSR. She looked over the rest of her e-mail, responded to a couple of forwards from a couple of friends and then signed off. Tomorrow was going to be a long day.

The doorbell rang, and Lacey shouted upstairs to Jake. "Jake, Susie's here." She swallowed the lump in her throat.

"I'm almost done, Mom."

Lacey opened the door. Susie came in, and they hugged.

"Are you doing okay?" Susie asked her.

"No, I'm really not." She swallowed another lump. "You want to help me with his luggage?"

"Absodarnlutely, as Nikki would say."

Lacey made an attempt to smile, and they each grabbed a bag and headed to Susie's car. "Thanks so much for being here with me, and for driving. The rental wouldn't have been too comfortable."

"So when are you getting your car?"

"I get to pick it up on Monday. At least that's something to look forward to," Lacey tried to smile again.

"You never did tell us what you're getting," Susie commented.

They were standing at the trunk of Susie's car and Lacey turned to Susie and grinned. "I'm actually getting a 325-I BMW."

"Get out!" Susie practically yelled. She opened up her trunk, and they both put the bags in. "I can't believe you haven't said anything about it."

"Yeah, well, there's been a little rain on my parade, if you get my drift."

Susie gave Lacey a quick hug. "And aren't you the one who tells us that there's always a rainbow after the rain?"

Lacey looked at Susie, surprised at her wisdom. "Thanks for that reminder." *Nothing like eating my own words!*

"Just remind me of that when I decide to march out of my own parade to find a rainbow."

"You can count on it," Lacey assured her. She started to close the trunk.

"Does he have any more bags?" Susie asked.

"Oh, yeah, but I think they're small, like a carry-on and one other one."

"Well, I'll leave it open, and he can put them in here if he wants to." They started to walk back inside, and Jake met them halfway.

"Hey, Susie," Jake came over, put another bag in the trunk, and gave her a hug.

Lacey left them to talk and went inside to lock up. She went upstairs first to check the windows when the doorbell rang. "Jake, did you lock yourself out?" she shouted as she ran down the stairs. She pulled open the door and stood there with her mouth open. It was Clint. "What are you doing here?" was all she could think to say.

"Well, that's a nice welcome."

"I'm sorry. I'm just a bit confused. Didn't we discuss me driving him up there to you?"

"We did, but I left you a voice mail last night. Didn't you get it?"

Lacey tried to remember if she had checked her voice mail after coming home from hanging out with the girls. "Did you leave a message on my voice mail here at the house or my cell phone?"

"I left it on your home phone."

"I must have forgotten to check it last night. I'm sorry."

"Well, I called you to tell you that Jenna actually had to come down here to see an AIDS specialist regarding some new medication, so we decided to just pick him up ourselves."

Lacey didn't know what to say. She looked out and saw Jake and Susie taking his bags out of her car and transferring them into Clint and Jenna's car. She stood up on her tiptoes to see over Jake and waved to Jenna, and Jenna waved back. "Is her daughter with you?"

"No. Courtney's staying with a friend for the weekend."

"Have you told her Jake's coming for the summer?"

"Yeah, she knows."

Lacey turned toward Clint. "And is she okay with that?" Lacey put her hand above her eyes to shield the sun so she could see his face.

"She's actually really excited." Clint walked over to the trunk of their car where Jake and Susie were, and Lacey walked over to Jenna's side.

Jenna started to roll down her window but obviously changed her mind and just got out of the car.

Lacey gave her a quick hug. "How are you doing, Jenna?"

"I'm good." She smiled.

"Are you sure you're up for this?"

Jenna obviously didn't understand her question.

"I mean having Jake there with you for the whole summer?"

"Actually, I think it's going to be good for Courtney and for Clint."

Lacey could tell she was being honest but she still wanted to scream, *What about me? How's it going to be good for me?*

Jenna interrupted her thoughts. "I'll make sure he calls you, Lacey."

Lacey could see Jake out of the corner of her eye. He was hugging Susie good-bye. Clint was getting in the car, and suddenly, Lacey felt as though her world was closing in on her and she was losing oxygen. She began to try and take deep breaths.

"Are you okay?" Jenna asked.

Lacey took a couple more deep breaths to shoo away her thoughts. *No, I'm not okay. I'll be okay at the end of summer when he's back.* She stared past Jenna. *It's not her fault,* she reminded herself. "I'll be fine, Jenna. Thank you for taking care of my boy." She gave Jenna a hug and turned to see Jake standing there. He reached for her and pulled her to him, and she hugged him back and didn't move. She held her sobs while she let him go. She heard Jenna get in the car, and she pulled him back to her. "Have a good time, Jake, and stay out of trouble."

"I will," he promised.

"And try and help Jenna, okay?" she added. She squeezed him one last time and let go. She walked toward her front door where Susie was standing and sucked in her breath so the tears wouldn't come. She heard the car start and turned in time to see them backing out of the driveway and Jake waving good-bye.

The Limo Driver

"Susie, would you get the door?" Lacey shouted from her bedroom.

"Got it," she yelled back.

A couple minutes later, Susie yelled upstairs. "Lacey, you got flowers."

"What?" She wasn't quite dressed, but stuck her head out of the bedroom door. She could see Susie holding an arrangement of lavender roses with a "Happy Birthday" balloon floating above them. "Who are they from?"

"Do you want me to open the little card?"

Lacey was truly curious. "Yes, please."

Susie set the roses down on the table at the entryway and opened the envelope.

Lacey watched her eyes get big and round. "Well…"

"Who is Giovanni?" Susie asked.

Lacey didn't answer her. Instead, she started to walk downstairs clad in only her underclothes. She held her arm out. "Let me see that."

Susie met her halfway on the stairs and gave her the envelope.

Lacey took it and read it: *Roses don't have to be red; they can be lavender too. That makes them special, just like you. Have an awe-*

some birthday. Love, Giovanni. Lacey looked up to see Susie still standing there waiting for an answer to her question.

"He's just a guy I've been chatting with online."

Susie had a big grin on her face.

"Please promise me you won't say anything to the girls," Lacey whined.

"Why don't you want them to know?"

Lacey responded with a silent plea.

"Okay, okay. I won't say anything." She handed the flowers to Lacey.

"Thanks, Susie.

"I'm going to cut up the snacks and get things ready." She started to walk down the stairs and glanced at her watch. "It's already four forty-five. Fifteen more minutes before everyone gets here," she reminded Lacey.

"I'm almost ready."

Ten minutes later, Lacey was dressed in a simple pair of black Ralph Lauren double-buckled pants that accentuated her slim waist and hips. They flared at the bottom perfectly to show off a pair of open-toed black shoes with a comfortable one-and-a-half-inch heel. She had topped it off with a red sequined sleeveless blouse that hugged her flat stomach. She put on her Brighton necklace and matching bracelet, just as Susie's voice called up the stairs.

"Nikki and Sophie are here, and Jillian just called my cell and said she's about thirty minutes away."

"Okay. I'll be down in a minute." The phone rang, and Lacey answered it.

The voice on the other end sang "Happy Birthday" to her and finished with "Happy birthday to my little Mama. Happy birthday to you."

Lacey was so excited to hear his voice she nearly started to cry. "Thank you, my favorite guy in the whole world. How are you?"

"I'm good, Mom. Are you having a good day?"

"Well, as a matter of fact, now that you've called, it just got better. I worked at my desk today, and then I treated myself to a manicure and pedicure. Now I'm getting ready for tonight because the girls are taking me out."

"Where are you going?"

"I'm not sure. All I know is they hired a limo driver."

"Wow, that's awesome, Mom. Try and have fun, okay?"

"I will, Jake. I miss you."

"I miss you too, but I'll see you soon, just four more weeks, right?"

Four weeks seemed like such a long time to wait to see him, and yet Lacey knew it was a short time to complete training for the show. "Right, four weeks."

"Well, I gotta go. I love you, Mom."

Lacey took advantage of his little pause. "More and most, buddy." She could feel his smile through the phone. "Talk to you soon, honey."

"Lacey, the limo driver's here," Nikki yelled up the stairs.

"Coming," Lacey yelled back and descended the stairs.

"Oh, geez, would you look at this! It's Barbie with muscles," Nikki exclaimed.

Everyone broke out in laughter, including Lacey. "You are too much, Nikki." She gave her and Sophie a hug.

"Lacey, this is our limo driver, Toby," Susie said.

"Happy birthday, Lacey, it's nice to meet you." He held out his hand.

Lacey shook it and tried not to stare at him. *Oh wow, he's adorable.* The voices in the other room broke her trance. "Who else is here?"

Susie looked as though she was going to pop with laughter. "Go into the living room and find out."

Lacey walked into her living room and screamed with delight as she looked at the faces of each of her friends. Closest to her was Anna-Maria, a fellow court reporter she'd known for a few years.

Beside her was Jenny, also a court reporter whom Lacey had met in court reporting school. She had become a great friend who had seen her through some tough times, including her divorce from Peter. Lacey hugged them both and thanked them for coming. She hugged and thanked Angie next, a fairly new friend that she had met at the church's high school ministry. She turned to the last two friends who were waiting patiently, Marie and her mom, Christy. She had met Marie at the gym and her mom shortly thereafter. Marie was going to court reporting school, and Lacey encouraged her however and whenever she could, which was how Lacey had become part of their family. She held her arms out, her heart overflowing with affection for them as she hugged each of them. "I had no idea you guys were coming."

"We had to fill up the limo," Susie said from behind her.

"Are you kidding? We wouldn't have missed this for anything," Marie insisted.

"That's right," Christy agreed.

"Thank you for helping me celebrate today." She turned toward all of them. "I have a bottle of champagne chilling and some appetizers. Do we have time for that, Susie?"

"There's always time for hors d'oeuvres and especially champagne," she said.

They gathered around the little bar off the kitchen while Lacey reached for the bottle.

The doorbell rang. "I'll go and get it. It's probably Jillian."

"Thanks, Susie." Lacey began to pour, and Sophie passed them out to everyone including Jillian who had just greeted the group and hugged Lacey. "Look who I found coming up your walkway," Jillian smiled as a familiar face stepped out from behind her, another friend from court reporting school.

"Valinue," Lacey exclaimed. She nearly ran to hug her. "It's so good to see you! How are you? How are Gary and the boys?"

"They're fine. They're growing so much."

Lacey looked out to the group and pointed to Val's recent family picture they had taken in the Scychelles, where she was originally from.

"Gary sends his love and birthday wishes."

"I'll have to come over soon to see them." Lacey handed Val a glass of champagne. "So, how do you like working at the courthouse?"

"It's great." She took a sip of her champagne. "I still think you should try out the next time the test comes around."

Lacey rolled her eyes. "Yeah, that will be the day when I'm good enough for court," she mocked. She changed the subject and began introducing her to the others as she poured her own glass of champagne.

"Just one more," Sophie said.

Lacey looked puzzled.

Sophie cocked her head as if to point to someone.

Lacey followed with her eyes and they stopped at Toby. "Oh, our limo driver," she exclaimed. "Toby, here, come have a glass of champagne."

Toby stepped forward. "I have to pass. I'm not allowed to drink on the job, I need to make sure I get you all to your destinations safely." He looked around at all the girls and his eyes came to rest on Lacey—and rest and rest and rest.

Lacey had to tear her gaze away from him. "Whew, it's getting warm in here."

Everyone laughed.

She held up her glass. "Here's to creating great memories with my friends." They drank their champagne and nibbled on the snacks while they visited. Lacey was laughing at Anna-Maria's latest family story when Susie stood up on a chair and asked for everyone's attention.

"Okay, everybody, pile into the limo. We've got to be at the Pasadena Playhouse in an hour and a half for the Late Nite

Catechism play, which means we have just enough time to go through In-N-Out for a bite to eat."

"We're going through In-N-Out for dinner?" Lacey exclaimed. "I can't eat In-N-Out."

"Oh, yes, you can, Peanut. You can get yours wrapped in a piece of lettuce." Nikki came over and gave Lacey a squeeze in the midst of the laughter. "How's that for our 'low-carb, no-carb' queen?"

"Let's go." Jillian was the first to the door.

Lacey grabbed her purse and camera, and headed to the limo. Nikki was just getting in, and Toby was standing outside holding the door for her. Lacey bent down and snapped a picture of her friends' faces amidst all the balloons. "Who brought the balloons?" Lacey asked. She stood back up when Toby answered.

"I did."

Lacey could see his warm smile and engaging eyes even through her sunglasses. "Thank you, Toby."

"You're welcome." He held her gaze. "I hope this is your best birthday ever," he added.

His sincerity tugged gently at her heart, and Lacey could feel the chemistry between them. *It's probably just part of the job.* She bent down to get inside the limo and nearly stepped on Sophie's feet as she plopped down on the seat. She felt the limo move forward and looked around. "This limo is awesome," she exclaimed, "and the limo driver's not so bad either." She giggled.

"And he's single," Susie announced.

All the girls broke out laughing. "How do you know that?" Sophie asked.

"I asked him," Susie declared.

Jillian interrupted the laughter. "Would you look at this," Jillian cheered. "It's a full-blown bar!"

Susie pointed to another compartment, and Sophie pulled out beautiful crystal glasses.

"Let the party begin," chimed Anna-Maria.

They had a difficult time finding the theater, and by the time they found it, they were a few minutes late. Everyone had scampered ahead, and Nikki and Lacey could see that the production had already started. The only lighting was coming from the dimly lit stage, which cast its shadow on a big nun wearing a huge habit standing in a classroom setting.

"Excuse me. Excuse me, class. It seems we have some late arrivals," Sister Mari-Pat announced to the audience. She walked off the stage, pointing her ruler toward Lacey and Nikki.

Lacey gasped and stopped walking as she realized that the spotlight was on both of them.

"Yeah, I'm talking to you," Sister Mari-Pat pointed to Lacey, and the audience's attention followed. Nikki seemed to have disappeared into a chair somewhere and was nowhere to be found. "Come on down here to the front row."

Lacey walked forward slowly, feeling like she was back in grade school.

"Hasn't anyone ever told you it's rude to be tardy to class, especially catechism? What's your name?"

Lacey just stared at her like a defiant student.

"Cat's got her tongue," she said to the audience.

The audience laughed as if on cue.

"Come on now. Tell Sister Mari-Pat your name."

"My name's Lacey."

Sister Mari-Pat mimicked Lacey's response.

The audience roared with laughter this time. *Why does this feel surreal?* Lacey wondered to herself as she stared up at the nun. *No telling what she's hiding under that habit.*

"Sit right there." Sister Mari-Pat gave Lacey a little push, and Lacey landed in a chair somewhat in a daze. *It's like I'm part of her act or something.* The pounding of the ruler on her desk lifted Lacey's attention to the stage, and she watched as Sister Mari-Pat began picking on another guy and then another. Lacey couldn't help but join in the infectious laughter. She looked in her purse for a tissue to wipe around her eyes. She pulled it out, and all of a sudden, her purse was snatched off her lap.

"Just what do you think you're doing? This is Late Nite Catechism. You don't get to rummage through your purse." Sister Mari-Pat put her ruler through the handles of Lacey's purse and held it up. She walked up the stage with it while the audience laughed. Lacey watched Sister Mari-Pat put it somewhere behind the podium and then make her way back to the front of the stage.

"Now, where was I?" She continued on with her lessons from the Bible, Catholic style, stopping every few minutes to scold someone. Filled with a mischievous streak, Lacey got up quietly from her seat, tiptoed to the stage, stopped, and turned around to make sure Sister was still where she had last seen her. She was, so Lacey made a beeline for the podium on stage, crawling up to it so as not to be seen by the Sister. When she reached the podium, she tucked herself neatly behind it so she could look for her purse. The auditorium broke out in heaps of laughter, and Lacey stuck her head out to see all eyes on her while Sister Mari-Pat looked bewildered. She grabbed her purse and crouched her way down the stairs. The laughter got louder.

"What in the world...!" screamed Sister Mari-Pat.

Lacey made it to her seat just as she heard the crack of the ruler crashing on the banister next to where Sister Mari-Pat was now standing. Lacey held her breath, quite sure she was about to get scolded again. "Silence, class!" she bellowed.

Lacey followed Sister with her eyes as she watched her walk to the middle of the auditorium to stand right in front of another girl who just happened to be well-endowed. Sister Mari-Pat spent the next few minutes of the class on a biblical rampage as she spoke of the lesson of lust and how to dress.

She moved on to another victim, a gentleman who looked to be in his fifties, as she began the lesson of impure thoughts. She barraged him with questions about his current thoughts and pulled out of him a confession of looking at another woman lustfully as recently as that evening. While the audience's laughter ricocheted throughout the auditorium, Sister Mari-Pat looked for her next victim as she announced the commandment of "Thou shall honor thy father and mother." After engaging a twenty-one-year-old female, she managed to pull from her a confession of being disrespectful to her mother just yesterday, to which Sister Mari-Pat vehemently responded with reminders of what happened when you talked back to your parents. That lesson ended with a broken paddle, which hit the audience in their funny bones again.

She was about to talk about the sin of eating meat on Friday when she heard someone pop their gum. Lacey giggled so much she was choking as she watched Sister Mari-Pat demand the piece of gum from the sinner, a guy that looked to be close to Lacey's age. When the last lesson was taught and the lights came up, Lacey's sides hurt from all the laughing. She stood there and began looking for her group of friends who had slyly ditched her.

Within a few minutes, all of them made their way over to Lacey. They stood there talking and laughing about Lacey and Sister Mari-Pat, trying to mimic her relentless lampooning and scolding. They all agreed that the highlight of the whole show was Lacey stealing her purse back from the crazy nun.

"You ready for the next part of the night?" Susie asked.

They walked down the stairs and out to the atrium, and Lacey saw Toby waiting for them. She walked up to him with her camera. "Could you take some pictures of us?"

He took the camera from her extended hand. "I would love to, but only if you have someone take one of us afterwards."

"I think that could be arranged." She smiled up at him. "Come on, girls. Toby's gonna take some pics of us." They gathered around the atrium's beautiful Toscana fountain. Toby took several group pictures, and then he handed the camera to Susie. "Would you mind?"

Susie shooed everyone away for the picture of Toby and Lacey. She took one from a distance and then a close-up. Lacey could feel herself beaming as his arm tightened around her waist, and he gently held her by his side. *Be still my heart.*

"Okay, let's go," Susie announced. "Our limo awaits us."

When they got close, Lacey thought she saw some more familiar faces.

"Surprise," the girls waiting at the limo yelled together.

Lacey let out a squeal of delight and turned to Susie.

"They're going to follow us to the next part of the party," Susie explained.

Lacey walked up to the group excited to see Flo and four of her coworkers from the agency. She gave each of them a hug, and felt a hand on the small of her back. Lacey looked up to see Toby leaning his head in close to hers. "Can I offer your friends something to drink?"

"Uh, sure," Lacey stammered.

"Everyone grab your glasses, and for the newcomers, here's a glass for each of you." He handed them each a glass while the others got theirs from the limo.

Lacey leaned over toward Susie and whispered in her ear, "Do you think he's just doing his job or that he's really this nice?"

Susie whispered back, "I think he's really that nice, and I also think he can't take his eyes off you."

Lacey nearly chocked on her leftover champagne. "You are so off base, Susie," she said louder than she intended.

Sophie walked up and joined them. "What is she off base about?"

Susie couldn't resist. "Our limo driver's smitten with our birthday girl. Just watch him, and you'll see he checks her out every chance he can."

Lacey glared at Susie. "You are so exaggerating." They stopped bickering when Toby approached them and refilled their glasses. He winked at Lacey as he poured the fresh champagne in her glass.

"I told you," Susie snickered.

The shaking of keys silenced Lacey's response.

"To the birthday girl," Toby raised the empty bottle and then looked over to her and smiled in the midst of the toast.

Lacey took a sip of her champagne and leaned over to whisper in Susie's ear, "Talk about eye candy, whew!"

Susie started laughing and Lacey walked over to visit with Flo, and her coworkers Robin, Laurie, Vicky, and Sarah. It wasn't long before Susie was interrupting them, banging her keys on her crystal glass to get everybody's attention.

"Okay, it's time for the next stop, or should I say stops." She giggled.

Lacey stopped talking

"Since Lacey loves to dance, Toby is going to take us club-hopping." She looked over to Flo. "Are you guys parked close to here?"

"We're in two cars and just around the corner, so we'll meet you here in a couple of minutes and follow you to wherever you're going."

Within an hour, they had visited two clubs and were on their way to the third, which turned out to be their final one. Toby knew the owner and was able to get them all in for free. The club was packed, so it took a while to find a couple of tables to accommodate all of them, but they had found a perfect corner with three tables under the outdoor patio. Lacey noticed right away that the dance floor was extremely crowded, but it didn't stop her. As soon as they got settled and she ordered a drink, she was off and dancing with a few of her friends. Three songs later, Lacey felt a tap on her shoulder. She turned around and was surprised to see Toby standing there. "What are you doing in here?" she yelled over the loud music.

Toby leaned into her so he could hear her.

"I thought you had to stay with the limo."

There was still a lot of noise, and Toby bent down to her ear. "I paid a guy to watch it for me." The music started again, and he began dancing.

Lacey watched him for a few seconds, taking in his rhythm. *There is definitely something enticing about a man that can dance*, she thought. She looked at the girls who were all giving her the thumbs-up sign and then turned back toward Toby and began to match his steps, almost competitively. When the music slowed, he pulled her to him, molding his body into hers, coming apart only when the song stopped and flowed into the next one, and the next until Toby felt a tap on his shoulder. It was the guy he had asked to watch the limo. Lacey kept dancing while they tried to talk, and then Toby leaned in and pulled her closer. "I think the boss is calling. I'll meet you outside when you're done." Lacey watched him walk toward the exit.

Lacey walked the girls to their cars. "Thank you so much. I had a blast."

"That's obvious, peanut," Nikki declared. "You wore me out just watching you."

Sophie broke in. "She was a dancing machine; that's for sure."

"No kidding," Susie chimed in.

"I'd better go," Sophie said. "I'm exhausted." Lacey hugged her good-bye and Nikki too.

She turned and walked Susie to her car, and Susie's phone rang. Susie ignored it. "Is it Jimmy?" she asked her.

Susie took her phone out of her purse. "Yeah. I'm sure he's ticked off because I haven't called him all night."

"Are you going to be okay?"

"I'll be fine," Susie dismissed.

"Well, I just want to say thank you for arranging everything for tonight, especially getting everyone together. It was so good to see everyone, and I had an incredible time."

Susie gave Lacey a hug and opened the door of her car. "It was fun. We just wanted to get you out and your mind off of Jake and the contest." She started to get in her car but then turned and looked at Lacey. "Don't do anything I wouldn't do with that limo driver." With a giggle she got in her car and waved good-bye.

Lacey shook her head and smiled. She watched her drive away and walked back into the house where Toby was still waiting. He was standing in the hall looking at all her pictures. "So, don't you have someplace to be right now?" Lacey teased him. They went into the kitchen, and Lacey poured him a glass of water and one for herself. They went and sat in her living room and began talking comfortably, interjecting a yawn here and there until finally at three-thirty in the morning, Toby announced that he should go.

Lacey looked at her watch and was startled at the time. "Holy smokes, I had no idea it was so late. The night was so much fun and went so fast."

Toby stood and held out his hand to help her up.

Lacey felt suddenly awkward. "Let me walk you out to your limo."

They walked outside and the moon was shining full and bright, and the sky boasted of scattered stars that looked like little twinkling lights. Toby unlocked the driver's side and then turned and faced her. "Do you mind if I give you a birthday kiss?"

Lacey was caught off guard. *No one's ever asked if they could kiss me before.* She didn't know what to say, so she didn't say anything. Instead, she reached her arms up and wrapped them around his neck as she stood on her tiptoes. She'd been battling this chemistry all night, and suddenly she found herself unarmed and unwilling to resist him. *It's just a birthday kiss.*

His mouth came down on hers, gently and slowly, at first, and then he gently prodded her mouth open and allowed his tongue to dance with hers, much like their bodies had danced on the dance floor just a few hours earlier.

Lacey's head was spinning when he finally ended the dance.

"Happy birthday, Lacey," he said, and he got in the limo and drove away.

Daniel looked at his watch. He had about fifteen minutes before Lacey's appointment. He pulled her chart and sat back in his chair to review his notes. Last week had been her first time back in three weeks. He wasn't really surprised at how much had been happening up to this point. Her anxiety was escalating and so was her inability to cope with her circumstances, especially with Jake going to his dad's for the summer. He went back to his notes and reviewed the sentence completion form she had filled out at the first appointment. He re-read the sentences that referenced Jake, nodding his head as he saw that there were several. He was suspecting that she was either hiding behind her son or so immersed in his life that neither one of them had a separate identity. She had finished "During my school days" with "I longed to belong." He nodded his head as he read the thing that made her mad, which was dishonest people. She felt that most men were frauds and frequently wished she could slow down. "Here it is," he murmured as he read aloud. "I feel miserable knowing my son's not doing well." He continued with the next sentence: "If I could only…" He stared at her answer. "…open the eyes of my son's heart," he finished. He looked through some of his other notes and then returned to the sentence completion. "Here's another one," he exclaimed aloud, "'I've always envied,' and she finished it with 'people with successful kids.' 'I admire' is completed with 'kids who make wise choices despite their circumstances.'"

He read that she worried about her son's direction and wondered why she cared so much and overextended her emotions, which could be referring to men and her son, he mused. He was convinced that her childhood was not only interfering with her relationships with men but her parenting as well. She was still projecting her own deeply hidden issue of abandonment onto Jake as well as her now not so hidden issue of shame. He would try to address this issue with her today, depending, of course, on the latest circumstances of her life.

Lacey sat across from Daniel in her usual spot on the couch. He listened to her as she recounted the events of the week, including her calls to Jake and her birthday party. He smiled with her as she animatedly spoke of the Late Nite Catechism production and then openly and honestly about the limo driver, their connection on the dance floor, his staying and talking after the girls had left, their many conversations throughout the week, including the final conversation where he had admitted to being married but separated and having a two-year-old daughter.

"So when you say your 'final conversation' with the limo driver, was that your choice or his?" Daniel asked her.

Lacey looked up with a smile on her face. "It was my choice, but looking back on it now, I think it was really eating at his conscience, and I think the fact that he brought it up was his way of trying to put a stop to it." Her expression became somber.

"At first you looked somewhat pleased about it and now you look sad. What just went through your mind?"

"Well, when he told me, naturally I was bummed, because it seemed like we had such a connection. But I told him he had to work it out with her, that the grass isn't so green on the other side. I also gave him this awesome book that I just read called *The Five Love Languages*."

"That's a great book."

"Yeah, it is. I wish I would have read it years ago. Anyway, I shared with him how hard it is being a single parent and I wouldn't wish it on anyone, and yet, I wouldn't change my situation either." She stopped herself and then continued, a little perplexed by her own words. "Does that make any sense?"

"As a matter of fact, considering your past, Lacey, it does." He watched as confusion danced in her eyes. He continued, "See, you have this habit of taking full responsibility for all of your situations, including what's happening with Jake."

"What does Jake have to do with this?"

Her defensive tone didn't go unnoticed. Daniel sat forward and looked right at her as he pushed forward ever so gently. "Well, he's not just another man in and out of your life, but you're afraid he'll abandon you, like the others have. He's your son, Lacey, and consequently, you see him as an extension of you. You think his life and all the crap in it must be because of you. And since you have a history of mess-ups, Jake is your ticket to validate the good in you by you being a good parent." He watched the confusion change to recognition and then she became defensive.

"What's wrong with wanting to be a good parent?"

"Nothing's wrong with it, Lacey. It's the way you're going about it. Your preoccupation with his life has become a way of rescuing your past, so you can prove you're a good person, or not an all-bad person. It's also a form of control to keep him from abandoning you, though control is delusional." He watched as her confusion surfaced, and he turned around and grabbed his notes. "Let me show you what I mean." He pulled out her sentence completion form. "So when you wrote 'have always envied people with successful kids,' you use the word 'success' as a way to make up for what you believe are your inadequacies and failures."

He watched as her eyes began to fill up, and he handed her a Kleenex and continued. He drew a tree with lots of branches and their veins within the trunk.

"See, it's like this tree. If we look at all these branches, we can trace them down to their root within the trunk of their tree, and if we look at your history, we can trace this shame you carry and this perception of what's wrong with you all the way back to the molestation." He directed her back to the tree. "See, all these branches represent all your efforts to make up for all that you feel is wrong with you because your trunk is full of junk, such as the inability to trust, a sense of insecurity which leads you to try and control your world and the people in it. The problem with this thinking is you were not in control of your molestation and the choice of your stepdad to do it, and you were not in control of Jake's dad who was equally selfish, and again, with Peter, you didn't make him choose another woman. Likewise, you are *not* in control of Jake and his bad choices. You can guide him by holding up the signs, so to speak, to point him in the right direction, but you can't choose for him."

He sat there for a minute as she wrestled with her tears, and then he got out of his chair and sat next to her. She looked up at him, her eyes so full of pain, tears streaming down her face. "So how do I change that?"

"For starters, there needs to be consequences that Jake needs to experience for his bad choices, and then you need to learn to let him struggle in those consequences."

"What do you mean?" Lacey stammered.

"Well, for instance, what were the consequences for stealing all that money from you?"

Lacey didn't have an answer.

"That's what I mean. There wasn't really any substantial consequence for that except to send him to his dad's, which is what he wanted anyway. When we as parents struggle to see our kids struggle, we enable them in codependency thereby sort of crippling them when it comes to the challenges of life. Kids not only need boundaries, but they like them."

"I don't know about that."

"It's true. Jake may rebel at first, but if boundaries are consistently set, he won't keep trying to push the line back. Instead, he'll learn to function within the boundaries set for him."

Lacey held her head down and let the tears fall. She brought her head back up, her face awash with more tears. "But what if it's too late?"

"I'm sure there will be many more opportunities to get it right, Lacey."

"It's so unfair that he should have to suffer because of all my issues that I didn't even know I had. I had no idea that I carry so much junk in my trunk as a result of what happened when I was a kid." Lacey just sat there, shaking her head, wiping the tears spilling down her cheeks.

"I know it hurts, Lacey, but these tears are the water that's needed to clean out all that mud." He paused. "There's a promise in the Bible that goes something like this: When you pass through the waters, meaning the storms in your life, He will be with you and they will not overflow, or overtake you."

Lacey looked at him, her eyes filled with hope.

"We'll pick up next time from where I left off. Let me pray with you."

Harrison looked at Lacey before he pressed the button on the CD player. "You ready?"

"I think so."

"Okay. Take it from the top. Show me what you've got."

Lacey began her routine. She had practiced it so many times that it was almost automatic. Even the strength moves were getting easier. The challenge now was keeping her head in the routine and not on the circumstances outside of it. She stayed focused through the end, her adrenalin taking her into her round-off down into the forward splits. She threw her arms up in a perfect

V-shape and her head followed. *I did it!* she exclaimed silently, and then she heard faint sounds of clapping, lots of it.

Harrison started laughing because of the completely bewildered expression on Lacey's face. "Look outside to the left, Lacey."

Lacey was in no way prepared for what she saw. There was a crowd gathered outside of the aerobic room, all with faces pressed up against the windows, and people in back of them, straining to see. Harrison was walking to the door to signal they could all come in and the clapping got louder. Lacey stood while looking at the many familiar faces walking toward her. One by one they congratulated her and wished her luck on her show just two weeks away. The crowd thinned, and Lacey saw an all-too familiar face lingering behind the two remaining people. Her pulse quickened and she felt herself begin to tremble as she hugged the last one good-bye and thanked her. She looked up to see Seth walking slowly toward her. She stood, frozen in her emotions.

He stopped within inches of her, so close that she could see the glistening on his forehead from his own workout. He looked up at her, his unforgotten smile unnerving her. "Hey, Seth," was all she could manage.

"Hey, yourself." He smiled. "Your routine looks pretty good."

"Thanks. I still need to perfect that planche move though."

"Anyway, I just wanted to say good luck. I'll see you there." He held her eyes one last time and walked away.

"Valentino Reporters, please hold."

Lacey didn't get a chance to say anything before she heard the click that switched her over to the music. She listened to nearly half of the upbeat song before Flo came back on the line.

"Hi, Flo. It's me, Lacey. I'm calling in for my job assignment for tomorrow."

Flo gave it to her and asked if she had a minute.

"Sure."

"Hold on. I want to go in one of the private offices so no one hears me," she whispered. She put her on hold, and Lacey waited, wondering what she needed to tell her.

"Are you still there?" Flo asked.

"Yeah, I'm still here. What's up?"

"Do you have a passport?"

"No. I've been meaning to get one, but I never have."

Well, we just confirmed a twelve-day job that's going to be in Seoul, Korea, for the first five days, and then Hong Kong for a week."

"Wow, Flo, that sounds like a great job." *But what does it have to do with me?*

"Anyway, Norm has a list of reporters he's looking over to see who he wants to send, and you're on it."

"What?" Lacey gasped.

"I just wanted to give you a heads-up. I know you have Jake and—"

Lacey interrupted her. "Actually, he's with his dad for the summer."

"Really," Flo interjected. "So would you go if he asked you?"

"How could I say no to that?" Lacey sputtered. "But then again, I guess it depends on when it is. I mean if it's while Jake's going to be gone…" She faded off.

"Right now it's tentatively set for the end of July, so about six weeks from now.

"Holy pooh," Lacey exclaimed. Her brain started to wrap around the possibility. "Doesn't it take eight weeks for a passport?"

"Usually it does, but you can get an expedited one, and our office will reimburse you for it."

They talked for a few minutes, and Lacey hung up the phone, somewhat in a daze. "What a trip," she said. She got up and did a little dance, throwing her arms up in excitement. "I'm leaving on a jet plane. Might be going to Korea, oh yeah. And then I'll get back on the plane 'cause I might be going to Hong Kong, oh yeah." She kept saying the words over and over, adding in beats as though she were a rapper. The ringing of the phone interrupted her silliness, and when she picked it up, she was a little out of breath. "Hello."

"Hello yourself," her sister said.

"Elaine, how are you?"

"I'm good. How come you sound as though you're out of breath?"

"I was just making up a silly song and doing a funky dance," Lacey admitted through her giggles.

"What were you doing that for?"

Lacey told her about the possibility of the international job, and Elaine congratulated her.

"Well, not yet. He hasn't chosen anyone. I'm just one on his list."

"That's still pretty awesome."

Lacey could hear her sister's envy.

"So what else has been going on? I hear Jake's up at his dad's."

Lacey was going to ask how she knew that but figured he must have called Alexandria. "Yeah, he's up there for the summer."

"Well, that's good, isn't it?" Elaine asked.

Lacey didn't want to get into all of her doubts and fears and regurgitate all that had happened since they had last been to see her, so she fibbed. "Yeah, it's good."

"So why didn't you call me when Jake totaled your car?"

Lacey let out a sharp breath. "I don't know. I guess I had so many things to take care of because of it that I really didn't have a lot of time to stop and talk about it." *Nor did I want to talk about it.* "Anyways, don't take it personal," Lacey encouraged.

"So when's this Ms. Fitness contest exactly?" Elaine asked.

Lacey grabbed her calendar and gave her the exact date.

"Crap," Elaine exclaimed.

"What's wrong?"

"I have to sing that weekend for Mass. I was going to try and surprise you and drive up to Vegas."

Lacey was touched. "Hey, maybe I'll do another one. They talked for a few more minutes before they hung up.

Lacey logged on to her computer and sent Gio an e-mail letting him know about the possibility of her traveling to Korea and Hong Kong for a job assignment. She pressed send and logged off. She needed to talk to a live voice, so she called Susie at her office but her voice mail came on. She left her a message and then called Sophie who was in a rush to get out the door so Lacey said she'd call her later. Nikki was out of town visiting her sister so she didn't want to bother her. She looked at the clock and saw that it was five thirty, her mom's dinner time, but she opted to try her anyway.

"Hello, Lacey," Mom answered on the second ring.

"Did I get you during dinner time, Mom?"

"No. we actually just finished. Dad was hungry for the first time in a few days, so we ate a little early. What's going on with you? Are you still coming up tomorrow?"

"Oh, yeah, I'm still coming. I just got some news, and I didn't want to wait until tomorrow to share it."

"Well, all right then. What's going on?"

Lacey repeated her conversation with Flo and got excited all over again. Lacey asked her questions about the passport process. "Listen to us, Mom. We're talking as if I'm going to get to go."

"There's not a doubt in my mind that you're the one he's going to choose, Lacey. Now what time are you coming out tomorrow?"

They talked a little longer and Lacey assured her she'd be out there in time for a nice visit before dinner. "I just have to do my workout, run a few errands, and straighten up around here, which won't take me long, especially since Jake's not here."

"Are you doing okay with that?" Mom asked.

"Yeah, I am. I'm staying pretty busy. Anyway, I should be out there by about three o'clock."

"Okay, then, we'll eat around five."

"See you tomorrow, Mom."

Lacey still had not programmed the garage door button in her Beamer to work for her garage, so she had to park in the driveway, go in through the front door, open up the garage, pull the car in, and then make sure she locked the front door. When she was all done with that, she got into her pajamas and poured herself a glass of wine and sat down in the living room. She was feeling really relaxed, especially having spent some time at Mom and Dad's. There was something about spending time with them that unwound her and made her feel at ease. She grew somber when she thought of her dad. He had looked so frail, and yet he still had a smile in his eyes, especially when her mom got close to him. They were still so kind and loving with each other, even after fifty-two years. Lacey let out a sigh, sad and content all at once. She reached for the phone so she could talk to the one and only person she knew she'd love for more than fifty-something years, but Daniel's words stopped her. *I won't put my emotional needs on him.* Instead, she grabbed her glass of wine and her journal and headed upstairs to her favorite chair to write about the day's events and look over what she'd written from her counseling session this past week.

She was so engrossed in recapturing the day with her mom and dad that when the phone rang, she nearly knocked her glass of wine over. "Hello."

"Hi, Mom." His tone sounded tired.

"Hi, honey. How are you?"

"I'm good," he assured her. "Just a little tired. I just got back from skateboarding and we're getting ready to watch a movie, but I thought I'd call you first."

"What are you going to watch?"

"We're gonna watch an Indiana Jones movie."

Lacey smiled because of the familiarity of it. "You two crack me up with your obsession about Indiana Jones."

Jake began to describe which Indiana Jones movie they had chosen when Lacey heard her doorbell ring. "Jake, let me call you back, honey. Someone's at my door." Lacey hung up the phone and put it on the kitchen counter. She looked at the time. It was just a little past nine o'clock. "Who in the world is knocking on my door at this hour?" she asked aloud. She turned the porch light on and looked through the peephole and gasped. She opened the door quickly, her hands already beginning to shake at the sight of her friend whose face was black and blue and her lips bloody.

Lacey threw the door open wide and started to reach for Susie, but she shrank away from her touch.

"Sorry," Susie cried. "It's just that my arm hurts."

Lacey held the door open and motioned for her to come inside. "What in the heck happened, Susie?"

Susie walked into the formal area and put her keys on the piano and leaned up against it.

"Susie, talk to me, please." Lacey followed her and turned on the lamp on the piano. "What happened?"

"I can't go back there anymore," she sobbed. "I'm done." She put her head down and let herself cry quietly.

Lacey, very gently, put her arms around her and let her cry, at a loss for words. She could only imagine, based on her own mother's routine beatings, what Susie had endured. She felt Susie move just a little. "You don't have to go back there anymore, Susie. You can stay here. You know I have that spare bedroom."

Susie pulled away slowly and turned so her right side was leaning back up against the piano and Lacey was able to see the bruising on her arm. She couldn't stop staring at it. The black, blue, and shades of red and purple began in her triceps area and went up. Lacey lifted up Susie's sleeve, needing to see the rest of it. She gasped. The colors went all the way up to her shoulder, stopped for just a few inches, and Lacey's eyes traveled to Susie's neck where the trail of bruising picked back up. She motioned for Susie to turn her head. Sure enough, there on the other side was a continuation of the splashes of cruel colors. Lacy began to tremble with rage. She dared herself to scrutinize Susie's face. Her bottom lip had crusted blood on it and had started to swell. There were a few scratches on her cheeks. The area around her right eye was free of bruising, but the anguish that came from both of her eyes took Lacey to a very painful place. Her left eye was framed in bruising and swelling. Lacey willed herself to not give in to her own emotions. "Let's get you some ice for your lip and your eye."

Susie followed her into the kitchen. Lacey quickly grabbed a sandwich baggie out of the drawer, filled it with ice and wrapped a clean dishrag around it. "Here, that's for your lip. Go in and try and relax on the couch while I make another ice pack for your eye."

When Lacey went into the living room, Susie was sitting up as if in a daze. "Here, let me fluff these pillows up so you can get comfortable."

Susie leaned back into the pillows and Lacey placed the ice pack gently on her eye. "Hold that right there for a few minutes. I know it probably doesn't feel very good, but we need to minimize the swelling."

"Remind me never to try out for boxing, huh," Susie tried to joke. She put the other icepack over her lip.

"You just rest for a few minutes. I'm going to call Jake and tell him good night."

Susie jerked upwards. "Please don't tell him about this, Lacey."

Lacey gently pushed her back on the pillow. "Shhh, I'm not going to say anything to anyone that you don't want me to. I just want to tell him good night." She watched Susie get the icepacks back in place, and when she appeared to be resting, Lacey turned to go upstairs, but changed her mind. She grabbed a cigarette and her lighter and went outside to smoke before calling Jake.

The cool night air collided with the flame on the lighter, and Lacey had to make a couple of attempts before lighting her cigarette successfully. She inhaled deeply and exhaled slowly, willing herself to relax for the first time since Susie's entrance almost an hour ago. Smoking was her way of escaping, but tonight, it wasn't working. She stubbed the half-smoked cigarette back and forth on the stucco wall and flicked it into the bushes. She let herself back in quietly and ran upstairs to call Jake. She picked up the phone and redialed Clint's number and almost hung it back up when she saw it was a little after eleven. Jake picked up right away.

"So who was at the door, Mom?"

"Oh, it was just Susie. She was just dropping off something I left in her car the other day," Lacey fibbed. *He's your son, not your friend. You don't need to confide in him,* her mom's word echoed. "Did you finish your movie?"

"Yeah," Jake said, yawning.

"Was it any good?"

"It was okay."

"And how is your dad doing?"

Jake yawned again, and he lowered his voice. "He seems to be doing pretty good, but he sleeps a lot," he admitted.

"I'm sure that's because of the meds, honey. And how are you and Courtney getting along?"

"Good. She introduced me to a lot of her friends."

Just what you need, a bunch of girls in your life.

"So how is Shellie doing.

"Good. Speaking of Shellie, Mom, can she come to the contest with us?"

"Jake, the contest is in Las Vegas."

"I know."

"I don't think her parents are going to go for her spending two nights with us in Las Vegas."

Jake didn't respond.

"I suppose I could get a suite and put you and Adam in part of it and the girls in the other," she thought aloud.

"We're not going to do anything, Mom. It's just that will be my only time to see her until I come home in September."

This time it was Lacey's turn to say nothing.

"*Please*," he whined.

"I'll think about it, Jake." She thought of Susie downstairs and told Jake she needed to get to sleep. "I'll talk to you tomorrow."

Lacey hurried downstairs and found Susie motionless on the couch. She crept closer to look at her.

Susie must have heard her getting closer to the couch because she removed the icepack on her eye and looked up at her. "Have you been smoking?"

Lacey blushed as if she'd been caught stealing. "Yeah," she stammered.

"I can't believe you're competing for Ms. Fitness and you smoke. That's kind of an oxymoron, don't you think?"

"Yeah, it is," Lacey said defensively, "but everyone's got a crutch; mine just happens to be a cancer stick."

Susie started to sit up. "Lacey, don't say that."

"Sorry," Lacey mumbled.

Susie managed to get herself all the way up. "How's Jake?"

"He's—he's good," she paused, "I guess."

"What's that supposed to mean?"

Lacey was relieved to hear a slight smile in Susie's voice. She repeated Jake's request about Shellie going to the show with them.

"So, just because he asked doesn't mean you have to give him what he wants. You can say no, you know."

"I told him I'd call her parents, but I'm almost positive that they're going to say no anyway. I know I would."

Susie sat up and handed Lacey the icepacks. "Here, I think that did the trick. I'm good."

Lacey took the icepacks and walked to the kitchen. She put them back in the freezer. "So when do we go get your stuff?" she called out from the kitchen.

"I actually brought a few things with me."

Lacey walked back into the living room. "That's good, but I think the sooner we get all your stuff out of that house, the better." She looked over at Susie when she didn't respond and saw her staring off as though she were in another place. She sat down on the chair across from Susie. "Susie, did you hear me?"

"Yeah, I'm sorry."

Lacey could see that she was struggling for words. "Do you think we should go over there tonight and get your stuff, or do you want to wait?"

"Oh, no, I'm not going back there tonight. I'm going to wait a couple of days, and then I'll go and get it. I want to make sure he's not there when I go."

Lacey looked over doubtfully at Susie.

"Don't worry; I'm really done letting him use me as a punching bag."

Lacey got up and went to her office and came back holding her camera.

Susie held up her hand to cover her face and turned away. "What are you doing?"

Lacey walked over to her and sat down beside her.

Susie turned back toward Lacey.

"I think it would be wise to take some pictures of these bruises on your face and arm, just in case there's any trouble." Lacey could see Susie thinking about the suggestion.

Susie broke the silence. "All right, but you have to promise me you won't show them to the girls. And, please," she pleaded, "don't tell them about this either."

Lacey promised. She took her camera out of the case and took several pictures of her arm and her face. She moved closer with the camera to get a few close-ups of the bruises.

"Okay, already. That's enough." Susie held up her arm over her face.

"All right, I'll take them into CVS tomorrow and get them developed." She put the camera back in its case and took it back to her office. She walked back into the living room, mulling over the events of the past couple of months and shaking her head in disbelief.

"What are you thinking about?" Susie asked.

"I'm just tripping out on the timing of it all. I mean, look, Jake's gone for the summer, and before he leaves, you begin to get strong enough to do what you did today. I've always wanted a roommate but never had one before. I mean, the timing is what's so amazing. Stuff like this makes me really know *someone* is watching out for both of us."

"You're right, Lacey—the timing is definitely not something we could have planned or dreamed up."

They talked into the night, and before going to bed, Susie announced that she was going to call in sick to work the next day.

"Well, I don't have a depo until one o'clock, so I can help you get settled in the morning. The biggest thing I've got to do this week is get water-weighed."

"Water-weighed?"

"It's a test to determine my body fat, and that way Harrison knows how to plan my diet the week of the show."

Susie looked sad again.

"What's wrong?"

"Are you sure the timing is good with your contest just around the corner?"

"Are you kidding? I think the timing's perfect. I'm going to need you here to help keep me sane from the carb depletion."

Susie smiled. "Yeah, maybe I could lose a few pounds, too."

Lacey nodded her head and stood up. "See, I told you. The timing is perfect for lots of reasons."

Susie put her hand out to stop Lacey. "Thank you," she murmured.

"Thank *you*, Susie, for being brave enough to leave."

Susie pointed her finger upward. "I think it's a God thing." She smiled. "And I think I'm going to sleep better than I have in months."

Ms. Fitness

Lacey was in the middle of a chat online with Gio when she heard Harrison honk the horn. She quickly told him she had to go. She signed off and grabbed her purse, ran out and locked the front door behind her. Harrison was leaning over, pushing the door open for her. She got in and had just buckled her seat belt when Harrison asked her where her towel and bathing suit were.

"Oh, crap. I forgot my whole bag. I'll be right back." She got out and ran back in and went right over to the bag she had packed just an hour earlier. She noticed the message light on the phone was already flashing but ignored it and ran back outside.

Harrison led Lacey into the Loma Linda Weight and Wellness Center. "Go ahead and sit down while I check you in."

Lacey turned to find a seat and sat in a little two-seater sectional and began looking through the magazines on the table.

Harrison joined Lacey a couple of minutes later and explained what was going to happen.

"And where are you going to be?"

"Don't worry. I'll meet you at the tank. I know the guy who runs it, so he's going to let me back there while you're being water-weighed."

"Did I ever tell you I almost drowned when I was twelve?"

"You're kidding, right?"

The fear on her face answered his question.

"There's nothing to be afraid of. The tank's really not that big, and we'll be right there."

"Lacey Thorton," the voice interrupted their conversation.

Lacey got up and walked slowly toward the guy that had called her name.

"Right this way." He led her through the hall and made a right and then another right into a small room. "Here's where you can change into your bathing suit, and when you're ready, you'll just go through that door right there, and you'll see the tank down a ways."

Lacey stared to where he was pointing, not saying a word. He left and she began to get undressed and into her bathing suit. She grabbed her towel and wrapped it around her and went through the door that the guy had pointed to. She looked straight ahead. Sure enough, there was the tank just a few yards away. Her movements became less robotic when she saw Harrison standing there talking to the technician. When he saw her walk up, he stopped talking to introduce Lacey to him. "Lacey, this is Scott. Scott, this is Lacey, my client."

Scott held his hand out to her and Lacey shook it. "It's nice to meet you." She had begun to shiver.

Scott offered a warm smile. "You'll feel better when you get in the tank," he encouraged. "The water's not cold. In fact, it's about eighty degrees."

"She's pretty nervous about this, Scott," Harrison interjected.

Scott looked at Lacey, surprised by Harrison's statement. "There's nothing to be nervous about." He went on to explain what Lacey needed to do, making it sound pretty simple. "So let's get you in there and used to the water first," Scott prompted.

Lacey walked toward the tank, her towel still wrapped around her.

Harrison cleared his throat. "Hey, Lacey, aren't you forgetting something?"

Lacey turned around, a puzzled look on her face.

Harrison pointed toward her midsection. "Your towel." He smiled.

"Oh." Lacey took off the towel as Harrison walked toward her and she handed it to him. Lacey turned her head to see that her suspicions were correct; they were staring at her, so she nearly ran to the tank. She got in and held on to the side as she kicked her legs in the water for a few minutes, willing herself to remain calm.

"Now, when I count to three, I want you to take a deep breath and go under and stay there until you hear this whistle. Don't forget to exhale slowly underwater so you can get as many tiny bubbles as possible. The less air in your lungs at the time of measurement, the more accurate this is going to be. We'll do that three times and take the average of the three." He looked down at Lacey. "You ready?"

"Sure," Lacey acquiesced.

Scott counted to three, and Lacey took a deep breath and went under. By the third time, Lacey was getting the hang of it and relaxing a little more.

"Your third one was your best one. Why don't you do it one more time, and we'll throw out the first one," he encouraged.

"Okay. Let's do it," Lacey agreed.

When she came up the final time, she saw Scott and Harrison smiling and talking. "Well?" Lacey asked, now really curious.

Harrison helped Lacey out of the tank. "Awesome," he said, handing Lacey her towel.

"You're pretty lean," Scott offered.

Lacey wrapped the towel around her and looked up to see the guy that had walked her back to the dressing room walking out toward them. "So, what's the verdict?" he asked as he stopped in front of Scott. "Was I right?"

Lacey looked to Harrison, an obvious question in her eyes.

Harrison smiled his boyish smile. "We had a bet going on."

Scott interrupted him. "You'd think that I'd be the one to win it, but it looks like John here nailed it. I said your body fat was at eleven percent, Harrison said eleven and a half, and John said ten."

Lacey looked to Harrison. "So is that good?" She really wasn't sure, but from the look on Harrison's face, she suspected it was. She stood there needing the affirmation.

Harrison nodded his head. "It's better than I thought. By the day of the show, you'll probably be down to about eight, which is awesome. Now your diet won't be as drastic the last week."

"I'm already on carb starvation; how much more drastic can it get?" Lacey rolled her eyes in disbelief.

Harrison laughed. "Trust me; it can get a whole lot worse, but we're just going to be decreasing your sodium next week."

John and Scott began to laugh, and Harrison joined them.

Lacey didn't like thinking she was being laughed at. "What's so funny?"

"Relax, girl. They're laughing because practically *everything* you eat has sodium."

Lacey's eyes widened and she was about to protest when Harrison put his hand on her shoulder. "It's not as bad as it sounds; it's really not. We'll talk about it on the way back."

Lacey took the hint and thanked the guys and walked back to the dressing room. "It's not as bad as it sounds," she mimicked Harrison. "Yeah, well, you're not the one that's nearly passing out from carb depletion, especially after a workout," she muttered. She closed the door of the dressing room a little harder than she intended.

Almost three hours later, Lacey let herself into the condo and dropped her bag in the laundry room. She was exhausted and starving. After being water-weighed, she had gone to the gym to complete her weight and cardio workout, and now she felt like she could eat the paint off the walls. She walked toward the kitchen, but the flashing light on the phone stopped her. *That's right; there was a message when I left earlier.* She dialed her voice mail and then pushed the speaker button and continued to walk to the refrigerator.

The voice on the recorder stopped her, and she walked back toward it. It was Sophie, and Lacey could hear she was crying through her words: "Lacey, it's me, Sophie. It looks like we're… It… Zach's dad woke up out of his coma today, but—but then his vitals started to drop, and he slipped back into the coma." Lacey waited while the pause continued, "His vitals are deteriorating slowly. They don't think he's going to make it through tonight." There was another long pause. "Call me."

Lacey pushed the speakerphone button off and picked up the phone to call Sophie. She counted the rings until her voice mail came on. "Sophie, I just got your message. Please call me back, and let me know where you are and what's going on. Call me on my cell if I'm not home. Love you, girl."

Lacey hung up and walked back toward the kitchen, not quite as hungry now. She mixed a can of tuna with some homemade salsa and put some on a rice cake. She reached for a bottle of water, and headed for her office to check her e-mail and finish up a transcript while she waited for Sophie to call her back.

Sophie didn't call back until later on in the evening after Susie had gotten home. They both listened as Sophie explained that the doctors didn't think that he would make it through the night. Sophie had decided to take Zach out of summer school, and they had headed up north to be there in case he passed away. Susie spoke up first. "Can we do anything for you, Sophie?"

Sophie sounded so tired. "No, I can't think of anything. But thank you, both of you."

Lacey couldn't imagine what her friend must be going through. She wanted to help but didn't know how. "Are you sure you don't need us to do anything? What about your dog? Do you want us to go over and feed him?"

"Oh," Sophie groaned, "I forgot about him. Yes, could you please go by and feed Max? You know where the key is, right?"

"Yeah, I know where it is," Lacey assured her. "Don't worry; we'll go by and feed him and play with him for a while."

"Thanks, guys. I'd better go."

Saturday marked the end of their first week as roommates, and Lacey couldn't believe how easy it was to live with Susie. They had spent the first few nights sharing life experiences, crying and laughing, strengthening their friendship more than either of them thought possible. Susie's physical signs of injury were fading, and when she asked Lacey to go with her to get the rest of her stuff, Lacey knew she was healing emotionally as well.

"I was wondering when that was going to happen," Lacey admitted to Susie after agreeing to go. They decided to meet back at the condo within two hours and head over to Jimmy's house, but when they were getting ready to leave, the phone rang. Susie picked it up. A couple of seconds passed, and Susie put her hand over the mouthpiece so she could tell Lacey that it was Sophie. "She's crying," she whispered.

Lacey put her purse down and waited to hear the news. She got the feeling it wasn't good. Sophie and Zach had really been through it last week. They had stayed up there longer than Sophie thought they would need to and then came home for a couple of days when they thought Zach's dad was stable, only to be called back again yesterday. Lacey looked up when she heard Susie. "I'm so sorry, Sophie. Yes, of course we'll check on Max. Do you need us to send you anything?" After a couple of minutes, she handed the phone to Lacey. "He's gone," she whispered.

Lacey exhaled slowly, not sure what to say to Sophie about something so final. "Sophie, I'm so, so sorry." She could hear Sophie crying. "How's Zach holding up?" Lacey listened as Sophie told her that Zach was pretty torn up, didn't understand why his dad never really woke up enough from the coma to be able to talk with him.

"Now I'm wondering if I did the wrong thing by letting him see his dad like that," Sophie choked out.

"Sophie, don't go down that road. You did what you thought was right at the time and that's what matters. He's a tough little guy, and he's got a great mom." Lacey decided to transition away from Zach. "So when's the funeral?"

"His parents are having a memorial service, but..." Sophie stopped midsentence.

"But what, Sophie?"

"They're pretty sure they're doing it next Saturday, which means we're going to miss your contest, Lacey. I'm so sorry."

"Don't worry about my contest, Sophie. I think this is more important. I'll miss you, but you'll be right here with me." Lacey held her left hand to her heart. "Now, go take care of Zach and we'll go check on Max. Call us if there's anything you need."

By the time they had finished playing with Max and feeding him, it was almost five o'clock and nearly dusk when they pulled up to Susie's old house in Pomona. Lacey took in the old and run-down neighborhood. They pulled into the driveway, and Lacey noticed that Jimmy's truck was gone. "Thank God for miracles."

"No kidding," Susie agreed after she let out a sigh of relief.

They moved quickly, first to the bedroom she used to share with Jimmy. They gathered her personal belongings from the closet and dresser. Susie went to the bathroom next, and Lacey went into the kitchen and shuddered at the grotesque sight. The counters were full of dirty dishes, splatters of food on the counters, empty beer and whiskey bottles. Lacey jumped when she saw something dart across the counter. "Susie, do you want me to get anything out of the kitchen?"

Susie came walking into the kitchen. "No, I don't want anything in here."

Lacey decided not to say anything about the cockroach or the empty beer and whiskey bottles. She walked from the kitchen into the dining room, which merged with the living room. "Isn't all the furniture in this place yours?"

Susie nodded.

Lacey walked toward the dark walnut high-top kitchen table and four equally high chairs. "This is a really nice kitchen set, Susie. Are you sure we can't take it for you?"

Susie just nodded her head.

Lacey looked at the living room furniture, which looked to be a little worn. She could see an extra worn spot on the end of the couch, no doubt where Jimmy sat every night. "Is that where he spends a lot of his time?"

Susie nodded her head in the affirmative. "Pretty much twenty-four/seven."

"I can see why you wouldn't want to take that furniture."

Susie was looking around the room, shaking her head. "I'll just have to start over. I don't want any reminders of all the years I've wasted here."

Lacey picked up two of the packed bags. "Okay. I guess we're ready to go, then." Susie grabbed the last of the packed bags and they walked out. She set her bags down and watched Susie lock up the house. *She sure seems to be holding it together*, Lacey thought.

As if to jinx it, a pair of headlights stopped them as Jimmy's truck pulled into the driveway. He shut the engine off, and Lacey saw a dog, a Jack Russell terrier, come running toward Susie. Susie dropped her bags, and Lacey quickly walked over to retrieve them and take them to the car. She could feel Jimmy's eyes on her back. She walked back toward the last two bags, intermittently staring at Jimmy and then at Susie who was bent down and putting her still-sore arm around her dog's little neck. Lacey watched as she buried her face in his short coat until he wiggled away from her and looked up at her and barked as if to say, "Where you going, Mom?" Lacey stood there, uncomfortable. She stared back at Jimmy who was now watching Susie and the dog.

"He really misses you," Jimmy said gruffly.

Lacey looked to Susie, willing her to stay strong. "You ready to go?"

"Yeah, let's go." Susie walked toward her car, her eyes avoiding him. Jimmy just stood there. Lacey threw the bags in the back seat on top of the others. Susie got in the front seat. Lacey ran to the other side and got in, and just like that, they left.

When Lacey looked back, Jimmy was still standing there, as if in shock, the little Jack Russell Terrier standing by his side. *So that's why they say a man's best friend is his dog, 'cause he sure don't have anyone else,* Lacey thought. She turned back around and sat in silence for a few minutes until they were completely out of Pomona, and then she asked Susie about her dog. "So why did you leave your dog there?"

Susie took a while to respond. "I guess because I actually feel sorry for Jimmy. He doesn't have anybody, and he really does love my dog."

Lacey let Susie's response linger in the air, humbled by her selflessness.

"When things cool off, I'll go by and see him." Susie sounded like she was assuring herself. "The dog, that is," she added with a half-hearted smile.

Lacey smiled back. "Well, I just want you to know if you decide you want to go get him, the dog, that is," she added with a wink, "you can bring him back to the condo. They do allow small dogs."

Susie took her eyes off the road for a second and looked at Lacey. "Thanks."

Less than ten minutes later, they pulled into the garage, and by the time they had gotten everything unloaded and put away, they were laughing and carrying on like sorority sisters.

The week of the show literally flew by. After work Monday, Lacey headed for her counseling appointment. She wasn't looking forward to it, but deep down she was hoping Daniel would leave her with a cup of courage for the competition.

When she got comfortable and they talked about her week, Daniel picked up from where they had left off the previous session; it was grueling. Eventually Jake was brought into it, and Lacey successfully veered away from her childhood by sharing Jake's request for his girlfriend to go to the contest with them.

"See what I mean?" Daniel asked. "Here's an opportunity to put into practice what you are learning about how to parent him versus trying to make sure he likes you." He let the words penetrate and then continued. "So what's your gut feeling about allowing her to go?"

Lacey sat there for a few seconds thinking. "Well, I don't think they'd do anything, but then again, as soon as he asked, there was something that went off in my head that said no, it wouldn't be a good thing."

"Then that's what you go with. Now you just need to figure out how to draw *your* line for *his* good."

Lacey's frustration was obvious.

"It's easier said than done; I know. But the more you do it, the easier it gets. Now, let's get back to you."

Lacey pulled into Starbucks after counseling. She had almost an hour to kill before meeting with Harrison for her second workout of the day. After receiving her blended iced coffee, she walked the few steps to her car to retrieve her journal and cigarettes and came back to a table outside. She made herself comfortable and let out a sigh of relief, thankful for the moments of downtime. She lit her cigarette, opened up her journal, and pulled out the notes she had taken during their session. She looked them over, trying to understand what her childhood had to do with Jake.

Daniel had reminded her that children are not born with shame. *That makes sense.* "They have this innate ability to trust and give love unconditionally." Lacey smiled as she retrieved glimpses of Jake as a small child from her memory bank, but when she tried to dig further and capture some sort of hint of who or how she was as a small child, the memory bank was empty. With a heavy heart, she returned to her notes and read the next sentence: "Their innocence enhances their belief that all expressions of love are good." Something inside Lacey hardened, but she couldn't quite put her finger on it. That same feeling returned, and her pulse quickened when she read: "Their desire and need to be close and want to be special allows for the mental compromise to believe even molestation is a way of expressing being special." Lacey felt a light turn on inside her head. *So that's where the shame comes from,* she thought, *but what does that have to do with Jake?* Lacey paused to put her cigarette out. *So what is the connection here? Why is Daniel having me delve so deep into this crap? Because I really don't see how it relates to my son.* She continued reading to herself. "There is a great deal of innocence and trust lost. The most significant loss of trust is the ability to trust ourselves and the judgments we make when it comes to letting people care for us and how we care for them. We learn to doubt the simple child-mindedness in life's moments."

She folded the notes back up, put them aside and reached for another cigarette. *This is too much,* she thought. She began to journal her thoughts:

> The realizations are coming more frequently now, and like pieces of a puzzle, they are forming a picture that is not only humbling me, but requiring from me a deeper understanding of my past in order to be complete. The funny thing about all of this was that I started counseling because I didn't know how to deal with Jake, and now it's becoming apparent that I need to learn how to not let my past have such a huge influence in the way I parent Jake and my need to have a man in my life.

She closed her journal and put her pen back in her purse. "Time to turn this stuff off," she determined. She headed for her car, her mind already on her workout.

Tuesday whizzed by with a morning session of cardio and weights, a midmorning deposition that had gone two and a half hours, and then an afternoon cardio workout. Lacey let herself in through the garage. Susie was already home from work, and as Lacey walked in, Susie was just coming in from the patio.

"I smell barbecue. What are you cooking?"

"Tonight we're having some chicken and veggie skewers."

"I am so blessed that you like to cook, Susie."

"Not cook, barbecue." Susie corrected her with a smile. She opened the refrigerator to take out stuff for a salad. "It's the least I could do."

Lacey washed her hands and started to help her. They chatted about their respective days, and then Susie announced that she had a phone call that day at work.

Lacey knew who it was before she even asked. "So who was it?"

"Guess," Susie countered.

Lacey stopped cutting the cucumber, not wanting to even let his name come out of her mouth. Instead, she played ignorant. "I give up. Who called?"

Susie took the cucumber slices and tossed them into the salad. "Jimmy."

Lacey was careful to not sound critical. "So what did he want?"

"He just wanted to offer the same empty promises, only this time he's gotten motivated enough to go out and consistently look for a job."

Lacey heard the bitterness in her voice. "Do you believe his empty promises?"

Susie didn't even hesitate. "Nope, sure don't." She threw in the diced tomatoes that Lacey had just finished cutting.

"That's good, Susie. Besides, you know how the saying goes, 'Actions speak louder than words.'"

"Ain't that the truth," Susie agreed. "Anyway, I wished him good luck. I don't want to be enemies with the guy. I just want my life back." She walked to the cupboard and took out two dinner plates and set them down. "I never realized how much of me I lost until I came here."

Lacey smiled and complimented her great attitude and her resolve that seemed to get stronger every day. "You truly inspire me, Susie, and make me realize that it's never really too late to start over."

Susie looked baffled at the compliment. "I'm going to go check the skewers." She took a plate and went out on the patio.

Lacey set the table, inwardly at peace as she offered up thanks for the gift of her roommate.

Wednesday Lacey woke up feeling like she hadn't been to bed yet. "Thank God this is my last day of weight-training," she remembered out loud. She lay in bed thinking about the conversation with Gio last night. He had been very talkative and shared more with her than he ever had. He told her about his ex-girlfriend who was still living with him, which sent the red warning lights flashing for Lacey. Those lights turned to yellow warning signals when he had forced the introduction and put her on the phone.

Lacey shook her head as if in a daze when she thought about it. "That was too weird," she admitted out loud, but nevertheless, she had gone with it, especially after Gio had been so open and seemingly honest to both of them.

She thought about the conversation with his ex, Donna. They had made small talk, both cautiously treading on mutual territory, but by the end of the conversation, Lacey really liked her. Donna had told Lacey that she wanted Gio to be happy and that they had made better friends than lovers. By the time Lacey had hung up the phone, she felt like she had received a sales call promoting Gio, and she knew in her gut that Gio was more into her than she was into him, and she wasn't really sure how she felt about that.

That last thought got her out of bed, and the realization that she'd have to back up from him followed her throughout the morning. It wasn't until she walked into the gym for her weight and cardio workout that Lacey was able to switch her focus. During her workout, several people came up and wished her luck in her competition, which really inspired her to train hard. When she left, she was exhausted but invigorated.

The rest of the day went by in a blur. There was lunch with the girls, a few errands to run, and then back to the gym for her second cardio workout. Then she went home and showered and met Mom and Dad for dinner on their way home from his doctor's appointment.

When Lacey finally tucked herself in, she remembered she'd forgotten to respond to Gio's e-mail.

Lacey slept in Thursday and took her time getting ready for the day. She checked her voice mail, returned phone calls, and then checked her e-mail. Gio had e-mailed her two more times. On one hand it felt good to be pursued, and on the other, it was getting annoying. She quickly sent him an e-mail explaining she'd be busy for the next couple of days with the competition, and she'd try and call him later. As soon as she sent it, she thought, *Why did I tell him I'd try and call? Wasn't that another mixed message?* She turned her computer off and got ready to go meet the girls for her final fitting at Fresh Peaches.

The bathing suit fit perfectly. The routine outfit had to be taken in an inch, which really shocked all of them, including Lacey.

"Peanut, you really need to go eat some carbs," Nikki exclaimed.

"You kidding? That's why she's lost that inch in one week." Susie marveled. "Now we know what I can do if I can't zip up my pants—just carb-deplete myself for a week."

"And just think," Sophie added, "we didn't even have to go to Hollywood for that secret." She shook her head as if seeing Lacey for the first time. "And to think I'm the one who introduced you to the gym. How come I don't look like that?"

The girls all giggled. Lacey pulled out her camera and asked the designer if she would take a picture of all of them. "Come on, guys, we need a group photo." They all gathered around Lacey as the designer took a picture of them.

"Okay, it's a wrap," the designer announced. "And, Lacey, you can pick your outfit up on the way out of town tomorrow."

Lacey thanked her and returned to the dressing room. When she came out, Sophie rushed up to her and gave her a hug. "I've got to go, girl. We're leaving tomorrow morning to go up for the funeral, and I've still got to get Zach packed. Be good to you and have a blast. I'll be home Tuesday, but don't forget to call me after the show and let me know how it went."

Lacey promised her she'd call. "Take care of you, Sophie."

"Excuse me, miss, step right over here."

Lacey looked up, startled to realize the guy was talking to her. She was standing in line waiting for her photo shoot before going on stage for the first part of the competition. She had been day-dreaming about their ride up to Vegas with Jake and her friends. The only damper on the whole event had been Sophie not being able to come, but everyone's support had been so amazing, that she hadn't come off cloud nine, not even for a minute. And when they had arrived at their room, there were flowers from Gio with a "good luck" message attached.

She walked toward the guy who had called her.

"Stand right over there."

Lacey walked to the center of the backdrop.

"Turn toward me, just a bit."

Lacey complied.

"So are you going to take that cover-up off?"

Lacey felt her cheeks burn like fire through the heavy coat of Pro Tan. She removed her cover-up to reveal her hot pink bikini.

The photographer smiled. "Now that's more like it."

Lacey tried to relax.

"Now, angle your hip, the one with the number on it, just a little bit forward."

Lacey awkwardly did as he asked.

"That's it. Now try and relax a little bit."

That's easy for you to say. She took a deep breath and exhaled slowly, rolling her shoulders back just a bit, trying to push her chest out while holding her abs in and squeezing her legs and buttocks tight.

"Perfect," he exclaimed.

Lacey could hear the click of the camera, *click, double click, click.*

"Now bring your left shoulder forward a bit and your right shoulder back."

Lacey felt as stiff as a board.

The photographer walked toward her and gently moved her shoulders to the position he was looking for. He stepped back and looked at her. "Move your right leg back in the same direction as your right shoulder, and your left leg forward, in front of the shoulder.

Lacey did as she was told, feeling more and more awkward by the minute. "No wonder I wasn't a model," she stuttered.

The photographer was smiling benignly. "Did you say something?" he asked.

"Oh, no, sorry. I was just thinking out loud." She took another deep breath and exhaled slowly.

"Perfect," he nearly shouted.

Lacey couldn't help but laugh, which brought more of the *click, click, click* of the camera. Finally, when she thought they were going to have to get paint thinner to remove the smile from her face, the photographer thanked her and wished her luck.

"Contestant number twelve oh four, Lacey Thorton," the announcer blared.

Lacey made her way out onto the stage, the lights blinding her from seeing much of anything until she was standing directly in front of the judge's table. She did what Harrison had told her to do and looked right at them, all four of them, and smiled, but it felt phony. She made the mistake of looking out into the audience, and all she could see was a sea of faces. She felt a little dizzy with fear. Just then, a voice shouted out: "That's my mama." The audience began to clap and whistle, and Lacey couldn't help but smile with pride and joy. She began her quarter turns, coming back full circle and then walked off.

"You did great, Lacey," Harrison assured her.

"Thanks," Lacey said breathlessly. She stood there, sneaking a peak at the contestant who was after her.

Harrison pulled her back. "Hey, you've got to go get ready for your routine."

"Already?"

"Trust me, the time goes by fast. When you're done, come back out here, and we'll get you warmed up."

Lacey made her way back to the dressing room, feeling like an alien in a strange world, even more so as several of the contestants stopped her to ask for help in pinning something, touching their Pro Tan up, fixing a loose strand of hair, a missing button. *Oh my gawd, they think I'm some stagehand or something. How self-centered is that!* Finally, Lacey was able to get to her own locker and retrieve her bag. She dressed quickly, completely unnoticed among the other contestants. She touched up her hair and makeup and walked back outside to Harrison.

He smiled when he saw her. "You look great."

Lacey let out a deep breath. "Thanks.

She spent the next fifteen minutes letting Harrison stretch her like a rubber band. She could hear the audience's applause for the contestant that was out on the stage performing her routine. Just two more contestants and it would be her turn. The butterflies in her stomach felt like they had grown into full-blown birds fighting inside her, and she could feel herself begin to tremble.

Harrison's voice broke through her stage fright. "Stretch your other leg. You don't want to be uneven."

She half-heartedly smiled up at him and switched legs.

"You're going to do fine," Harrison encouraged her. "Your routine is awesome and very creative."

Lacey looked down and took a deep breath as she pulled her foot closer to her butt and exhaled slowly. "I sure hope so."

Harrison lifted her chin. "Just go out there and have a good time, Lacey."

His words stayed with her as she got into position for her routine. She stood bent over her court reporting machine frozen like a mannequin until the first beat of the music, and then she turned toward the audience, ripped off her dress, which brought shouts and whistles, and lost herself in the routine.

The last time on stage was with all of the contestants. Lacey noticed there were only seven of them. *That's weird,* she thought. *How come there were so many more backstage?* Lacey turned her focus to the audience, trying to see if she could see Jake or any of her friends, but the stage lights made it impossible so she quit trying. She was having a heck of a hard time standing still, especially when her bladder screamed for relief. *Oh, this is just great. Please don't let me make a fool of myself.* Suddenly the girl to her right leaned a little closer and said through her teeth, "You're supposed to step forward."

Lacey looked confused and then she heard the announcer: "Well, I guess she's not used to being called by her number, so we'll try this again, " he said with a chuckle. "In fourth place for the master's division of Ms. Fitness Las Vegas is Lacey Thorton."

What the heck is "master's division"? She looked at the girl who had told her to step forward, and this time instead of looking irritated, the girl flashed Lacey a plastic smile. Lacey turned and gave her a phony smile right back as she walked toward the emcee to receive her trophy. He handed her the trophy and indicated she was to step back, which she did. The previous year's Ms. Fitness placed a bouquet of flowers in her right arm and gave her a congratulatory hug while whispering for her to move to the left of the stage. Lacey moved to the left and watched as the third-, second-, and finally the first-place winners were announced. All the contestants from the other division came up and congratulated each of them, and then the photographers stepped forward and begin taking pictures. Finally, just when Lacey was figuring out how to wear a permanent smile without looking phony, they were excused, and the stage was cleared for the final division announcements. Lacey walked backstage, and she could see Harrison looking for her amongst the crowd. When he saw her, he waved, and she walked toward him. He greeted her with a big hug. "Good job, Lacey."

"I'm really not sure I understand what just happened," she admitted over the backstage noise and excitement. "What is the 'master's division'?" she said emphasizing *master's*.

Harrison started to smile. "Don't minimize your achievement," he nearly shouted so she could hear him. "I put you in the master's division so you wouldn't have to compete with all the twenty-something-year-olds, especially since it was your first competition."

Lacey realized at once that he had done her a huge favor and admitted as much to him. She leaned in closer to him so she wouldn't have to shout. "And don't think I didn't pick up on your little hint of a future competition." She smiled at him.

He winked at her. "We'll see." He led them toward the exit and held the door open for her.

Before Lacey walked out, she stopped in front of him. "I just want to say thank you for believing in me and not giving up on me, even when I wanted to give up on myself."

"Well, from the sounds of the audience, I'm not the only one who believes in you. Was that your son I heard out there?"

Lacey felt like her grin reached from ear to ear. "Uh-huh."

"Well, I'm looking forward to meeting him. Now let's go celebrate and eat some carbohydrates."

"Sounds like the best thing I've heard all week."

New Beginnings

Lacey hit the snooze button on her alarm Monday morning. Several snoozes later, she poked her head out from her pillow, and the bright sun glared in at her and jolted her up. "What time is it?" She nearly screamed when she saw it was already seven-thirty in the morning. She had overslept and would have to get in high gear so they wouldn't miss Jake's 9:08 train. She jumped out of bed and ran down the hall to wake Jake up. "Jake, we're late, honey. Get up. Rise and shine."

An hour later, they were pulling out of Starbucks, which Lacey had bribed Jake with to get him to move faster. They made it to the train station with only a few minutes to spare. Lacey grabbed his bag while Jake strapped his guitar to his back. "You got your ticket?"

Jake reached into his pocket and pulled out his ticket and held it up, and in his newest impersonation of Forest Gump, said, "Yep, all I need is my Starbucks and my ticket, Mama."

Lacey couldn't help but laugh. "Come on, you goof. I think I hear the train."

Jake picked up his pace and began singing, "She'll be coming round the mountain when she comes…"

Lacey joined in the song, and when they came to the second verse, they both stuttered and stammered and then Jake made up a new ending, and by the time they made it to the platform, they were both laughing at each other. When Lacey saw the train coming closer, she willed herself to keep smiling. She pulled him to her.

He hugged her back. "Bye, Mom,"

"I'll see you soon, honey." Lacey pulled herself out of his embrace and watched him board. He waved to her and she walked to her car. She pulled out of the driveway of the train station and headed home. It had been so good to have him with her this weekend. It hadn't started out too well when he had found out that Shellie wasn't going with them, but by the time they had gotten to Vegas, and he had called her three times from Lacey's cell, he seemed to have gotten over it.

There hadn't really been any time to talk until just last night. They had gotten home from Vegas about nine thirty in the evening. Susie had gone right to her room, pleading exhaustion, and after getting their pajamas on and getting ready for bed, Lacey went into Jake's room, sat down on his bed, and they began talking. Jake confessed to being really mad at her for Shellie not being able to come with them. Lacey admitted that Shellie's mom had said no, but that she had agreed with her decision.

That had really irritated him, but Lacey didn't let that intimidate her. "Jake, it boils down to the fact that I'm the parent, and one of my jobs is to draw boundaries for your own good. You don't have to like it, but you are going to have to choose to dwell within those boundaries or bust out of that protection and make foolish choices." He had rolled his eyes at her but listened, so she had continued, "Believe it or not, honey, it will help you appreciate the value of making good choices now and trying to see the whole picture. That way, when you're older, doing the right thing won't be so hard." She had stopped after that and bent down to kiss him on his forehead and tell him she loved him. She went to bed hoping he had recognized a change in her and would think about what she had said.

Lacey's cell phone rang and brought her out of her reverie. "Hello," Lacey stammered, sighing away the rest of her thoughts.

"Lacey, it's Flo. Are you okay?"

"Yes, I'm fine." She stopped herself from saying more and looked at the clock on her dashboard. "It's too early for job assignments," she said. "Is everything okay?"

"Everything's fine," Flo assured her. "I just wanted to be the first to tell you that Norm has chosen you for the job in Korea and Hong Kong."

"Shut up!"

Flo laughed. "It's true."

"Wow, what timing," Lacey exclaimed breathlessly.

"Norm wanted me to go through a checklist of things you'll need to do to get ready, the most important being the passport."

Lacey jumped in. "I actually started that when you first told me about this. It's all taken care of. As a matter of fact, I should have it any day now."

"Well, that's good because you leave exactly two weeks from this coming Saturday, so call me when you get home and we'll go over the rest of this checklist."

"Thanks, Flo."

"You're welcome." She paused. "Congratulations, Lacey."

The rest of the week went by slowly. Now that the contest was over, Lacey didn't know what to do with all her free time, especially since Harrison had told her to take a few days off from the gym. There were moments of being uncomfortable in her skin and feeling directionless. The absence of Jake added to it.

She had taken care of her immunizations, ordered the electrical adapters she'd need for her equipment, checked into international calling with her cell phone carrier, informed American

Express that she would be traveling abroad, and confirmed the use of her card while there.

She started back at the gym on Thursday after work, but even that didn't cure the restlessness. After her workout, she called to check on Sophie who had just come home the night before. She told Lacey that things were getting back to normal, "Whatever normal is." She laughed.

"Yeah, I know what you mean. I'm feeling pretty abnormal myself these days, and I'm not sure if it's because I'm not training for the show, or because Jake's gone, or what," Lacey admitted.

"It's probably a little bit of both," Sophie assured her. "You've been working really hard for the contest for a long time, and now it's your time to rest, especially since Jake's with his dad."

"Yeah, you're probably right." She changed the subject. "I'm sorry, Sophie, I've been a bit self-absorbed. How is your new boyfriend?"

Sophie admitted that things were getting pretty serious and that he had been incredibly supportive while she was up north helping to take care of the funeral arrangements for Zach's dad.

Lacey asked how Zach was doing.

"He's doing okay, I guess. I mean I've never been in his shoes because my dad's still around, so I can't even pretend I understand what he must be going through. I just try and get him to talk about it and let him know it's important not to hold it in."

"I'm sure you're doing great, Sophie." Lacey thought about Dad's recent prognosis but wasn't ready to share that with anyone.

"Nikki told me you got chosen for the Hong Kong job. Congratulations, girl. Looks like we have another reason to go out and celebrate soon."

Lacey laughed. "Yeah, I guess we do, but since when do we need an excuse?"

Sophie agreed with her. "I better go. I've got to pick Zach up from a friend's. I think we're getting together a week from tomorrow, but I'll see you before then."

Daniel was standing at the opened door, waiting with a big smile. "So, how was it? How did you do?"

Lacey smiled at Daniel's enthusiasm. They walked into his office, and she sat down and put her journal and notepad down beside her. "Well, it was interesting."

Daniel laughed. "Well, I don't know if I expected that response."

"I came in fourth in the"—she held her fingers up to indicate quotation marks—"the 'master's' division."

"That's great, Lacey. Why do I get the impression you're not too thrilled with the results?"

"Well, there were only seven contestants in that division."

"Were you expecting to come in first?"

"Actually, I didn't have any expectations, or at least I don't think I did. The only thing that was a bit disillusioning was the phoniness and the self-absorption of the other competitors."

"Ahhh, now *that* is interesting," Daniel agreed. "But why do you minimize your achievement?"

"I don't know," Lacey said honestly. "I guess the real prize was what I became while striving for the goal of competing. The training is what produced the rewards, like self-discipline, confidence, better eating habits and of course being several dress sizes smaller now." She smiled. All of that means more than coming in fourth place."

"You are getting so wise, Lacey." Daniel smiled as he pulled some papers out of his file. "So let's pick up from last week. We were reviewing your sentence completion form, so we're going to pick up with those that go along with the 'men' pieces of your life as well as a couple more issues concerning Jake."

Lacey turned her focus to what he was saying. "You know, I spent some time going over this after our session, and I don't think I get all of it."

He held the form out so they could both look at it, and Lacey scooted forward on the couch. "When you look at how you completed the sentence 'during my school days,' you said that you 'longed to belong.' And then the thing that made you more upset than anything in life was dishonest people."

Lacey nodded her head and smiled. "They still do."

Daniel continued, "And of course when it comes to men, we know, in your eyes, they're all dishonest. In fact, you described most men as 'frauds.'"

"I still don't see what this has to do with Jake, though." Lacey watched as Daniel turned around and reached for something. He turned back around, with a puzzle box in his hands. He picked up a cluster of pieces laced together.

"These three pieces create the illusion that you're really independent." He repeated her words: "You long to belong, but since most people are 'dishonest' and most men are 'frauds,' that leaves you trusting no one, including Jake because trust equates to you anything you can control." He pointed to the cluster of three pieces. "So these pieces here are belonging, trusting and attaching."

Lacey nodded her head in understanding. "I think I'm starting to get it."

Daniel smiled and continued, "But in order not to feel the need of belonging or attaching or trusting, you keep moving, which brings us to your next sentence that you completed. The partial sentence was, 'you frequently wish,' and you completed it with you wished you could slow down."

Lacey knew where he was headed before he said it.

"If you did slow down, you would feel, and because of the effects of the child/sexual abuse, you don't allow yourself to feel; instead, you keep moving to survive."

That veracity of his statement rendered Lacey speechless.

"Is this making sense so far?"

"Uh-huh," Lacey stammered.

Daniel took another piece out of the box. "Now you see that this is one piece, and in fact, it's one of the pieces of the frame, right?

"Yeah, so it's a pretty important piece, I'm thinking?"

Daniel smiled. "It is. This piece represents your observing ego, which is the part of us that watches what we do and say in some objective manner, but because of your painful childhood, your sense of reality often differs from actuality."

Lacey sat up straight. "Are you saying I'm nuts?"

Daniel shook his head and chuckled. "No, that's not what I'm saying at all. It's just that these other pieces have hindered your ability to realize how you come across to others and sort of blinded you to your own defensive attitude, which causes you to push people away on one hand. On the other hand, you continue to perpetuate the cycle by trying to prove yourself indispensable to others under the guise of nurturing, which is what fuels you and moves you on in your mode of survival. You run further and further from your true self and the ability to see yourself accurately, let alone recognize the effect your projections of your unfulfilled needs have on others. See, Lacey, your sense of self-awareness has been blocked because of the amount of pain endured by others' behaviors, and the 'others' started with your mom and your stepdad and perpetuated to the men in and out of your life."

Lacey sat there, convicted by the honesty and clarity of it all, yet fighting it. "So how did you get all this with that little test?"

"This little test tells me things about what your mind is not conscious of, things that have been inside you a very long time and yet you live your life as if they are the truth."

"So you're saying that all this stems from my childhood?"

"Well, a child's basic needs are nurturing, trust, predictability, safety, and your child sexual abuse betrayed that. See, Lacey, the effects of child or sexual abuse are analogous to these puzzle pieces. It's hard to see one piece at a time and yet, it's hard to separate them because one effect usually creates another." Daniel picked out another clump of pieces from the box and held them up.

Lacey just looked at them.

"This is what I mean about hard to separate. Going back to the child/sexual abuse, initially there is an internal tension about what's happening, meaning you're not sure if it's right or wrong. The pressure to choose has to resolve on one side or the other, and the child in you would rather not be alone than to confront the shame and guilt as well as helplessness and the feeling of powerlessness. As you get older, that eventually leads to anger or rage." Daniel handed her a Kleenex and continued, "For example, a child wants to feel special. You thought when your stepfather was molesting you that you were special; therefore, you, as a child, defined that behavior or activity through your desire to be special and close and safe. As a child, we have this innate tendency to trust implicitly that whatever's happening at the hands of our parents is under the umbrella of love or value."

Lacey shook her head and put her hand out as if to say stop. Her tears were coming down faster than she could wipe them. "I think I'm done," she managed to choke out.

When her crying had subsided, Lacey sat there in silence, listening to the seconds of the clock ticking away. "Will I ever be okay?" she stammered.

Daniel lifted his head and answered with a hint of a smile. "Yes, you will. It's going to take a while because there are still pieces to take from the box that will complete the puzzle of your life, but week by week we'll discover how and where those pieces fit in." He looked at his clock. "Let me pray with you."

Revelations

When Lacey got home after counseling, she felt emotionally drained. Susie had left a message on her cell phone saying she was going to dinner and a movie with her parents, so she was on her own tonight, and that was okay with her.

She saw that there were messages on her home voice mail but she didn't feel like talking to anyone. She had a lot to think about. She looked at the clock. It was already six thirty. *Shouldn't I be hungry?* she asked herself. She fixed something to eat but could only eat a few bites. The things on her mind pushed her appetite away. She tossed the rest of her dinner down the garbage disposal and poured herself a glass of wine. She grabbed her journal and headed upstairs to her room and her oversized, comfy chair. She set her wine and journal down and put the new Christian CD in the player. She turned the volume on low and sat down and let the music soothe her. She opened her journal and began to read Daniel's words as well as the notes she had taken during the counseling session.

How come I never made the connection between my childhood and relationships with men? She was beginning to understand that the effects of her childhood were the driving force behind many of her emotional needs. They were also revealing her subconscious need to have a man in her life. Something else that was now more obvious to her was the fact that she had never really dealt with the pain of her childhood. No, she had packed it and left it hidden, but now, as each piece was revealed and removed through counseling, the excruciating pain was coming out of hiding, offering healing and freedom…but freedom comes with a cost. Eventually, she'd get there, far and away from the effects of her childhood, but for now, she was content in the realization that she didn't need to be married or be dating to be happy and whole. Daniel had told her that the hole in her heart that longed to be filled with love could only be filled by God because His love was perfect and would never leave her or forsake her.

"Does that mean I shouldn't date anymore?" She knew the answer as soon as she asked the question. She would continue to go out and have a good time, but before she allowed another man into her heart, she'd have to clear out all the scar tissue and make room.

Her thoughts went to all the men in and out of her life that had made their mark on her heart with permanent ink. Her first love had been Jake's dad and though their ending had been painful, Lacey was able to see the good that had come from that relationship—Jake and her determination to finish court reporting school. Peter had been just a year and a half after her divorce. Obviously, there had not been any healing time before jumping into that marriage. As she rewound the beginning of their marriage, she realized that she had allowed herself to become vulnerable with him. It was her unresolved and hidden anger that had tipped the scales and he just wasn't equipped to balance them.

She took another sip of her wine. "And now, here I am, back to single," she said aloud to the silence. Her thoughts returned to the men she'd dated in the past year. Ian had been fun, but she hadn't really invested anything there. He sure had soothed her bruised ego, though, and he had been a great way to launch into the dating world.

She sure couldn't say that about Seth. Her heart still hurt when she thought about him. She felt like they had been finished before they even started, and yet, every time she saw him, the chemistry brought back all the questions, and the memories of that night, the night that had left her with a hole in her heart. A groan of frustration escaped. "Why, oh why did I give in to that intimacy?" Her mistake had definitely brought more clarity, though, and she realized that there were reasons that God teaches that two people should wait until marriage to share the profound intimacy that they had shared.

She sat and listened to the music for a few seconds, reveling in its positive message, letting the rhythm take her back in time equipped with the pieces of the puzzle of her life that she was beginning to put together, thanks to Daniel.

And then came Daryn. She had nearly jumped into that one because of his son, a sweet kid starving for approval, just like Jake. That little boy had definitely taught her that kids don't ever give up on the idea of their mother and father being together, happily ever after. His pain had mixed too well with Jake's and had created a poison, and her need to fix and control and be valued had definitely hindered her judgment.

Lacey finished her glass of wine with thoughts of Toby. The situation with him had been different in a sort of whimsical kind of way. Lacey smiled as she reminisced her birthday outing. *Would it have been as fun without him?* she wondered. Lacey was honest with herself. *No, because he was part of the magic that night; that's for sure.* No telling what would have happened if he hadn't been honest about his separation from his wife. The temptation to condemn herself was huge but she was learning that condemnation only took one further away from the truth and love of God.

She fast-forwarded to the ending, knowing in her heart that she would never want to be a part of the emotional crime of adultery after having been a victim of it.

It was a tough pill to swallow, but the truth was her urgency to control had been the genesis and the end of each one of those relationships. And with each ending, the emotional baggage had become heavy-laden with bitterness and unforgiveness. "Whew, have I got some unpacking to do," she admitted aloud.

She looked at the journal entry from the night before about Gio. He had called her his soul mate, and that had definitely sparked something in her heart. Now she understood that that was the piece of needing to belong somewhere with someone and be more deeply connected. He was so nurturing and gentle at times, and as she thought about it more and more, Daniel's words began to make more sense. The truth was she had been cheated of the nurturing while growing up and therefore, she craved it and tried to find it in men. "Yes, Gio, for now, you'll just have to stay out there in cyber space," she mused aloud, and maybe that was where she'd keep him, at least until more pieces of her puzzle were put in place and she was free from more of the effects of her childhood.

Her thoughts turned to her son. Her eyes welled over as she thought about the ways she tried to manipulate Jake by trying to manipulate his choices under the guise of parenting him as best she could. Daniel had said it was a dangerous pattern that would create a similar experience for the person she was caring for—Jake—while becoming like the ones she had come from, her mother and stepfather.

The last revelation was so powerful, it unleashed the tears. She got up out of her chair, her arms clutching her stomach, and dropped to her knees. "Oh, God, I'm so sorry," she cried out in anguish. She put her face into the cushion and sobbed, asking God to help her get through all of the pieces and be free from all the effects that threatened to keep her victimized and never experiencing true joy. She remained on her knees and lowered her face to the floor, and her sobs began to subside. One by one, she saw the faces of the men in and out of her life, and she resolved to forgive them for their part of her wounded heart.

Several minutes later, Lacey heard her cell phone ring. She just sat there and let it ring, awash with emotion, yet quiet and calm. She got up off her knees and stood up and let out a big yawn. She felt tired and less burdened at the same time. She reached for her journal and put it in her drawer and got ready for bed. One by one she took all of the pillows off the bed and got in. For the first time that Lacey could remember, she was fast sleep within minutes.

"Lacey, it's time to get up," Susie plopped down on the bed.

Lacey woke up and sat up slowly and startled. "What's going on? Is everything okay?"

"That's what I should be asking you." She gently shoved Lacey back down. "You never sleep this late."

Lacey looked over at the clock on her nightstand. "Holy moly, it's almost nine o'clock!" She sat up, this time much more quickly.

"So are you okay?"

"Yeah, actually, I'm good. And how about you, did you have a nice visit with your mom and dad?"

"It was good. We went to our favorite Mexican restaurant, and we were there talking so long that we decided not to go to the movie, but I followed them home and we watched a movie there." She was quiet for a few seconds. "It felt good to be with them. I hadn't realized it had been so long since I'd been home."

Lacey could see that Susie was basking in the contentment from the visit with her parents. "You're very lucky, you know, to have them."

Susie's eyes watered up. "I know, and they are so grateful that I've broken free from Jimmy and that you and I are roommates.

Mom told me she and Dad have been praying for me since the day I moved in with him…" She faded off and then held out her hand.

"What's that?"

"Two tickets for a concert that's sponsored by Calvary Chapel of Chino Hills. It's at the Anaheim Stadium. My mom and dad got them for us because they thought we'd like it. They said the music's more for our age, not theirs."

Lacey laughed. "So when is it?"

"It's tomorrow night." Susie hesitated. "Are you busy?"

"No, as a matter of fact, I'm free." She let out a big sigh. *In more ways than one*, she realized. "So what time does it start?"

"I think it starts at seven, but we should be there by six thirty."

"Well, that leaves plenty of time to go to church and do whatever we have to do, shopping, our usual Sunday errands."

"That will work. So what are you doing today?"

"I think I'm going to go to the gym." Lacey hesitated before asking Susie if she wanted to come with her. She had joined a week after moving in and as far as Lacey knew, she had gone just a few times, so Lacey wanted to encourage her, not push her. "Do you want to come to the gym with me today?"

"Absodarnlutely," Susie smiled

Lacey wasn't prepared for her enthusiasm. "Okay, then."

"I've actually gone three times this week on my lunch hour."

"Susie, that's awesome."

Susie pushed the compliment aside. "But don't ask me to give up my pizza and French fries."

They both laughed. "You're incorrigible, Susie."

Two and a half hours later, they walked into 24-Hour Fitness. Lacey got a locker for their gym bags. "So what do you usually do when you come?"

Susie didn't hesitate. "I just do thirty minutes of cardio and some abdominal work. That's all I have time for, usually."

"That's good, though. Cardio is really important for burning calories and helps keep your lungs and heart healthy. So today, we'll do thirty minutes of cardio, and then we'll do an upper-body workout."

Susie started to laugh. "This ought to be good."

"Stop it. We'll make it fun. We need to do weights so we can tone the muscles, which will also help us burn more fat."

"I'm all for that."

At the end of the thirty minutes, both of them had really broken a sweat.

Susie got off her treadmill first. "I've just broken my calorie-burning record. If I keep coming to the gym with you, I may be the next one competing in a Ms. Fitness contest."

Lacey laughed as she watched Susie practically gasp for air. "You're such an exaggerator, girl. You did great."

Susie rolled her eyes.

"Come on. Let's go on over to the weight machines." They began walking toward them, and Lacey heard her name called. She turned around and saw a girl she had gotten to know at the gym. She waved and said hi and began walking again, backwards, until she bumped into someone. She turned around, startled, and came face to face with Seth. "I'm sorry, I wasn't—"

Seth was smiling. "Isn't that how we met almost a year ago; you bumped into me?"

Lacey joined his smile. "Yeah, I think so." She looked past Seth and saw Susie watching. She motioned for her to come over. "Susie, this is Seth. Seth, this is Susie."

Susie's eyebrows shot up. "It's nice to meet you, Seth." She looked over to Lacey. "I'll be right over here."

Lacey offered up a silent thank you and then looked back to Seth. "So how did you do at the show?"

"Not bad," he answered somewhat modestly. He looked right into her eyes. "I haven't gotten a chance to congratulate you, though, for getting fourth place. That's great, especially for your first show."

Lacey brought her eyes level with his. "Thanks. I missed seeing you there. Did someone tell you about it?"

"I was there. I watched your competition before getting ready for mine."

Lacey didn't know what to say.

"So what are you doing later? Do you want to get some dinner—my treat? We can celebrate your victory." He waited. "And mine," he added.

Lacey caught the last part of his sentence and made eye contact again. "So then you placed?"

"Yep, second in two divisions."

Lacey noticed him put his gym bag in his other hand.

"So are you busy later?" he asked again.

Oh, is this tempting, or what? "As a matter of fact, I am." She watched him put his head down. "Seth, can I tell you something?"

His head came up quickly.

Lacey almost got lost in his expression, trying to determine what he was thinking. She continued, "I just want to say I'm so, so sorry for how I reacted after that night. Every time I—"

"You don't have to say you're sorry, Lacey," he interrupted her.

"Yes, I do."

He set his gym bag down and shifted positions, obviously uncomfortable.

Her words came out nonstop, like a river gushing down a mountain. "It's just that I have never experienced such connection in intimacy, and it freaked me out, and I really didn't know why it freaked me out so bad until recently, and to make a long story short, it's because I still have a lot of junk in my trunk that I need to unpack." Lacey tried to smile at her own attempt at lightheartedness.

Seth wasn't saying anything, so Lacey continued, only much more slowly. "Every time I think about it, I can't help but admit it was amazing in so many ways…"

Seth was nodding his head. "Yeah, it was," his voice was like a whisper, the expression on his face agreeing loud and clear.

Lacey continued, "But I never should have gone and crossed that line, not only because of my personal convictions, but because of my own issues." Lacey let her head drop and watched a tear fall to the ground and then another. She started to raise her hand to wipe at them when she felt his hand touch her face and wipe them away before she could. She looked up and saw that his eyes were like pools threatening to overflow and take her in. She let him wipe at her tears and then gently moved his hand. "So will you accept my apology, Seth?"

He bent down and picked up his gym bag and stood up again, making sure he looked right at her. "Yes, I accept your apology, but…" He faded off and turned his head away, obviously struggling.

"What is it, Seth?"

He turned toward her again. His words came out effusively. "I think I need to thank you."

"Thank me for what?"

"For getting me to realize I have my own baggage to unpack."

Lacey was completely stunned and couldn't even find her tongue when he said, "See you around," and then turned around and walked away. She watched him go out the door, and a sense of unexplainable relief came over her. She turned around and walked toward Susie.

The girls walked out of the gym to Susie's car. After Susie had unlocked the doors and they had gotten in, she looked over at Lacey. "Is everything okay?"

"Yeah, actually, it is. At least I feel as though there's more closure now."

"That's a good thing, then." They drove for a few minutes in silence, and then Susie reached for the volume knob on the radio and turned it up.

Lacey turned it down.

"What did you do that for?"

"I just heard something right before you did that."

"What do you mean you heard something?"

"I just heard the words 'Jeremiah twenty-nine eleven,' I think."

Susie looked over at Lacey, perplexed.

Lacey felt as perplexed as Susie looked.

Susie took her eyes off the road long enough to glance at Lacey. "You know that's a verse in the Bible, right?"

Lacey hesitated. "I think so, but I've never read it."

"I have, a long time ago, when I was a little girl, but I don't remember what it says."

They were both quiet for a moment.

"What's wrong?" Susie asked.

"Nothing's wrong. I just remembered that when we were older, before we got taken away from my mom, my brother Robert and me used to walk to Sunday School. It's like I've always known about God and in some ways that He's always been with me.

Well, I just can't wait to get home and read it now. It just reminds me of when you shared about hearing that other verse after Peter left you. It gives me the chills and comforts me at the same time."

Lacey smiled. "Yeah, I remember that. 'Surely He carries all of your pain; He dries all of your tears,'" They rode the rest of the way home quiet, each of them lost in their thoughts.

Susie let them in through the front door and headed to the kitchen.

Lacey headed for the stairs. "Hey, I'm gonna go check that verse out. I'll be down in a while."

"Take your time. We have a couple of hours before we need to leave for the concert."

Lacey went upstairs to her bedroom and closed the door. She smiled to herself because this time she wouldn't have to go searching for the Bible; she knew right where it was. She got it and sat in her chair as she looked in the index. She found Jeremiah, turned to the chapter and verse and read it aloud: "For I know the plans I have for you, says the Lord, plans of peace, not of evil, to give you a future and a hope."

Lacey was stunned and excited at the same time. She smiled, convinced of the reality of God and the truth of His having a plan for her. It was hard to explain, but she knew that she wanted to learn to trust Him. She had no idea what His plan was, but she knew she had much to look forward to: the trip to Korea and Hong Kong, which she knew was an opportunity of a lifetime. Then there would be Jake's homecoming. She knew she had a lot to learn in the area of parenting, but things would definitely be different with him now because *she* was changing. Yes, change could be a good thing. She smiled as she remembered that she had even accepted the invitation, at Val's insistence, to take the court reporter test for L. A. Superior Court, just two weeks after Jake came home in September.

She felt an unfamiliar sense of contentment. Yes, her life was looking up and taking her in a different direction. She realized that none of her plans included a man in her life, and the amazing thing about it was she was okay with that.